D0362632

Praise for *Driftwood Bay*

"Ranging in tone from harrowing to heartwarming, *Driftwood Bay* is character-driven, thought-provoking, and highly recommended for connoisseurs of the genre."

Midwest Book Review

"Readers will delight in this pleasant romance. Hannon's take on loss and survival is simpatico with Debbie Macomber's Blossom Street series."

Booklist

"Full of faith and characters that readers will want to root for until the end."

Publishers Weekly

"*Driftwood Bay* is beautifully layered. It's the kind of story that becomes better and better with each turning page."

Interviews and Reviews

"Rambunctious beagle alert!!!!! Perfect for comic relief, exasperating interruptions, and copious warm fuzzies! But there's so much more to this divinely magical story (the whole series, really) that elevates it to the absolute top of my everyone-in-the-world-should-read this-book-NOW list."

Best Reads (2010–2019)

Books by Irene Hannon

HEROES OF QUANTICO

Against All Odds

An Eye for an Eye

In Harm's Way

GUARDIANS OF JUSTICE

Fatal Judgment

Deadly Pursuit

Lethal Legacy

PRIVATE JUSTICE

Vanished

Trapped

Deceived

MEN OF VALOR

Buried Secrets

Thin Ice

Tangled Webs

CODE OF HONOR

Dangerous Illusions

Hidden Peril

Dark Ambitions

That Certain Summer

One Perfect Spring

Hope Harbor

Sea Rose Lane

Sandpiper Cove

Pelican Point

Driftwood Bay

Starfish Pier

Starfish Pier

A Hope Harbor Novel

IRENE HANNON

a division of Baker Publishing Group
Grand Rapids, Michigan

© 2020 by Irene Hannon

Published by Revell
a division of Baker Publishing Group
PO Box 6287, Grand Rapids, MI 49516-6287
www.revellbooks.com

Printed in the United States of America

All rights reserved. No part of this publication may be reproduced, stored in a retrieval system, or transmitted in any form or by any means—for example, electronic, photocopy, recording—without the prior written permission of the publisher. The only exception is brief quotations in printed reviews.

Library of Congress Cataloging-in-Publication Data
Names: Hannon, Irene, author.
Title: Starfish Pier : a Hope Harbor novel / Irene Hannon.
Identifiers: LCCN 2019039591 | ISBN 9780800736149 (paperback)
Subjects: GSAFD: Love stories.
Classification: LCC PS3558.A4793 S73 2020 | DDC 813/.54—dc23
LC record available at https://lccn.loc.gov/2019039591

ISBN: 978-0-8007-3782-5 (casebound)

This book is a work of fiction. Names, characters, places, and incidents are the product of the author's imagination or are used fictitiously. Any resemblance to actual events, locales, or persons, living or dead, is coincidental.

20 21 22 23 24 25 26 7 6 5 4 3 2 1

To my niece, Catherine Hannon,
as you graduate from high school.

I am so proud of the young woman you've become.

Wherever the road ahead may take you,
hold fast to your dreams and values—
and may all your tomorrows
be filled with joy and love.

1

Maybe coming back to Oregon had been a mistake.

Expelling a breath, Steven Roark moved to the stern of the twenty-two-foot fishing boat where he spent his days and double-checked the cleat hitch knot on the mooring line.

Secure.

Which was more than he could say for his place in the world—or in Hope Harbor.

He ducked into the foldaway canvas enclosure that offered a modicum of protection to charter clients on blustery, cold days—like this late March Saturday—and dropped into a deck chair, massaging his forehead.

From a business standpoint, the day had been productive. For this early in the spring, steelheads had been running better than usual on the river at the north end of town, and his customers had left satisfied with their catches. One of them had even hooked a twenty-pounder.

On the personal front, however, the day was a total bust.

Steven leaned forward, flipped the latch on a storage compartment, and retrieved the envelope he'd found in his mailbox yesterday, the address penned in Cindy's fluid, curvy handwriting.

He pulled out the card, reread the printed verse, and skimmed the best wishes jotted inside by his sister-in-law under a crudely drawn smile icon that had to be his nephew's handiwork.

His brother hadn't bothered to sign his own name. Cindy had done the honors for both of them.

Stomach kinking, Steven shoved the card back in the envelope and hunched forward, elbows on knees.

Some birthday.

No one but fish, a couple of pesky seagulls, and three taciturn customers for company. No cake or festive dinner shared with friends or family. No recognition of the day by his kid brother—nor any progress in their relationship.

And if he hadn't made any inroads with Patrick after almost a year, there wasn't much chance his sibling would come around in the future unless the status quo changed.

Steven sighed.

While mustering out of the army had seemed like the right decision twelve months ago after Cindy's disturbing letter arrived in the Middle East, in hindsight—

"Hello? Is anyone on board?"

Steven jerked upright and squinted through the isinglass window.

A slender, thirtysomething woman stood on the dock beside his boat, a folder clutched against her chest. As the gusty wind whipped strands of her longish, light brown hair across her face, she brushed them aside and peered into the deck enclosure.

Given the shadowed interior on this gray day—plus the fog that had rolled in—she might not be able to make out his form.

That left him two options.

He could sink lower and ignore her . . . or give himself a birthday treat and chat with an attractive woman for a few minutes.

No contest, in light of the solitary evening that loomed ahead—providing she wasn't here on some sort of bothersome business.

He set the card down, pushed aside the canvas that covered the opening, and emerged into the stern.

The woman hugged the folder tighter and gave him a wary once-over.

Understandable, given his disheveled state after a full day on the water and the coarse stubble that would be darkening his jaw by now.

"Can I help you?" Taking into account her poised-to-flee posture, he remained where he was.

"Steven Roark?"

"Guilty."

"My name is Holly Miller. May I speak with you for a few minutes?"

"Depends."

Faint creases dented her brow. "On what?"

"On the reason for your visit. I'm not in the mood for a sales pitch."

"I'm not selling anything."

"Then we can talk." For as long as she liked, since he had nothing more exciting to do.

How pathetic that the bright spot of his birthday was a visit from a nervous woman who looked as if she couldn't wait to escape.

But it beat going home to an empty apartment.

"Um . . ." She surveyed the marina. "Could we sit somewhere? Like . . . back there?" She motioned toward crescent-shaped Dockside Drive, where benches and planters were placed along the sidewalk at the top of the sloping pile of boulders that led to the water.

"I have a few chores to finish here before I leave. Why don't you come on board?"

She gave the craft a dubious sweep. "My sea legs aren't the best."

"There isn't much motion in the marina." Extending a hand, he moved toward her, toning down his usual take-charge manner. Based on her rigid stance, that sort of approach could frighten her off. "She's easy to board, and we can sit there." He indicated the unprotected bench seats along the edge of the stern.

It would be warmer—and far less windy—inside the portable

enclosure he'd erected for today's charter trip, but despite the windows it was safer to stay in the open. With all the misconduct allegations flying around these days, why take chances?

"Okay." She swallowed . . . grasped his hand . . . and eased one foot onto the gunwale.

The craft gave an almost imperceptible bob as she transferred her weight, and she gasped. Tightened her grip.

"You're fine. I've got you. Just step down."

She followed his instructions, but the maneuver was downright clumsy, and the instant both her feet were on the deck she groped for the seat and collapsed onto it in an awkward sprawl.

Pretty as his visitor was, she seemed to have been shortchanged in the gracefulness department.

And the pink hue that crept over her cheeks suggested she knew that.

He took a seat at the far end of the stern, leaving plenty of space between them. "You have the floor . . . or the deck." He hiked up one side of his mouth. Holly Miller appeared to be wound up tight as the ubiquitous black turban snails that clung to the rocks on Oregon beaches. Perhaps a touch of humor would help her chill.

Didn't work.

Her lips remained flat—and taut—as she set the folder in her lap, picked a speck of lint off her jeans, and zipped up her windbreaker as far as it would go. "Are you familiar with the Helping Hands volunteer organization here in town?"

"Yes."

"Well, I'm on a committee that's putting together a dinner auction to raise funds for a new pro-life initiative. Everyone involved is soliciting auction items. Reverend Baker at Grace Christian mentioned you as a potential donor. That's why I'm here."

Steven stifled a groan.

This was the thanks he got for letting Cindy not only pressure him into helping with the holiday food drive at a church to which he didn't even belong, but allowing her to drag him across the room for an introduction to the minister.

Proving the truth of the old adage that no good deed went unpunished.

Worse yet, of all the causes his visitor could be soliciting for, why did it have to be this one?

When the silence lengthened, she cleared her throat. "I was, uh, hoping you'd consider donating a charter fishing trip for two—or four, if possible. Everyone we've contacted has been very generous. I spoke this morning with the owner of the Seabird Inn B&B, and he offered a weekend romance package for one of his rooms."

If she was hoping to guilt him into donating, it wasn't going to work.

"What will the money you raise be used for?" He could guess, but the stall tactic would buy him a few seconds to figure out how to decline without coming across as a heartless jerk.

She opened the folder on her lap, withdrew a sheet of paper, and held it out to him. "This explains the effort in detail, but topline, we'll establish a fund to support efforts that protect life in all its stages. One example would be providing financial assistance to abortion alternatives, like paying expenses for women who agree to carry their babies to term and linking them with adoption agencies. We may also get involved in issues like capital punishment."

He narrowed his eyes. "What's your beef with capital punishment?"

She met his gaze square on. "Killing is killing."

"Putting a guilty person to death is called justice. And it keeps that person from taking other innocent lives."

"A lifetime prison sentence does too."

"At a huge expense to taxpayers."

"How do you put a price on a life?"

"There are practical considerations."

"Also ethical ones."

Squelching the temptation to continue the debate, he skimmed the sheet she'd handed him. This wasn't a subject on which they were going to agree, so why argue on his birthday . . . or extend an encounter that was going south? This day had been depressing enough.

"Let me think about it." He folded the sheet into a small square, tucked it in the pocket of his jacket, and stood.

She gave a slow blink at his abrupt dismissal—but after a slight hesitation she rose too.

And almost lost her balance.

Again.

He took her arm in a firm grip. "Steady."

"Sorry. I'm a landlubber through and through." She flashed him a shaky smile.

That could be true—but it didn't explain her equilibrium issues.

The same kind Patrick had on occasion.

Yet this woman, with her clear hazel eyes, didn't strike him as the type who would struggle with his brother's problem.

Appearances could be deceiving, though. That's why you had to fact find, then make decisions using the evidence you uncovered . . . always keeping the greater good in mind.

At least that's how he'd justified some of his choices in the past.

As Holly tugged free of his hold and turned to disembark, he shifted gears. "Let me go first."

Without waiting for a reply, he hopped onto the dock and held out a hand.

After a nanosecond's hesitation, she took it and climbed up onto the seat. Swayed. Stabilized after he tightened his grip.

"One more step." Steven gave a little pull, and she heaved herself up.

He maintained a firm grip until she was on the dock beside him and wiggled her fingers free.

Although the lady still didn't appear to be all that sure-footed, he relinquished his hold—but stayed close.

She tucked the folder tight against her chest again. "I appreciate your time today. If you decide to donate, you can contact Helping Hands at the number on the sheet I gave you."

"Could I call you instead?"

The instant the words spilled out, he frowned. Where in blazes had *that* come from? Why would he want to have any further contact with a woman who'd run the other direction if she knew his history?

Her raised eyebrows indicated she was as surprised by the query as he was. "I, uh, suppose I could give you my phone number and email."

No backtracking now.

He pulled out his cell. "Ready whenever you are."

As she recited them, he tapped in the phone digits and the professional rather than personal email address. "You work for the school district?"

"Yes."

She offered nothing more.

Fair enough. He was a stranger, and she was smart to be cautious.

But he was no threat to her.

Nor was there much chance she'd ever hear from him again. Willing as he was to support charitable causes, this particular endeavor didn't fit with his history.

He motioned toward Dockside Drive. "I'll walk you to solid ground."

"No." She edged away, leaving a faint, pleasing floral scent in her wake. "I've delayed you from your chores too long already."

"I don't mind."

"Thank you, but I can manage on my own." Her chin rose a notch. "I may not have perfect balance, but I'm perfectly capable of taking care of myself. I'll let you get back to whatever you were doing on your boat."

With that, she pivoted and wobbled down the dock toward Dockside Drive.

Steven folded his arms, reining in the urge to follow along behind her in case she started to tumble. The lady had made it clear she didn't want an arm to hold.

All she wanted was a donation.

Too bad he couldn't accommodate her.

But after everything he'd done, God might smite him with a bolt of lightning if he tried to contribute to a pro-life cause.

Don't fall! Don't fall! Don't fall!

Holly concentrated on putting one foot in front of the other as she traversed the wooden planks.

While walking on firm surfaces posed few problems, a slightly undulating platform could be dicey.

Despite all the falls she'd taken in her life, for some reason doing a face-plant with Steven Roark watching would be the ultimate humiliation.

And the man was definitely watching her. That intent gaze of his was drilling a hole in her back.

Just a few more feet, Holly, and you'll be on terra firma. You can make it.

She focused on her destination, exhaling in relief as the soles of her shoes made contact with the concrete sidewalk.

From here, getting to her car was a stroll in the park.

She picked up her pace, furrowing her brow at a sudden urge to glance over her shoulder for one last glimpse of the charter fisherman. What was *that* all about? Why would she want to see Steven Roark again?

It wasn't as if he'd gone out of his way to be charming, after all. Yeah, he had decent manners—but he'd gotten downright argumentative during their brief exchange about capital punishment.

That was a hot-button issue for many people, though—and both sides had compelling arguments.

Given his abrupt end to their conversation, however, he wasn't open to continuing the debate. He couldn't have hustled her off his boat any faster.

No wonder she was flustered—and unsettled.

On top of all that, Steven Roark was nothing like she'd expected. There wasn't a lick of similarity between the taciturn man and his amicable six-year-old nephew. Nor did he resemble—in appearance or manner—the boy's sandy-haired, low-key father who'd come to the recent first-grade parent-teacher conference with his wife.

Yet the temptation to look over her shoulder remained.

Holly skirted two gulls that stared at her from the middle of the sidewalk and held their ground.

There could be only one explanation for her reaction.

Brusque dismissal aside, the man exuded magnetism—and no one with his commanding presence had ever entered her orbit. Certainly none with a tall, toned physique, strong jaw, wind-mussed brown hair, and piercing chestnut-colored eyes.

He was the type who would appeal to women attracted to tall, dark, and dangerous men.

But that description didn't fit *her*. Steven Roark was one-eighty from the romantic hero of her dreams. There was nothing about him that should set off a buzz in her nerve endings.

Yet there it was.

Go figure.

As another powerful temptation to turn around swept over her, she huffed out a breath.

Enough.

She'd gone to his boat to make a pitch for a donation. Period. The next step—if there was one—was his.

Keeping her eyes aimed straight ahead, she continued toward her car—until the distracting aroma of grilling fish tickled her nostrils.

Salivary glands kicking in, she surveyed the small waterside park abutting the river at the far end of Dockside Drive. The serving window was open on the taco truck that was a permanent fixture beside it on the wharf, and Charley Lopez was leaning on the counter, deep in conversation with a customer.

She hesitated.

It was early for dinner . . . but after that disconcerting encounter with Steven Roark, Charley's tasty tacos might help calm her.

And she wouldn't have to cook tonight either.

Sold.

She switched direction and approached the window with the owner's name emblazoned above in colorful letters against a white background.

As she drew near, the customer picked up his order, lifted a hand in farewell to Charley, and strolled away.

"Ah. If it isn't my favorite teacher." Charley's lips curved up as she approached, a fan of lines radiating from the corners of his eyes.

"I bet you say that to all the teachers." She smiled back at the man with the weathered, latte-toned skin who was wearing a Ducks cap over his long, gray ponytail.

Strange how easy it was to chat with Charley despite the childhood shyness she'd never been able to shake.

"I have many favorites—all for different reasons."

"Smooth answer."

"But sincere." He grinned at her. "Did you stop by to say hello, or are you in the mood for tacos?"

"Tacos. I caught the aroma as I was walking back from the wharf and couldn't resist."

"My best advertising. That, and word of mouth." He pulled two fillets out of a cooler and set them on the grill. "What took you to the wharf?"

She gave him a quick recap of her visit. "But I'm afraid my sales skills aren't as polished as yours. He didn't commit to a donation."

"Could be he wants to mull over how best to contribute." Charley tossed a handful of diced onions and red peppers on the griddle and began chopping a chipotle.

"I don't think so. I got the impression he wasn't receptive to the cause."

"Is that right?" He finished with the chipotle. "That surprises me. He seems like a nice fellow."

"You know him?" Holly kept her tone casual. Curious as she was about the charter fisherman, that didn't mean she wanted anyone to *know* she was curious.

"Don't you?"

"No. Should I?"

"Maybe not. From what I can tell, Steven keeps to himself." Charley pulled a lime out of the cooler and began cutting it into wedges. "I don't see you very often either."

"It's not a reflection of your cooking, trust me. I've just been busy learning the ropes on my new job and settling in. Church is about the only place I socialize."

Sad but true.

While she'd successfully demonstrated her independence since moving from Eugene in January, so far she was batting zero on her resolution to spice up her social life.

"I expect Steven's busy too. That may be one of the reasons he keeps a low profile. Of course, people also tend to do that if they have a lot on their mind . . . or they're insecure." He gave her a fast scan and went back to cooking.

She squinted at his back. Was the latter part of that comment meant for *her*?

No.

What a ridiculous notion.

She and Charley had no more than a passing acquaintance. He knew nothing of her history.

Besides, her self-confidence was growing by the day.

"Why do you think he has a lot on his mind?" Best to shine the spotlight back where it belonged.

Charley laid three corn tortillas on the grill and shook his special spice onto the fish and veggies. "Call it intuition. In any case,

I expect he could use a few friends. Don't you think so, Floyd?" He aimed the question over her shoulder.

Holly swiveled around. There was a fair amount of activity on the other side of Dockside Drive, where storefronts with colorful awnings and containers waiting to be filled with spring flowers lined the street. But no one was anywhere close to her.

Who was Charley—

A loud squawk erupted at her feet, and she jumped back.

Two gulls stood less than a yard away. One inspected her as his companion made a cackling noise that sounded like a laugh.

Charley leaned over the window. "Hey, Gladys. I didn't know you were here too."

Holly took a calming breath as amusement displaced fright. "You're acquainted with these gulls?" The town sage was living up to his reputation as an eccentric artist/taco chef.

"We're old friends. Right, you two?"

Gladys cackled again, and Charley chuckled as he straightened up and began assembling her tacos.

"You have unusual friends." Holly pulled out her wallet, keeping tabs on the twosome that was a bit too close for comfort.

Kind of like the pair on the sidewalk that had refused to budge as she walked away from the wharf.

Was it possible they'd followed her here and—

Rolling her eyes, she cut off that fanciful line of thought.

As if seagulls had agendas.

"Friends come in all shapes and sizes, and from all manner of backgrounds." Charley began wrapping the tacos in white paper. "Lots of people write off potential friends who seem too different at first glance. The trick is taking a second look—and checking out their heart as well as their face."

Holly counted out her money. "That sounds reasonable in theory."

"Works in practice too. Doesn't it, Floyd?"

In response, the gulls rose into the air with a screech and flutter of wings, then flew off in the direction of Steven's boat.

Or more likely, toward the harbor in general—the readiest source of a meal, thanks to the fishing crafts anchored in the sheltered waters between the pair of islands on the right and the breakwater on the left.

But they stopped and circled in the vicinity of his boat.

Odd.

Judging by his thoughtful expression as she turned back to pay for her order, Charley had reached the same conclusion. "Curious." He continued to watch the feathered duo.

"How so?"

He flashed his white teeth. "Floyd and Gladys usually hang around here until I toss them a handout—unless another mission takes priority." Without giving her a chance to question him further, he passed over her order. "Enjoy."

"Always." She handed him the bills.

"Let me get your change."

She waved away the offer. "The amount's too small to worry about. But you wouldn't have to make change if you took credit cards." She tapped the cash-only sign taped to the serving window.

"Why muddle up a simple transaction with computers and encryption and cloud technology? People today have a tendency to make things more complicated than they have to be. When I think of a cloud, that's what I want to picture." He swept a hand toward the heavens, where fluffy white billows and blue sky were appearing through the mist.

"I wouldn't expect anything less from an artist." Holly inhaled the savory aroma wafting up from the sack.

"Ah, but we're all born artists. The challenge, as Picasso pointed out, is how to remain an artist once you grow up."

"Not everyone has your talent with a brush, though."

"Yet we can all see with the eyes of an artist if we leave preconceived notions behind, open ourselves to possibilities, listen with our heart—and take a leap of faith." Charley grinned. "And there you have my thought for the day. Enjoy those tacos."

Holly relinquished her place in line to a hand-holding couple and continued toward her car, her step lighter. As usual, her short visit with Charley had lifted her spirits and provided food for both mind and stomach.

But she hadn't learned a thing about Steven Roark.

While the taco chef seemed to know an inordinate amount about Hope Harbor residents, he epitomized the word *discretion*.

Meaning if she wanted more background on the fisherman, she'd have to find another source.

First, however, she needed to determine why she was so keen to ferret out info on a man who'd been a stranger less than an hour ago.

At the door to her Civic, she angled back toward the marina. Steven's boat was too far away to distinguish—but the two gulls continued to circle in their holding pattern over a craft in the vicinity of his.

Despite Charley's assessment of the fisherman as a nice guy, if she was a betting woman she'd wager he'd already decided not to contribute to the Helping Hands event.

Too bad. A charter fishing trip could bring in a hefty sum at the auction.

Jiggling her keys, she tipped her head and watched the gulls.

If she wanted to venture outside her comfort zone again—take a leap of faith, as Charley had put it—she *could* pay Roark a second visit, make another appeal. After all, she believed in the cause heart and soul.

But that wouldn't be your only motivation for returning, Holly.

At the chiding reminder from her subconscious, she yanked open her door and slid into the car.

Fine. She could admit the truth.

Her reasons for going back—if she decided to follow through on the impulse—wouldn't be entirely altruistic.

Because despite his daunting personality . . . despite an intuitive sense that it would be safer to walk a wide circle around him . . . Steven Roark was the most intriguing man she'd ever met.

And she wanted to see him again.

2

Easing back on the gas pedal, Steven drove past the small house his brother's family called home.

The driveway was empty—as expected.

Cindy always went to church on Sunday, and with a six-year-old and an infant to feed and get dressed, she preferred the later service.

Or so she'd told him.

No way he'd know that from personal experience, since he hadn't attended a Sunday service with any regularity for too many years to count—and none during his tenure in Hope Harbor.

At the end of the block, he made a U-turn and retraced his route, parking in front of the house that was tucked into a quiet neighborhood a few blocks from Dockside Drive.

Steven killed the engine and sat unmoving, the knot in his stomach tightening.

This impromptu visit could end up being a fiasco.

But with the twelve-month anniversary of his arrival approaching, he and Patrick were past due for a long talk. He hadn't moved to Hope Harbor for his health—not primarily, anyway—and his mission to save his brother was floundering.

That had to change.

Beginning today.

Lips pressed together, he shoved the door open, got out of his Wrangler, and marched toward the tiny front porch.

He bypassed the two steps in one leap, pressed the bell—and reined in his temper.

Stay cool, Roark. Keep this calm and rational. Today is all about breaking down barriers and making a fresh start.

Check.

His hard-nosed approach had not only failed, it had driven a deeper wedge between them—and unless they resolved their differences and got back on civil footing, he wouldn't be able to help Patrick tackle his problem or lend the family a helping hand.

Helping hand.

An image of Holly Miller flashed across his mind, her wavy hair blowing in the salt breeze, expression earnest, eyes vibrant.

The corners of his mouth rose a fraction.

She was a pretty woman—and her visit had been the highlight of his birthday . . . until she'd ventured into restricted territory with her Helping Hands request.

His lips flattened.

He ought to forget about their brief encounter. What was the point of a combat-toughened, seen-it-all warrior thinking *those* kinds of thoughts about a woman who radiated idealism? Who came across as an optimist. As the sheltered type who believed the best about everyone.

She was no match for a guy who'd lost his rose-colored glasses long ago.

Expunging her image from his brain, Steven pressed the bell again.

Waited another thirty seconds.

Gave it one more try.

Nothing.

Anger nipped at his composure.

If Patrick continued to avoid him, how would they ever smooth out the turbulent waters between them?

Gritting his teeth, he pressed the bell again . . . and again . . . and again . . . and again . . . and—

The knob rattled, and an instant later the door was flung open.

His brother glared at him from the other side. "What's with the noise blitz? I was trying to sleep in."

Steven took a quick inventory of the man across from him—uncombed hair, bloodshot red-rimmed eyes, shaky hands, baggy sweats, bare feet—and folded his arms. "Sleeping in . . . or sleeping it off?"

Spots of color appeared on Patrick's cheeks. "None of your business."

His brother attempted to shut the door, but Steven grabbed the edge of it and stuck his foot in the jamb. "If it affects my sister-in-law and nephew and niece, it's my business."

"Did Cindy put you up to this?" Patrick shaded his eyes, squinting against the muted light on this cloudy day.

More evidence he was hungover.

"She has no idea I'm here." He let a beat pass. "Thanks for the birthday card, by the way."

A muscle twitched in Patrick's cheek. "That was Cindy's idea."

"So I gathered. Your chicken scrawl was nowhere in sight. You going to ask me in?"

"No."

"Tough. I'm not leaving until we talk." He shouldered past his brother, into the tiny but tidy living room, and claimed a seat on the couch.

Spewing out a rude term, Patrick slammed the door and followed him in. "You're trespassing."

"So call the cops."

Several charged moments passed before he capitulated. "What do you want?"

"I want to know what's stuck in your craw." Steven kept his tone neutral. "I've been back almost a year, and our relationship has gone from bad to worse. Every overture I've made, you've thrown back in my face. We need to talk."

"Overture?" Patrick barked out a laugh. "I don't call telling me how to run my life an overture. Let's get this straight—I don't answer to you. I don't even have to talk to you." He kept his distance, hands clenched at his sides.

At the simmering rage radiating from his brother, Steven slowly filled his lungs and tamped down his own anger. If Patrick shut down, they'd get nowhere.

A change of tactics was in order.

Gentling his voice, Steven leaned forward. "Look, I care about you, okay? I don't want you to end up like Dad."

"Dad was a good guy."

"Yeah, he was—but he had a problem. A problem that killed him . . . *and* Mom. He ran into that tree head-on—and his BAC was double the legal limit. Is that the kind of trauma you want for *your* family?"

"I don't have Dad's problem."

"Patrick—he denied it too."

His brother shoved his fingers through his hair and began to pace. "Dad couldn't regulate his drinking. I can. Yeah, I like to have a couple of scotches on Friday night with the guys after work. That's not a big deal."

"It is if two drinks become three or four or five . . . or you drink every night."

"I don't drink every night. I've got this under control. I know when to stop."

"Do you?"

"Yeah." He clamped his hands on his hips, posture rigid, jaw hard.

"Drinking can escalate."

"I know that." Patrick closed the distance between them and got in his face, antagonism contorting his features. "I also know that I don't appreciate my war-hero big brother swooping onto my turf telling me how to live my life or coming to my rescue. Not everyone can be a top-gun high-achiever hero with an MBA and a closet full of citations and sports trophies and academic awards—but I'm doing fine. I don't need your help." His nostrils flared. "So why don't you go back to the Middle East, earn a few more medals, and leave us mere mortals alone?"

Steven sucked in a breath.

Whoa.

That was the longest speech his brother had made in the past year—and the most enlightening.

How long had he been nursing what appeared to be a formidable inferiority complex?

Was *that* the source of their rift?

Was that also one of the reasons he'd sought solace in alcohol?

And had his big brother's homecoming exacerbated the situation?

Spirits tanking, Steven flexed his stiff fingers as he continued to grapple with the implications of Patrick's rant. "I'm picking up a boatload of resentment."

An understatement if ever there was one.

Patrick swiped the back of his hand across his eyes and retreated, shoulders drooping. "You are who you are. It is what it is. I thought I'd accepted that—but when you showed up, all the old feelings came rushing back. I'm working on them . . . but it's hard to live in the shadow of a rock star."

His defeatist tone was more worrisome than his fury.

"I'm a charter fisherman, Patrick. Not a rock star . . . or a corporate executive or sports celebrity or movie idol. And my military days are over."

"You fish by choice—and I bet not forever. You'll move on to bigger things after you finish your current mission to straighten me out. But I don't need straightening out—no matter what Cindy's told you." Patrick slumped into a chair on the far side of the room. "I know she wrote to you. I know that's why you came here."

How to respond?

Steven balled his fingers and studied the framed family photo on a side table, no hint of the turbulence in this house visible beneath the smiling faces of the foursome. Cindy *had* asked him to keep her letter confidential, but she hadn't summoned him to Hope Harbor. She'd merely laid out her concerns and sought his advice. It had been his choice to muster out and show up unannounced.

In view of what he'd just learned, however, riding into town in a white hat may not have been the best choice.

"You don't have to respond." Patrick let his head drop back against the upholstery. "I assume they train you special forces guys to keep secrets. But one day, when her hormones were all over the place while she was pregnant, she admitted she wrote to you. Didn't matter. I'd already figured it out."

"She didn't ask me to come. That was my idea."

"I know. She told me. I wasn't surprised. You always did have the hero gene."

Hero gene?

Not a term that had ever crossed his radar—yet Patrick could have him pegged. Growing up, his make-believe games had all revolved around superheroes and saving the world. As an adult, he'd simply transferred that mind-set to a broader stage.

Given the five-year spread in ages, plus their different sets of friends, he'd never considered the impact of his achievements on Patrick.

But in hindsight, he should have. Living in the shadow of a brother who seemed larger than life couldn't have been easy for a kid who was more inclined to bury his nose in a history book and hide behind the lens of a camera than to work out at the gym or study weaponry.

His spirits continued to plummet.

If that was the source of their conflict, the challenge was far bigger than he'd feared. You couldn't erase decades of memories in a few months—or even a year.

Maybe never.

Yet his brother *did* have issues—and he needed help now.

What a mess.

"I can hear the gears whirring in that precise military mind of yours." Patrick crossed his arms, watching him from across the room. "Save your brainpower for someone else. I may not be perfect, but I'm capable of taking care of myself."

Not perfect, but capable.

Almost a verbatim replay of Holly Miller's parting comment yesterday, after he'd raised her hackles.

Odd fluke.

Or was it?

Perhaps there was a message in there he should heed.

Since tough love hadn't worked, it might be time for a kinder, gentler approach with Patrick. Give him support and encouragement instead of grief. Let him find his own path instead of trying to run the show and ramrod his own ideas through. Demonstrate he had faith in him, that he considered him capable despite his flaws.

That wasn't how a take-charge kind of guy would choose to handle the situation—but he was on a new kind of battlefield here, and different tactics could be more effective than the ones he'd employed overseas in pursuit of real-life villains.

Steven exhaled and clasped his hands. "I had no idea the friction between us went back that far."

"Doesn't matter." Patrick gave a taut shrug. "It's history."

"If it's still affecting us, it matters. It never occurred to me that my life had had such an impact on yours. You were just a kid when I left for college, and I didn't see much of you on my summer breaks, thanks to my fishing jobs."

"I saw *you*, though—and so did everyone else in our circle. I also heard about you from teachers in high school, who encouraged me to get stellar grades—like you did . . . find a niche or two to excel in—like you did . . . and go to college—like you did."

Steven cringed.

That stunk.

"I'm sorry you had to deal with that." What else could he say?

"I survived—and I created my own life here, with Cindy. Close enough to Coos Bay to feel at home, but far enough away to leave comparisons behind."

Until his big brother had shown up, charging into the fray, resurrecting old resentments—and changing everything.

Patrick didn't have to say the words. The message came through loud and clear.

"I didn't mean to disrupt your world. I came because I cared."

The hard line of Patrick's jaw softened a hair. "I get that—and I appreciate your good intentions. But you know what they say about those."

Ouch.

If Patrick was comparing his presence to fire and brimstone, maybe he ought to leave.

But if he did . . . if he gave up . . . his mission here would be unfinished—and leaving a job undone wasn't in his DNA.

Besides, where would he go? With Mom and Dad gone, Coos Bay was just another town filled with strangers. At least he'd met some nice people in Hope Harbor—and reacquainted himself with a few others. Like Charley at the taco stand, who'd been a fixture here forever. And Eleanor Cooper, the oldest resident, who'd welcomed him to town with a special delivery of one of her famous fudge cakes.

The truth was, since his days of crewing on a fishing boat, Hope Harbor had felt more like home than anywhere he'd lived after bidding farewell to childhood.

And he didn't want to leave.

"Look. You're all the family I have left." He swallowed, struggling to put together a plan that would be acceptable to both of them. "I want to see Beatrice and Jonah grow up, be part of their lives. I want to be part of *your* life. Let's figure out how to smooth the waters, make this work. Nobody here knows my background, and I don't have to talk about it. I *won't* talk about it if you prefer I don't. And I *can't* talk about my military service. That's classified."

"It's not fair to ask you to ignore your accomplishments."

"Family means more to me than any award I've received or job I've done. It's not a sacrifice to keep all that to myself. I view it as a fair trade. I'll also butt out of your business."

Patrick narrowed his eyes. "You'll stop trying to fix my so-called problem?"

The problem wasn't so-called. It was real.

But he bit back the reply poised for launch on the tip of his tongue.

"If that's what it takes." Hard as it would be to step aside, look the other way when someone he loved was on the road to disaster, he'd honor his promise. Keeping tabs on Patrick would be much easier if they were talking than if they remained estranged.

"You really think you can stay hands-off?" Patrick didn't try to hide his skepticism.

"I never break a promise."

As the seconds ticked by, the temptation to hurl a plea for assistance toward the heavens was strong.

But God wouldn't be interested in the likes of him.

Instead, he waited—and hoped.

"So let's be clear." Patrick locked gazes with him. "No more lectures. No more storming into the bar and reading me the riot act or laying a guilt trip on me. No more texts or emails with links to AA material or articles about the dangers of alcohol and signs of addiction. No more calling Cindy to get status reports on me. Agreed?"

Rattled off machine-gun fashion like that, his typical let's-get-results-fast, hard-nosed, shape-up-or-ship-out style did sound a mite overbearing.

And who knew? If the pressure was off, Patrick might be less stressed—and less inclined to seek solace in alcohol. Without regular infusions of booze, it was possible he'd see the light on his own and get his act together.

"Agreed." He rose and held out his hand.

After a moment, Patrick stood too, and returned his firm clasp.

"To celebrate our truce, why don't you let me take you all out to dinner in Bandon or Coos Bay tonight? I'd suggest the Myrtle Café, but I doubt Cindy would consider that much of a treat with all the hours she spends there waitressing."

"Thanks, but she put a stew in the crockpot this morning before she went to church."

Steven waited—but no reciprocal invitation came.

He stifled a foolish surge of disappointment. Perhaps in time he'd be welcome here, but it was too soon to expect such rapid progress. "If there's a night this week that would work for all of you, give me a call. My schedule is wide open."

"I'll have Cindy check our calendar." A beat ticked by. "Thanks."

Steven fished out his keys. Much as he'd like to prolong this visit, there was nothing else to say. His business was finished for today. "I'll get out of your hair. I have to run down to the wharf for a few minutes."

"I'm surprised you aren't out on a charter this morning." Patrick followed him to the door.

No reason to share that he'd declined a last-minute booking to keep his morning free for this visit. Giving up a few hundred dollars was a small price to pay for a chance to get his relationship with his brother on more solid footing.

"March can be tricky. The weather is iffy, and the majority of people don't want to spend hours damp and cold on a boat."

"Put me in that camp. Don't those conditions bother you?"

"I'm used to worse."

"Yeah. I suppose you are. The Middle East couldn't have been a picnic. Especially in your line of work."

Steven winced.

Outside of his Delta cohorts, only Patrick knew what he'd

done in The Unit. Operators didn't talk about their jobs to anyone. Period.

If the two of them hadn't gone drinking on that terrible day four years ago—and downed a few too many shots—he'd never have let it slip.

An indiscretion that had led him to swear off alcohol.

He paused at the door. "Take care of yourself—and text me a date for dinner."

"I will."

Steven nodded and turned to go—but a hand on his arm stopped him. He angled back.

"For the record, I do appreciate all you gave up to come here." The expression of gratitude was grudging—and not entirely deserved.

"Don't saddle yourself with a guilt trip, Patrick. I was ready for a change, and Cindy's letter gave me the excuse I needed to muster out. I don't have any regrets." About coming to Hope Harbor anyway.

"I'm glad to hear that. Talk to you soon."

"Count on it." He lifted his hand in farewell.

As the door closed behind him, Steven returned to his car and started the engine, the tension in his shoulders diminishing.

The meeting had produced far more positive results than he'd dared hope.

And Patrick had displayed keen insights on several fronts—including his speculation that charter fishing wasn't part of his brother's long-term plans. While his months on the water in the open air had helped him regroup, de-stress, and ease back into civilian life, fishing wasn't how he wanted to spend his future. The fickle, sometimes fiendish, coastal weather was better appreciated from land than from sea.

Maybe he was getting soft, but his tolerance for cold and wet was nosediving.

He cranked up the heater.

One of these days he'd have to think about what he wanted to do with the rest of his life—and whether he should find someone to spend it with.

For the second time in less than thirty minutes, an image of Holly Miller materialized on his internal screen.

He frowned.

That was nuts.

Other than the quick glimpse of fiery passion she'd given him while they sparred over capital punishment, his awkward visitor had come across as a timid introvert.

That kind of woman typically didn't merit a second glance from him.

She was, however, one of the few young, eligible females he'd met in Hope Harbor—and their encounter was very recent.

That had to explain why she was lingering in his mind.

You sure about that, Roark?

At the prod from his subconscious, he put the car in gear and released the brake.

Yeah. He was sure. There was no other reason for her to be popping into his mind.

Except she managed to rev your engine, didn't she?

"Oh, shut up."

As he muttered that response and tuned out the annoying voice in his head, he lowered the heat and pointed the car toward the wharf.

Holly Miller may have stoked his libido for reasons that eluded him, but they were at opposite ends of the philosophical and ethical spectrum. Whatever appeal she held for him had to be some hormone aberration.

End of story.

In fact, even if they were compatible on every level, the chances anything would come of it were slim.

Fighting back a wave of melancholy, Steven flipped on his turn signal and scanned the rearview mirror, watching the house his brother shared with his wife and children recede.

Despite Patrick's issues with alcohol and self-esteem, he had a family that loved him.

That was more than his older sibling with the alleged hero gene had.

More than he might ever have.

Because until—or unless—he came to terms with his past, he was doomed to a solo existence.

3

She had a new neighbor.

Tires crunching on the gravel, Holly swung her Civic into the driveway of her rental house on Sea Rose Lane and surveyed the small moving truck in front of the adjacent bungalow.

The white clapboard cottage next door with the miniscule front porch was the smallest dwelling on the dead-end street, but the unobstructed view of sea and sky from the patio on the double lot was to die for.

Too bad it hadn't been available three months ago.

On the bright side, though, her house had been completely renovated, and it was charming despite the more restricted view. Plus, there was less yard work.

She parked and slid out of her car as two uniformed men exited the house next door, followed by a gray-haired man with a cane. After a brief exchange and handshakes, the movers continued to their truck and climbed aboard.

The older gent glanced over at her from his porch as the van pulled away from the curb, and she smiled and waved.

Without acknowledging her greeting, he turned his back and disappeared inside, closing the door after him.

Well.

She may not have gotten to know the previous occupants all that well given the long hours the couple had worked, but at least they'd been pleasant whenever they'd seen her.

This guy didn't appear to have any interest in striking up an acquaintance—or even exchanging a civil greeting.

In fact, he was as off-putting as Steven Roark—without the saving grace of the fisherman's inexplicable tingle-inducing charisma.

Holly retrieved her work satchel from the back seat, locked her car, and trudged toward the house.

What a day.

First, two upchucking six-year-olds that had *not* been part of her lesson plan, now a new neighbor who seemed about as sociable as the reclusive mole crabs that burrowed into the sand at the first hint of an interloper.

Not the best start to her week.

But she could veg for an hour before dinner and try to—

At the sudden vibration from inside her purse, she fumbled the key as she inserted it in the lock.

Good grief.

Ever since that unsettling encounter on Saturday with Steven Roark, her nerves had been—

She froze.

Roark.

Could this be him, calling to donate to the auction?

If so—and she let it roll—he could change his mind.

She pushed the door open, dropped her satchel to the floor, and scrambled to retrieve the cell before voicemail kicked in.

But it wasn't the charter fisherman.

Quashing an irrational surge of disappointment, she pressed the talk button and put the phone to her ear. "Hi, Mom."

"Hi, honey. Everything okay?"

Same question her mother always asked.

"Fine." No way was she going to share the news about the virus outbreak at school that was felling students and teachers alike. Her parents would only worry more than they already did. "The kids are wonderful, and every day is a joy." Well . . . most days, anyway.

"You sound a little less perky than usual." A thread of worry wove through her mother's comment.

"It *is* Monday." She injected a touch of humor into her inflection and changed the subject. "What's new with you and Dad?"

As she listened to her mother recount a story about one of her cousins back East, she wandered into the kitchen and over to the back window that offered a view of the sea beyond the house next door.

The scene was calming, as always—until her new neighbor emerged onto his patio, a folding chair in one hand, his cane in the other.

She frowned.

At fifty-five degrees, with gray skies and a fine mist in the air, it wasn't the best day to sit outside. Yet he opened the chair, faced it toward the sea, and eased into the seat.

"Don't you think so, honey?"

Whoops.

She angled back toward the kitchen. "Sorry, Mom. I was distracted for a minute. I have a new neighbor, and I was watching him out the window. What did you ask me?"

"A new neighbor? What does he look like?" Her mother's tone was half worried, half hopeful.

Better quash the worry and dash the hopes.

"I'd estimate he's in his late seventies. He moved in today."

"Oh." Hard to tell if her mother was disappointed or relieved. "You'll have to go over and introduce yourself. I always do that with newcomers on our street—and I bring along a plate of homemade cookies."

"I remember." She perused the man over her shoulder. "I don't know about this guy, though. He ignored my wave as I pulled in from school."

"He could be exhausted. Moving can be trying—and tiring. Worse if you're doing it alone. Have you seen anyone else?"

"No."

"All the more reason to make him feel welcome. He may be overwhelmed—and lonesome. It wouldn't hurt to give him a second chance. Sometimes the least friendly people are the ones in greatest need of a friend."

An image of Steven Roark popped into her mind.

Could that be true for him too? Hadn't Charley suggested as much on Saturday?

Perhaps the fisherman's usual disposition was agreeable and she'd just caught him at a bad time. His customers may have been demanding or irritable, and he could have been tired and frustrated after spending hours on the water.

If she paid him another visit, would he be more receptive to her—

"Holly?"

At her mother's prompt, she blew out a breath.

Man, she was so not focused on this conversation.

"Sorry again. It was a busy day, and part of my mind is still on school."

And on a certain fisherman—though there was no reason to share *that* excuse with her mom.

"I'll let you go, then, so you can unwind. Call me later if you're in the mood for a chat."

"I think I'll make it an early night. But we'll touch base tomorrow." At least once, if her parents' typical communication pattern held.

But how could you fault people for caring too much?

And short of hurting their feelings, what choice did she have except to hope they'd eventually become more confident she was fine on her own—and worry less?

"Dad or I will call you after school if we don't hear from you. What are you having for dinner tonight?"

"Um . . ." What was in the fridge? She pulled open the door and took a quick inventory. Eggs, turkey, lettuce, cheese. "An omelet and a salad."

"That sounds healthy. We're having pot roast."

Her favorite—as her mom knew.

"I wish I was there to eat it with you."

"So do we."

There was no missing the wistful note in her mom's voice, and guilt nipped at her conscience—as usual.

She leaned against the window frame and studied the solitary man next door, who appeared to be watching the silver-white harbor seal perched on the rocks offshore.

After all her parents had done for her, after all they'd sacrificed, had it been selfish to move away, create a life apart from them? Was it wrong to deprive them of daily contact with the daughter they loved more than life itself?

The same questions she'd grappled with as she'd struggled with her decision about whether to take the job in Hope Harbor.

Yet prayer and reflection had led her to this choice—for better or for worse.

She was thirty years old, for heaven's sake. If she'd stayed in Eugene, her sheltered, comfortable existence would have continued in the same pattern until she was forty . . . and fifty . . . and sixty. Much as she loved her job, what was wrong with wanting a personal life too? A little excitement, a dash of romance, and—if it was in God's plan for her—a family of her own someday.

One thing for sure.

She'd never have met someone like Steven Roark in Eugene.

Whether that was good or bad remained to be seen, but if nothing else, their encounter had added a touch of zing to her quiet days, spiced up her—

"Honey?"

Sheesh.

How long had she been zoned out this go-round?

"I'm here, Mom."

"I didn't mean to give you a guilt trip with that last comment. You know your dad and I want you to be happy. We just miss you—and worry about you."

"I know you do. I miss you guys too. But moving here has been a confidence booster for me."

"You're not lonely?"

"With fourteen six-year-olds occupying me seven hours a day?"

"I know they keep you busy during working hours—but what about at night and on the weekends?"

"I've only been in town three months, Mom. I'm still getting the lay of the land and settling in. And speaking of being new in town, I may take your advice and bake a batch of cookies for my new neighbor."

"Can't hurt. We should never give up on people too soon. You may want to wait a day or two, though. If he moved from any distance and he's older, he'll be too tired for visitors tonight. So . . . any chance you can come up this weekend?"

Holly muffled a sigh. The almost six-hour round-trip drive was too tiring for a one-day visit after a busy week, but if she stayed overnight, there wouldn't be much left of her weekend to work on improving her social life here.

"I haven't thought that far ahead yet, Mom. Depending on what comes out of the meeting Thursday night for the Helping Hands project, I may be tied up."

"If that's the case, your dad and I could always drive down for an afternoon instead. He's fond of Charley's tacos, and we could catch up in person for an hour or two."

That would be easier to manage than driving to Eugene and would leave a large part of her weekend intact—but it would eat up her parents' whole day.

"I hate for you to make the long drive for such a short visit."

"We don't mind. Any chance to see you, no matter how brief, is worth it."

Another jab of guilt pricked her conscience.

After all the years Mom and Dad had devoted to her to the exclusion of almost everything else, they deserved a hefty dose of carefree time with each other at this stage of their lives.

But letting go after three decades would take a while. Just as her transition to a new life in Hope Harbor remained a work in progress, their adjustment to an everyday life that didn't include her physical presence would be a slow process.

She needed to work on her patience.

"I know, Mom. And I appreciate it more than I can say. Let's talk about the weekend Thursday night, after my meeting. I'll know more about my schedule then."

"That's fine, honey. We don't have any other plans. A last-minute decision will work for us. You take care."

As they said their good-byes and Holly ended the call, she wandered back to the window. The fine mist had intensified to a soft rain, but her new neighbor showed no signs of going inside.

Why would the man sit unprotected in a cold drizzle? He could end up with a bad case of the sniffles—or worse.

But she wasn't his keeper. He was old enough to make his own decisions.

Yet half an hour later, after she threw in a load of laundry, reviewed tomorrow's lesson plan, and passed the window again en route to the fridge, the man was still there.

As far as she could tell, he hadn't moved a muscle.

Okay.

This was weird.

She caught her lower lip between her teeth as she watched him through the swirling gray shroud of fog that had begun to obscure the sea view.

Was it possible he was sick? Unable to get back inside? Hoping someone would come to his aid?

If so, she was the sole candidate. Given how the houses were situated, no one could see him except her.

Great.

Apparently she was going to have to venture outside her comfort zone and traipse over there whether she liked it or not.

At least she'd had recent practice approaching a man she'd never met.

But unless this exchange went better than the one with Steven Roark, she'd be sent packing in a matter of minutes.

Sixty seconds later, slicker buttoned and hood pulled up, she stepped out the back door and assessed the situation.

If she approached the man from behind, she could scare him. Why not circle around the front and come down the driveway on the ocean side of the house? That way, he'd see her as she came around the corner and wouldn't be as startled.

Armed with that plan, she shoved her hands in the pockets of her jacket, dipped her head against the steady rain, and followed a U-shaped route—driveway to street to driveway.

Despite the slicker, in the short span it took her to reach the front corner of his house, her jeans were damp.

The breeze picked up, and a shiver rippled through her.

Gracious.

Her new neighbor had to be freezing.

Bracing for probable rejection, she picked up her pace as she drew near the back of the house. Unlike the man on the patio, she wanted out of this miserable weather ASAP.

As she rounded the corner and approached him, he shifted his gaze from the direction of the sea to her, his expression . . . vacant was the word that came to mind.

A niggle of unease crept up her spine, and she halted.

Whatever that look in his eyes, it wasn't normal.

Maybe this hadn't been her best idea. What if the man had mental issues?

Yet he didn't move or display any threatening behavior.

So she'd do what she'd come to do—but keep her distance while doing it.

"Hi." She forced up the corners of her lips. "I'm your neighbor from next door, Holly Miller. I noticed you sitting out here in the rain without a coat or umbrella, and I wanted to make sure you were all right."

He blinked, as if rousing himself from a stupor, and his light blue irises cleared. With a bony finger, he plucked the fabric of his slacks away from his thin legs and examined it, as if he'd just realized his clothes were wet.

But he made no effort to rise or go inside. Nor did he speak.

As the silence lengthened, Holly transferred her weight from one foot to the other. "I, uh, have an extra umbrella at my house, if you'd like to borrow it."

He fingered the wet material again. "Too late for that." His voice was gravelly, as if he didn't use it often. "Doesn't matter anyway."

Yes, it did. While it was true the man couldn't get any wetter, the longer he stayed out in the chilly air in soggy clothes, the higher the odds he'd get sick.

"It's kind of cool today. You may want to go inside and change into dry clothes." She maintained a friendly, conversational tone—but if the man took offense at her suggestion, she was out of here.

He lifted his chin, and at the sudden desolation in his eyes, her heart faltered. "I suppose I should, or my neighbors will think a lunatic has moved into their midst."

After setting the cane against the chair, he grasped the arms and pushed himself to his feet as if he were weighed down with weariness.

The cane began to slide, and he fumbled for it—but it slipped to the ground.

Holly hurried to his side. If he bent to pick it up, he might pitch onto the stone patio face first and end up with far worse problems than a bad cold.

She scooped up the cane and held it out.

"Thank you." His fingers brushed hers as he took it.

Wow.

Hands that icy had to be numb.

No wonder he'd lost his grip.

He needed dry clothes and a bowl of warm soup or a hot drink.

Fast.

But he hadn't made a grocery run as far as she knew. His kitchen could be bare.

As he started toward the back door without so much as a goodbye, she hesitated—but compassion won out.

"Sir."

He paused . . . then half turned her direction.

"I, uh, have a supply of soup at home. Canned, not homemade." She flashed a smile.

No reaction.

She forged ahead anyway. "If you'd like me to bring a couple of cans over until you stock your kitchen, I'd be happy to do that. Soup is perfect on a day like this."

"I'm fine." He resumed his trek to the door but did toss a grudging thank-you over his shoulder.

She remained where she was, hands jammed in her pockets, until he disappeared inside.

The instant his door closed, however, she took the shortcut across his yard to her own house, suppressing a shiver.

That had certainly gone well.

Rolling her eyes, she pushed through her own door, hung her slicker on the hook by the door, and crossed to the fridge, doing her best to forget about the incident with her new neighbor. Why dither over a rude man who hadn't even bothered to introduce himself?

But erasing the image of his forlorn expression—or ignoring a person who exuded such . . . defeat—proved difficult.

Dinner fixings in hand, she stopped by the window and surveyed the solitary chair on his rain-drenched patio. It looked lonely . . . and forsaken. Like its owner.

What was his story?

Why were no family members around to lend a hand and help him settle in?

What had brought him to the tiny town of Hope Harbor?

Was he the sole occupant of the house—or was there a wife

inside who didn't find dreary skies and cool temperatures as appealing as her spouse?

The questions tumbled through her mind, one after the other—but given the man's reticence, odds were they'd remain unanswered.

Holly continued to the counter, set down the carton of eggs, gave the bottle of spicy vinaigrette a vigorous shake—and fought back a wave of discouragement.

Based on her strikeouts with both Steven Roark and her new neighbor, it would appear her social skills were lacking when it came to the male of the species.

Yet John Nash at the Seabird Inn had been cordial during her visit to request a donation.

So maybe it wasn't her.

Maybe she'd simply run into two difficult men back to back.

She set the bottle on the counter and picked up an egg. Tapped the shell on the edge of a bowl.

It didn't give.

She tried again, with more force.

This time it yielded.

Hmm.

Steven Roark and her neighbor seemed to have hard shells too—but would they crack if she exerted a bit more force?

Not her usual style—but hadn't she come here to expose herself to new experiences, take some risks, be more adventuresome?

And what would be the harm in trying? Worst case, they'd shut her out and write her off—but since they'd already done that, she had nothing to lose.

She tapped another egg open and discarded the shell.

No reason to rush a decision, though. Why not think about it for a day—or two?

And by Wednesday, if she could gather up sufficient courage, perhaps she'd have another go at the two new men in her life who seemed as if they could use a hefty dose of TLC.

4

He needed a taco.

Bad.

Even worse than he needed a shower—which was saying a lot.

Steven stepped off the wharf and made a beeline for Charley's stand. Since Patrick had never gotten back to him about setting up a meal with the family—and it was too late today to coordinate dinner plans—a taco would be the perfect comfort food.

Thank goodness the renowned artist had decided to cook instead of paint on this quiet Wednesday afternoon.

"Steven." The man lifted a hand in greeting as he approached, his perennial upbeat nature on display as he flashed a smile. "You just caught me. The lunch rush is long over, and my muse was beginning to call. Five minutes later, you'd have found a closed window."

"Are you willing to put your muse on hold long enough to make me tacos? I had more cleanup than usual after today's trip and missed lunch. I'm starving."

"Always. I never leave a hungry customer in the lurch. One order?"

Odd question, considering that in all the months he'd been here, he'd never varied his order.

"Yes—as usual."

"Never hurts to check. Circumstances can change. How was the fishing today?"

"My clients were happy."

"Glad to hear it." Charley set a few fillets on the grill. "What do you think about all the excitement in town?"

He arched an eyebrow.

Lou at the bait and tackle shop or his fellow wharf-dwellers could usually be relied on to pass along important tidbits, but they must have fallen down on the job with this one.

"What excitement?"

"The big find up your way after Sunday night's storm. At Starfish Pier."

"I'm out of the loop on this piece of news. What's the story?"

Charley retrieved an avocado from the cooler and began cutting and skinning it. "You've been out to the pier, haven't you? It's only a short stroll from Sea Haven Apartments."

Steven frowned.

Had he ever mentioned to Charley where he lived?

Not that he could recall.

Then again, the resident sage seemed to have the inside scoop on everyone in town.

"I walk down there once in a while." Not that there was much left of the old fishing pier. Just a few rotting pilings sticking above the water.

"Have you gone as far as the tide pools at the far end of the beach?"

"No."

"They're worth a visit. Best I've ever seen, filled with starfish and anemones and sea urchins. They're a smorgasbord of beauty for people who take the time to venture onto slippery, rocky terrain and look close."

"I'll have to do that. Tell me about the big find."

Charley finished with the avocado and flipped the fish. "Well,

Logan West—the doctor at our local urgent care facility, if you haven't had the pleasure of meeting him—and his wife took their daughter out there Monday evening to see the tide pools I mentioned. They came across what they thought was a log that had washed ashore, but Jeannette—Logan's wife, who runs the lavender farm—noticed something odd about it." Charley pulled out three corn tortillas and laid them on the grill.

As the silence lengthened, Steven's lips twitched. With his storytelling ability and knack for building suspense, Charley could have been a mystery writer.

"Are you going to leave me hanging?"

"Nope." Charley grinned and sprinkled his special seasoning on the fillets. "But I don't want to shortchange your lunch, either. The current obsession with multitasking is a sad commentary on the frenetic pace of today's world."

"I won't disagree with that. But everyone's busy, and dialing back is hard."

"Possible, though. You did it."

Now how did Charley know *that*? Not once during his months in Hope Harbor had he discussed his history with anyone, other than a brief reference to being in the service.

But the military was known to be hard-driving, no matter your job . . . so maybe that's what the man was referring to.

What else could it be?

"I'm trying, anyway. What was odd about the log?"

"There was rust on it."

Steven furrowed his brow. "Wood doesn't rust."

"Bingo." Charley began chopping green onions. "After they dug around it for a few minutes, they realized it was very old and could have historic value. So they contacted a ranger at Bullards Beach State Park up the road, who concurred. He brought in someone from the Oregon Parks and Recreation Department. They cordoned the area off, and a state archaeologist was supposed to weigh in today."

That would account for the higher-than-usual traffic on the beach road in front of his apartment complex.

"Anyone know what it is?"

"So far, the consensus seems to be that it's a cannon."

Steven arched his eyebrows. "That's not your typical beach find."

"Far from it." Charley began assembling the tacos, adding a generous dollop of salsa to each. "Nothing this exciting has washed up on our shores since one of our residents found a seventeenth-century Spanish piece of eight about twenty, twenty-five years ago."

"What happens now?" Steven dug out several bills.

"We wait for the archaeologist to weigh in. If it's real and worth preserving, I expect the state will claim it. Put it in a museum somewhere, even though it was found on one of *our* beaches." He began wrapping the tacos.

"I suppose." Steven laid his money on the counter as Charley slid the wrapped tacos into a bag and passed them over. With everything else going on in his life, who cared about the fate of an old cannon?

"I hear Holly paid you a visit on Saturday."

At the non sequitur, Steven froze. "How did you . . . who told you that?"

Eyes twinkling, Charley counted out his change. "She did. She stopped here for tacos after her trip to the wharf."

Oh.

Not a mystery after all.

But how much else did Charley know about her visit?

"Yeah, she did." He took his sack and closed his mouth. Rule number one when seeking information—see how much the other person offers before you start pushing. That technique often produced even more data.

"Nice woman."

"Uh-huh."

"A little on the shy side—with a heart that's easily bruised, I imagine. That can make it hard to meet people in a new town. And it doesn't help if you spend your days with first graders, either."

First graders?

Holly Miller was a first-grade teacher?

"Does she teach at the school here?"

"Yes. Took over the class in January. They were fortunate to find someone with her experience on short notice after the previous teacher and her husband relocated to Sacramento for his job."

So Jonah was in her class.

How about that?

"Her work on the Helping Hands project should give her a chance to meet more people her age—and I expect everyone she's met has been gracious." Charley wiped the already spotless serving counter. "You have to admire how she's dived in and taken an active role in the community."

Steven squinted at the taco chef.

Was Charley complimenting Holly—or censuring a certain charter fisherman who'd kept to himself during his twelve-month tenure in Hope Harbor . . . and been less than gracious to one of the town's newest residents?

Had to be the former.

Charley was more the type to praise people's positive attributes than criticize their shortcomings. Reading too much into the remark said more about his own guilt complex than the other man's motives.

Let it pass, Roark. Take the comment at face value.

"She seems passionate about the cause."

"That she is. And a worthwhile cause it is—don't you think?"

"Uh-huh." He took a step back and lifted the bag. "Thanks for these. I'll enjoy every bite."

"Music to a taco maker's ears." Charley motioned toward the gazebo in the pocket park behind him, where a pair of seagulls were strutting around. "The picnic table over there has your name on it." He leaned down and retrieved two bottles of water from under the counter. "These will help you wash down the tacos."

Steven hesitated. Lingering on the wharf with his late lunch hadn't been in his plans—but why not? It beat dining alone in his empty apartment.

"I think I'll claim that table. But one bottle will be fine." He reached for his wallet again.

"Water's on the house—and take both. You'll find your lunch a bit on the spicy side today."

Before he could protest, Charley began to lower the window.

"Thanks." He snatched the two bottles from the counter.

"My pleasure. Enjoy."

Lunch in hand, Steven skirted the taco truck and strolled over to the tiny, wedge-shaped park bordered on one side by the river where he spent his working hours, and by Dockside Drive and the open sea on the others.

Not a bad place to eat a solitary meal.

Well, not quite solitary. The two gulls moved away from the table as he approached, but stayed close.

No problem.

They could hang around and enjoy the view of Pelican Point lighthouse on the soaring headland in the distance so long as they didn't become a nuisance.

He sat, back to the town, and opened his tacos.

The aroma set off a loud rumble in his stomach, and he chuckled.

"Lucky no one's around to hear that except me and you, isn't it?" He aimed the comment toward the avian duo.

They waddled closer, watching him.

"You guys hungry?"

One of them cackled.

"I'll take that as a yes." He broke off two small chunks of fish, tossed them to the couple, and focused on his own meal.

If he couldn't eat with his brother's family, this was the next best thing. A peaceful meal with delicious food, a world-class view, and amiable feathered companions.

He was going to relax and enjoy every bite.

He'd laughed—and fed the birds.

Those had to be positive signs, didn't they? Indications of a fundamentally good nature—and a decent mood?

Holly hesitated at the entrance to the small park with the tiny manicured lawn and white gazebo, clutching her bag from Sweet Dreams bakery as she studied Steven Roark's broad shoulders.

Funny how fate had a way of pushing you into decisions.

Despite her constant dithering over the past two days about whether to visit her neighbor and the fisherman again, she'd been no closer to a verdict by the end of school today than she'd been Monday night.

Hence the quick detour to Sweet Dreams for comfort food.

Who knew she'd spot Roark in the park?

And that sighting had to be providential. After all, what were the odds he'd be sitting in the gazebo at this hour of the day?

So march over and speak your piece, Holly.

Inhaling a lungful of the salty air, she squared her shoulders and gathered up her courage.

She could do this.

Crimping the top of the bakery bag in her fingers, she forced her legs to carry her toward him—but stopped several feet away. "Excuse me."

He stiffened a hair . . . then slowly turned.

It was impossible to read his expression.

"I, uh, saw you as I was passing by and wondered if you'd given my donation request any more thought."

His brow wrinkled.

Uh-oh.

She braced for an abrupt dismissal.

But instead of sending her packing, he looked past her, toward the shuttered taco stand. Glanced at the two bottles of water on the table. Expelled what sounded like a resigned breath.

"Why don't you join me?" He stood and motioned to the picnic table.

Join him?

Her pulse picked up.

"Um . . . I don't want to intrude."

"I hate to eat alone."

"Oh." She adjusted the strap of her shoulder purse. If she wanted to plead her case again, this was an ideal opportunity. "I can sit for a few minutes."

He moved down, leaving her ample room to slide onto the bench seat that faced the sea.

She eased onto the wooden plank, put the bakery bag on the table, and set her purse beside her.

Roark sat and slid a packet wrapped in white paper toward her, along with a bottle of water. "Help yourself."

"Oh . . . no. I can't take your lunch . . . or dinner." She slid it back.

"You don't like Charley's tacos?"

"I love them, but—"

"Have one." He pushed it toward her again and fished a few paper napkins out of the bag to go with it.

The man didn't appear willing to take no for an answer.

"I'll tell you what." She opened her purse, felt around inside, and withdrew a plastic knife encased in cellophane. "I'll eat a taco—if you'll take half of my brownie." She tapped the brown bag.

"Is it from Sweet Dreams?"

"Yes."

"Deal." He picked up his taco. "You always carry eating utensils with you?"

Was that a touch of amusement in his tone?

"I believe in being prepared."

"Not a bad trait." He went back to eating.

She unwrapped her taco, sending him a sidelong peek. Was he

going to respond to her opening comment about a donation—or force her to bring it up again?

It might be best to wait a few minutes and see. Maybe he wanted to eat his meal in peace before they launched into business.

He concentrated on his taco, and she did the same, only the occasional boat whistle and the distant caw of a gull breaking the placid silence.

When she was halfway through her taco, he turned to her. "I hear you're new in town."

She almost choked on the bite she'd just swallowed.

Where had that comment come from?

Trying to suck in air, she grabbed her water, unscrewed the lid, and took a long swallow.

"Sorry. I didn't mean to startle you. If it's any consolation, I do know the Heimlich maneuver."

There was no missing his amusement this time.

So he had a sense of humor.

Another plus.

And another indication he might be more receptive to her appeal today than he'd been on Saturday.

"A handy skill—but I hope you haven't had much reason to use it."

"Not that one."

Meaning what? That he possessed other medical skills too—and had been called upon to use those?

If so, was he talking about the kind of basic first aid he may have learned in case an emergency came up during a charter fishing trip—or did he have advanced training?

The latter, if her instincts were correct.

Since he didn't offer anything more, however, her curiosity wasn't likely to be satisfied today. And it wouldn't be wise to risk shutting him down with questions he might not want to answer.

"I moved here right after Christmas. How did you know?"

"Charley mentioned it."

What else had the taco chef shared?

She picked up a stray piece of shredded lettuce and tucked it back in the tortilla. "I came here to teach first grade."

"So Charley said. My nephew, Jonah, is in your class."

"I know. Lovely family."

"Yeah."

He fell silent again as she finished her taco, wiped the sauce off her fingers, and dug out the brownie.

"I got the last one." She cut it in half and passed his share to him.

"Thanks."

It was now or never.

"So . . ." Her pulse accelerated, and she took a steadying breath. "I was wondering if you'd decided to donate a fishing trip to our auction now that you've had a few days to think about it."

He put the last bite of taco in his mouth and chewed. Swallowed. Took a swig of water.

On the far side of the table, the two seagulls that had been hanging around edged closer—kind of like those two at the taco stand had done on Saturday.

They stared back at her as she scrutinized them.

Were they the same ones?

Impossible to tell. They all looked alike to—

"I could do a trip for two."

She jerked her attention back to the man beside her.

Yes!

"That would be fantastic! Thank you." She pulled a pen out of her purse. "If you'll give me your address, I'll send you the form to fill out."

As he recited it, she jotted the information on a paper napkin.

"When's the dinner auction?" He polished off his brownie.

"The first Saturday in August, up at the lighthouse banquet facility. I'll send information about that too, with the form."

"Don't bother. I don't attend many social events."

"Okay." She had what she'd come for. Why push her luck? "Well . . . I should be going. Thank you for sharing your tacos."

"I came out ahead on the deal. A brownie for dessert from Sweet Dreams—and pleasant company while I ate."

A foolish warmth spread through her, and she dipped her head, rooting through her purse to hide the telltale flush on her cheeks. "You had those two." She motioned toward the gulls.

"Birds don't count."

With a loud squawk that sounded indignant, the two gulls levitated in a flutter of wings and flew out to sea.

"I don't think they liked your comment." She slid off the bench and stood.

He rose too. "I'm more concerned about my effect on the human species." He shoved his fingers in the back pockets of his well-fitting jeans. "And speaking of that—I'd like to apologize if I was a bit gruff on Saturday. My manners are on the rusty side."

"Your manners are fine." She met his gaze directly. "And we all have off days. No offense taken."

He gave a quick nod. "Thanks."

Her cue to exit.

But she didn't want to go.

Get those feet moving, Holly. Don't overstay your welcome.

Summoning up her willpower, she extended her hand. "On behalf of Helping Hands and the auction committee, thank you for your donation, Mr. Roark."

He took her fingers in a grip that was firm—and warm. "Make it Steven."

A bevy of butterflies took flight in her stomach.

Why would he bother to suggest the use of his first name unless he hoped to see her again?

"If—" Her voice choked, and she cleared her throat. "If you like."

Several beats passed before he let go of her hand.

Too many.

Was he reluctant for their impromptu lunch to end as well—or was that wishful thinking?

Whatever the reason for his lingering release, it put a spring in her step as she left the park behind and walked toward her car—as did the donation their unplanned lunch had produced.

Strange how that impromptu picnic had come about.

If she hadn't happened to notice Charley closing up shop . . . and spotted Steven in the park beyond . . . and dredged up the courage to take a second chance with him . . . she might have chickened out and never contacted him again.

She pressed the autolock button as she approached her car.

Was it possible she'd have similar success with her next-door neighbor? The man hadn't shown his face since that night on the patio—at least not while she was home—nor given her any encouragement to initiate another conversation.

But surely he didn't want to alienate his neighbors.

If she baked him cookies and showed up at his door, perhaps he'd be more welcoming and gracious this time around.

She slid onto the driver's seat and started the engine.

It was worth a try.

So tomorrow night after work, she'd pay him another visit bearing a plate of her tasty ginger cookies.

If he wasn't receptive to that overture? Her students would devour the offering.

But much as she loved the children in her class, they didn't need the cookies—or what they represented—as much as her neighbor did.

For while she didn't know a thing about him personally, it was obvious the man was running on empty in terms of TLC.

Cookies could help remedy that situation—but before she left she'd also do her darndest to coax a smile from him.

Assuming, of course, he didn't shut the door in her face.

5

"I'm hungry, Mommy."

"I know, sweetie." Cindy dropped to one knee and gave Jonah a squeeze. "Daddy will be here soon. Would you like a biscuit while we wait?" She motioned toward the tray on the counter.

"Are they hot?"

"No, they're a little cold." Like a lot of things. "But I could warm one up for you."

"Okay." He climbed onto his chair, a piece of paper clutched in one hand, three crayons in the other. "I'll draw till Daddy gets home."

"Great idea." She moved his place setting aside, then nuked and buttered the biscuit. Lowered the heat in the oven—again. Checked on Beatrice, who kicked her feet and beamed from the playpen in the corner of the kitchen, the picture of contentment.

Must be nice.

But it was far easier to conjure up happiness at seven months old than at twenty-seven.

And a husband who drank too much was a major source of angst at any age, no matter how much you loved him.

Cindy began to pace.

Had Patrick stopped at the bar, downed a few too many, and lost track of the time—again?

Should she call his cell, see if—

The faint hum of a car engine registered, and she swung toward the rear of the house. Gripped the top of a kitchen chair. Braced.

Please, Lord, let him be sober.

Less than sixty seconds later, a smiling Patrick pushed through the back door.

She studied him.

The sparkle in his eyes wasn't from alcohol. Spirits had the opposite effect, dulling rather than brightening his vibrant blue irises. And there was an undercurrent of excitement and energy about him that had nothing to do with booze.

"Sorry I got delayed. The time slipped away from me, and when I realized how late it was and tried to call, my phone was dead. Guess where I've been?" He grinned at her.

"I have no idea." She folded her arms tight against her chest.

"Hi, Daddy!" Jonah slid off his chair and ran toward his father.

"Hey, sport. How's my man?" He swooped the boy up into his arms.

"I got a gold star at school today."

"That's what I like to hear."

"Can we eat? I'm hungry."

"I am too. And I bet your mom made a delicious dinner." He set Jonah down and turned back to her with another smile.

Lord, it was hard to be angry with him when he looked at her like that.

But life on an emotional seesaw took a toll on good humor and affection . . . and trust.

"It's ready, if you want to sit."

"I'll help you put it out." He detoured to the playpen and tickled Beatrice, who chortled.

"Chicken's in the oven. I'll nuke the biscuits and get the potatoes and green beans."

He snagged an insulated mitt off a hook and opened the oven door. "So guess where I was."

"I have no idea. All I know is you're an hour late."

"I'm sorry, hon." Contrition softened his features, and he touched her arm. "I didn't mean to cause problems."

"You never do."

Some of the luster faded from his face at her sharp rebuke, and he lowered his volume. "I wasn't drinking. I ran down to Starfish Pier on my way home. I only meant to stay a few minutes, but it was fascinating."

Starfish Pier.

His excuse was credible, at least. Her history-buff husband had mentioned the big news often in the past couple of days.

"You went to see that old cannon everyone's talking about?"

"Yeah. An archaeologist happened to be there, and we ended up having a long conversation. We also exchanged emails, and he promised to keep me in the loop on developments. I took photos too." He set the roasting pan on the counter and transferred the chicken to a serving platter. "I could show them to you later, if you're interested—or want proof about where I was."

She kept her face averted as she put the potatoes in a bowl, lowering her volume another few decibels. "You've never lied to me . . . that I know of."

"I never have—and I never will." He touched her arm again. "You believe me, don't you?"

After a tiny hesitation, she looked over into his earnest eyes. "I'm trying, Patrick. It's just been hard, and—" Her voice choked.

"Mom?"

At Jonah's tenuous query, she clenched her teeth. She was *not* going to break down in front of her children. They needed stability and joy in their home, not worry and uncertainty. Those were her lot. Negative emotions shouldn't mar the carefree days of childhood.

Forcing up the corners of her mouth, she swung toward her son. "What is it, honey?"

He scrutinized her, his demeanor solemn. "You sounded kinda . . . funny. Are you sad?"

She forced a laugh and bent to kiss the top of his head. "I'm more hungry than anything else. My stomach is growling so loud I could scare away a bear."

That elicited a giggle.

Thank you, God.

"Your daddy has a story to tell us during dinner about the cannon that washed up on the beach."

"I love stories!"

"I do too." She transferred the beans to the table and motioned for Patrick to sit. "Let's say grace first."

Although his excitement had dimmed, as they ate her husband did fill them in about his after-work detour and his chat with the archaeologist.

"Was the cannon from a pirate ship, Daddy?" Jonah watched him, wide-eyed.

"They don't know yet. It could be. The archaeologist told me they're going to take it to a lab to study it. There are several markings that are partly visible, and once they clean it up, those may give them a clue about where it came from."

"Are there pirate ships here now?" Her son's brow knitted.

"No." Cindy jumped in. No nightmares allowed in this house—for her children, anyway. "There haven't been any in this area since long before any of us were born. The cannon is very old." She tapped his plate. "Eat your chicken."

Jonah poked at a piece with his fork. "Are you going to show us the pictures you took, Daddy?"

Cindy tipped her head toward their son's barely touched dinner, and her husband picked up the cue.

"After we're done eating. Tell me about school today."

For the next few minutes, Jonah regaled them with stories from his first-grade class, raving about his teacher as usual. Staff changes midyear were never ideal, but Hope Harbor elementary had lucked out with Holly Miller. She seemed to have charmed every child in her class.

As soon as their plates were clean, Patrick pulled out his camera and began showing them both the photos he'd taken at the beach.

Although her husband's photography was stellar, as usual, Jonah lost interest fast in the hard-to-decipher pictures of the sediment-encrusted cannon and wandered off to watch a video.

"You want to see the rest?" Patrick glanced over at her. "The archaeologist thought they were decent and asked me to email a few to him."

"Sure." While history wasn't one of her passions, it would be heartening to see again the spark of enthusiasm that had brightened her husband's eyes as he'd come through the door.

He ran through them quickly, then pocketed the phone and began gathering up their plates.

"How was work today?" She collected the utensils.

"Same old, same old."

"It pays well." While a lumber mill job wasn't the most exciting career, it provided steady work—and every constant in her life these days was a godsend. "And you did get a promotion four months ago."

"I know. That was a comment, not a complaint. How was your day?"

"The lunch crowd was noisy—and demanding. And that *is* a complaint. They weren't our typical Myrtle clientele. I think they were part of a tour that was passing through. Believe me, I was glad to hang up my apron at three and clock out." She opened the dishwasher and began slotting plates. "Of course, as soon as I came home, I was back in the kitchen preparing dinner."

"I wish you didn't have to work outside the home. Motherhood is a full-time job."

"We can use the income." And the security, given her husband's issues—and where they could lead.

"Speaking of cooking . . ." Patrick fitted a piece of cutlery into the dishwasher with more care than necessary. "Steven stopped by on Sunday. He invited us to dinner."

Her jaw dropped. "And you waited three days to tell me?"

He shrugged. "We've been busy. It's not like we have much opportunity to talk alone in the evenings."

They had enough for him to share that piece of news—but she let his excuse pass.

"Does that mean you two had a cordial conversation?" After a year of almost total radio silence, that would be a miracle—and the answer to countless prayers.

"I wouldn't go that far—but it ended on a civil note."

She leaned a hip against the counter. "What did you tell him about dinner?"

"That I'd talk with you and get back to him. What do you think?" He angled away to scrape a plate.

She waited until he had to face her or risk scrubbing the glaze off the ceramic. "I think I'd like to know what you two talked about—and why you let him in."

"I didn't let him in." He dipped his chin and went back to loading the cutlery. "He barged in."

Yeah, she could see that. Steven's patience with the whole situation had to be wearing thin. If he didn't care so much about his kid brother, he'd have left long ago.

A fact her husband refused to acknowledge.

"Yet you talked to him."

"He did most of the talking."

"You must have listened if you agreed to a family dinner."

"I didn't make any commitments. I only said I'd discuss it with you."

"How did you get from him barging in to a dinner invitation?"

She listened as he gave her what was no doubt an abbreviated—and edited—version of the exchange.

"In the end, he promised to butt out of my life if I let him be part of our family."

"And you agreed to that?"

"If he keeps his end of the bargain."

"Steven's the honorable type. He won't go back on his word."

"Yeah." Patrick shoved a plate in the dishwasher with more force than necessary. "Heroes have a boatload of stellar qualities."

They were back to that—the childhood resentment Patrick couldn't shake and which was totally unwarranted, as far as she could tell. Steven wasn't the sort to lord anything over a younger sibling.

But being constantly compared to a high-achieving older brother by teachers, coaches, and other authority figures took a toll on an impressionable child—one even loving parents couldn't totally mitigate.

"Heroes come in all shapes and sizes, Patrick. You don't have to have a chest full of combat medals or a roomful of trophies to prove you're brave or admirable or courageous."

"Right." His jaw hardened into a stubborn line.

Her usual argument to try and convince him he was as worthy as his big brother wasn't any more effective now than it had been on previous attempts.

Time to switch gears.

Cindy gripped the edge of the counter behind her and chose her words with care. "I'm happy he came over, and that you two reached a truce. Although I'm a little surprised he's willing to compromise." Surely a difficult challenge for a hard-driving, results-oriented man like Steven. "But I imagine he's been kind of lonely this past year."

"And that's my fault?" Patrick scowled at her across the dirty plates in the dishwasher.

"I didn't say that. There's blame on both sides. You both have strong wills. But it's sad to let stubbornness disrupt families. We're the only relatives he has."

"He doesn't have to be lonely. Hope Harbor is full of pleasant people. He could have made friends, found a niche."

"He didn't come here for that. He came here for you. Because he cares."

"So he claims." Patrick slammed the dishwasher closed, and she flinched. "But I'm not letting him run my life."

"Patrick." She moved closer and touched his face, gentling her tone. "No one's trying to run your life. We're trying to save it."

"Why does everybody think I need saving?" Red splotches mottled his complexion. "I have a steady job, two fantastic kids, and a beautiful wife who loves me. Or she used to."

"You know I still do. But some days . . . it's hard." She swallowed past the tightness in her throat. "The nights you come home after you've had too much to drink, I . . . it scares me sometimes." Her last syllable hitched.

Some of the color leeched from his skin. "I've never laid a hand on you or the kids."

"That's not what I mean." She knuckled away the moisture misting her vision. "I worry about you when you're—" She bit back the term *drunk*. It would only exacerbate his tension. "When booze muddles your thinking. I worry about what will happen as the kids get older and begin to realize their dad drinks too much. I worry about you getting a DUI—or having an accident and hurting yourself or someone else. I worry about our marriage if this continues."

"You always knew I liked to have a few drinks. I never hid that from you."

"I know—and I can handle you stopping at the bar for a drink or two with your buddies at the end of the week. But it's gone far beyond that."

"I have it under control, Cindy."

"Do you?"

"Yes."

"Could you stop tomorrow? Cold turkey?"

"If I wanted to."

"What about if *I* wanted you to?"

The question slipped out before she could stop it, and her stomach twisted.

Asking him to stop completely was a giant step toward an ultimatum—one that could have serious, life-changing consequences for all of them.

The very reason she'd never issued one.

Patrick crossed his arms. "My drinking has never caused trouble for anyone in this house. Have I neglected you or the kids? Missed work? Created a public scene?"

"No—but I'm afraid any of those could happen if the situation continues to escalate."

"I told you I've got it under control. Why can't you trust me—like you trust Steven?"

"This isn't about him. It's about you." She clenched her fists until her fingernails dug into her palms. "I know you think you have it under control—but that's a typical attitude of people with addictions."

There.

She'd said the A-word.

"I don't have an addiction." Patrick's denial came through gritted teeth.

Yes, he did.

But until he was willing to admit it, seek help, the merry-go-round would continue—and no amount of badgering from her or Steven would change that. It would only fuel his anger. All the reading she'd done about the subject was clear on that point.

"Would you consider going to an AA meeting? Talk to the people there, see if that might give you a different perspective? It's anonymous, and you can find one up in Coos Bay, where no one will know you."

He glared at her. "How often do I have to tell you? I don't need help. Steven's, yours, or AA's. I've got this."

"Would you attend one meeting? For me? Just to listen?"

"You're beginning to sound like Steven—and I don't want to fight with you like I fight with him."

His warning was clear.

They were on a collision course with an even bigger argument if she didn't back off.

Meaning their discussion on this topic would end as usual.

In a stalemate.

But at least there was one positive development. If Steven became part of their life, he'd be on hand to bolster her efforts and provide moral support.

And with him on the scene, perhaps exerting subtle influence—along with massive amounts of prayer from her end—maybe Patrick would come around.

If he didn't?

Cindy eradicated that thought. She wasn't going there.

Yet.

Dishcloth in hand, she moved to the table and wiped it down. "Instead of Steven taking us out to eat, why don't we invite him here for Sunday dinner? He can't be getting rich doing fishing charters, and I'm not a bad cook." She flashed Patrick a stiff smile.

He didn't return it.

"Between your job and keeping us fed, you spend half your life in kitchens as it is. Let him take us out if he wants to."

"I'm not opposed to a restaurant meal, but he probably doesn't get much home cooking, and I have a pork tenderloin in the freezer. It could be more relaxing to eat here."

Not by much, though. The tension between the two brothers wasn't going to dissipate overnight, even if progress had been made.

"Fine." Patrick pulled out his keys. "I'll text him." He started toward the back door.

"Where are you going?"

He stopped on the threshold, posture taut, tone defiant. "I want some fresh air."

No, he wanted a drink.

He was going to the bar by the mill—and one scotch would lead to more . . . unless she gave him a reason to come back before the drinking got out of hand.

"I was hoping you'd read Jonah a bedtime story. That always makes his day."

Patrick hesitated. Scanned his watch. "I can be back in an hour."

A significant amount of liquor could be consumed in an hour—but less than if he stayed out two or three.

It was the best she was going to get.

"I'll tell him. Be careful."

"I'm not going far." He grasped the edge of the door as his suddenly weary gaze searched hers from across the room. "I don't want the drinking issue to come between us, Cindy. You—and the kids—mean everything to me."

Pressure built again in her throat. "I don't want it to, either, but I'm afraid it will unless . . ." Her voice broke, and she swallowed. "I keep thinking about your dad, and how it ended with him."

A flicker of pain shot through his eyes. "I'm not my dad, Cindy."

But he was, in many respects. Not only in appearance, but in mannerisms and disposition. Even their jobs at Fisher Lumber were similar.

Pointing all that out, however, would accomplish nothing. Patrick had to recognize the similarities himself.

Including the weakness he shared with his father.

So she said nothing.

Shoulders slumping, Patrick turned away. "I'll be back soon."

He closed the door behind him with a quiet click, his anger gone.

Yet in its place was a more dangerous emotion.

Despair.

Which usually led to more alcohol.

Cindy crossed to the kitchen table, sank into a chair, and rubbed her eyes.

Deep inside, Patrick had to know he was on the road to destruction. He was a smart man, and you could only play the denial game so long. In time, God willing, he'd accept the reality that he and alcohol didn't mix and leave booze behind.

There was just one problem with that scenario.

The clock was ticking.

And unless he reached that realization soon, he could find himself out of time—and in deep, deep trouble.

6

She was back.

Sighing, Pete Wallace peered through the tiny crack in the blinds as the young woman from next door rang his bell for the second time.

She was a persistent little thing.

Not only had she returned despite his rude behavior on Monday, she was holding a plate of cookies.

And he couldn't pretend he wasn't here. His car was in the driveway.

Rubbing his forehead, he glanced toward the marble urn on the coffee table. "What should I do, Sal?"

"You know what to do, Pete. There isn't enough kindness in the world as it is. We should commend those who offer it and return it whenever we have the opportunity. No act of thoughtfulness should ever be ignored."

As his wife's sweet voice echoed in his heart, the bell rang again.

Once more he peeked through the slat in the blinds.

The woman . . . Holly something or other . . . was biting her lip, as if she wasn't certain what to do next.

A moment later, her chest heaved and she turned away to descend the single step from the porch to the walk, holding on to the railing with one hand while juggling the plate of cookies in the other.

She was leaving.

Problem solved.

Except . . . just because he was in a sour mood didn't mean he should take it out on her—especially after she'd gone out of her way to welcome him to the neighborhood with home-baked sweets.

Sal would have a fit if she knew he'd thrown the kind gesture back in the young woman's face.

Resigned, he moved to the door, flipped the lock, and twisted the knob.

His neighbor swiveled at the bottom of the step, eyebrows arched. As if she couldn't believe he'd answered the door after all.

He couldn't either.

Hadn't he planned to keep to himself after he came to Hope Harbor? Have as few interactions as possible with the locals? Avoid any socializing that could lead to invitations or prompt questions he didn't want to answer?

Yes, yes, and yes.

But he hadn't counted on happy-faced Holly, who seemed determined to become acquainted.

So fine. He'd give her five minutes.

He wasn't asking her in, however. He'd take her cookies, thank her, be clear he liked his solitude, and send her on her way.

That should put a damper on any future outreaches.

"Good evening." She offered him a cheery smile, turned herself around, and climbed back up the step to the porch—a maneuver that appeared to require more effort than it should. "I was about to throw in the towel."

"I was, uh, occupied."

"No worries. I don't always move fast myself. I'm Holly Miller, from next door." She tipped her head toward the house on his right.

What did she think he was, senile?

"I remember." Even if her last name *had* escaped him.

A faint pink stain tinted her cheeks. "Well . . ." She held out her free hand. "It's nice to meet you officially."

Unless he wanted to be a jerk, what choice did he have but to reciprocate?

"Pete Wallace." He gave her fingers a quick squeeze and released them.

She lifted the plate. "Welcome to the neighborhood. I hope you like ginger cookies. They're my specialty."

"Thank you." He held out his hand.

She passed the plate over . . . and waited. As if she expected him to invite her in.

It would be a long wait.

After a few silent seconds, she spoke again in a too-bright tone. "I, uh, won't keep you. I hope you enjoy those. And if I can be of any help as you settle in, don't hesitate to let me know. I taped my cell number to the top." She motioned to the plastic-wrapped plate.

He dipped his chin and found a slip of paper with her number written under a smiley face.

All at once, a gust of wind whipped past, and the leaden skies opened.

"Oh my word!" Shock flattened her features. "This came out of nowhere. I better go."

She angled back toward the step and grasped the rail—but at the rate she was moving, she'd be soaked before she reached the sidewalk.

"Ask the poor girl in, Pete."

He heard the directive as clear as if Sal had spoken from behind him.

"Miss . . . why don't you come in until this passes? Otherwise, you'll be as wet as I was on Monday."

Without hesitating, she reversed course and eased past him into the front room. "Thank you. I've had one shower today, and I don't need another. But I can't stay long. I have to attend a meeting in half an hour."

Best news he'd had all day.

He closed the door and retreated to the center of the room, plate of cookies in one hand, cane in the other.

Now what?

"I like your house." She gave the space a sweep. "To be honest, if it had been available when I moved to town three months ago, I'd have snapped it up."

She was a newcomer too?

That gave them one thing in common.

Most likely the only thing.

"Sorry you didn't get it. I don't much care where I live. This happened to be the first place that popped up in my price range."

"Lucky you. I bet you'll love it after you settle in." She gave the sparse room another scan, her gaze lingering on Sal's urn.

"I'm about as settled as I plan to be." The furnishing might be meager, but he'd kept the essentials—and various charities had benefited from the rest.

Why haul a bunch of stuff to another state if you weren't going to need it for long?

"I'm sure you'll feel more at home after you unpack and—"

"Already done."

"Oh." She studied the recliner with the reading lamp beside it, the sofa, the coffee table holding the urn. Gave the bare walls a once-over. "I, uh, like the open look myself. I'm not into clutter. Those pillows are lovely, by the way." She motioned to Sal's needlepoint creations, tucked into each corner of the sofa. The lone spots of color—and life—in the room.

"My wife's handiwork."

"Wow." Holly walked over to the couch and bent to examine one in more detail. "They're beautiful."

"She had many talents."

Holly straightened up, her demeanor softening. "I noticed the urn. Has she been gone long?"

"Three years."

"I'm sorry for your loss."

"Thank you. It's been . . . difficult." He swallowed past the tightness in his throat. "We were married for fifty-two years."

The instant that disclosure slipped out, he frowned.

Now why had he shared that piece of personal history with this young woman who, kind as she appeared to be, was nothing more than a stranger?

Nor would she ever be more than that.

He hadn't come to Hope Harbor to make friends.

"Fifty-two years." Holly smiled. "That's a testament to true love. We don't see enough of that these days."

"I agree. Sal—my wife—always said people today expect marriage to be a stroll down the garden path, and as soon as weeds begin cropping up among the blossoms, they give up instead of plucking them out."

There he went again. Running off at the mouth.

This had to stop.

Holly beamed at him. "I love that analogy. I have a feeling I would have liked your wife."

He did too.

But this time he kept his response brief and noncommittal. "She was easy to like."

"Do you have any other family in the area?"

"No. Not in the area. Not anywhere."

A few beats of silence ticked by—but he clamped his lips shut. He was done talking.

His neighbor finally spoke. "So, uh, would you happen to have an umbrella I could borrow? I'll return it as soon as the rain stops."

"Yes. Give me a minute." He left her standing in the living room and escaped to the kitchen. After depositing the plate of cookies on the café table, he retrieved the umbrella from the stand beside the back door and rejoined her. "Don't hurry to bring it back. I won't be setting foot out the door in this kind of rain."

"I don't blame you. After growing up in Eugene, you'd think I'd have learned to travel everywhere with one of these—even next door." She lifted the umbrella. "Are you from Oregon?"

"No." He was *not* going to share any more of his background.

"I love everything about this state—other than the rain." She didn't appear to be in the least offended by his abrupt answer. "If we Oregonians were made out of metal, we'd all be rusty. Oh!" A spark sprang to life in her irises. "Speaking of rust—did you hear about the amazing find this week at Starfish Pier?"

"Where?" And what did that have to do with anything?

"A beach just north of town, with tide pools and the remnants of an old fishing pier. An antique cannon washed up after Sunday night's storm. At least that's what everyone's speculating it is. Can you imagine the tales it could tell?"

"Yes." He grimaced. "Stories about war and killing and aggression."

Her forehead knotted. "I was thinking more about the places it may have traveled and the adventure of being out on the high seas. But I see your point. It *is* a weapon."

For whatever reason, ruining her romantic fancies didn't sit well.

"Maybe there *is* a story of a grand adventure somewhere in its past, though." As he threw her that crumb, he started toward the door. "Let me show you out."

She followed, opening the umbrella as she exited. "I'll return this soon."

"Like I said, no hurry. You can leave it on the porch. I'll put your plate out here too, in case I'm away or unable to get to the door when you come back."

"That works. I hope you enjoy the cookies."

"I will."

With a lift of her hand, she maneuvered down the step and set off at a brisk, if slightly uneven, pace, following the sidewalk toward the street rather than taking a shortcut across the soggy grass.

As she disappeared from view, he shut the door and trudged toward the kitchen. Without bothering to flip on the light, he pulled a can of instant coffee out of the fridge and nuked a cup of hot water.

Steaming brew in hand, he sat at the café table, unwrapped his neighbor's cookies, and picked one up.

The spicy scent of ginger wafted up, whetting his appetite, and he bit into the soft confection.

Mmm.

Sal would have liked these.

Appetite vanishing, he stared out the window at the dismal, gray weather.

A perfect match for his mood.

And sitting in a dim, half-furnished house with no one for company wasn't improving his spirits.

How sad that the gift of cookies from a stranger was the nicest thing that had happened to him in years.

But feeling sorry for yourself was foolish and self-indulgent. His situation was what it was, and there was no changing it. Flipping on the lights, adding more furniture, tuning the radio to a station with cheery music, finding new friends—none of that would make any difference in the long run.

Or, more accurately, the short run.

He'd come here for one purpose, and that required nothing more than four walls and a bed to sleep in.

Now that he had those, it was just a waiting game.

"Any other comments or discussion before we adjourn?"

As Michael Hunter posed that question to the dinner auction committee, Holly refocused on the Helping Hands director seated at the head of the table in the Grace Christian meeting room.

Drat.

Although Michael had kept the meeting moving with practiced efficiency, she'd missed half of what had been said.

And it was all Pete Wallace's fault.

Hard as she'd tried to forget about it, her brief visit to his sad, forlorn house two hours ago remained front and center in her mind.

It was no wonder he seemed down, living in a cave like that.

The man should turn on the lights, open the blinds, put a splash of color on the walls.

But unless her intuition was failing her, he had no intention of doing anything that would add cheer to his life.

Was he still deep in mourning for his wife—or was there another reason for his crankiness and reclusive tendencies?

As she pondered that question, Michael fielded one final question and wrapped up the meeting.

"Again, thank you all for the hard work you've put in on the dinner auction, and for the great items you've convinced businesses and individuals to donate." Michael directed the comment to everyone at the table. "We're off to a fantastic start. Please continue to be on the lookout for other auction items as we move into the next phase of planning. Reverend Baker . . . Father Murphy . . . any final comments?"

The pastor of St. Francis motioned for his Grace Christian counterpart to speak first.

Reverend Baker folded his hands. "I'll add my thanks and remind everyone that the power of prayer can work miracles. As we continue our efforts to respect and foster life in all its stages, let's not be reticent to call on God for assistance. And following the example in Ephesians, let us also pray for those who fail to see the merit of our cause, that the eyes of their hearts may be enlightened. Father Murphy." He motioned to the other cleric.

"Amen to that. I would also suggest we put our trust in the Lord, for as Job reminds us, 'I know that you can do all things, and that no purpose of yours can be hindered.' That would be chapter forty-two, verses one and two." He directed the final comment to the minister, eyes twinkling.

"I'm familiar with Job. And in case you're wondering, the citation on my example is—"

"Ephesians 1:18." Father Murphy grinned at him.

Reverend Baker's eyebrows peaked. "You've been boning up on the Bible."

"Let me remind you which church won our most recent Bible Trivial Pursuit tournament."

"You got softball questions." The minister gave a dismissive wave.

"I'd hardly call naming the three men thrown into a fiery furnace by Nebuchadnezzar a softball—"

Lips twitching, Michael cleared his throat as several other committee members attempted to mask their amusement. "I think it's safe to say that both Grace Christian and St. Francis congregations are well versed on the Bible."

"Spoken like the diplomat you are." Father Murphy chuckled.

"True—and more evidence of why you're the perfect man to direct Helping Hands." Reverend Baker slapped him on the shoulder.

A flicker of—consternation?—scuttled across Michael's face, gone so fast Holly would have missed it if she'd blinked.

What was that all about?

And what was with the good-natured banter between the clerics, who were obviously friends?

Whatever the source, it was a hoot.

"We'll continue our theological debate on the golf course next Thursday." Father Murphy leaned forward to speak to the minister, who flanked Michael on the other side.

"It's a date."

"I hope you'll all stay for a few minutes to enjoy a piece of Eleanor's legendary fudge cake." Michael stood and motioned toward a table at the back of the room, where a luscious-looking cake and a pot of coffee waited. "And thank you, Eleanor, for supplying tonight's treat."

A round of applause ensued, and Holly joined in. The older woman, who'd introduced herself one Sunday after church, acknowledged the enthusiastic expression of appreciation with a dip of her head.

Holly rose and perused the cake, her taste buds revving up.

But after a busy day of teaching, followed by a cookie-baking session, a troubling encounter with Pete, and an evening meeting, a battery recharge took precedence over socializing.

As she slipped on her jacket, Eleanor approached, pushing her walker ahead of her. "My dear, I wanted to say hello before you got away. I imagine you're exhausted after dealing with a roomful of six-year-olds all day."

She coaxed up the corners of her mouth. "They can be a handful."

"I remember that from my Sunday school work, in my younger days." Eleanor patted her arm. "I asked Luis to cut a piece of cake for you to take." She indicated the fortysomething Cuban man who shared her home as part of the Helping Hands companion program. "I hope you're finding life pleasant in our lovely town."

"Yes. Everyone's made me feel welcome."

"I'm glad to hear that—and congratulations on all the donations you've secured for the auction. I'm particularly impressed by the charter fishing trip. Steven keeps such a low profile these days, he's a hard man to pin down. I haven't seen much of him myself since he's been back."

"Back?"

"Oh. Sorry." Eleanor patted her arm. "Of course you wouldn't know anything about his history, being new to town yourself. And *back* isn't quite accurate. He never lived in Hope Harbor, but during his high school and college summers he crewed on fishing boats here."

"How did you two meet?"

"He drove by my house one day while I was trying to start my lawnmower. Not only did he help me get it going, he insisted on cutting my grass. He did that every week for many years—and refused to take a dime in payment. He always smiled and said it was his good deed for the day. Such a nice boy. And he still is, from what I can tell. He hardly had his charter business up and running last year when he hired the father of the refugee family from Syria that the town adopted. I doubt he even needed the help back then."

Impressive.

"Is he from around here?"

"Coos Bay. I missed that boy after he went off to war."

Eleanor was a font of information.

"I didn't realize he'd been in the service."

"For many years. No one was more surprised than me when he showed up in Hope Harbor twelve months ago. Except maybe his brother." She adjusted her position as the darker-skinned man joined them, doing the introductions while he handed over the cake.

Holly responded by rote, anxious to continue their conversation.

But another committee member commandeered Eleanor, leaving Holly to retreat to her car in the darkness with more questions than ever whirling through her brain.

What had brought Steven back to Hope Harbor?

Why had his brother been surprised by his return?

If he had family in town, why did Steven come across as a loner who lived a solitary life and communed more with fish than people?

Shaking her head, she slid behind the wheel and carefully placed Eleanor's offering on the seat beside her.

For such a small town, Hope Harbor had more than its share of residents with intriguing histories and mysterious secrets.

While it was possible she'd make progress with Pete, thanks to their close proximity, Steven was a different story. Despite his insistence on first names, it was doubtful he'd initiate any further contact.

Yet the man seemed as much in need of a friend as her neighbor did.

She started the engine—and blew out a breath.

Too bad she wasn't more outgoing, like Marci at the *Hope Harbor Herald*. No challenge was too intimidating for that dynamo. Why, if it hadn't been for her, Pelican Point light would have been wiped off the earth by now, according to Charley.

Charley.

Now there was a man who seemed to know a lot about the people in her adopted town.

She shifted the car into drive but kept her foot on the brake, the sonorous, muffled blare of the foghorn on the jetty the only sound on this quiet evening.

With his keen insights, might the taco-making artist have a few nuggets of wisdom to offer about how to draw out the two men who were disturbing her thoughts—for far different reasons?

If her parents came down this weekend and they paid his stand a visit, could she corner him for a chat while her mom and dad enjoyed their tacos?

It was worth a try, anyway.

She released the brake, backed out of the parking spot, and drove down Dockside Drive, slowing as she passed the wharf.

All was quiet here too—and empty. The boats were at rest for the night, the water dark save for a reflection of a light here and there.

What was Steven doing this evening?

More important—why should she care?

She rolled her eyes.

Being fixated on a man with whom she had no more than a passing acquaintance was ridiculous. She ought to put him out of her mind. Transitioning to a new life in Hope Harbor was a more than sufficient challenge. Why add other people's problems to the mix?

And Steven and Pete had problems, no question about it.

Except . . . she wasn't wired to walk away from people who were hurting.

So where did that leave her?

Hard to say.

Yet as she left Dockside Drive behind and picked up speed toward Sea Rose Lane, she did know one thing.

Both men would benefit from prayer.

And that she could offer—until, God willing, a concrete opportunity to assist presented itself.

7

He shouldn't have had those shots last night after Cindy went to bed.

Patrick lifted his safety goggles, rubbed the grit out of his eyes, swallowed past the sour taste on his tongue, and resettled the glasses on his nose—all while trying to focus on the parade of boards rolling past him on the conveyor belt.

"You okay?"

As the question registered through his ear protection and the deafening din of the sawmill, he spared his grading partner a quick glance.

Jack had already shifted his attention back to the passing boards, evaluating every other one with a decisive scan before marking it with a quick stroke.

He could ignore the query, but his coworker would corner him later if he didn't answer.

"Yeah." He tried to concentrate while he continued to examine and mark every other plank.

But his assurance was a lie.

It had been much easier to cope with the aftereffects of his drinking in his previous job on the gang saw, where occasional lapses in concentration weren't as noticeable and the margin for error was less tight.

Here, missed boards—or mismarked boards—could come back to haunt you.

As they had ten days ago when his supervisor had pulled him aside to remind him that if the company footed the bill to train you for a plum job, they expected the investment to pay off.

Meaning he had to be on the ball.

The break whistle blew, and the conveyer belt came to a halt.

Perfect timing.

A cup of black coffee and fresh air would help clear his mind.

Jack pulled off his helmet and goggles and appraised him. "A few got away from you."

His neck warmed. "I know. I'm sorry."

"I caught them. Misses happen with new people. That's why they always pair greenhorns with old experienced hands like me." The mill vet flashed him a quick smile, then grew more serious. "But this is supposed to be a team effort. You should be up to speed at this point. If there are any issues keeping you from pulling your weight, you may want to talk to Peg."

Confide in the mill's HR/office manager?

Not a chance.

She was one tough cookie who didn't put up with sloppy work and had zero sympathy for excuses. She'd have him demoted in a heartbeat—or worse—if he so much as suggested he had a problem.

Which he didn't.

"I'm fine. Just a little tired. You know how it is with a baby in the house. Getting a full night's rest can be a challenge."

True—but Beatrice was sleeping eight hours at a stretch these days. His sweet daughter wasn't to blame for her father's mistakes at work.

"Yeah. I've been there. When my own were babies, there were days I went straight home from here, ate dinner, and fell into bed.

If I hadn't done that, I would never have gotten enough shut-eye to be up to speed the next day. It's not a bad technique."

Patrick scrutinized the man. Jack was as straight as they came. He never socialized with the crew, instead spending his spare time with his family or volunteering with Helping Hands. Not once had he seen the man at the bar where a bunch of the guys hung out.

But the rumor mill was alive and well at the lumber company. Jack could have heard stories about his partner's frequent stops for a drink after work.

Was his comment about going directly home after work a suggestion—or a warning?

"I'll have to consider that. In the meantime, I'm going to get a cup of coffee and some fresh air." And pop a couple of aspirin.

"Not a bad idea."

Patrick left him at the conveyor belt, grabbed his java, and headed outside to join several of his coworkers, who were already lounging in the sun.

"Hey, Patrick." Ryan lifted his disposable cup in greeting. "We're thinking of going to Bandon to check out the new place on the wharf. It's running a happy hour deal. You in?"

Any other day, his answer would have been a no-brainer. But with Jack's comments looping through his mind, he hesitated. "I don't know."

"It's Friday, man. We gotta celebrate."

"I'll think about it. What's the deal?"

As Ryan rhapsodized about the two-for-one drinks and dollar appetizers, a familiar craving for the taste of booze began to gnaw at him.

Craving.

He frowned.

The word was accurate—but a craving wasn't the same as an addiction.

Was it?

He tossed the aspirin in his mouth and washed them down with a sip of coffee.

No, it wasn't.

People who craved chocolate or the adrenaline rush of a challenging ski slope or relaxing beach time weren't addicted. It just meant they enjoyed those treats.

And that's all it was with him and booze. Scotch was merely one of life's simple pleasures.

Maybe he overdid it a tad on occasion—like last night—and paid the price with a fuzzy brain and a pounding headache the next day, but that didn't mean he was addicted.

He could quit drinking tomorrow if he wanted to.

Could you, Patrick?

The voice in his head came out of nowhere, and he scowled.

Stupid question.

Of course he could.

He took another long slug of coffee.

There was nothing wrong with having a few drinks with the guys at the end of the week—or any other night. He worked hard, and chilling out for an hour after work was fine . . . as long as he didn't let it get out of hand.

And he wouldn't.

"So are you in or not?" Ryan nudged his arm.

"I'm in—but I can't stay more than an hour. I have to be home for dinner."

"I hear you. If I had a wife like yours, I'd hightail it home too."

The whistle blew again, and Patrick downed the rest of his coffee in two long gulps. He'd have to text Cindy to let her know his plans . . . but he could do that later.

She wouldn't like his detour—but he'd spend the evening with her and the kids after that. And he could promise to stay off booze the whole weekend to help smooth out the domestic waters. That would make her happy. It had been a while since he'd had an alcohol-free weekend.

In fact, how long *had* it been?

Patrick dug deep into his memory as he tossed his cup in a trash can by the door and tried to come up with a date.

Failed.

Come to think of it, when was the last *day* he'd gone without booze?

That answer eluded him too.

A twinge of doubt rattled his self-assurance.

Was it possible he was beginning to start down the path that had led to tragedy for his dad, as Cindy and Steven claimed?

He gritted his teeth and returned to his place on the grading line.

No.

He could quit anytime.

And he'd prove it this weekend by staying away from booze.

After all, how hard could it be to go two days without alcohol?

"It's such a lovely afternoon—why don't you folks enjoy your tacos in the gazebo?"

As Charley waved a hand toward the pocket park behind him and pushed a large brown bag across the counter, Holly reached into her purse.

"My treat." Her dad touched her arm and extracted his wallet.

"You don't have to do that."

"We want to, honey." Her mom picked up the bag. "Besides, we'd happily pay twice this much for such incredible tacos. In case you haven't figured it out, Charley, you have two new fans. Now that we've discovered these"—she lifted the bag—"we'd drive down whether Holly was here or not."

"I'm flattered." Charley gave a slight bow.

"And I like your idea about eating in the park. What do you think, Tom?"

"I'm all for it." Her dad slid his wallet back into his pocket. "We Oregonians have to savor every sunny hour we get. Ready, Holly?"

"I'll get a few extra napkins and lemon slices and be along in a minute. You go ahead and claim our table." If she wanted to pick Charley's brain about Steven, this could be her best chance. There wasn't a customer in sight on the wharf.

"Shall I wait and walk with you?" Her mother touched her arm, concern etched on her features.

"I'm fine, Mom. I wander around down here often. I know where all the uneven spots are."

"I suppose that's true." After a brief hesitation, she followed her husband toward the park.

"Nice people." Charley wiped a rag over the pristine counter.

"Very. A bit on the protective side."

"Understandable."

Odd comment, given that she'd never shared her background with anyone in Hope Harbor.

"Why do you say that?"

He shrugged. "Isn't that par for the course with loving parents?"

Oh.

Maybe she'd overreacted.

"I suppose so." She plucked several paper napkins from the dispenser on the counter.

"Did I hear you mention extra lemon?"

"Yes. Dad likes lemon." It was as convenient an excuse as any to linger with Charley for a minute or two. "Now all we need to complete our meal is a piece of Eleanor Cooper's fudge cake." Not the smoothest segue to the topic on her mind . . . but it would work.

Charley grinned as he sliced a lemon. "I have to agree that would be the icing on the cake—pardon the pun."

"I saw her at the auction committee meeting Thursday night. She sent a piece home with me."

"That sounds like Eleanor."

"We had a brief chat." Holly kept her tone casual. "She congratulated me on convincing Steven Roark to donate a charter fishing trip. I didn't realize he'd been in the military."

"He doesn't talk about it much. War isn't a pleasant business."

"No. I suppose not."

"I expect a lot of men and women who serve come back from overseas with scars the world can't see or begin to fathom. Trauma comes in many forms—and can sadly keep people apart." Charley put the lemon slices in a small disposable container, pushed it toward her, and flashed his white teeth. "Tell your folks I said to enjoy."

"I will. Thanks."

She picked up the cardboard tub and circled around to the back of the stand, mind churning.

While Charley's comments had been general, as usual, they'd somehow seemed personal. As if he knew more about the new schoolteacher in town and the reclusive soldier-turned-charter-fisherman than logic suggested he should.

But just as she'd read too much into his comment about loving parents, she was probably overdramatizing his last remark about trauma too.

Nevertheless, it had whetted her appetite for more background on Steven.

Unless another source presented itself, however—or the man himself happened to appear out of the blue and was more talkative than usual—there wasn't much chance her curiosity was going to be satisfied anytime soon.

Steven stopped at the end of the wharf and cast a longing glance down Dockside Drive as the aroma of Charley's tacos tickled his nose. After working seven hours without a break, a fish taco would hit the spot.

But with Patrick and Cindy expecting him in an hour, he'd be late unless he hustled home to shower and change.

Quashing his hunger pangs, he set off at a fast clip toward his car. Better make a wide loop around Charley's, though, or he'd be tempted to—

He came to an abrupt halt as three people circled around from behind the stand—one of them familiar.

Holly caught sight of him and jolted to a stop too.

The older woman beside her grabbed her arm, and the middle-aged man's hand shot out to steady her, alarm registering on both their faces.

Holly recovered first.

After offering a comment he couldn't hear to the older couple, she aimed another tentative look his direction.

He couldn't stand there and gawk at her, nor could he ignore her and run the other way without being rude.

That left him one option.

Putting his legs in gear, he walked toward the small group.

Holly offered him an uncertain smile as he drew near. "Hello, Steven."

"Holly."

"Um . . . these are my parents, Joan and Tom Miller, from Eugene. Mom and Dad, Steven Roark."

He shook hands with both of them as they gave him a critical once-over.

Kind of like his commanding officer had done the day he'd returned from a mission gone bad, sporting a scraggly beard, longish hair, and a simmering rage that had earned him a forced leave.

"Nice to meet you." Tom Miller's mouth flexed, but her mother's lips remained flat. "So you're a charter fisherman."

That must have been the piece of intel Holly had passed on as he approached.

"Yes. For now."

As the words spilled out, Steven furrowed his brow.

What in blazes had prompted that caveat when he'd been careful for months to play his cards close to his vest and let everyone in town assume he had no intention of changing careers?

Why would he share such a telling piece of information with these strangers?

Only one answer came to mind.

He wanted to impress them. Wanted them to realize he expected to have a more secure career down the road. One with a steadier income that was more than capable of supporting a wife—and family.

But that was ridiculous.

He had no romantic interest in their daughter.

Did he?

As he pondered that question, Holly spoke again. "Are you planning to get tacos? They're exceptional today."

"Uh, no. I'm having dinner with my brother and his family later."

She offered him a bright smile. "How nice. Tell Jonah I said hi." She added an aside for her parents. "Steven's nephew is in my class."

"I'll do that." In the background, Charley held up a soda, and Steven lifted a hand in acknowledgment. "Our resident taco maker has a soft drink with my name on it that will help tide me over until dinner. It was a pleasure to meet you." He included both her parents in his parting comment.

They murmured a return sentiment, and after they each took one of Holly's arms, the threesome strolled down the sidewalk.

He remained where he was, hands shoved in pockets, watching them. As a bicyclist approached, Holly's dad darted in front of her, shielding her until the bike passed. And as they turned away from the wharf, toward a car parked along Dockside Drive, they slowed their pace after her mother pointed out the cobblestones edging the sidewalk. At the car, her dad was more than solicitous while helping her into the back seat.

Why were they fussing over her?

Were the balance issues he'd noticed on the wharf the day she'd approached him about a donation an ongoing problem? Had she suffered an injury that had left her with a permanent disability?

When her father angled back his direction and caught him staring, Steven pivoted and continued toward the taco stand, questions racing through his mind.

"I had a feeling you were thirsty." Charley set the soft drink on the counter.

Not really—but claiming the drink Charley had offered had been a welcome excuse to end the exchange with Holly's parents.

"Thanks. It will help fill the gap until dinner." He counted out the change in his pocket and pushed it across the counter.

"You want tacos too?"

"Not today. I'm eating with Patrick and Cindy." He popped the tab on the soda and took a long pull.

"Is that right?" Charley folded his arms and leaned a shoulder against the side of the cabinet inside the serving window.

"Yeah." Steven took another drink.

"That should be fun."

Fun could be a stretch . . . but at least their get-together was progress.

Or it would be if he and Patrick could hold on to their tempers and he didn't end up being thrown out on his ear before dinner was even served.

"I hope so."

"Life tends to be what we make it. If you go to your brother's expecting fun, that's what you should have."

If only it was that simple.

Nevertheless—going in with a positive attitude couldn't hurt.

"I'll keep that in mind." He finished off his soda in several long gulps and handed Charley the can. "I assume you want to recycle this."

"Always." He took it and dropped it into a bin behind him. "We all have to do our part, however small, to take care of this beautiful world the good Lord blessed us with. Enjoy your dinner."

"Thanks."

Steven struck off for his car, glancing toward the spot where Holly and her parents had parked.

It was empty.

What were *their* plans for the rest of the day?

No doubt far more relaxing than his.

Yet maybe his visit to his brother's home didn't have to be stressful. If he took Charley's advice and went with an upbeat attitude and a firm resolve to remain pleasant no matter what Patrick said or did, the dinner could end up being a new chapter in their relationship.

He pulled out his keys and hit autolock as he approached his jeep. A muffled click confirmed the door had opened.

Too bad it wasn't that easy to open the door between him and his brother.

But in forty-five minutes, he'd cross the threshold with an optimistic mind-set, give it his best shot—and hope Charley's advice proved to be sound.

8

Shoot.

Pete cast another surreptitious glance next door as he poked at a weed with his cane.

If he'd noticed Holly sitting on her patio with an older couple, he'd never have ventured into the backyard, saw in hand.

But now that he was here, he couldn't very well pretend he'd come out just to admire the view.

He could, however, ignore his neighbor and her guests—and finish his chore as fast as possible.

Turning his back on the trio next door, he trekked to the rear of the property, where a large spruce branch had fallen during Sunday night's storm. Disposing of it was beyond the scope of his responsibilities as a tenant—but why initiate an exchange with his landlord if he could handle the chore himself?

Up close, however, the downed limb was bigger—and thicker—than it had appeared from the back door.

Maybe he ought to let someone else take care of it after all.

But as long as he was back here, why not give it a try?

He knelt as gracefully as his arthritis-stiffened knees allowed and laid his cane on the ground. Bracing himself on the limb with one hand, he began sawing with the other.

It was slow going—and he broke a sweat way too fast.

He paused and took a deep breath. Nice and easy was the key here. He didn't want to have a heart attack on top of everything else he was—

"Excuse me . . . Mr. Wallace?"

He smothered a groan.

Of course his neighbor had come over. Her do-gooder instincts were becoming the bane of his existence.

He shifted around.

The older man who'd been sitting on the patio next door was with her.

"I hope you don't think we're butting in, but my dad wondered if he could help you with that." As she introduced her father, Pete struggled to his feet.

The other man clasped his fingers in a firm grip. "Nice to meet you. I had a limb come down myself two weeks ago. Cleanup is much faster if more than one pair of hands pitches in."

"I don't want to intrude on your visit with your daughter."

"Don't worry about it. She and I talk every day—and we'll have this done in a jiffy. To tell you the truth, I always feel guilty sitting around watching other people work. You wouldn't want to add to my guilt complex, would you?" The man grinned at him.

Holly's father was as pleasant as she was.

And given how he'd positioned his offer, it was hard to refuse.

Besides, this job was a little more taxing than he'd expected. Back in the day, he could have easily handled it alone. But he wasn't a strong, healthy young man anymore—hard as that was to accept.

"If you're certain you don't mind."

"Not at all." The other man was already rolling up his sleeves. "Holly, why don't you go keep your mom company? I'll be back in a few minutes."

"I could help."

"Pete and I can handle this. And we wouldn't want your mom to get lonely, would we?"

A beat passed. "Okay."

"Want me to walk you back?"

"No. I'm fine." A touch of starch crept into her voice.

After a brief hesitation, he nodded. "All right—but be careful crossing the lawn."

Tom Miller watched her until she reached her patio, then leaned down and picked up the saw. "Let's see what we've got here. Do you have any twine we can use to bundle this?"

"Yes. My yard supplies are in the tool shed."

"Why don't you find the twine and I'll dive in here?"

"I'll be back fast."

"No reason to hurry." After giving the branches a quick perusal, Holly's father set to work while Pete headed for the shed.

It took longer than he expected to unearth the roll of twine in the box where he'd dumped a handful of yard-maintenance items before moving, and by the time he returned, the other man had almost completed the job.

Within ten minutes, they'd bundled up the boughs and the bigger pieces of the limb.

"Where would you like these?" His neighbor's father secured the last knot and stood.

Pete motioned to the back of the yard. "We can stack them there. I believe the town has a few pickups every year for yard waste." Details about services he wasn't likely to use much hadn't been on his radar screen while researching the town, but for whatever reason that piece of information had stuck.

The other man went about the task with quick efficiency.

Pete tried to assist, but after it became apparent he was hindering more than helping, he backed off and let Holly's father finish the job.

"All done." Tom examined his fingers and made a face. "I'd shake your hand again, but I'd rather spare you all this sap. Spruce trees give new meaning to the term sticky fingers."

"I appreciate your help."

"My pleasure. That's what neighbors are for."

"You're not my neighbor."

"My daughter is. That counts." The man flashed him another smile. "Would you like to join us for a drink and dessert?" He motioned toward the adjacent patio.

"No. Thank you. I, uh, have a few chores to do inside."

"Ah. The never-ending to-do list. I have one too. Enjoy the rest of your Sunday." With a lift of his hand, he returned to the two women on the patio next door.

Pleasant man.

Like daughter, like father.

There was a time he would have cultivated their friendship—but that time was long past.

As for enjoying the rest of his day?

It was a kind thought—but enjoyable days were also long past. That's how it was when everyone you loved was gone . . . and hope died.

Fighting back a wave of despair, Pete trudged toward the house, taking one last peek at the family group next door.

Once upon a time, he'd have accepted Tom's invitation.

But planting the seeds of friendship was a wasted effort if there was no harvest to look forward to.

He continued to the house, slipped into his solitary world, and clicked the door shut behind him, isolating himself from the people next door—and any new attachments.

It was better this way.

For everyone.

So far, so good.

Steven picked up his spoon, surveying the table as he dived into the warm brownie and vanilla ice cream drizzled with chocolate sauce Cindy had set in front of him.

His sister-in-law nibbled at her tiny portion, while Patrick confined his sweet treat to sugared coffee. Baby Beatrice gurgled happily in her high chair as Jonah tackled his dessert, both children content and relaxed. Neither appeared to have picked up on the subtle thread of tension running under the careful veneer of politeness and cordiality among the adults.

"The dessert's delicious, Cindy." Steven scooped up a second bite.

"I'm glad you like it—but it's hard to compete with Sweet Dreams. Their brownies are spectacular."

"They don't come with ice cream and chocolate sauce, though."

"True."

An awkward silence fell, as it had too often during the meal.

As Steven searched for a new topic, Jonah piped up.

"Did you see that cannon they found on the beach, Uncle Steven?"

"No—but I heard about it."

"Daddy saw it. He took pictures and talked to the arcologist."

"Archaeologist." Patrick winked and tousled his son's hair.

"Yeah. That." Jonah kept shoveling in his dessert.

"You went out to see it?" Steven directed his question to his brother.

"I stopped by after work."

Not surprising. Patrick had always had an avid interest in history, and he'd done a fair amount of research into their family tree.

"I haven't heard anything more about it. Are there any updates?"

"It's been transported to a university in Texas that has a nautical archaeology program. That reminds me—I noticed as we were sitting down to dinner that an email came in from the state archaeologist I met here, who promised to keep me in the loop. Do you mind if I skim it?"

"Not at all."

While Patrick pulled out his phone and scrolled through his email, Steven gave Jonah his full attention. "What's your favorite subject in school?"

"I like them all."

"A promising start to his academic career." He directed that comment to Cindy.

"I agree—but I think it has more to do with the teacher than the topics being studied. The kids love her."

"That would be Holly Miller, right?"

"Yeah!" Jonah beamed at him. "She's awesome."

Cindy cocked her head. "Do you know her?"

"Not really. She came to the dock to ask me to donate a fishing trip for the benefit auction Helping Hands is doing for its pro-life program—and our paths have crossed on occasion since."

"Did you contribute?"

"Uh-huh." At Cindy's quizzical look, he scooped up a large bite of brownie and ice cream and shoved it in his mouth.

"How come you—"

"This is amazing." Patrick stared at his cell.

Saved by . . . whatever it was, he'd take it.

"What's amazing?" Steven spoke around the chunk of brownie.

Patrick continued to gape at his phone. "I think we own a cannon."

Steven looked at Cindy, who appeared to be as bewildered by her husband's comment as he was. "You want to explain that?"

His brother set the phone aside, expression dazed. "It seems the cannon that washed up here is from Jedediah's schooner."

Jedediah.

Steven rolled that name around in his head. "He was a relative, right?"

"Yes. Great-great-great-grandfather. I mentioned the photo I have of him standing on the ship to the archaeologist, and he asked to see a copy. After the university found a date on the cannon from 1852, he emailed them the scan I sent."

"Why would there have been a cannon on his ship? Wasn't he into shipping?"

"Yes—and many of the merchant vessels back then were equipped to defend themselves against pirates."

"But how do you know *his* ship was armed?" Steven could barely recall any details about their long-ago sailor relative, let alone information about his schooner.

"In the photo I have from 1874, he's standing on deck, next to a cannon. Would you like to see it?"

"Sure." Steven finished his dessert. History wasn't his thing, but if it could direct Patrick's attention to something other than booze, a lesson in family lore was tolerable.

Patrick scrolled through his phone and held it out. "Someday I'm going to get the original photo restored and framed."

Steven's gaze flicked to his brother's fingers.

They were trembling.

He shifted his focus to Patrick's face.

A slight flush stained his sibling's cheeks, and he set the phone on the table in silence.

Let it go, Roark.

Heeding that advice, Steven picked up the cell.

The photo would definitely benefit from restoration, but the image of a cap-wearing, broad-shouldered man with a trimmed beard and mustache was clear—as was the view of the cannon beside him.

"What do you know about him?"

"He was born in 1826 and served in the navy on the USS *Shark* at the time it sank. Some of the cannons from that ship washed ashore up the coast near Cannon Beach as recently as 2008. But that kind of find is rare."

"How did Jedediah end up in Oregon—and owning a merchant ship?" Steven handed the phone back.

"I'll have to pull out his journal and take another stab at reading it to flesh out the details. That old handwriting is a challenge—but from what I've been able to decipher, after he got out of the service, he came back to this area because it had appealed to him while he was serving on the *Shark*. He worked on a merchant schooner, ascended through the ranks, and eventually saved enough money to buy his own ship."

"Which sank." That much he remembered.

"Yes. It foundered in a gale offshore of Hope Harbor in 1875." Patrick took another sip of coffee. "But he'd made his money and was ready to retire. He spent the rest of his life here as the keeper at Pelican Point lighthouse."

"You've done your homework on this."

"History fascinates me. Always has. If it would pay the bills, I'd be happy to spend my life buried in old photos and historic papers and artifacts."

"I wish you could do that for a living, honey." Cindy laid her hand on his.

Patrick shrugged. "Like you've said, the mill pays well and it's steady work. I can indulge my love of history on the side." He patted her fingers. "Anyway, after comparing my photo with the cannon from the beach, the university is certain it's from Jedediah's ship. Which means it's ours, since we're Jedediah's only direct relatives."

"What are we supposed to do with a cannon?" Steven pushed his dessert plate aside.

"Maybe you could donate it to a museum." Cindy sipped her coffee.

"Hope Harbor doesn't have a museum—and a cannon from a private merchant ship isn't a find of great historical significance, like the ones from the *Shark*. If we donate it, it could end up gathering dust in storage." Patrick tapped a finger on the table. "It would be nice to keep it here—if the town wants it."

"Restoration would probably be expensive. I doubt Hope Harbor has the budget for that." Cindy dabbed her napkin at a dribble of ice cream running down Jonah's chin.

"We could ask."

"Where would they put it?" Steven laid his napkin beside his plate.

"I don't know . . . maybe on the wharf, or the park behind Charley's—or up at the lighthouse?" Patrick began to warm to the topic. "Some place where everyone could see it, with a small historical marker in Jedediah's honor. He had quite a history."

"I suppose it wouldn't hurt to ask." Though Steven agreed with Cindy. From what he'd heard, the town budget was always tight.

"I'll make a few calls tomorrow." Patrick stood. "Why don't we all help clear the table and go out on the deck while the weather holds?"

"I can handle cleanup." Cindy rose too. "You and Steven go ahead. I'll join you in a few minutes."

Steven pushed his chair back. "I'm not used to being waited on. Let me help with—"

"Not today." Cindy shook her head, her tone brooking no argument. "Next visit, I'll accept all help offered. Today is special. Humor me."

Patrick rested his hands on his hips. "Let's compromise. You and I can clear the table, and Jonah can keep Steven company. I'll join them while you finish the cleanup."

"That works." Cindy began gathering up plates.

"Come on, Uncle Steven." Jonah slid off his chair and took his hand, pulling him toward the back door. "You can tell me a story about the army."

He grinned at the boy. Thank heaven Patrick hadn't objected to Cindy and the kids meeting him on occasion over the past year for ice cream at the Myrtle. Without those visits, he'd be nothing more than a stranger to his niece and nephew.

"Go on out." Patrick's lips quirked. "Cindy rules the kitchen, and once she makes up her mind, the safest course is to fall in line."

"Come *on*, Uncle Steven." Jonah pulled harder.

He let his nephew drag him out to the deck, where they settled into two adjacent chairs.

"Tell me about fighting the bad guys." The youngster's eyes lit up.

Not a subject suitable for a six-year-old—especially the type of work he'd done—but if he wanted to build rapport, he couldn't shut the boy out.

"What would you like to know?"

"Did you carry a bunch of guns?"

"If I had to."

"Did you drive a tank?"

"No."

"Did you fly a helicopter?"

"No."

"Did you shoot people?"

His gut clenched, and he shifted in his seat. "Most days were pretty quiet. I did a fair amount of reconnaissance."

Jonah's forehead puckered. "What's that?"

"Information gathering. Kind of like . . . like being a spy."

"Wow! I didn't know soldiers could be spies too."

"It depends on what job they assign you." A change of topic was in order. "Now tell me more about school. Your mom said you like your teacher."

"Yeah. She's fun. This week it's my turn to be her helper."

"What does her helper do?"

"If her back gets tired and she has to sit down, her helper does different jobs—like collecting papers or getting her a pencil or passing out tests."

"Why does her back get tired?" Could that have anything to do with the kid-gloves treatment her parents had given her earlier today . . . and her slightly off-kilter gait?

Jonah lifted his shoulders. "I dunno. Old people can get tired, I 'spose."

Old people.

Steven stifled a smile.

Thirtysomething was hardly old—except to a youngster like Jonah.

Patrick joined them, putting an end to the conversation—but after the rest of the evening passed without incident and they all said a pleasant good night, Steven's mind returned to his brief chat with his nephew.

What was Holly's story?

He dug his keys out and slid behind the wheel of the jeep as he pondered that question.

Came up empty.

He was an expert at finding answers, though. That had been a critical part of his job in The Unit, and he'd learned to ferret out information under the most adverse conditions.

Yet this reconnaissance challenge was as tricky as any he'd faced overseas.

It also had ethical issues.

Digging around behind Holly's back wouldn't be honorable. That meant he'd have to go to the primary source—Holly herself.

But that wouldn't work either.

He started the engine and put the jeep in gear.

If he sought her out, began asking questions, she might think he was attracted to her. And giving her the impression he thought there was potential for them as a couple would be wrong.

Because based on their brief but instructive encounters, every instinct in his body told him they came from two very different worlds that could never, ever be compatible.

Cindy's eyelids flickered open, and she blinked at the dark ceiling. Shifted onto her side toward the nightstand. Peered at the bedside clock.

Twelve-thirty.

What had awakened her?

She rolled back toward Patrick's side of the bed.

Empty.

Had he heard Beatrice stirring, perhaps, and risen to see to her?

She listened.

The house was silent.

For half a minute, she lay there, straining to detect any sound that would give her a clue to her husband's whereabouts.

Nothing.

But Patrick always tried to be considerate during late-night rising—unless he was hungover, in which case he tended to fumble doorknobs and bump into furniture.

That wasn't the case tonight, however.

Still, if he was moving about, she ought to be able to discern *some* sound. As she'd learned after Jonah was born, mothers developed supersensitive hearing—especially in the wee hours of the night.

Giving up the guessing game, she rose, clapped a hand over her mouth to cover a yawn, and tugged her sleep shirt down. She'd find Patrick, confirm everything was fine, and fall back into bed. While the evening with Steven had been far more amiable than she'd dared hope, the underlying fear that the situation would implode had taken a toll—and every muscle in her body was tired.

Hopefully the next visit would be less stressful.

Aside from the success of their family get-together, though, the best part of the weekend had been Patrick's promise to stay away from the scotch.

A promise he'd honored.

Lips curving up, she padded into the hall. Peeked in on Beatrice and Jonah. Continued past the living room, to the kitchen.

The instant she spotted her husband, her spirits tanked.

He was sitting at the table playing with his phone, a glass filled with golden-hued liquid in his hand, a bottle on the counter within reaching distance.

As if sensing her presence, he lifted his chin.

"Oh, Patrick." She didn't attempt to mask her dismay.

"What?" His jaw jutted out, as it always did when he got defensive. "I kept my promise. The weekend is over."

"It's twelve-thirty. Half an hour past the end of the weekend. Are you so desperate for a drink that you had to get up to track one down at this hour?"

"I didn't get up. I've *been* up. I'm just having a nightcap before I come to bed. And I'm not desperate."

"How many have you had?"

His cheeks grew ruddy. "Tonight was stressful, okay? I'm too wired to sleep. This will relax me."

"Booze isn't the best way to unwind. We could have cuddled. That used to help you chill if you were tense."

"You were asleep."

"I wouldn't have minded being woken up if it would have saved you from that." She motioned toward the glass.

"Saved? Isn't that being a bit dramatic?"

"It fits." She crossed to the table. *Lord, please let him hear my message. Let him realize I have his best interest at heart*. "Your hands were shaking at dinner tonight—and you didn't eat much. You even skipped dessert."

"I was nervous. That can cause the shakes and dampen your appetite."

"So can withdrawal. Two days without booze can have an impact."

"You're overreacting."

"Am I?" She filled her lungs. Tried to stay calm. "The signs are all there, Patrick. You're in serious trouble. This"—she waved a hand toward the glass and bottle—"is telling. You had to have a drink as soon as your promise expired."

"I told you. It's been a stressful day." He picked up the glass and finished off the scotch in one gulp. "Go back to bed. I'll be there in two minutes."

She hesitated—but only for a few seconds.

There was nothing else to say.

Fighting back tears, she retraced her steps to the bedroom.

Words weren't going to work with Patrick. It was going to take a traumatic event for him to realize the extent of his problem.

Climbing back under the covers, she suppressed a shiver as she sent a prayer heavenward that her husband would receive a wake-up call soon.

And that no one would get hurt if and when it arrived.

9

Getting laid off on April Fool's Day was like a bad joke.

Except no one in the small office was laughing.

Not him.

Not his boss, Harv.

Not Peg, wearing her HR hat.

Patrick twined his fingers together in his lap and regarded Harv across the desk as he attempted to wrap his mind around the shattering news.

"Let me be certain I understand this." He tried to keep breathing. Tried to swallow past the bile rising in his throat. "You're laying me off because I missed marking a few boards?"

"More than a few, Patrick. On several occasions."

"I'm still learning the ropes on the new job."

"You should be up to speed by now."

The same thing Jack had said last week.

As the throbbing in his temples intensified, he gritted his teeth. Man, he needed a chaser. Bad.

Rewarding himself for a booze-free weekend by indulging in a midnight binge after Steven's visit yesterday hadn't been his most brilliant idea.

"I'll try harder, okay?"

Harv folded his hands on his desk and leaned forward, his expression pained. As if he was finding this session difficult and uncomfortable too. "Trying harder at work isn't going to fix the problem, Patrick. The source is elsewhere. I've talked to a few of the guys, kept my ear to the ground. I'm sure you know what I heard."

Some of his friends had ratted on him about his frequent trips to the bar?

If he found out who they were, they weren't going to be his friends much longer.

But in case Harv was talking about an issue besides alcohol, he ought to play this cool until the man spelled it out.

"I don't know what you mean."

His boss raked his fingers through his thinning hair. "Look . . . I'm not here to judge what you do in your personal life. But if it starts affecting your job—and this company—I have to step in. You've been here eleven years. You've worked in most areas of this operation. You know our equipment can be dangerous. We can't have people who are less than . . . alert . . . putting themselves, or others, at risk."

"I've never done that."

Harv exhaled and picked up a piece of paper from his desk. "Two years ago, you had a near miss when you slipped while trying to clear a jam in the bander. You walked away with a dozen stitches, but it could have been much worse."

"Accidents happen. Like you said, a mill can be a dangerous place."

"Last year, there was another near miss, this one on the debarker. You and a coworker entered the drum to clear an obstruction. You told your coworker you were going to lock out the debarker. You didn't. Nor did you hit the stop button. Fortunately, the third employee who joined you did. You know what would have happened if you'd removed the obstruction and he hadn't done that."

Yeah, he did.

Just thinking about it could make him break out in a cold sweat.

Once they'd cleared the jam, the hydraulically operated drum would have begun to rotate—and from the infeed end of the unit where they'd been, the only escape from the rotating logs had been back through the drum or up a steep chute.

They would have been trapped . . . and crushed.

That was a story he'd never shared with Cindy.

But most of the guys didn't bother to lock out the debarker to deal with jams—and forgetting to hit the stop button wasn't proof that drink had impaired his thinking that day.

Even if it had.

No one knew that other than him, though—and after that incident, he'd cut back on the booze.

For a while.

No reason to share any of that with Harv, however.

He had to stick with the story he'd told at the time.

"People do forget procedures once in a while. And two slipups after working in a high-risk environment for eleven years isn't that unusual."

"Patrick." Harv set the paper on the desk in front of him. "We all know mistakes can happen. That's why there weren't any repercussions from those incidents. But after we began to see lapses on the grading line . . . and started asking questions . . . we connected the dots. Alcohol and mill work don't mix."

So his boss *had* nailed the source of the mishaps on the job.

That didn't mean he had to admit it, though—and going on the offensive would put him in a stronger position

"A lot of the guys enjoy a few drinks after work. If visiting the bar was an issue, you'd have to lay off most of the workforce."

"No one has a beef with an employee having an occasional drink—but from what we've gathered, it's gone beyond that with you."

"That's hearsay. And laying someone off for drinking is . . . it's got to be illegal. Discriminatory, even."

His boss's mouth thinned and his voice hardened. "We're not

laying you off for drinking. We're laying you off for poor job performance."

"Without giving me a chance to improve."

"We *are* giving you a chance to improve." Peg spoke at last. "If we weren't, we'd fire you. But you have a long tenure with us, and for most of your years here you've been an excellent, reliable employee. We wouldn't have sent you for grading training if that hadn't been the case. We want you back."

That was positive news.

But there was a catch. He could feel it in his bones.

"So what do I have to do to *get* back?" He didn't try to mask his caution.

She opened a folder, pulled out a printed sheet and several brochures, and handed them over. "These are resources we recommend through our employee assistance program. The company will pay for you to see any of those counselors."

Patrick skimmed the sheet of paper . . . riffled through the brochures . . . but it was all a blur.

Only one word kept looping through his mind.

Counselors.

They were forcing his hand.

Forcing him to admit he had a problem.

Forcing him to acknowledge he was addicted to alcohol.

His stomach bottomed out.

Harv and Peg were communicating the same message Cindy and Steven had been trying to beat into his brain for the past twelve months.

But this time, ignoring it was going to have serious consequences.

Like . . . how was he supposed to take care of his family if he wasn't bringing home a paycheck—and health insurance?

Panic clawed at his throat.

"What if . . . what if my wife or kids get sick while I'm laid off?"

Peg's demeanor softened. "Your benefits will remain in place during the layoff period."

Relief coursed through him. At least that gave him breathing room.

"How long is that?"

"Six weeks. If you see a counselor on a regular basis and we get a positive report, your job will be waiting for you—but on a probationary basis for six months."

Probation at his age. After all his years of experience.

How depressing was that?

Yet if he was honest . . . if he viewed the situation impartially . . . they were being fair with him.

Fairer than they had to be.

Still, the whole mess left a sick feeling in his gut.

Head down, he fingered the pieces of paper in his hands as the truth he'd been shunning refused to be suppressed any longer.

If the powers-that-be at work, and the people he loved most, all agreed he was hooked on booze . . . maybe he was.

Especially after his mighty struggle over the weekend to lay off scotch for a mere forty-eight hours.

And he sure didn't want to end up like Dad. Much as he'd loved the man, his father's weakness had been apparent to everyone but him. Denial had always been his dad's crutch.

Kind of like it had become his.

"Patrick—are you on board with this plan?"

At Harv's question, he lifted his chin and forced out the hardest words he'd ever said. "I'll see one of the counselors."

"Good." Peg stood, and Harv followed her lead, signaling the end of the meeting—and the discussion. "Let them know you're on our dime. They can fill out all the paperwork. I'll be in touch with you in a couple weeks to see how it's going."

He nodded, feeling as off balance as if he'd downed one too many scotches, and walked through the door.

Outside the mill, he paused and filled his lungs with salt-laced air. But the cloudless blue dome above and bright sunny weather didn't lift his spirits.

What was he supposed to do now? Being at loose ends on a Monday morning during a normal workweek was . . . weird.

Glancing again at the papers in his hand, he sighed. Closed his eyes. Swallowed.

Might as well pick a name on the list and set up an appointment.

First, though, he needed to clear his head.

A hike to Pelican Point light, where the view was expansive and you could almost touch the sky, should do the trick.

Perhaps while he was up there he could also figure out how to deal with the questions that had started gnawing at him as Harv's message began to register.

How were they going to survive on a part-time waitress salary for the next six weeks?

What if he couldn't convince the company he'd licked the problem everyone said he had—and he ended up losing his job permanently?

How was he going to tell Cindy he'd been laid off?

And what was this going to do to their marriage?

That looked like Holly's car.

But what was she doing in his neck of the woods?

Steven pulled in beside the red Civic parked at the end of the road that wove past his apartment toward Starfish Pier and set the jeep's brake.

Odd that his visit had coincided with hers.

Odder yet that half an hour ago, when he'd stopped for tacos after taking care of chores in town on this Monday afternoon, Charley had urged him again to visit the tide pools.

A timely suggestion after the stressful if uneventful dinner at Patrick's yesterday. Wandering among the rocks had seemed like a relaxing way to spend an hour.

Now . . . not so much.

Not with Holly here.

He tapped a finger against the steering wheel.

Go or stay?

As he debated, two seagulls swooped low over the small dune that hid his view of the beach and the tide pools at the far end, circled twice . . . and landed on top of the sand.

After staring at him for a few seconds, one ruffled his feathers and the other began to cackle. Like the gull in the pocket park by Charley's had, the day Holly joined him for an impromptu lunch.

Was he being stalked by seagulls?

One corner of his mouth turned up at such a fanciful notion.

A moment later, the gulls put that idea to rest. With a flutter of wings, they took off again—toward the tide pools.

Where Holly likely was.

After all, there were plenty of beaches prettier and more accessible than this one. The big draw here was the tide pools, according to Charley.

Tide pools the man had said were nestled among slippery, jagged rocks.

Steven frowned, and his pulse quickened.

Given Holly's apparent balance issues, that kind of terrain could be dangerous. If she fell and hurt herself . . . hit her head, twisted an ankle . . . no one would know. She could be trapped there as the tide came in. There wasn't much chance anyone would be rambling around out there at three-thirty on a Monday afternoon.

Fumbling for the door release, he tried to quell his rising panic. Overreacting was nuts. Holly didn't seem like the type who would put herself at risk. A woman who had to be coaxed to board a boat secured in a slip on the dock wasn't going to take any chances.

Nevertheless, he pushed through the door and ascended the small dune at record speed.

As he crested the rise, he gave the beach a sweep.

He spotted her immediately in the distance, standing at the edge of the rocky shoal area that was only exposed at low tide, her back to him. She hadn't yet ventured out onto the mottled gray rock bed dotted with pools of water.

She was safe.

But she also wasn't going to see much of the incredible sea life Charley had raved about unless she decided to tackle the uneven surface and pick her way across to peer down toward the pools of water among the rocks.

All at once, she moved onto a flat boulder that abutted the beach and took a few tentative steps.

Wobbled.

His heart stuttered, and he lurched forward.

She must be more of a daredevil than he'd thought.

Still, there was a fine line between daring and foolish—and she was crossing it.

He broke into a jog, passing the line of rotting pilings from the long-gone pier as she continued to inch forward, the crash of the surf masking his approach.

Ten feet away from her, he stopped.

Now what?

If he called out, she might be so startled she'd lose her balance and pitch headlong onto the rough rocks.

Surprising her close up, where he could grab her if she showed any signs of taking a nosedive, would be more prudent.

Steven jumped onto the rock and covered the distance between them in several long strides. He didn't speak until he was within snatching distance.

"Fancy meeting you here."

She lurched sideways—and teetered.

Before she could topple, he sprang in front of her and grasped her upper arms. "Steady. I've got you."

Gasping, she stiffened and stared up at him, eyes wide.

Somehow he got lost in their hazel, gold-sprinkled depths.

And no woman should have eyelashes that long and curvy without the benefit of mascara—which Holly didn't appear to be wearing. In fact, other than a touch of lipstick, her face seemed to be cosmetic free.

The sole non-natural substance on her skin was a faint purple chalk mark on her chin.

As for the translucent sprinkling of freckles across her nose, invisible except at this close proximity, they only added to her girl-next-door appeal.

"Wh-what are you d-doing here?"

Over the keening gulls and the boom of waves against the outer edges of the rocks, her breathless question registered in the distant recesses of his mind.

Get a grip, Roark. You're here to save her *from falling—not to fall yourself.*

He managed to conjure up a smile. "Checking out the tide pools. We both must have had the same idea." He released one of her arms. "Walking out here is a bit tricky, though."

She moistened her lips . . . swallowed . . . and surveyed the rocks. "More than I thought it would be. But I wanted to see the pools. Charley says they're spectacular."

"Did you talk to him about this today?" Wouldn't that be a strange—and somehow suspect—coincidence?

"No." She put that notion to rest with a definitive shake of her head. "He told me about them not long after I moved here. I've been meaning to come out and wander around, and since I got away from school earlier than usual today—and the weather was perfect—I decided to swing by." She scanned the area again. "I didn't realize how precarious it could be."

"Exploring tide pools should probably be done with a partner." He hesitated, but the invitation tumbled out before he could stop it. "We could team up. For safety reasons."

Surprise—and indecision—flickered in her irises. "I, uh, wouldn't want to slow you down. Navigating this kind of terrain isn't my forte. I could just wander around the periphery, back by the beach." She gestured to the spot where sand met rock.

"You won't see much staying at the edges."

"No." Her expression grew wistful. "You miss a lot watching life from the sidelines—and letting fear hold you back."

Unless his intuition was off, she wasn't talking about tide pools anymore.

Whatever her physical issues, they must have made her super cautious—and her parents' hovering, however well-intentioned, didn't nurture confidence.

But he could help give it a boost.

"Then come explore with me." He angled his elbow her direction and gave her his most persuasive smile. "I have a strong arm if you want something solid to hang on to."

Longing and trepidation duked it out in her eyes as the turbulent sea in the distance thundered against the rocks.

Steven waited. He'd pushed enough. If she declined, so be it.

Truth be told, that might be the best outcome.

For if she agreed to venture out with him into new, unknown territory . . . if she placed her trust in him to keep her safe . . . if she aimed those big eyes his direction in wonder as they discovered all nature had to offer here at Starfish Pier . . . he could be the one who lost his balance.

And while falling on rocks could cause physical injuries, falling for a woman like Holly would put his heart at serious risk.

Because as soon as she learned his history, she'd head the opposite direction as fast as a sandpiper scurried away from a breaking wave.

So maybe it would be best if she turned him down flat and stayed by the shore, where it was safer.

For both of them.

Even if his traitorous heart yearned for her to accept.

10

Go off on an adventure with Steven—or play it safe and stay on shore?

As Holly debated her choice, the wind whipped her hair across her face, obscuring her view of the tall ex-military man who was maintaining a firm grip on her arm.

Thank goodness.

It was hard to think straight while looking into eyes the color of melted chocolate and admiring the strong line of a chiseled jaw darkened with a hint of five o'clock shadow.

While she untangled her hair, she forced the left side of her brain to engage.

Because if she followed her heart, the decision was straightforward.

Go.

The problem was, if she *did* go, her mobility issues would become much more apparent. Steven had already witnessed her clumsiness on the boat and had surely noticed her not-quite-normal gait. He would also have picked up on her parents' protectiveness on Sunday. And who knew how long he'd been watching her timid approach to the tide pools before he'd made his presence known?

If she accepted his invitation, she'd have to offer a credible reason for her awkwardness. Ignoring the elephant in the room wasn't going to make it disappear.

"Everything all right?"

At his question, she shoved her hand in the pocket of her jacket and groped for one of the elastic bands she kept on hand to restrain her longish locks if they became a nuisance while she was teaching.

"Fine. I, uh, need to corral my hair in this wind. I should have done it back at the car."

She pretended to feel around for the band after it was in her grasp, buying herself another few seconds.

What to do?

Much as she wanted to downplay her physical issues and lead a normal life, she did have some limitations—and while she'd developed all kinds of coping mechanisms to deal with them under normal circumstances, they'd be obvious if she wandered around on sharp-edged, slick rocks.

But how much detail would she have to share with this man?

How much *should* she share?

She swept her hair back into the band—and found him watching her. Waiting for her response.

Go for it, Holly. One of your reasons for moving here was to beef up your social life. This could be your chance. You can decide how much to tell him after you venture out onto the rocks.

That was true. She didn't have to finalize her strategy this minute.

Pulse picking up, she took the plunge. "Let's give it a shot."

A couple of beats passed as she tried in vain to decipher his expression. Then he hiked up one corner of his mouth and tightened his grip on her arm. "This should be interesting."

To say the least.

He led her out onto the precarious terrain, farther than she would ever have ventured alone, adjusting his stride to accommodate her slower pace, finally pausing at the rim of a tide pool.

"Now those are spectacular starfish."

She peered over the edge of the rock, at the spot he indicated . . . and gasped in delight.

Half a dozen of the huge beauties were clinging to the side of the rough stone, bright orange and brick red, stippled with an intricate network of lace-like white lines that appeared to be studded with tiny pearls.

"Oh my." She leaned closer.

"Come on down." Beside her, Steven knelt on one knee and gave her arm a gentle tug. "They're even more impressive up close."

"Um . . . I may not be able to get up if I do that." No reason not to be honest. He'd find out the truth if she attempted it.

"I'll help you."

Out of excuses, she eased down—with far less grace than he had.

If he noticed, though, he was kind enough not to comment.

And he was right about viewing the scene closer. From this proximity, the contrast between the starfish and the gray rock they were clinging to was more dramatic. And she was able to spot tinier sea life not visible from higher up.

After they had their fill of the starfish, they moved on to other pools filled with spiky, bright purple sea urchins, brilliant yellow sea lemons, and several varieties of sea anemones, ranging from large clusters of vibrant green giants to a small grouping of the creatures with gray centers and a delicate fringe of white, mauve-tipped, petal-like tentacles.

"Those are incredible." From her crouched position beside the pool she stared at the flowers of the sea, any self-consciousness over her lack of grace receding as she drank in the bounty of beauty.

"Yeah, they are. Also very shy and cautious. Watch."

Steven leaned over the pool, dipped his finger in the water, and gently touched a mauve-edged petal.

Instantly the anemone closed up into a tight bud. Hiding. Protecting itself.

Steven withdrew his finger but remained hunkered down beside her.

Petal by petal, the anemone began to open again.

"That is amazing." Holly continued to inspect the pool. "Charley was spot on about this place. I'm glad I decided to—oh!"

As a spray of water flecked her cheek, she surveyed the sea.

The tide was coming back in—at a decent clip.

"That's our cue to return to dry land." Steven stood and helped her up, putting more muscle into the assist than the average person would require.

After she was on her feet and steady, he took her arm and guided her back over the rocks, toward the beach.

She stumbled once near the end of their trek, and his grip tightened.

"You okay?" He paused to scrutinize her. Though he asked no other questions, they hovered in the air between them.

This was her opening.

Should she take the leap and share her story—or stick to her original plan to disclose as little as possible about her background to the people in her new town?

As a pelican on a flight path toward the lighthouse dipped low, giving her a clear view of its oversized orange beak, she brushed back a few strands of hair that had escaped and thrust her brain into warp speed.

She'd come here to start fresh, in a place where people didn't know her background and wouldn't be as inclined to treat her with kid gloves. Where she could spread her wings, test her limits, without anyone bending over backward to accommodate her because of her history. Where she was defined by what she *could* do rather than what she couldn't do.

The logical choice was to zip her lips.

Besides, if she confided in Steven, he might treat her differently afterward. Lose interest in her.

If it had happened once, it could happen again.

Still . . . wouldn't it be better to know now if her condition was a deal breaker rather than let herself get carried away with romantic fantasies that had no chance of ever coming true?

"Holly?"

At his prompt, she filled her lungs . . . gave her choice another moment of thought . . . and made her decision.

Steven watched an array of emotions play tag on Holly's face. Even without interrogation training, she'd be a cinch to read. Her eyes were a window to her soul.

She was trying to decide whether he was worthy of her trust.

Truth be told, he was as conflicted as she was about the verdict.

Not because he'd betray any confidences she shared. That would never happen.

But once people opened their hearts, they could pull you in—ready or not.

And he was nowhere near ready to let someone like Holly into his life.

"I'm fine—but I've always been more stable on flat terrain, like that." She motioned toward the hard-packed sand a few feet away, her fingers not quite steady. "You, uh, probably noticed I have a few issues with balance."

"Yes." He wasn't going to play games with this woman. If she asked a question, he'd give an honest answer.

"Thanks for not sugarcoating the truth." She offered him a quick smile. "Most people seem to think I'll be offended if they admit the obvious. But I prefer to deal with realities straight on—and this is my reality." She indicated a large log that had washed up at the back of the beach. "If you have a few minutes, I could tell you a little of my story. Assuming you'd like to hear it."

A rush of warmth filled his heart at her willingness to confide in him—followed immediately by a red alert . . . which he ignored.

"Yes, I would—and I have no other plans for the day." He exerted a hint of pressure on her arm, urging her toward the log.

As soon as they reached hard-packed sand, however, she wiggled free of his grasp. "I'm fine on firm ground."

Rather than fuss over her or hover too close, as her parents had, he let her go and fell into step beside her.

The grateful glance she sent him suggested she appreciated that.

At the log, Holly carefully lowered herself to the sun-bleached, wind-polished surface.

He sat beside her—close, but not too close. Unless he was misreading her, she put a high value on personal space.

Two seagulls joined them, huddling together a few yards away. No personal space issues between those two. They were nestled as close as two honeymooners.

A wave of yearning swept over him at the images that term conjured up.

What would it be like to get that cozy with the woman beside him? Would her skin be as silky beneath his fingertips as he suspected? Would her eyes fill with longing if he drew her close? Would her mouth soften beneath his if he claimed a kiss? Would she—

Wait.

This was nuts.

He'd only met Holly a week ago. It was way too premature to let his mind wander in such dangerous directions. The attraction he felt had to be hormones, pure and simple.

Stretching his legs out in front of him, he crossed his feet at the ankles and braced his palms on the log. "The tide's coming in fast." The innocuous words rasped past his tight throat.

She squinted into the distance, where the last set of rocks they'd explored was already submerged.

"Yes. It won't take long for the whole area to be covered. No one would ever know such beauty lies beneath those dark waters."

"Unless they sought an opportunity to check out what was underneath." He transferred his attention to her.

Her forehead wrinkled, as if she wasn't quite certain how to interpret that comment.

That made two of them.

Thankfully she didn't dwell on it.

"So . . . switching to the reason for this conversation, you may have noticed on Sunday that my parents are very . . . attentive . . . toward me."

"Yes."

"Most people who see us together do." She picked up a broken sand dollar and ran a finger over the jagged edge. "Especially after they watch me walk and realize my gait isn't quite normal."

Silence fell, as if she was having second thoughts about the wisdom of continuing.

He was too—but now that they'd taken a few steps down this road, he wasn't settling for a dead end.

"Was there an accident?" Maybe a question would jump-start the conversation.

"No—although that's the usual assumption. My problems began before I was born." She looked over at him. Took a deep breath. "Do you know anything about spina bifida?"

He rolled the name around in his head as alarm bells began to jangle. "I know it's a serious medical condition—but that's it."

"That's all most people know." She tossed the sand dollar aside and linked her fingers into a tight knot. "Cutting to the chase, SB is a defect in the spine. It forms in the womb. The mildest form can go undetected forever, while the most severe form can cause paralysis of the legs, learning disabilities, and a host of other problems. I have a rare type known as lipomyelomeningocele. How's that for a mouthful?" She flashed him a nervous grin.

He tried to return it, but his lips refused to budge as he grappled with the news that while Holly seemed normal except for a slight limp and a few balance issues, she had a severe medical condition. "Tell me about the form you have."

At his serious tone, her smile faded. "Let me back up a bit first.

Myelomeningocele is the most common and severest form of spina bifida. For babies who have that, part of the spinal cord pushes out with the meninges—that's the membrane around the spinal cord—through an opening in the spine and forms a sac on the back. The spinal cord and nearby nerves are damaged, resulting in disabilities. With the lipo version I have, an abnormal growth of fat attaches to the spinal cord and its membranes and forms a pad under the skin. As a result of that padding, there tends to be less damage."

"Is it curable?"

"No. Any disabilities from damage to the spinal cord and nerves are permanent. But there are treatments to help with some of the secondary problems."

"Such as?"

"In my case, primarily surgery. My first operation, a few days after I was born, lasted eight hours. More surgeries followed to treat a variety of problems—tethered spinal cord, tendon issues, a cyst on my spine."

He curled his fingers into his palms. "How many surgeries have you had?"

"Twelve. The last one was when I was twenty-four—six years ago. These days, I lead a mostly normal life—or try to."

Normal?

Not even close.

Nothing about this woman's day-to-day living had been normal.

While he'd been running track and shooting baskets and working on the fishing boat in the summer, Holly had been in the hospital having surgery or trying to recover from her latest visit to the operating room.

He'd faced major challenges in his life, but none of them came close to what she'd dealt with.

No wonder her parents fussed over her.

"Hey." She touched the back of his hand. "It's not as bad as it sounds. As a kid, I was able to do most of the activities my friends did. I roller-skated, rode my bike, went on campouts with my church youth group. All under the superwatchful eye of my parents, of course—which made me kind of self-conscious." She wrinkled her nose. "These days, I struggle on occasion with walking and balance—and I avoid being the center of attention like the plague—but beyond that and a few other inconveniences, it's all good."

He exhaled . . . pulled his feet back . . . and rested his elbows on his knees as he studied her. "I had no idea your story was that . . . complicated." Or that it would burrow deep inside him and wrench his heartstrings.

She lifted one shoulder. "I've tried to keep it quiet since I moved here. I wanted to be independent. That's hard to manage with people hovering over you—which they tend to do after they know my background. Like my parents do. I've asked Mom and Dad to pull back, and they're trying their best, but it's difficult for them to let go."

"I can understand that."

"I can too. After shepherding me through all those medical procedures and devoting themselves to caring for me, I totally get why they want to do everything in their power to keep me safe."

"But that kind of care and attention can also smother."

"Exactly. I had a fine life in Eugene, but it had gotten kind of . . . stale. And insulated. I knew unless I shook up the status quo, nothing would ever change. So when I came across the job opening here not long after my thirtieth birthday, I applied. I didn't expect to be chosen, but after beating out the competition, I decided this was where I was supposed to be."

"Any regrets about moving?"

"No. There've been a few challenges—like dealing with yard work. That's tougher than I expected—for me, anyway. But I've managed to cope, and that's empowering."

"How are your parents handling the separation?" After seeing the three of them together and listening to Holly's story, it wasn't hard to predict her answer.

She sighed. "They call every day—multiple times—and come down frequently. I know they miss me, and that's a major guilt trip. In fact, there are days it makes me second-guess my choice."

He knew all about the heavy burden of guilt and second-guessing.

But hers wasn't deserved.

"I'm sure they appreciate your desire for independence. I didn't pick up anything but love in the few minutes I spent with them."

"They've always wanted what's best for me—but they're having difficulty letting go. I'm hoping once they see I'm capable of surviving on my own they'll worry less about me."

"So what prompted you to shake things up at this point—aside from turning thirty?" He'd be willing to bet there had been more of a precipitating incident than a milestone birthday and a vague discontent with her life.

She regarded the two snuggling seagulls, the faint parallel lines on her forehead deepening as the silence between them lengthened.

Just when he thought she was going to shut down, she spoke again, her voice subdued. "I dated a guy from church for close to a year. It got serious, and I began to think a proposal was in the offing. But it didn't work out. Getting involved with someone who has SB can be . . . messy. And difficult."

Steven narrowed his eyes.

Some guy had seriously dated her knowing she had health issues, only to get cold feet and dump her?

Anger began to simmer in his gut.

This woman deserved better than that.

Relationships could be messy and difficult even between people with normal health. But if you loved someone, you didn't bail. You worked through problems, discussed them, dealt with the challenges together and—

Hypocrite.

As the well-deserved rebuke smacked his conscience, he winced.

Given his track record, he fell into the same camp as her boyfriend.

She peeked his direction, and he curbed the impulse to spew out a negative comment about her ex. That would be disingenuous. Best to keep it simple—and sincere.

"I'm sorry, Holly."

And he was—about a lot of things.

"I kind of expected it all along, to be honest. Anyone who gets involved with me would have to be willing to put up with a bunch of hassles. Too many for most people. I mean, I could marry, have children—but there would have to be . . . accommodations."

"That should be par for the course in *any* marriage."

She cocked her head, apparently picking up on nuances he hadn't intended to communicate. "That sounds like experience talking."

Not territory he'd intended to venture into today—but after all she'd told him, he should be upfront about that piece of his past, at least.

"I've been married. My wife died." He stood, cutting off any further conversation on the topic.

She gave a slight gasp at his abrupt move—but recovered quickly and pushed herself to her feet. For an instant she faltered, but he restrained the urge to grab hold of her. Acting like her parents would *not* endear him to her.

And until he'd had a chance to digest everything she'd told him, decide if he should let their relationship progress beyond the casual acquaintance stage, he didn't want to jinx himself.

"I'm sorry about your loss."

Her gentle sympathy was more than he deserved.

"Thanks." He swallowed past the lump in his throat and tried for a dispassionate tone. "She's been gone four years, so I've learned to deal with the grief." He motioned toward the parking area. "I'll walk you back to your car."

"No need. Stay awhile if you want."

"I'm ready to go. I came to see the tide pools, and they're disappearing." After giving the rocks that were still visible above the water a quick scan, he refocused on her. "But the treasure beneath the surface was worth the trip."

She looked up at him, and he locked gazes with her. Willed her to realize he was talking about more than the secrets the tide pools had revealed. That he appreciated how she'd opened up to him—even if he wasn't willing to reciprocate.

Her lips parted slightly as she searched his face, and the tiniest hitch in her breathing gave him his answer.

Message received.

Dipping her chin, she made a project out of removing the band from her hair, stowing it in her jacket, and retrieving her keys.

When she lifted her head, she seemed to have regained control of her emotions—though the tiniest tremble in her fingers betrayed her.

"Shall we?" He indicated the far end of the beach.

He fell in beside her as she trekked down the hard-packed sand, shoving his hands in his pockets so he wouldn't succumb to the urge to take her arm.

At the small, loose-packed dune that led to the cars, however, she paused.

"May I offer an arm here?" He crooked an elbow.

"Thanks. I managed to cross this earlier, but it wasn't pretty."

It wasn't pretty going back, either. Sand wasn't easy to walk on for anyone—especially uphill. For Holly, it required a major effort.

If he wasn't 100 percent certain she'd object, he'd sweep her into his arms and carry her across.

By the time they reached the cars, she was winded.

"Sorry." She tucked her hair behind her ear. "Shifting sand and SB don't mix."

"You got through it. That's what counts."

"With a little help from a friend." She unlocked her door and brushed remnants of sand off her slacks. "Thanks for the tour out there." She pointed toward the sea. "If you hadn't come along, I'd have chickened out after a few more steps and missed a fantastic show."

"You can thank Charley for my opportune arrival. I hadn't planned to come out here today until he reminded me about the tide pools while I was at the stand buying tacos."

"Must have been fate."

Or something more.

God might not have much interest in him these days, but perhaps he'd been watching out for Holly on the treacherous rocks. If ever there was a woman who deserved special blessings and graces, she was it.

"Whatever the reason, I'm glad I had company." He opened her door for her. "Enjoy the rest of your day."

"I'll try—but I think the best part is over."

Leaving that enigmatic remark hanging in the air, she slid behind the wheel, started the engine, and backed out. After executing a U-turn, she drove away.

For a long while after her taillights disappeared, Steven remained where he was, mulling over her last remark.

Had she meant the best part of her day was seeing the tide pools—or spending an hour with him?

Based on the undercurrent of electricity thrumming between them—and her willingness to tell him her story—his money was on the latter.

And he'd sent *her* several signals that he'd enjoyed their impromptu excursion too.

Not smart.

Exhaling, he leaned back against the jeep and folded his arms.

The two of them wouldn't be a good match—for reasons unrelated to the disability that had been the kiss of death in her previous relationship.

This stumbling block was with him.

For despite the medals he'd won overseas for bravery, he was no hero. Nor was he worthy of a woman like Holly. Given the odds she'd overcome and all she'd gone through to achieve a normal life, s*he* was the real hero.

No way did she deserve to be hurt by another man—a likely outcome if he caved and asked her out.

And that wouldn't be fair to her.

Maybe he couldn't change the past or redeem the mistakes from his marriage, but he *could* ensure no other woman was ever again hurt by his insensitivity.

Meaning it would be dead wrong to encourage the interest of someone who would run the other direction if she knew his history.

It wouldn't be easy to walk a wide circle around Holly, but that was the honorable course.

He pushed off from the car and opened his door.

Besides, now that he was making progress in his relationship with his brother, that had to be his priority. He'd come here to help Patrick, not pursue a romance. Getting involved with a woman would only distract him.

Even if a certain teacher with sparkling hazel eyes was already playing havoc with his concentration.

11

Why was Patrick's car in the driveway at four o'clock on a workday?

As Cindy swung in behind her husband's Focus, a tingle of worry rippled through her. His shift at the mill didn't end for half an hour, and he was supposed to pick up Beatrice from the sitter and Jonah from aftercare while she cooked dinner.

Only once before in their marriage had he come home early, after an accident at the mill had resulted in a dozen stitches.

Had there been another mishap?

Pulse accelerating, she jammed the brake to the floor, yanked her keys out of the ignition, and dashed toward the house.

The back door opened as she reached the stairs to the stoop.

"I've been watching for you." Patrick moved aside so she could enter.

She ran up the steps but stopped on the threshold to give him a quick scan.

There were no visible bandages, cuts, bruises, or plaster casts.

That was a positive sign.

Yet the charged vibes in the air spelled trouble.

"What's wrong?"

"Come on in. We can talk over there." He motioned toward the kitchen table, where a cup of tea was steeping with her favorite, soothing chamomile blend.

Her heart picked up speed again. “Tell me what’s wrong.”

“Not out here.” He took her arm and gently tugged her inside, closing the door behind her. “Let’s sit.”

Whatever he was about to tell her was bad.

Maybe she *should* sit.

After depositing her purse on the counter, she crossed to the table, dropped into her chair—and braced.

Patrick retrieved a mug from the microwave and joined her, gripping it with both hands when the coffee inside sloshed close to the edge.

Panic bubbled up inside her. “Did the mill close?” Hard to believe, after four generations of Fishers at the helm. But stranger things had happened.

“No.” Patrick took a sip of coffee, set the mug down on the table, and stared into the dark depths. “But I’ve been laid off.”

Laid off.

The message registered . . . but it didn’t compute.

“I-I don’t understand.” She rubbed her forehead, trying to make sense of the news. “You were just promoted four months ago—and you have more tenure than most of the employees. If they had to lay off people, why would they include you?”

A muscle twitched in his cheek, and he slowly lifted his head. “There weren’t any other layoffs. I was the only one.”

“The only one?” She gaped at him. “Why would they—”

As understanding dawned, the question died in her throat.

His drinking had caught up with him at last.

“Oh, Patrick.” She wrapped her cold fingers around the ceramic mug to warm them as a million questions—and worries—tumbled through her mind. “What happened?”

“I made a few mistakes on the line. They talked to several of the guys and put two and two together.” He laid his hand on her arm, his fingers as icy as hers. “I’ll make this right, Cindy. I promise. As long as I see a counselor and they're confident I've got this under control, they'll let me come back in six weeks."

"Are you willing to do that? See a counselor?"

"Yes. I called this afternoon and set up an appointment."

At least there was one constructive outcome from this experience. Plus, her prayer had been answered—no one had gotten hurt in the wake-up call.

But how were they supposed to feed the kids and pay the bills for the next six weeks? Her major car repair last month and the trips to the urgent care center for Jonah's asthma episodes had eaten up their meager cash reserve.

"I can try to get a few more hours at the Myrtle—but they don't need another full-time employee." Her temples began to throb. "We don't have enough money saved to tide us over."

"I'll do my best to hustle up odd jobs around town."

"You need to focus on detox."

"I can't do that twenty-four hours a day. I have to find something else to occupy myself. A few odd jobs will help fill in the gaps. And I can work on the cannon project too. I talked to the city manager today, and Marci at the *Herald*. They were both interested in the idea of finding a public home for it here." His Adam's apple bobbed. "I'm sorry, Cindy. I never meant for it to come to this."

"I know." Yet this day had been inevitable. People on a downward spiral eventually hit bottom.

The scariest part was, some of them stayed there—despite their best intentions to lick the problem.

Would her husband be one of them?

"It'll be okay." He squeezed her arm. "As long as you stick with me, we'll get through this."

At the fear lurking in his eyes, a ripple of shock shuddered through her.

Was he actually afraid she'd leave him?

"Patrick—we took vows. Through better or worse. I meant them. If you're serious about beating this, we'll figure out a way to manage for six weeks."

"I'm serious." He rubbed the tip of his index finger across a scratch in the oak table. "I went up to the lighthouse today after they let me go. I sat there for hours, thinking. And I realized that if everyone—my family and the people at work—is convinced I have a drinking problem, it's possible I do." He swallowed. "To be honest, that kind of freaks me out. I mean . . . drinking killed my dad—and he took Mom with him."

"But he never admitted he had a problem. Taking that step is huge." She picked up her tea, downed a soothing sip, and broached a subject sure to be touchy. "You know, I bet Steven would be willing to help us out with a small loan if our funds run low."

Patrick's face reddened. "I don't want to ask my brother for money."

"It would only be a short-term loan."

"He may not have any excess cash either."

"More than us, I expect. His charter business keeps him busy, and I doubt he had much opportunity to spend money during his military career overseas. It may be worth asking."

"Let's see how we do on our own first."

"Okay." No sense pushing the issue if Patrick wasn't receptive. Besides, the day could come when they had no choice. "You may want to tell him about the layoff tonight, though. Hope Harbor is a small town, and the grapevine is active. This isn't the kind of news a family member wants to get secondhand."

"I suppose I could text him."

He could—if he wanted to take the easy way out.

Instead of voicing that opinion, she sipped her tea.

"You think I should call him, don't you?" Patrick sent her a sidelong look.

At the very least.

"Or you could swing by his place. You've never been to his apartment."

He grimaced. "A phone call would be less—complicated."

"Also less considerate. You may not have been happy about

him showing up here after I wrote that letter, but a man doesn't travel halfway around the world for someone who isn't important to him. We launched a new chapter yesterday. Got a fresh start. Going to his place to share this news might mean a lot to him."

"He'll lord it over me. Say I told you so." Patrick's jaw hardened, like it always did when he was getting ready to dig in his heels.

Her signal to back off. Further discussion now would be fruitless.

"I doubt that's how he'd respond, but fine. Do whatever you want." She rose. "I can go get the kids."

"No." He stood too. "That's my job. You work on dinner." He pulled out his keys. "I'll think about visiting Steven."

"Okay."

She began to swivel away, but he stopped her with a touch on the arm. When she angled back, his brief prickliness was gone. Instead, contrition—and gratitude—softened his features.

"I really am sorry about this, Cindy. And about all the worry I've put you through for too long. I'm going to turn this around. I love you—and the kids—more than anything in the world, and I don't want to risk"—his voice hoarsened, and he cleared his throat—"I don't want to risk becoming my dad and losing everything." He held out his arms but remained where he was, leaving the choice about whether to hug up to her.

She didn't hesitate.

Resting her hands on his chest, she moved into the familiar embrace that had always felt like home.

"I love you too, Patrick. Always have, always will."

And as they stood in the kitchen on this quiet Monday afternoon, in the modest house containing everything she needed to be happy, she sent one more prayer heavenward.

Please, Lord, let him stick with his pledge to beat this—and hold him up if he stumbles.

Someone was knocking on his door.

As Steven shut off the shower and began towel drying his hair, he frowned.

No one ever visited his apartment.

And who would come calling at eight o'clock on a Monday night?

For a brief moment, an image of Holly standing on his doorstep flashed through his mind—but that was stupid. He'd seen her less than four hours ago, and she'd have no reason to seek him out again.

Even if the notion of spending a few more minutes in her company was far too appealing.

The bell rang, and he went into action, pulling on jeans and a T-shirt. If whoever was out there had resorted to both knocking and ringing, they must be determined to see him.

Jogging barefoot to the living room, he gave his face one last swipe and slung the damp towel over his shoulder.

At the door, he peered through the peephole.

No one was on the other side.

Had his caller given up?

He opened the door—and from several yards away his brother turned.

"Patrick?" He did a double take. "What are you doing here?" Even as he asked the question, his pulse picked up. After all these months of keeping his distance—and despite the tentative step forward they'd taken yesterday—nothing but an emergency could coerce his sibling to come here. "Are Cindy and the kids okay?"

"Yeah. Everyone's fine." His brother jingled his keys. "I, uh, had news I wanted to share. Looks like I caught you in the shower."

"I'm done now. Come on in." He pulled the door wide.

After a slight hesitation, Patrick walked back and entered the apartment. "Sorry to disturb you."

"Nothing to disturb. I didn't have any plans for the evening." Steven closed the door. "You want a soda?"

"Yeah. That'd be fine. But I can't stay long. I promised Cindy I'd be home by nine."

Steven led him to the tiny kitchenette in his one-bedroom apartment, ditched the towel, and pulled two soft drinks from the fridge.

After handing Patrick one of the cans, he motioned to the living room. "Have a seat."

As Patrick walked over to one of the side chairs in the furnished unit, Steven studied the rigid line of his shoulders.

His brother was clearly stressed—and here under duress.

Since there wasn't much chance Patrick would chill out until he'd completed whatever mission had brought him here, why not cut to the chase?

"So what's your news?" Steven sat on the couch and popped the tab on his soda.

"It's, uh, work related." Patrick's soda hissed as he too released the tab.

Steven took a swig and waited.

"It's, uh, not good." Patrick gulped the fizzy drink, avoiding eye contact.

No kidding.

His brother's posture was as stiff as the dress uniform the brass had insisted operators in The Unit wear on the rare occasions requiring formality—like medal ceremonies.

"What happened?" Whatever it was, ten chances to one alcohol had played a role.

"I got laid off today."

A shock wave ricocheted through him, but Steven managed to maintain a neutral tone and expression. "Why?"

He listened without interrupting as his brother briefed him, absorbing the news—and the daunting ramifications.

The one positive takeaway was that Patrick sounded as if he intended to finally address the problem he'd been refusing to acknowledge.

When he finished the story, Steven chose his words with care. "I'm sorry it came to this."

"Yeah. Me too." His brother swiped a tear of condensation off his can. "Go ahead and say it."

"What?"

"I told you so."

"Why would I do that?"

"Because you were right."

"This isn't about who's right and who's wrong. It's about fixing the problem. It sounds like you're committed to doing that."

"I am."

"Tell me how I can help."

"I think it's up to me at this point."

"The hard work is. But I want to be part of the support team." He took another drink, debating how to broach the next subject. No matter his approach, it would be tricky. "I don't know how you're fixed for cash over the next six weeks, but I've got some money in reserve if you run low."

"We should be able to manage—but thanks."

The exact response he'd expected.

"You're welcome—and it's a standing offer. Don't hesitate to let me know if a few bucks would come in handy down the road. How soon are you meeting with the counselor?"

"Tomorrow."

That was fast.

But when you were dealing with addiction, every hour . . . every minute . . . counted—and the pros knew that.

"You going to be able to hold out until then?" The lure of alcohol—or any addiction—could be a powerful force, and an appointment twelve or more hours away could feel like a lifetime once withdrawal symptoms kicked in.

"Yeah. I think so. Today was . . . it shook me up pretty bad."

I think so wasn't the most reassuring response.

Having the foundation of your world shaken could have a positive impact—but it could also make you susceptible to the very thing you were trying to overcome. In a state of anxiety, it would be easy for a person hooked on booze to justify having one more drink.

Steven gave his watch a surreptitious skim. Eight-twenty. As early as he got up for his charter fishing trips, eight-thirty was his typical bedtime.

But if Patrick left now and temptation struck, that would give him a window to stop by the bar before heading home.

He could sacrifice a little sleep if it kept his brother on the straight and narrow—for tonight, anyway.

"I hear you about being shaken up—but remember what Mom always used to say. Whenever you don't understand what's happening in your life, close your eyes, take a deep breath, and trust that it's part of God's plan for you."

Patrick arched his eyebrows. "I don't remember her saying that."

"No?" Funny, the advice was etched deep in his memory, even if he hadn't consciously thought about it in years. "She may have only said it to me, since I was the one who tended to end up in all the scrapes."

"Yeah. That I remember. Like when you were thirteen and decided to explore a sandbar that formed offshore, then ended up stranded after the tide came in. As I recall, the Coast Guard got pulled into that one."

Steven gave a dismissive wave. "Someone on shore overreacted. I could have swum to the beach."

Maybe.

"Mom and Dad didn't think so. You were grounded for weeks. Near as I can recall, you complained nonstop that your sense of adventure was being stifled."

"It was. But they were luckier with you. You were always the obedient, toe-the-line brother who never raised their blood pressure."

Patrick leaned back in his chair and took another sip of soda. "Your life's been more exciting than mine, though."

"Excitement is overrated—and it doesn't hold a candle to a wife and family." Not even close. "I envy you the home you've created."

"Yeah?" Patrick squinted at him, as if trying to discern whether that comment was truth or fiction.

"Yeah." Steven met his gaze straight on. "I'd trade all my medals and all my travels for what you have."

"Huh." Patrick swirled the soda in his can. "You could still have it, you know. There's no reason you couldn't remarry someday. I doubt Laura would begrudge you that."

Strange how his wife had come up in conversation twice in the space of a few hours after months with no mention of her.

"Marriage isn't top of mind these days." He finished off his soda and changed the subject. "Want to play a couple of hands of poker before you head home?" That could eat up twenty minutes.

"You have cards?"

"Always." Solitaire was less mind-numbing than surfing the net or watching TV.

"I'm in." Patrick rose and strolled toward the small table for two in the combination living/dining room. "That quote from Mom about God having a plan for you . . . you really believe that?"

Steven opened the drawer where he kept the cards. "Mom did."

"I know. She and Dad never missed a Sunday service."

"You still go to church?"

"Sometimes. Cindy goes every week, with the kids."

"Why don't you start going with her again on a regular basis?" He might not attend church anymore, but it couldn't hurt Patrick to put in face time with God as he traveled the road to sobriety.

"I'll consider it—if you go too."

As Patrick threw down that gauntlet, Steven's hand froze for an instant.

Of all the comebacks his kid brother could have lobbed at him, why did it have to be that one?

He closed his fingers around the cards and pulled them out. "My church habits don't have anything to do with you."

"Mom and Dad always encouraged us to go to services every week. We could make it a family activity—and it would be a good example for the kids."

Steven tossed the deck of cards on the table and propped his hands on his hips. "Did Cindy put you up to this?" His sister-in-law wouldn't be above using a little bribery to encourage church attendance for a sheep who'd strayed. She never missed a Sunday and made no secret of the fact she considered weekly worship a sacred duty.

"Nope. My idea. And to be honest, I have no clue where it came from. Let's forget the whole thing and play cards."

That would be his preference too—but the notion of getting Patrick back to church was taking root. Despite his own lack of urgency to reconnect with God, his brother would need every source of support he could get in the weeks and months ahead.

And if the only way to get Patrick to agree to his suggestion was to attend too—so be it.

Even if he lost his Sunday morning charter revenue.

Even if a bolt of lightning hit him as he approached the church.

God might be willing to forgive sinners, but a mere "I'm sorry" didn't seem anywhere close to adequate for all the transgressions he'd committed.

"Fine. I'll go with you." He sat across from Patrick and began to shuffle the deck.

His brother's jaw dropped. "Seriously?"

"Yeah."

"I didn't expect you to call my bluff."

"I know you didn't." Steven managed a grin. "Now let's see if I can best you in poker too."

He didn't—but as he saw Patrick off at the door at seven minutes to nine, he *had* accomplished his mission.

There would be no bar visit tonight. Not if Patrick kept his promise to Cindy.

And despite his problems, his brother's word had always been gold.

Even without the promise to his wife, however, he may have resisted a bar visit. The layoff had clearly thrown him. Forced him to admit he had issues—and take stock of his priorities.

But one day without booze was doable.

After the shock wore off, though—and the craving for alcohol set in—the going would get tougher.

Steven closed the door and wandered back to the table to collect their empty soft drink cans. If he didn't get a few hours of sleep, he'd be dragging all day tomorrow—and after forking over big bucks, his customers deserved a guide who was at the top of his game.

Except he wasn't tired anymore.

Between his impromptu tide pool excursion with Holly and Patrick's unexpected visit, he was too wired to sleep.

Expelling a breath, he sat at the table again and laid out a solitaire game, playing on autopilot as his mind grappled with other, more pressing matters.

Months ago he'd arrived in Hope Harbor with the best of intentions. But very little had gone as he'd expected. His charter business was thriving—but between battling loneliness and bombing out on every attempt to help Patrick, his personal life was a mess.

Or it had been, until recently.

Then he'd met Holly . . . and had a breakthrough with Patrick.

But the woman who'd caught his eye should be off-limits, and the uneasy peace with his brother could be short-lived if he made one wrong move.

Some would call his attitude pessimistic.

He preferred to think of it as realistic.

Because of all the lessons he'd learned during his years in the service, one in particular had been validated time and time again.

Just when you thought you had the situation under control and everything was going well, disaster was often lurking in the shadows . . . waiting to pounce.

12

This was stupid.

As Holly drove slowly down Dockside Drive, scanning the wharf, she blew out a breath.

Steven's charter trips ended long before her school day did—yeah, yeah, she'd checked the schedule on his website—and there was no reason to think he'd be hanging around the boat at this hour.

Nor was there any reason to expect him to call her, despite their outing to the tide pools three days ago—and the confidences she'd shared with him. Snatching up the phone every time it rang for the past seventy-two hours had been silly.

He might be attracted to her . . . surely she hadn't misread his cues . . . but that didn't mean he'd feel any urgency about pursuing his interest.

In fact, despite his assertion that he'd learned to deal with the loss of his wife, it was possible he was still in mourning and had no intention of initiating another romance anytime in the near future.

And who knew what other kinds of wounds he was nursing? The soldier-turned-charter-fisherman was a complex man. One who no doubt bore the kind of battle scars Charley had mentioned during their conversation not long after she'd met Steven. He probably also carried secrets he'd shared with very few.

Perhaps many of them dark.

Yet some quality about him continued to draw her in, despite her mother's warning on the patio the day her dad had helped Pete with the downed branch.

"Be careful with that young man, Holly. He likes you. But there's an air of . . . danger . . . about him. And while the brooding, mysterious type may be romantic in a novel, it can be disastrous in real life."

It was possible her mom had been justified in sounding a note of caution—but it was also possible she was being überprotective. It wouldn't be the first time they'd been down that road.

Not that it appeared to matter. Steven was nowhere to be seen on this sunny afternoon.

As she neared the end of Dockside Drive, Charley smiled and lifted a hand in greeting from behind the counter of the taco truck.

She eased back on the gas pedal.

It was early for dinner—but nothing was more comforting than a Charley's taco . . . or a conversation with the man himself.

And she could use comforting today.

She pulled into the first available parking spot and trekked toward the stand.

Halfway there, she spotted Marci from the *Herald* also making a beeline for Charley's.

The editor grinned and sent her a cheery wave as their paths converged. "I see we're both indulging in a late-afternoon treat on this beautiful day."

"Guilty as charged. I caught a whiff as I was driving past . . . and the rest is history."

"I hear you. Imagine working up the street from this place. I'm surprised I haven't gained twenty pounds since I moved here." She patted her flat stomach. "I try to resist, but I had an extra strong craving today."

Some nuance in her inflection sent Holly's antennas up. "A craving, huh?"

Marci chuckled and gave her a shoulder nudge as they reached the stand. "You're the first outside the family to hear the news—other than Charley. He figured it out last week."

The taco chef's lips curved up as they drew up to the counter. "That glow you were sporting was easy to interpret."

"Congratulations." Holly touched her arm. "I'm happy for you."

"Thank you. We're both excited. And I'm hungry."

"Two orders coming up—I assume you're eating too, Holly?"

"Yes."

"Any late-breaking stories this week, Marci?" Charley opened his cooler and began pulling out fish fillets.

"As a matter of fact, I have a big one. You know that cannon that washed up on our beach? Turns out it's from a ship that was owned and captained by one of our residents back in the mid-to-late 1800s. The heirs contacted Brent at City Hall to see if the town wants it."

"That's an intriguing proposition." Charley retrieved an avocado from a bin that was out of sight. "I wonder where we could put a cannon?"

"Several locations were suggested—including our wharf-side park." Marci motioned toward the tiny green space with the gazebo behind the stand.

Holly wrinkled her nose. "Why would we want something that represents war and killing and aggression in such a peaceful place?" Pete had been right about what the find on the beach symbolized.

Marci and Charley both turned to her.

"I never thought about it like that." Marci cocked her head. "But if public money is involved for restoration costs, citizens should have the opportunity to weigh in and opposing viewpoints should be heard. That's a critical part of balanced journalism."

"Does the town have enough in its coffers to fund an undertaking like that?" Charley directed the question to Marci.

"It could be a stretch, according to our city manager. Brent says the budget is tight. But he may be able to scrape up the funds if there's a strong consensus we should display it. Holly, would you consider writing a few paragraphs about your feelings that I could run on Tuesday, along with the update on the cannon? I'll find someone to represent the other side too."

Good heavens, what had she gotten herself into?

"I'm, uh, not sure I should weigh in on this publicly. I mean . . . I'm too new here. I wouldn't want to alienate anyone this early in my tenure."

"Don't worry about being new." Marci gave a dismissive wave. "Once you move to Hope Harbor, you're one of us. I think residents would appreciate the opportunity to hear both sides. Don't you, Charley?"

The man's expression remained impassive. "I like to think everyone in town has a heart large enough to accommodate different opinions."

"There you go." Marci pivoted back to her, as if Charley had given his blessing.

Holly wasn't certain about that. The man's response hadn't sounded superdefinitive to her.

"A couple hundred words would be perfect." Marci stepped into the silence. "Why don't you give it a shot, and if you decide not to follow through, let me know by Saturday. But you do have a point a lot of people in town may agree with. We ought to get a reading on opinions before we go too far down any road—and the *Herald* feature could generate discussion that will help the city determine whether to pursue this."

Charley went back to cooking while Marci waited for an answer, her eyes dancing with enthusiasm—as usual.

Also as usual, it was hard to say no to the effervescent editor.

"So I could decide as late as Saturday?" Holly tightened her grip on her purse.

"Absolutely."

Given that out, how could she say no?

Besides, it would be easier to back out by email than in person.

"Okay. I'll give it a try."

"Wonderful!" Marci swiveled back to the counter. "What do you think about having a cannon in the park, Charley?"

"I don't expect I'll notice it much. I'm too busy cooking."

"I mean, would it bother you to have a weapon nearby?"

He began assembling the tacos. "Its days as a weapon are long past. Now it's just an artifact from a different era."

"I imagine the history buffs in town would get a kick out of having it here. The fact it washed up at Starfish Pier after more than a century and a half is incredible."

"It did defy the odds." Charley wrapped their tacos in white paper. "It may be prudent to find out more about the story behind it before we rush to any judgments." He slid the first three tacos into a brown bag and set it on the counter. "There you go, Holly."

For a brief moment, his gaze held hers, his intent look at odds with his kindly demeanor.

Was he trying to send her a message? Suggesting she give her position more thought?

Or was she reading too much into his quick scrutiny?

Who knew?

As he broke eye contact and began wrapping up Marci's order, Holly exhaled. She hadn't committed to this yet—and she wouldn't until she examined it from every angle . . . jotted down her ideas . . . and prayed about it.

But no matter what she decided to do about the *Herald* piece, she wasn't going to change her mind about the cannon.

Why glorify a weapon that maimed and killed, when there were far more uplifting ways to honor history?

Hmm.

That could be the perfect theme for her opinion piece.

And who could argue with such a logical position?

"Well, I'll be." Patrick ended the call with the city manager and set his phone on the table, willing the withdrawal headache and jitters that had dogged him all day to subside. Thank heaven the cannon situation was giving him something to focus on besides the powerful lure of alcohol.

Cindy added another dash of pepper to the stew that was destined to be their dinner on this Friday night and glanced over at him. "What was that all about? I couldn't get the gist listening to your end of the conversation."

"It seems an anonymous donor has come forward and offered to foot the bill for the restoration of the cannon if the town displays it in a public location. This benefactor will even spring for a historical marker about Jedediah."

Cindy arched an eyebrow. "Who would do that?"

"Brent has no idea. The offer came through a third party. He assumes it's from a resident who's a history lover. There was one stipulation, though—our family has to promote the cause and do everything we can to support the effort."

"You've already spoken with Marci for the feature she's going to run next Tuesday. What else can you do?"

"I suppose if there's serious opposition, we'll have to try and convince everyone it makes civic sense to honor one of the town's illustrious sons."

Twin furrows appeared on his wife's brow. "Why would anyone balk at such a generous offer?"

"When Marci interviewed me yesterday for the article, she said she'd gotten some negative feedback. She's going to give both sides a chance to sound off in her feature."

Cindy put the lid back on the stew. "What kind of feedback?"

"There's some opposition to displaying a weapon of war in a public space."

She joined him at the table. "But isn't this more about displaying a historic artifact from a merchant ship owned by a Hope Harbor resident than glorifying a weapon of war? It's about him and his history, not the cannon—right?"

"Yes."

"Besides, wasn't the cannon on the boat when he bought it? I mean, he never fired it, did he?"

"Not that I know of—but I'm going to dig deeper this weekend."

"How can I help?"

"Go through the journal with me. It's been a struggle trying to decipher that old handwriting."

"I can do that." She folded her hands—meaning she was about to suggest an idea he wasn't going to like. "Do you think Steven would pitch in on the project too, if you asked him?"

Probably—but he didn't want to ask.

"He might, but I don't have a job for him at this stage."

"How about calling on him for moral support? Besides, if this anonymous donor wants the family to present a united front, that would include your brother. Jedediah was his great-great-great-grandfather too."

Impossible to argue with that—and if there was a fight ahead, having a former special forces soldier on their side couldn't hurt. Those guys were trained in tactical diplomacy and information gathering as well as weaponry.

He massaged his temples and swiped away the film of sweat on his forehead—another unpleasant withdrawal symptom. "I suppose I ought to fill him in on the situation so he's not blindsided by the article on Tuesday."

"I agree." She rose and returned to the stove. "Why don't you give him a call while I finish supper? You've got about fifteen minutes—and in case he has any plans for his Friday night, you'll catch him before he leaves."

Hard as he tried to come up with an excuse to delay, none popped to mind.

"Yeah." He stood and moved toward the back door, pausing at

Beatrice's playpen to ruffle her hair as she gurgled in delight. "I'll call from the porch. It's quieter out there."

He slipped outside, filled his lungs with salt-laced air, and tapped in Steven's number. This call was *not* going to ease the anxiety the counselor had warned could plague him.

His brother answered on the first ring. "Hey, Patrick. I was just thinking about you and was planning to call later. How's it going?"

"Holding my own." A twinge of guilt nipped at his conscience. He should have offered more than a one- or two-word response to Steven's encouraging text messages over the past several days. After all, his older sibling was holding up his part of their bargain by toning down his high-handed approach.

"Glad to hear it. What's up?"

"Am I, uh, keeping you from anything?"

"Nope. I'm home for the night—and I'm in no hurry to embark on a solitaire marathon."

Another pang of guilt stabbed him. He hadn't yet done much to honor their agreement to include Steven in his family circle.

"I wanted to update you on the cannon situation."

As he filled Steven in, his brother listened without interrupting, speaking only after he finished.

"Any suspicions who this benefactor is—and the reason for the stipulation?"

"No. Anyway, I didn't want you to read about it in the *Herald* without a heads-up."

"I appreciate that."

"I'm hoping, if we have to take a public stand on this as a family, you'll be in my corner."

"Count on it. I have Jedediah's blood in my veins too. How much do you know about him?"

"A fair amount. I could fill you in on his background, if you're interested."

"History was never my thing, as you know—but I'll make an

exception if it's family-related. Why don't we get together sometime soon and you can brief me?"

Patrick edged toward the door. "Actually, Cindy and I were going to dig into his journal tonight—and I have a box of other stuff that could help us round out his background. Hang on a sec." He muted the phone and stuck his head in the door. "Do we have enough food for one more?"

She pivoted toward him, the surprise on her face quickly morphing to approval. "More than."

"You mind if I invite Steven for dinner?"

"I think that would be great."

He retreated to the porch, unmuted the phone, and issued the invitation.

Several silent seconds ticked by.

"I'd like that very much." Steven cleared the huskiness from his voice. "Cindy's cooking beats mine any day. When should I come?"

"As soon as you can get here. I'll ask Cindy to hold everything until you arrive."

"I can be there in fifteen minutes."

"That works."

The line went dead without a sign-off—as if Steven had shifted into fast-forward to get ready for his unexpected dinner engagement, grateful he didn't have to spend another Friday night alone . . . and lonely.

Slowly Patrick pocketed the phone and reentered the house.

"Is he coming?" Cindy stood beside the table, a fourth place setting in her hands.

"Yes."

Relief smoothed a bit of the tension from her features, and she set the cutlery on the table. "Good. I get the feeling he's hungry for companionship."

"With a little effort, he could have a wide circle of friends—and guys like him are chick magnets, if they send the right signals."

"I don't think he's ever gotten over Laura."

That wasn't the problem, based on the confidences Steven had shared that night in the bar after Laura's funeral, once drink had loosened his brother's tongue. The impediment to a new relationship ran far deeper than grief, if everything Steven had alluded to had been true.

Guilt—deserved or not—was what was holding him back.

And guilt was almost as tough a demon to shake as alcohol.

"What do you think, Patrick?" Cindy looked over at him. "I mean, he and Laura were married for less than two years. They were almost newlyweds."

"I suppose that's possible."

His wife studied him. "There's more to it than that, isn't there?"

There shouldn't be secrets between a man and wife—but this wasn't his secret to share. "Yeah. I think so."

"That's what I thought." She set a napkin at each place. "But I won't push for details. I respect confidences between siblings. I just wish Steven could find a nice woman and start over."

"That could happen." If he ever got past the shackles holding him back.

Would solid grounding among people he loved help him shake them loose?

Not out of the realm of possibility.

Lips pursed, he retrieved another glass for his brother and set it in the extra place Cindy had set.

Funny.

Steven may have come home to help his kid brother, but maybe, if they included him more in their family life, he'd get past his loneliness . . . and find a door to his own future.

And wouldn't it be ironic if the biggest beneficiary of Steven settling in Hope Harbor was Steven himself?

13

"Well, crud!"

As the wind wafted the female voice toward his patio, Pete sighed.

Holly must have come out after he'd settled into his folding chair facing the sea—and her exasperated exclamation suggested she'd run into a glitch with whatever she was doing.

Not his problem—even if she *had* baked him cookies and her father had given him a hand with that downed limb last weekend.

She could fend for herself.

In his peripheral vision, a white sheet of paper fluttered by.

Then another.

Apparently whatever she'd been working on had been snatched by the wind—and if someone didn't rescue those sheets soon, they'd end up in the drink.

Crud was an apt sentiment.

After all her kindness, he couldn't very well sit by and ignore her plight.

Muttering under his breath, he pushed himself to his feet, picked up his cane, and trudged toward a wayward piece of paper lodged in a bush.

As he collected the sheet filled with childish letters and numbers, he glanced toward his neighbor's house.

Holly was dashing around her yard like a kid at an Easter egg hunt, snatching up the scattered sheets of paper, chasing after the ones that eluded her first attempt to retrieve them.

Or trying to.

Trouble was, the woman didn't move fast—or gracefully. And her ungainliness seemed more than mere awkwardness. As if it was caused by a physical disability.

Not that he cared.

He had more than his own share of problems to worry about.

Gripping his cane tighter, he snagged another sheet of paper and trailed after a third, no faster or more nimble than his neighbor—who had to be less than half his age.

A woman in the bloom of youth shouldn't be constrained by such physical limitations. It wasn't fair.

Then again, who said life was fair?

It sure hadn't been for him.

"Thank you, Mr. Wallace!"

At the call-out from next door, Pete swiveled around. Holly waved a sheaf of papers at him and continued to pluck the renegades from the grass, following a path toward him.

Great.

He managed to corral the half dozen sheets that had trespassed onto his property before she reached him, her cheeks flushed.

"Wow. It was calm when I came out. I didn't expect the wind to pick up all of a sudden. I'd say we both had our exercise for this Saturday."

"Weather on the coast can be unpredictable." He handed her the sheets he'd collected.

"I'm finding that out. Thank you for pitching in with this. My students would be very upset if I told them their papers had become fish fodder." She tried to coax the jumbled sheets into a neat pile but gave up when they refused to cooperate. "I hope we didn't miss any." She surveyed their yards again.

"I got everything that came over here."

"I appreciate that. I would never have been able to gather up all of them by myself. Half would have ended up on the beach—or in the water."

He peered down at the back of her hand, where a scratch was beginning to ooze blood. "What happened there?"

She gave it a dismissive scan. "One of the papers got stuck on the thorns of a gorse bush at the back of my property."

"You should get rid of it—or the owner should. Gorse are invasive."

"I know. But my landlord lives in Medford, and I'm not certain I could tackle that job without getting far worse than a scratch. I suppose I could try to find someone to deal with it."

"In the meantime, you should take care of that." He motioned toward the cut.

"Yeah. I'll have to poke around and see what kind of first aid supplies I have. If nothing else, soap and water works in a pinch."

"That should be treated with antibiotic ointment."

"You think so?" She examined the scratch again.

"Yes." And he had a tube inside.

"For pity's sake, Pete, offer it to her. It's unkind to turn your back on those in need."

As Sal's voice echoed in his mind, he drew in a lungful of air. Her advice was sound—as always. Once upon a time, it wouldn't have taken a prod from beyond for him to be solicitous.

"You can borrow mine." He forced out the words. "It's never been used."

"I don't want to impose."

"It won't take more than a minute or two to dig it out." He walked toward the door.

"I appreciate that." She followed along behind him. "At home, my mom always had a fully stocked medicine cabinet. She said it paid to be prepared."

"Smart woman."

"Yes—but sometimes you can be overprepared . . . you know what I mean?"

No, he didn't.

Nor did he want that comment explained to him.

"The tube's in the bathroom. I'll be back fast." He stopped at the back door and turned.

Blood was seeping from the cut, and as he watched, a large drop plopped onto the concrete walk.

"Oops." She flung her arm out over the grass. "Sorry about that. I'll clean it up for you later."

"Don't worry about it. I'll take care of it. Listen . . . why don't you come into the kitchen and rinse that off in the sink? You can cover it with paper towels until you get home."

"Not a bad idea. Otherwise I'll leave a trail of blood all the way to my house. Thanks, Mr. Wallace."

"Call me Pete." He pushed the door open and held it as she entered, motioning toward the sink. He might not want to be friends with her, but there was no reason for formalities. "Go ahead and clean it up while I get the ointment."

Without waiting for her to respond, he trekked down the hall and rummaged around in the medicine cabinet. At least his neighbor didn't appear to be squeamish. Unlike Sal, who used to get dizzy at the tiniest speck of blood. His wife would have been useless in this situation.

But that had been her biggest peccadillo, God rest her soul. In every other respect, she'd been the perfect partner.

Lord, how he missed that woman.

Throat tightening, he gripped the tube and retraced his steps, pausing at the living room doorway that framed the urn on the coffee table. It wasn't like having her here with him, filling his life with love and laughter—but it was better than nothing.

Taking a fortifying breath, he continued down the hall. He wouldn't let grief overwhelm him. That would be foolish. He and Sal would be together again in the—

He came to an abrupt halt on the threshold of the kitchen as Holly raised wide eyes from the paperwork he'd left on the end of the counter, her complexion a few shades paler than it had been minutes ago.

Blast.

How could he have been so careless?

In his defense, though, he hadn't been expecting any visitors.

Didn't matter now, though. His secret was out.

But that didn't mean he had to answer the questions hovering under the shock in Holly's eyes.

"Here's the ointment." He crossed to her and held it out.

She took it, her gaze flicking from him to the paperwork and back again. "I, um . . . this should, uh, do the trick."

Thank goodness she had enough tact not to ask any questions.

"No hurry to return it." He pulled a couple of paper towels from the roller and offered them too. "I'd appreciate it if you didn't spread this around." He tapped the papers.

"Sure. Of course." She tucked the ointment in her pocket, wrapped the towels around the cut, and picked up her school papers. "But don't you think there may be other—"

"You ought to go take care of that scratch." He crossed to the door and pulled it open, cutting her off.

"Yes. Yes, I will." She joined him on the threshold. "If you need anything at all . . . or want to talk to someone . . . don't hesitate to call or come on over. I'm happy to help with . . . whatever."

"I'm fine—but thank you for the offer."

She hesitated . . . then slipped through the door.

Rather than stand there and watch her trek across the yard, he closed the door and moved to the counter.

The documents were arranged exactly as he'd left them, suggesting she hadn't touched them. That meant she'd seen nothing but the top page.

But that sheet was sufficient to reveal more than he'd planned to tell anyone in this town.

There was no going back, though.

He could only hope his kindhearted neighbor would honor his wishes about confidentiality—and that she wouldn't get it into her head to try and convince him to rethink a decision he'd made months ago after long and careful thought.

Because no matter what plan she might concoct, it wasn't going to work.

She needed comfort food—again—and nothing beat Charley's tacos for satisfying the stomach . . . or soothing the spirit.

As she pulled into a parking spot on Dockside Drive, Holly surveyed the colorful stand.

Drat.

The window was closed.

Meatloaf at the Myrtle would have to suffice . . . but as a pick-me-up, it was a distant second to Charley's food—and the man's encouraging conversation.

After leaving the parking place behind, she circled the block and found a spot a few storefronts down from the café.

The place was bustling as usual on Saturday night, but since she'd arrived early it didn't take long to be shown to a booth.

She perused the offerings on the menu, but meatloaf remained her choice. Maybe she'd add a side salad, though. A Caesar would give the meal an extra—

"Evening, Holly. What can I get you tonight?"

She looked up from the menu at the waitress standing by the booth, pen poised.

It took her a moment to identify Cindy Roark in this out-of-context setting. While Jonah had mentioned that his mom worked at the café, their paths had only crossed at church and parent-teacher conferences.

"Hi, Cindy. I'm not used to seeing you here."

"I usually work the lunch shift, but I'm taking on extra hours." She hesitated. "It's a small town, so if you haven't heard already, you will soon. My husband got laid off from the mill."

First the upsetting discovery at Pete's house, now a job loss. Was there no end to the bad news on this Saturday?

On top of that, she still owed Marci an answer about the opinion piece on the cannon for the *Herald*.

"I'm so sorry."

Cindy was too, given the concern tightening her features. Did her almost palpable worry suggest there wasn't much of a nest egg to draw on during this crisis?

If that was the case, there were resources available. Surely Cindy, who'd been in town much longer than she, was aware of that. In case she wasn't, though . . .

"Did you know Helping Hands has an emergency fund for people who need short-term assistance?"

"Yes—but Patrick won't take charity."

That probably meant he didn't want to ask Steven for help either.

"Are there any other similar businesses in the area where he could get a job?" As far as she knew, Fisher Lumber was the sole such operation nearby, but she wasn't yet familiar with the surrounding area.

Cindy transferred her weight from one foot to the other, as if the subject made her uncomfortable. "To tell you the truth . . . we think the layoff is temporary. Instead of searching for another full-time position, he's trying to fill in the gap with handyman-type jobs. I've been spreading the word, and he's already got a few grass-cutting and home maintenance gigs lined up."

Grass-cutting. Yard work.

Getting rid of an unwanted gorse bush.

She may not have figured out how to deal with Pete's issue yet, but she could help out the Roark family.

"Why don't you have him call me? I could use a hand with those kinds of chores too. And my new neighbor might also be interested in hiring him." If his struggle with the downed branch was any indication, Pete wasn't up to much yard work either.

Understandable, after what she'd discovered earlier today.

"That would be wonderful. Thank you." Cindy acknowledged another patron who was signaling her.

"Go ahead and take care of your other customer. I could use another minute anyway."

Not to decide on her dinner order, but to come up with a plan to hook Steven's brother up with her new neighbor. Pete shunned interaction with other people—for reasons that were now clearer. Yet if he got to know more people, began to put down roots and form friendships, he might have second thoughts about the course of action he intended to follow.

In fact, his isolation could be a big part of the problem. Without human connections, a person was more susceptible to loneliness. Depression even.

Especially this man.

And people who were down could make decisions they later regretted.

When Cindy hurried back over, she relayed her order—and extracted a promise that the woman would have her husband call in the next few days.

That ought to give her time to lay the necessary groundwork with Pete.

While the likelihood of her neighbor being receptive to the notion of hiring a handyman to help him with his yard was low, if she did manage to get the two of them together there could be benefits all around—companionship for Pete and a financial assist for Patrick.

It was a small gesture—but as the quote from Mother Teresa on the plaque in her parents' home said, "Not all of us can do great things. But we can do small things with great love."

So she would do her small part to infuse a ray of light into the darkness next door—and in the Roark family.

As for Marci's request . . . she'd do that too. Maybe some residents would disagree with her opinion, but Hope Harbor should live up to its name and uplift. Remind people that life was worth living, not put an implement of death in a prominent location.

Especially in their peaceful little pocket park on the wharf.

"This is amazing."

As Patrick spoke from the bedroom, Cindy swiveled away from the bathroom sink.

Her husband was sitting on the edge of the bed, staring at his cell, a glass of Gatorade in hand.

"Was amajing?" The question came out garbled, thanks to the toothbrush stuck in her mouth.

"I heard from the state archaeologist again. Get this. He wants to know if he can pass my photos on to a magazine that's doing a story about the find. They're higher quality than the ones the park service took, despite the fact I was using my phone rather than my camera. Plus, this magazine is willing to pay me for them!"

"Thash great." She rinsed and spat. "I'll join you in a sec."

After finishing her bedtime ritual at record speed, she padded into the bedroom, giving him a surreptitious once-over while she put away her clothes.

Five days into detox, he was holding his own, thank the Lord. Not only had he seen the therapist twice, he'd also visited their doctor on the counselor's recommendation.

Nevertheless, it had been a stressful period—for both of them.

Though Patrick wasn't experiencing any of the more severe withdrawal symptoms, he'd had most of the others. Anxiety. Nightmares. Headaches. Tremors. Sweating. Insomnia.

And those were just the ones she could detect.

She couldn't begin to imagine the psychological ones—like the waves of craving he'd been warned to expect, and which he battled mightily.

But he'd been following all the instructions his counselor and doctor had given him—drinking fluids with electrolytes, taking cold showers if an urge to relapse hit, eating lots of fruit, staying away from his drinking buddies, emptying the house of alcohol, taking daily walks, staying busy.

He was doing everything by the book.

Yet prevailing in a few battles didn't win the war—and this was a long-haul fight.

She sat beside him on the bed and took his hand. "Are you going to sell the pictures to the magazine?"

"Why not? We could use the money—and it would be a kick to see my photos in print."

"Yeah, it would. And speaking of money . . . I may have found more work for you."

As she told him about her conversation with Holly earlier in the evening, he nodded. "Another couple of jobs would help. I'll talk to her Monday when I pick up Jonah from school."

"That works. I agreed to a double shift, so I'll be late. But I'll leave dinner for all of you in the fridge. Will you be okay watching the kids alone for that long?"

"Yes." There was no hesitation in his assurance.

Still . . . it was hard to shake her apprehension.

Yet what choice did they have?

Except . . . maybe to enlist Steven's help?

"Why don't you see if Steven wants to keep you company?" She tried for a conversational tone. "You know he loves being around the kids. Watching him with Jonah and Beatrice last night, it's obvious he'd make a great dad."

Patrick set the phone on the bed and gave her his full attention. "Cindy . . . you can trust me to take care of our children. I would never, ever do anything that put either of them at risk. If a craving hits, I'll take a cold shower—and bring them into the bathroom with me. That'll let me keep tabs on them. Please trust me."

She wanted to.

Desperately.

But all the reading she'd done had emphasized that it was far too easy for an alcoholic to slide back into old patterns if the thirst for booze hit with overwhelming force.

What if that happened while she wasn't here? The children were too young to be left unsupervised—or to have to deal with a father who was drunk.

"Give me a chance, Cindy. I promise I'll call you if I feel myself slipping."

His heartfelt entreaty was hard to resist—and her husband had never lied to her . . . or broken a promise.

She had to trust him on this.

"Okay." She rose. "Want to check on the kids with me before we call it a night?"

"Yeah."

He took her hand as they walked down the hall and peeked through the door at Jonah, who was sprawled across his twin bed, the stuffed whale he always slept with tucked under his arm. In the nursery next door, Beatrice was sound asleep, her thumb stuck in her mouth.

Both were the picture of innocence—and the most priceless gift she'd ever received . . . apart from Patrick's love.

As if he'd read her mind, he leaned close and spoke in her ear. "We may not live in a palace, but I've always felt as rich as a king when I survey our domain."

Pressure built in her throat as she choked out a response. "Me too."

"You know . . . I used to be jealous of Steven and the adventurous life he led, but the night I stopped by his place after I got laid off, he told me he envied *me*."

At his speculative inflection, she angled toward him in the shadowy hallway. "Did you believe him?"

"Not at first. But he convinced me he was sincere. And the more I've thought about it, the more I've realized that despite all the places he's been and the experiences he's had and the medals he's won, I wouldn't trade my life for his. What I have is worth more than any of those things—and I'm not going to throw it away, Cindy. I'll stick with the plan—whatever it takes—as long as you stick with me."

"I will—but it wouldn't hurt to put God in the equation either." Not much chance he'd latch on to that suggestion, considering how unreceptive he'd been to such notions in the past . . . but it couldn't hurt to keep trying.

He led her back toward their bedroom, his face hidden from her view. "I agree. That's one of the reasons I'll be going to church with you every Sunday from now on."

What?

She stopped abruptly at the threshold to their room, tightening her grip on his hand, forcing him to swing back toward her. "Are you serious?"

"Yeah."

"Why the sudden change of heart after all these months?"

"Are you complaining?"

"No." But he *was* deflecting. Why? Her brain shifted into high gear. "You said putting God in the equation was *one* of the reasons you're going back. What else happened?"

A faint flush stole over his cheeks. "Steven called my bluff."

"You'll have to explain that."

As he relayed his conversation with his brother, Cindy sent a silent thank-you heavenward. For not only had the Lord answered her prayer to bring her husband back into the fold, Steven would be coming to church too.

Hallelujah!

They were both fine men. Believers at their core, and morally solid based on everything she knew and had observed. That wasn't the issue.

But weekly church attendance was important. A visible sign of faith that told the world you were proud of your beliefs—and a reminder to yourself to live the values every day that were preached from the pulpit on Sunday.

One more positive outcome of the layoff that had sent their world spinning out of orbit.

"I don't really care how it came about, Patrick—I'm just grateful." She rose on tiptoe and kissed him. "With God in your corner, you'll get through this."

"Not to mention a wife who loves me." He tugged on her hand and winked. "Let's go to bed."

She knew that look—and her pulse picked up, as it always did when he flashed her his come-hither smile.

"Sleepy?" She let him tow her toward the bed, feigning innocence.

"Not yet. I have excess energy tonight. Want to help me get rid of it?"

She batted her eyelashes. "I think that could be arranged."

And as he drew her close to express his love with the wordless eloquence that always made her heart sing, she prayed that the worry hovering over her like a menacing specter was unfounded—and that nothing was waiting in the shadows to send them tumbling back into turbulent water.

14

How dumb could she be?

As her ankle twisted on the uneven pavement, Holly expelled an exasperated breath.

If she hadn't been so busy gawking at Steven arriving for church with his brother's family, she'd have noticed the jagged piece of concrete in her path.

Now she was in for a fall.

A hard one.

As she pitched sideways, Steven glanced toward her—jolted to a stop—and launched himself her direction.

Too late.

No matter how fast he ran, he wasn't going to reach her in time for a save, even though the fall felt like one of those slow motion dives in a movie.

But the wrenching pain in her left wrist as it connected with the cement when she tried to cushion herself was all too real.

Somewhere in the recesses of her mind, the sound of running feet pounding against pavement registered, but until Steven knelt beside her, all she could focus on was the throbbing ache radiating up her arm.

"Holly?" He touched her shoulder, his voice tight. "Are you hurt?"

She forced herself to concentrate on his question, rotating the ankle that had folded. No issue there. "Only my wrist." A crowd began to gather, and warmth stole over her cheeks. Nothing like making a spectacle of yourself in front of half the town. "If you could help me up, I'll be fine."

He gave their audience a sweep . . . and lowered his volume. "Are you certain? If there are any other issues, you could compound them by moving."

"No. Nothing's hurt but my wrist—and my pride. I'm tuned in enough to my body to recognize malfunctions."

After subjecting her to another thorough scrutiny, he gave a clipped nod, stood, and grasped her uninjured hand. "On three."

With a large assist from him, she was on her feet an instant later—but she couldn't contain a slight groan as her wrist protested the sudden change in position.

He tucked her against his side, urging her with gentle pressure to lean into him as he absorbed her weight.

She didn't protest.

"I think we have the situation under control, folks. Thank you all for your concern." Steven sounded calm as he spoke to the worried group gathered around them . . . but beneath her ear, his heart was beating in double time.

That was encouraging.

Steven didn't seem like a man who spooked—or lost his cool—easily. If concern about her well-being had goosed his pulse, that had to be significant.

Didn't it?

As the crowd began to disperse, Steven eased back to scrutinize her. "Let's claim that bench over there." He motioned toward the wooden seat on the side lawn of the church, near the fellowship hall.

"I don't want to hold you up. Your f-family will be waiting for you, and the service will be starting any minute."

He took her uninjured arm and led her toward the bench. “They’ll understand and go in without me. As for God—he’s waited this long to see me. He can wait another week.”

Holly didn’t argue. If he wanted to sit with her for a minute, why not let him? Hadn’t she been hoping to run into him again since that day at the tide pools?

Although a tumble in front of church wouldn’t have been her preferred method of bringing about another encounter.

She remained silent, cradling her injured wrist as they slowly walked toward the bench.

Once they were seated, Steven angled toward her and touched the long sleeve of her sweater. “May I? I have first aid training.”

So her assumption that day in the park during their impromptu taco lunch, when he’d referenced the Heimlich maneuver, had been correct. He did have medical knowledge.

And the quick but thorough inspection he gave her rapidly swelling, tender wrist suggested it was more than rudimentary.

If pain wasn’t stalling her brain, she might be able to ferret out the reason for his knowledge—but as her wrist ballooned and discolored, her thought processes became more and more sluggish.

“I see an X-ray in your future.”

Her stomach bottomed out. “You think it’s broken?”

“No—but I’m not a doctor. An expert should weigh in. What happened to the back of your hand?” He touched the bandage.

“Close encounter with a gorse bush in my backyard. I’m hoping your brother will get rid of it for me.” She briefed him on her encounter with Cindy at the Myrtle.

“If he doesn’t take care of it, let me know. Those bushes can be—”

“Morning, folks.” Logan West strode toward them across the lawn. “I heard there was an accident. I take it you’re the patient, Holly.” The town’s urgent care center physician gave her exposed wrist a scan.

"Guilty."

"You okay otherwise?" He shifted his attention to her face, concern etched on his features.

"Yes." Thank goodness she'd had the foresight to pay the urgent care facility a visit soon after moving here so they'd have her medical background in case of an emergency. Logan knew all about her SB issues.

"We should check you out anyway." He turned to Steven and introduced himself as the other man stood.

"Sorry." Holly did the return honors for Steven. "I thought you two would have met."

"No. I'm a healthy guy." Steven shook the other man's hand.

Also a loner, from what she'd been able to gather. Despite her short tenure in Hope Harbor, it appeared she knew far more people than he did.

"I can come to urgent care later, after you open." Holly adjusted the position of her wrist, but the pain didn't dissipate.

"Let's run over now." Logan pulled out a set of keys, jingled them, and grinned. "Being the director has certain privileges. And given that we're a small-town facility with a tiny staff, I even know how to run all the equipment. I'll have you x-rayed, treated, and out the door within an hour."

"But you'll miss church."

"I think God will understand. That has to be painful"—he indicated her wrist—"so why don't I give you a lift to the clinic and run you home afterward? We can deal with your car later. I assume you drove to church?"

"Yes. I can—"

"I'll drive you to urgent care and take you home in your own car. Then you won't have to worry about logistics." Steven rejoined the conversation.

"But . . . how will *you* get home?"

"I'll text Patrick. They can pick me up at your place after church and run me back here to get my car."

"Sounds like a plan. I'll see you both at the office in a few minutes." Without waiting for a response, Logan strode off.

As if everything was settled.

Steven held out a hand, apparently under the same assumption.

She narrowed her eyes.

Having decisions made for her didn't sit well.

However . . . while their take-charge manner rankled her independent streak, she probably ought to cut them some slack. A former big-city ER doctor and an ex-soldier were no doubt used to being in command. Plus, they both had her best interest at heart and were going above and beyond to help her.

But would either be doing as much if she didn't have SB? Was their kid-gloves treatment due to her condition?

Impossible to know.

Whatever their motivation, though, she should be grateful. Her wrist hurt like the dickens, and getting to the clinic or home without their assistance would be a huge hassle.

"If you're concerned I'm doing this because of your SB, the answer is no."

She did a double take.

Was Steven a mind reader, or what?

He hitched up one side of his mouth. "In your shoes, that's what I'd be wondering. I may not have attended church much in recent years, but I was raised with a firm foundation in Scripture—including the story of the good Samaritan. I'd have stepped in to help even if you were a stranger. Since you're more than that, I hope I can also convince you to stop at the new coffee shop after we're done at urgent care for a caffeine infusion—unless the wrist is too sore."

A coffee date with Steven?

The definite highlight of this day.

And a little pain wasn't going to stop her from accepting his offer.

"I'd like that. Thank you."

"You're welcome. Shall we?" He leaned down and cupped her elbow.

"Yes."

The short ride to the urgent care center was mostly silent, and she let her eyelids drift closed as the pulsing ache in her wrist intensified.

Yet Steven's presence beside her was more soothing than any pain-killing drug Logan could recommend.

It was also an opportunity.

Today's meeting may have been happenstance—but if she wanted to get to know him better, this was her chance. All she had to do was muster up her courage and take the lead. Let him know in no uncertain terms that she'd like to see more of him.

Easier said than done—but she'd manage it.

Maybe he wouldn't respond as she hoped, but if he didn't, it wouldn't be from lack of interest. Despite her minimal experience with men, she hadn't imagined the electricity zipping between them at the tide pools . . . or read too much into the couple of loaded comments he'd made that day . . . or imagined his pounding pulse today after he feared she'd been injured.

The man was interested in her, no question about it.

If he walked away after she made *her* interest clear, lack of attraction wouldn't be the cause.

And unlike her ex's excuse, she'd be willing to bet Steven's reason wouldn't have a thing to do with her SB.

The question was—if he backed off, could she unearth the reason why he was skittish . . . and also find a way to overcome his reservations so they could explore the sparks that had ignited the first time they met?

Suggesting they have coffee together had been a mistake.

As Steven dropped into a chair in the waiting room at the urgent care center, he stared out the window at the tendrils of fog swirling past.

If she hadn't given him that uncertain look—as if she suspected his kindness had been prompted solely by concerns about her spina bifida—he wouldn't be in this pickle.

Horse manure, Roark. You wanted to ask her to coffee for one reason and one reason only. You like her.

Huffing out a soft snort, he retrieved his cell and began thumbing a text to Patrick to arrange pickup.

Fine.

He liked her.

That was not, however, sufficient reason to act on his feelings.

But now that he had, he was stuck.

They didn't have to stay long, though. And what harm could there be in having a cup of coffee together?

His phone dinged, and he skimmed Patrick's response.

No problem. Text when ready. Ingenious bail from church BTW

He shot off a reply.

Stop texting. Listen to sermon

I am

Expect elbow jab if u keep this up

Just delivered. Done 4 now

Lips quirking, Steven opened his browser and used the waiting time to supplement the research he'd done on spina bifida after Holly had dropped her bombshell.

None of what he'd learned was pretty—and today's intel was no different.

While Holly didn't have any major difficulty walking on level terrain and seemed to lead an otherwise normal life, SB could bring a host of other problems—and inconveniences, as she'd termed them—that weren't readily discernible.

Ones that a potential suitor—like the jerk who'd dumped her—might not want to deal with.

But Holly claimed none of them would keep her from being a wife and mother, and there was no reason to doubt her. There were quite a few women on the net with SB who were married or in relationships and who blogged about it or posted videos that dealt frankly with issues related to the condition.

Holly's SB wouldn't be a game changer for him, as it had been for her ex.

His issues were the game changer in this relationship.

If he gave in to the temptation to spend time with her . . . if they clicked, as he suspected they would . . . in the end, he wouldn't be the one doing the dumping.

Unless he'd totally misread her the day she'd come to solicit a donation for Helping Hands' pro-life initiative, Holly would drop him cold once she learned his personal—and professional—history.

So why was he wasting any energy researching SB . . . and why was his traitorous mind trying to come up with another excuse to see her again after today?

It didn't make sense.

For a man who thrived on logic, who scoped out every move to the *n*th degree and considered all the ramifications of every step he took, his irrational behavior was more than a tad disconcerting.

And thirty minutes later, as Holly emerged from the treatment area, her wrist wrapped in a compression bandage, he was no closer to figuring out how to deal with his illogical inclinations than he'd been when they arrived at the urgent care facility.

He rose, putting his dilemma on ice for the immediate future. Until he delivered Holly to her house, her comfort was his top priority.

"What's the verdict?"

"It's not broken." Holly joined him, Logan on her heels.

"What grade is the sprain?" He directed his question to the doc.

"One. It could have been much worse."

Yeah, it could have. Pain and swelling were far preferable to a torn ligament or the loss of function characteristic of higher-grade sprains.

"So it will heal on its own." He slid his phone into his pocket.

"More or less. As I told Holly, she can help the process by resting the wrist and using ice packs for the next forty-eight hours. It should be back to normal in two to four weeks." Logan refocused on his patient. "Remember to keep your wrist elevated above your heart whenever possible, and don't try to tough out the pain. Take over-the-counter anti-inflammatory medicine if it gets too uncomfortable."

"Got it. Thanks again for opening up early for me on a Sunday."

"I took the Hippocratic Oath seriously." He grinned. "Besides, during my tenure as an ER doctor, Sunday morning emergencies were par for the course."

He walked them to the door, and Steven took Holly's arm as they exited.

"You still up for coffee, or would you rather go straight home? I know how painful even minor injuries can be."

Cradling her wrist, she searched his face. As if she wondered whether he was having second thoughts about his offer.

Smart lady.

But despite any qualms she picked up, she didn't let him off the hook. "A cup of coffee would hit the spot."

Relief and dismay butted heads—but dismay triumphed. Spending another hour in Holly's company wasn't going to benefit either of them in the long run.

So he'd conjure up an excuse about not wanting to interrupt his brother's Sunday any more than necessary and keep this short.

"Okay. Let's do this." He coaxed up the corners of his lips. No reason to ruin Holly's morning coffee. "Have you been to the new shop yet?"

"No. I was hoping to stop by for the grand opening last week, but school was crazy and I was too tired at the end of the day to do anything but go home and crash. Have you tried it?"

"Yes. I swung by after a charter fishing trip—but since I reeked of fish, I didn't linger. I doubt the owner would have appreciated me stinking up his shop. The java was first class, though. It's about time Hope Harbor had a real coffee shop."

He opened the door of her car, helped her in, and took his place behind the wheel. The shop on Main Street was walking distance—what wasn't, in a community the size of Hope Harbor? But hiking around town under normal circumstances might be taxing for Holly . . . and with an aching wrist it would be torture.

Less than five minutes later, he pulled up in front of the Perfect Blend and peered into the dark interior. "Huh. It doesn't seem to be open. Sit tight and let me find out what's going on."

He slid out of the car, noted the hours on the placard in the front window, and rejoined her.

"What's the story?" She hiked up an eyebrow.

"Closed on Sunday." He scanned the shop again as he shut his door. "He's losing serious revenue by shutting down on a weekend. That's when we have the bulk of our tourists."

"Could be he believes in honoring the Sabbath. Did you meet the owner?" She examined the storefront.

"Yeah. Zach Garrett. Pleasant guy. I'm sorry I couldn't introduce you to his barista skills."

"We could always try again another day."

He let her comment pass and twisted the key in the ignition. "You should probably elevate your wrist anyway—and that will be easier to do at home. You'll have to direct me."

She did, leading him north of the business district to a small street on the fringe of town that dead-ended at the sea.

"I'm the second house from the end." She indicated the tiny bungalow as they approached.

He swung into the driveway and set the brake as a car pulled out of the driveway next door, an older man behind the wheel.

Holly lifted a hand in greeting, and the man gave her a brief wave. "I'm hoping to hook him up with your brother."

"Does he need help with yard work too?"

"Not that he's admitted—but yes, he does." Twin creases dented Holly's brow as she surveyed the small house next door. "He has . . . issues." She sighed and turned back to him. "Thanks for bringing me home."

"My pleasure."

"I guarantee my coffee won't live up to our new barista's, but let me make you a cup while you wait for your brother."

"Thanks, but I'll text him after I walk you to the door, then stroll back toward town. I may get to church before the service ends and save him a trip."

"It's a long walk."

For her, perhaps. Not for someone who'd trekked mile after grueling mile in high desert and harsh mountain terrain toting a ton of gear—and on red alert for a sudden attack.

"I prefer to think of it as a chance to give my leg muscles a workout. I'm still not used to being confined to a boat for hours at a stretch."

She bit her lip. "I wouldn't want to interfere with your fitness regimen . . . but I could use some advice about my neighbor if you have a few minutes to spare. I won't delay you long."

Now how was he supposed to turn down *that* request without coming across as rude or uncaring?

Not that her opinion of him should matter if he wanted to keep her at arm's length.

Yet it did.

Besides . . . while she was picking his brain, he could do a bit of digging too. Try to determine the strength of her pro-life commitment. After all, being on the Helping Hands committee didn't have to mean she was radical about her position. It was possible she had a broader perspective than he'd given her credit for.

Before he wrote her off, it couldn't hurt to have a go at finding out.

He checked his watch. Church wouldn't be over for another fifteen minutes, at the earliest, and Patrick and Cindy could always take the kids to the fellowship hall for donuts until he was ready to be picked up.

There was no reason to refuse.

"I can stay for a few minutes."

"Great." She gave him a taut smile—as if she too was nervous about their tête-à-tête.

Odd.

Why would she be on edge?

That answer eluded him—but one thing was certain.

When he walked out her door after their conversation, he'd leave with a definite game plan for the future.

And while the probability that he'd misread the woman sitting in the car beside him was low, he couldn't quite extinguish the tiny glimmer of hope that maybe . . . just maybe . . . a woman like Holly would be willing to overlook his past and give him a chance.

15

Her house had never been roomy, but with Steven's dominant presence and broad shoulders filling the space with energy, electricity—and a heaping dose of testosterone—it suddenly felt downright cramped.

"Um . . . why don't we sit in the kitchen?" Holly restrained the urge to fan herself as she motioned toward the back of the house and took a discreet step away from her guest. "You can catch a glimpse of the sea from the table." And the big window would help the room feel less claustrophobic.

"Works for me."

He followed her back, pausing on the threshold to survey both the living room behind him and the sunny kitchen.

"The decorating is a work in progress." She gave the rooms a critical sweep. To her eye, the neutral palette was restful, and the patterned rugs she'd selected for the polished hardwood floors warmed the space. The colorful accent pieces throughout, from a batik wall hanging in the living room purchased at a fair trade shop to the crockery in an assortment of bright colors displayed in glass-fronted cabinets in the kitchen, added spark and personality to the space.

It all worked together to create a pleasing, welcoming ambiance.

At least she thought it did.

"Looks finished to me. I like it. It feels homey—and inviting."

A warm rush of pleasure filled her at his compliment. "I suppose it's not bad for a first foray into large-scale decorating—if you can call this tiny bungalow large scale." She indicated the table for two tucked beside the window, a small vase of wildflowers in the center. "Make yourself comfortable while I put on the coffee. I don't know if you're one of those people who can get by without caffeine in the morning, but I'm hooked on the stuff."

The planes of his face shifted, and his demeanor darkened for a split second—but it happened so fast she couldn't be certain if his momentary mood change had been real or imagined.

"Why don't you let me do it? Your wrist has to be hurting."

Yeah, it was. But Steven had done enough for her already today. She could brew their coffee.

"I can manage. It won't take long."

"Where do you keep the mugs and spoons and everything else?"

A man who didn't like to sit while others worked.

Admirable.

"It's all over there, including paper napkins." She waved a hand toward a wall of cabinets and drawers. "There's cream in the fridge. I have a feeling you drink yours black, but I have to cut the strength a hair."

He went about his task with quiet efficiency but remained standing after he finished as she prepared the coffee and put a plate of cookies on the table.

Not until she poured their java and took her seat did he claim his chair.

Also admirable.

No one could fault this man's manners.

"Help yourself." She touched the edge of the plate. "These are my specialty. Ginger." She took one herself.

The cookies were the perfect lead-in to the subject she'd claimed she wanted to talk to Steven about—but while his take on Pete's situation could be helpful, luring him inside had been more about conveying her interest in him than soliciting advice.

That, however, was going to require a different kind of lead-in. One she hadn't come up with yet.

He took a cookie and bit into it, examining the treat as he chewed. "You could give Sweet Dreams a run for their money with these."

"Nope. I'll leave the professional baking to them. I think my neighbor appreciated them, though. I took a dozen over a couple of weeks ago to welcome him to town."

"So you've just met?"

"Yes. And I discovered something very . . . disturbing . . . about him on Saturday."

Steven stopped eating, and his posture tensed. "Something dangerous?"

Her cookie froze halfway to her mouth. "Good heavens, no."

He narrowed his eyes. "He hasn't been bothering you, has he?"

It took her a few beats to get his drift. "No. Nothing like that. If anything, the opposite is true. I'd be willing to bet he views me as a pest, with all the trips I've made over to his house. The truth is, he's kind of a recluse—and I think I found out why on Saturday." She gave him a quick rundown on the gorse bush attack that had earned her entrée to his kitchen. "What I saw there . . . it kind of blew my mind."

When she hesitated, he tipped his head. "Now you have me intrigued."

She bit her lip, suddenly beset by misgivings. Was she about to renege on a promise? "The thing is . . . he asked me not to spread around what I'd discovered."

"Have you told anyone else about it?"

"No."

"I don't think sharing the information with one person constitutes spreading it around—and I'll give you my word that whatever you tell me won't go any farther."

She studied him. While she didn't know the man sitting in her kitchen all that well, he reeked of integrity. Deep inside, she knew she could trust him with this confidence—along with much, much more.

Decision made, Holly rested her injured wrist on the table and wrapped both hands around her mug, drawing comfort from the warmth seeping through the ceramic as she gave voice to her fear. "I think he's planning to kill himself."

A shock wave rippled through Steven as he absorbed Holly's revelation.

That was *not* what he'd expected.

"Okay. You're going to have to back up. Why do you think that?"

"Because of a stack of paperwork I saw on the kitchen counter. Only the top sheet was visible—an official-looking form—and the heading said, 'Request for medication to end my life in a humane and dignified manner.'" A slight shudder rippled over her.

Steven did the math. "He must have moved here to take advantage of Oregon's assisted suicide law."

"That's my take. I did some research after I saw the form. I never realized assisted suicide has been legal here for more than twenty years. I'm assuming Pete's very sick. From what I read, a person has to be diagnosed with a terminal illness that will lead to death within six months in order to legally get the necessary drugs." She sighed. "My heart aches for him."

Yeah, it would.

Not just because she had a pro-life bent, but because she was Holly. From everything he'd observed and heard, the woman sitting across from him was compassionate and caring and kind. Learning that her neighbor wanted to end his life would freak her out.

Careful how you proceed, Roark—unless you want to be shown to the door before you can determine whether her pro-life position is a deal breaker for the two of you.

Fortunately, talking about her neighbor gave him the perfect opening to dig in and find out.

"Any idea what illness he has?"

"No. He appears to get by on his own without any trouble. I do know he misses his wife."

He listened as she told him about the urn in the living room, and the man's comments about his late spouse.

"There could be depression at play here too."

"Exactly. For all we know, there may be a treatment out there he's written off because he doesn't see any reason to keep living. If he had friends to support him through whatever it entails, though, he might rethink his decision. That's one of the reasons I'm hoping to convince him to let Patrick do yard work for him. That would be one more person in his life to care about what happens to him."

"But what if there aren't any treatment options left? No hope?" Steven brushed a few stray crumbs from the cookie into a neat pile, keeping his voice neutral. "How would you feel about what he's doing?"

"My position wouldn't change." Her tone was firm. "God chose when to give us life. He should choose when it ends."

Her answer wasn't surprising—but it sent his spirits spiraling.

He took a sip of coffee as he geared up to ask the hard questions.

The ones that could lead to answers that might snuff out any hopes he harbored about pursuing this woman.

Yet putting them off wouldn't change the outcome.

"Have you always been this pro-life?"

"Yes." Again, her answer was firm.

"On religious grounds?"

"That's a big part of it. But I have personal reasons too."

"Care to share?"

She broke off a piece of cookie one-handed but didn't eat it. "Given that you already know most of my story, I suppose you may as well hear the beginning." She took a deep breath. "Are you familiar with the passage from Psalms that begins, 'You formed my inmost being; you knit me in my mother's womb'?"

"No." He tightened his grip on his mug, a sense of foreboding squeezing the air from his lungs. "Why?"

"My mom and dad believed it heart and soul, along with other similar passages from Isaiah and Jeremiah. Otherwise, I'd be an abortion statistic."

Steven's gut clenched.

Suspicion confirmed.

"They knew you had spina bifida before you were born."

"Yes. Seventeen weeks into Mom's pregnancy, an ultrasound indicated I had key indicators for the condition. Her doctor was very negative about what my parents—and I—could expect, and suggested they consider terminating the pregnancy."

"Obviously they didn't." Somehow he managed to maintain a conversational tone.

"No. They were appalled by the idea—even though almost 70 percent of babies with SB are aborted. So they ditched that doctor fast and got a second opinion. The new specialist ordered a fetal MRI, which indicated I was a best-case scenario. The opening was small and low on my back. There was potential for a good outcome—but it wasn't a guarantee. And this doctor, while far more optimistic, was very clear that even best-case, there would be ongoing issues for them and for me."

"But that didn't deter your parents."

"No. They believe life begins at conception. I don't think they ever had a single regret about their decision, despite all the problems they had to contend with after I was born. Neither have I."

"All the surgeries and pain you've had to endure have been worth it?"

"Yes." Not one iota of hesitation in her response. "My life is rich and full. Every day is a blessing. Do I wish it had been easier? Sure. Was my condition so negative I wish I'd never been born? No. That's why I couldn't refuse Reverend Baker's request to serve on the Helping Hands pro-life committee. What could be more important than protecting innocent life in the womb—or protecting life in general? That's why I'm concerned about Pete."

Of course she was—for clear reasons, now that she'd shared her early history with him.

And as she'd recounted the story, underscoring her belief that the choice to end a life should be God's alone, his last hope that there might be potential for them had withered and died.

Steven folded his hands on the table beside his half-eaten cookie and tried to forget about himself, to concentrate on her neighbor's situation. "I don't know what you can do to change his mind. He's a grown man, and if this is his choice, in the end you'll have to accept it."

"We're not at the end yet—I hope. I intend to keep showing up at his door, letting him know I care about him—and I'm going to introduce him to your brother. Who knows? He may be more receptive to friendship with a man."

Steven took a tiny bite of the cookie he no longer wanted and chewed it slowly as he composed his response. "Patrick may not be your best candidate for that."

"Why not? From what I've seen of him at parent-teacher conferences and school functions, he seems like a nice guy."

"He is—but he has problems of his own."

"I know." Her features softened in sympathy. "The layoff had to be a shock to him and his family."

Steven took another sip of the cooling coffee. How much should he tell Holly about his brother's troubles? It wasn't as if the reason for his layoff was a secret. During their impromptu dinner Friday night, both his brother and Cindy had mentioned that half the town already knew drinking had led to his dismissal. Holly would hear it soon enough through the grapevine anyway.

"It's more than the layoff."

She let a beat tick by. "To borrow your earlier phrase—care to share?"

"He has a drinking issue. It was affecting his job performance. That's why he was laid off."

Her eyes widened. "I had no idea."

"You would have soon. Nothing stays secret in a small town." Except the truth about his marriage—and what he'd done in The Unit.

No one other than Patrick knew any of those details.

"Is he getting help?"

"Yes. And the odd jobs are keeping him busy, which is beneficial. But I wouldn't count on him to help your neighbor see the light, since he's battling his own demons."

"Thanks for the heads-up. I'll have to mull over how that could impact his relationship with Pete." She exhaled. "It's funny. People think I've had such a hard life because of my SB, but everyone faces problems and difficulties. I was fortunate to have a strong support system in my parents. That can make a huge difference."

"Cindy's been a rock for Patrick."

"I expect you've done your part too."

"Not as much as I'd have liked. Patrick and I have issues that go back to childhood. He wasn't too happy to find me on his doorstep a year ago. But I think we've finally agreed on a path forward and are mending our fences."

"Going to church together ought to help."

No way was he telling her how *that* had come about.

"Let's hope so." He checked his watch. Much as he'd like to spend the next hour or two sitting at Holly's table, sharing cookies over coffee, he didn't belong here.

He never would.

It was time to go.

Putting his thumbs to work, he tapped in a message for Patrick as he spoke. "Church should be over. I'll be out of your hair in a few minutes."

"You don't have to rush." She motioned toward his napkin. "You're not finished with your cookie."

He picked up the uneaten half and shoved it in his mouth, washing down the crumbs that stuck in his throat with several gulps of coffee. "I don't splurge on dessert too often."

"You liked the brownie from Sweet Dreams the day you shared your tacos with me in the park." She flashed him an uncertain smile.

"I do indulge my sweet tooth on occasion." He maintained eye contact—and her breath hitched.

Blast.

He'd done it again.

Sent another subtle signal he was interested.

She tucked her hair behind her ear, the slight tremble in her fingers a dead giveaway she was as aware of the charged particles zipping through the air as he was. "I, uh, think you realize I've led a pretty sheltered life. Aside from my one so-called romance, I've dated very little. That means I'm not too adept at flirting or repartee. So I'll just be honest. I understand if you're not ready to think about dating after the loss of your wife, but I've enjoyed getting to know you—and I'd love to see you socially if you ever decide to get back into circulation."

Her last sentence came out in a breathless rush, as if it had taken every ounce of her courage to deliver that lay-it-all-out-there speech, with its inherent risk of rejection.

And it probably had.

Of all the women he'd ever dated, Holly was the least sophisticated. The least experienced. The least flirtatious.

And apt to be the most easily hurt.

In other words, she wasn't at all the type that would have appealed to him in his thrill-seeking special forces days.

Why she did now was a mystery.

One that might always remain unsolved if he followed the noble course and bowed out of her life.

At least she'd given him a legitimate reason to do so.

"I appreciate that." He wiped his fingers on the napkin. Wadded the flimsy square into a tight ball as his phone dinged with a text.

He scanned Patrick's message.

On our way. See u in 2 min

Perfect timing.

"My ride." He stood.

After a moment she did too, shoulders drooping a smidgen, her voice subdued as she cradled her injured wrist. "I'll walk you out."

She started toward the door.

Double blast.

He couldn't let her think he didn't care. After her last experience with romance, it would have taken a boatload of bravery for her to initiate the first move—and leaving her with a bruised ego for reasons that had nothing to do with her appeal would be wrong.

"Holly." He caught up to her in two large strides. The instant he touched her arm she froze . . . turned slowly . . . and gave him a wary look. "I want you to know that if I was in the market for a relationship, you'd be top on my list."

The corners of her mouth flexed up a hair. "You don't have to offer excuses. My ego isn't that fragile."

"It's not an excuse. It's the truth." And it was. Not once since coming to Hope Harbor had he sought female companionship. Between getting his business up and running, worrying about Patrick, and dealing with the psychological fallout from his military job and the mess-up in his marriage, romance had been his lowest priority.

Yet somehow, with her unique charm and appeal, Holly had managed to wriggle around all the garbage blocking the entry to his heart and dive straight in.

She scrutinized him for a few seconds . . . then dipped her chin. "Okay. I'll accept that." She continued to the door and pulled it open.

He followed. "Thanks for the coffee and cookies."

"Cookie. Singular. You didn't eat much. And it was small repayment for ruining your Sunday morning."

"My morning wasn't ruined. Just the opposite." No reason not to be honest, now that he'd been clear he wasn't interested in pursuing a romance—for reasons that had nothing to do with grief over Laura, despite Holly's assumption.

"Thanks for saying that." Her knuckles whitened as she gripped the edge of the door. "I know you're busy with your family and job, but if you ever want to get together as friends, let me know. No strings attached, no expectations." She offered him a tentative smile.

"I'll keep that in mind."

Among other things.

Like a pair of lush lips that were destined to play a recurring role in his dreams for the foreseeable future.

A sudden temptation to brush his mouth over them hit him upside the head.

Hard.

Too hard to ignore.

Without any conscious decision, he leaned toward her and—

Gravel crunched behind him, and he jerked back, pulse pounding.

Close call.

Too close.

Holly swallowed and flicked a glance toward the driveway. "Your b-brother's here."

"Yeah."

Thank goodness.

Two more seconds, he'd have undermined all the groundwork he'd laid in the past few minutes to exit Holly's life without adding to the battering her ego had already taken—despite her claim to the contrary.

No one who got dumped emerged unscathed.

Especially a gentle, tenderhearted woman like the one standing inches away.

He backed through the door. "Take care of your wrist."

"I will."

With a clipped nod, he turned and jogged down the walk to the driveway.

Cindy had squeezed into the back between the car seats, leaving the front passenger spot for him, and he slid in beside Patrick.

His brother gave him a once-over. Repeated the exercise with

Holly, who was still standing in the doorway. "I hope I didn't interrupt anything."

Steven concentrated on buckling his seat belt. "Nope." *Change the subject, Roark.* "She's expecting you to call her, you know."

"I told him." Cindy spoke from the back seat. "In case you haven't figured it out, she's very nice."

"Yeah." Jonah rolled down his window and waved. "Hi, Ms. Holly!"

She smiled, lifted her hand, and slipped back into the shadows as she closed the door.

"*Have* you figured that out?" Cindy leaned forward and nudged him.

His sister-in-law was as tenacious as a barnacle.

"She seems to be."

"The kids all love her. Right, Jonah?"

"Uh-huh. She smiles a lot and makes me feel happy, even on rainy days. She says if we carry sunshine in our hearts, it will be bright on the inside no matter how yucky it is outside."

That sounded like Holly.

"Maybe you could get to know her better, Steven." Cindy settled back in her seat. "She can't have much of a social life yet, being new in town. I bet she'd appreciate another friend."

Or something more.

The lady might lack experience with men, and she may have been coddled by her parents most of her life, but here in Hope Harbor she'd apparently developed a strong independent streak and a willingness to take charge of her life and ask for what she wanted.

Commendable qualities.

Too bad he couldn't accommodate her.

But as her house receded in his side-view mirror, he put any lingering hope of that to rest.

Because nothing shy of a miracle could bring about a match between a woman committed to protecting lives and a man who'd destroyed far too many.

16

She was back again.

Through a slit in the blinds, Pete watched Holly approach his front door—but as she drew closer, he retreated.

Had he known his neighbor would be Miss Sociable, he'd have insisted his rental house have a garage where he could stash his car so no one would have a clue whether he was home or not.

Instead, the black sedan in the driveway broadcast his presence as effectively as a billboard.

The bell chimed, and he let out a slow breath.

If he ignored her, maybe she'd go away.

Then again, having seen the paperwork on his counter, Holly might call 911, thinking he was incapacitated and required assistance.

Having a police car and ambulance speed down Sea Rose Lane with sirens blaring was not how he wanted to end his Monday.

That left him one option.

Heaving a resigned sigh, he trudged to the door and pulled it open.

"Hi, Pete." The corners of his neighbor's mouth rose—but her hesitant tone indicated she wasn't certain of her welcome.

Good. That could discourage her from staying long.

"Holly." The elastic bandage around her left wrist registered, and he frowned. "What happened there?" He motioned toward it.

"I took a tumble at church. My klutziness in action." She flashed him another nervous smile. "The sidewalk in front of Grace Christian is uneven, and I wasn't watching where I was walking. Be careful if you're in that area."

Not likely. He hadn't darkened a church door in three years.

"I won't be. I don't go to church anymore."

"Well, if you decide to reconsider, I'd be happy to take you any Sunday. Reverend Baker's sermons are wonderful—and we serve delicious doughnuts after the services."

"Thanks, but I don't think that will happen. What can I do for you this afternoon?"

She took the hint and dropped the subject of church. "I wanted to let you know I found someone to help me with yard work. A godsend, thanks to this." She tapped her wrist. "He's coming by tomorrow afternoon to get rid of my gorse bush, and I thought you might be interested in talking with him."

"I'm managing on my own."

Her demeanor remained cheerful. "I was too—except for that gorse bush. But heavier stuff can be tricky. Like the downed limb you had in your backyard."

"That was a fluke. I can get help if it happens again, or call my landlord. And I've always cut my own grass."

"My dad has too—but last summer he hired a lawn service. He said at this stage of his life, he'd rather play golf or tennis than push a mower. They do a fantastic job too. All the edges are trimmed with military precision, and they blow all the clippings off the sidewalks and driveway."

Pete didn't have to scan his yard to know it didn't come close to living up to that description. In the old days, he'd been meticulous about his lawn too. To the point Sal used to kid him about having a grass fetish.

No more.

Who cared if the edges weren't quite straight? And the stray clippings would dry up in a few days and blow away.

He was not going to be railroaded into hiring someone to pretty up a house he didn't own.

"I'm glad your father found a service that does an excellent job." He eased the door closed an inch or two. "I hope the man you found is as diligent."

"So do I. He can use the income." Her cheeriness faded. "His son is in my class, and he has a new baby at home. His wife works at the café in town, but waitresses there don't make much—and he just lost his job at the lumber company."

Pete tightened his grip on the door.

Losing a job was tough. Been there, done that, years ago.

Thankfully he and Sal had been able to weather the dry spell—but being out of work with a young family to support was a much dicier predicament.

"Is this man looking for another job?"

"Not yet. His wife told me the layoff may be temporary. They're hoping he'll be able to return in a few weeks." She tucked her hair behind her ear. "I believe he made mistakes on the job that were alcohol-related—but he's working hard to get back on the right track. I figure if someone is trying to turn his life around, the least I can do is support the effort." She offered him a sheepish shrug. "And to tell you the truth, I'm not all that fond of yard work anyway."

Neither was he, these days.

And it wasn't as if paying this guy a few bucks a week to keep his lawn in shape would strain his budget. Far less than it would an elementary schoolteacher's in a town the size of Hope Harbor. Holly couldn't be earning a fortune—yet she was spending her hard-earned money to assist someone in need.

A twinge of guilt tweaked his conscience.

Should he consider helping the guy out? After all, if the charities he'd designated in his will got a few less dollars, they'd never miss them. But those same dollars could make a world of difference to the man Holly had taken under her wing—and to his family.

Besides, he'd benefit too. His stamina was declining, and yard work took a toll.

"What's this man's name?"

Holly's demeanor brightened. "Patrick Roark."

"I suppose you could bring him over tomorrow, let me meet him. If I like what I see, I may hire him."

"That would be wonderful!"

"No promises."

"That's fine—but I know he'll appreciate having the chance to talk with you."

"You didn't tell him about the . . . what you saw in my kitchen, did you?"

Worry dimmed the brightness in her eyes. "No—but I've been thinking about it."

"I'm past the thinking stage. Rehashing a well-thought-out decision is a waste of brainpower. What time is Patrick coming?"

"He said he'd stop by after school, around four."

"I'll be here." He half closed the door. "Take care of your wrist."

"I will."

She remained on his porch, biting her lower lip, as if she wanted to talk more about the other subject.

Not on his agenda.

He edged the door toward the closed position. "I expect I'll see you around."

"Yes. In fact, I'm going to swing by Charley's on my way home tomorrow afternoon and get tacos. Have you been there yet?"

"I've seen the truck, but I haven't stopped." And what did that have to do with anything?

"You're missing an amazing meal. The order is three tacos, and I can never eat more than two, tops. Since they don't improve with age, I'll drop my extra one off for you and you can give it a try."

"You don't have to do that."

"My pleasure. You'll thank me forever once you sink your teeth into one of his creations."

Doubtful. His taste buds had gone on strike months ago, and eating was more a chore than a pleasure these days.

"Don't bother. I haven't got much appetite anymore."

"It's no bother at all. What are neighbors for? And I bet a Charley's taco will jump-start your appetite." With a cheery wave, she descended the porch step and followed his walkway toward the street.

Pete closed the door and swiveled toward the urn on the table. "She's a firecracker, isn't she, Sal?"

In the recesses of his mind, he could hear his wife's soft chuckle of agreement.

"She's not going to change my mind, though."

The chuckle faded.

He crossed to the sofa and sat, placing his hand on the urn. "Don't be mad at me, Sal." His voice rasped, and he swallowed. "I know you don't approve, but there's no sunshine in my world without you. I want us to be together again—sooner rather than later. Why should I try to postpone the inevitable?"

Silence was the only answer.

Just as God had responded with silence to his angry questions after Sal died. After illness robbed him of his health. After the flame of his faith . . . and hope . . . sputtered and died.

Through all that anguish, God had ignored him.

And what good was a God who paid no heed to the pleas of his sons and daughters? Who turned a deaf ear even to prayers for consolation?

Maybe, after he passed to the other side, he'd have to answer to the Almighty for his lack of trust and faith.

So be it.

If you were abandoned, you had to fend for yourself. If no guidance was offered, you had to make your own life-and-death decisions.

He'd made his, and he wasn't changing course. The paperwork was filled out, his medical records had been forwarded, and there were just a few more hoops to jump through. An appointment with the doctor he'd selected in Coos Bay. Another appointment fifteen days after that to sign the form in front of witnesses. Confirmation of his diagnosis and prognosis by a consulting physician. The writing of a simple prescription.

Once he had that script in hand, he could choose the day for his departure.

His neighbor wouldn't approve.

Sal wouldn't approve.

God wouldn't approve.

But short of a message emblazoned in the sky telling him to do otherwise, in less than a month he was saying good-bye to the heartache and hurt that had become his lot on planet Earth.

Oh no!

As Holly read the *Herald* article in the teachers' lounge, her stomach dropped to her toes.

The cannon she'd dissed belonged to the Roark family?

Well, crud.

"You okay, Holly?"

She pulled in a lungful of air and looked over at the fourth-grade teacher, who'd lowered the novel she was reading and stopped eating her lunch. "Yes."

Liar.

"You sure? You're a little pale. Is your wrist bothering you?" Twin furrows creased the other woman's forehead.

"The pain's subsided, and I'll be done with the compression bandage after today. I'm fine." She took a bite of her chicken salad sandwich as proof, praying it wouldn't stick in her throat.

After her coworker went back to reading, Holly washed down

the mouthful of food with a gulp of water and went back to reading the center-spread feature Marci had written.

As usual, the woman's journalistic skills were impeccable. The article was sprinkled with quotes from Patrick, the state archaeologist who'd come to town after the cannon washed up, and a member of the state historical society.

The sidebars expressing the opposing viewpoints about putting the cannon on public display bookended the article—her negative piece, and one with a positive spin from Greg Clark, who'd lost a leg in the Middle East and now managed the Pelican Point Lighthouse Foundation.

Spirits tanking, Holly reread the article. Steven was only mentioned in passing, and he'd offered no quotes, but Patrick's enthusiasm for the project was clear.

Setting the paper down, she exhaled.

Steven had been clear in their conversation on Sunday that he wasn't interested in romance at this stage in his life—for understandable reasons, despite the electricity pinging between them.

Perhaps in time, that might have changed—the very reason she'd left the door open with the offer of a no-strings friendship. At least that would have kept her on his radar screen.

But she'd shot herself in the foot with her opinion piece. If push came to shove, Steven was going to side with his brother on this issue—and that put them in opposing camps.

Not exactly the sort of positioning conducive to romance down the road . . . or ever.

Blowing out a breath, she massaged her temple.

Why, oh why, had she let Marci talk her into this?

And why hadn't the *Herald* editor told her who owned the cannon?

Why didn't you ask *her, Holly?*

Yeah, that would have been the smart move. Her dilemma wasn't Marci's fault. The woman wouldn't have had any idea the players were acquainted.

What a mess.

Stomach twisting, she wrapped up what was left of her sandwich and put it back in the fridge for tomorrow.

Not even the tacos from Charley that were on her menu for tonight were likely to tempt her.

Come to think of it—that's where all this trouble had begun. If she hadn't run into Marci that day at the stand, it might never have occurred to the editor to run opposite opinion pieces with her article.

Holly picked up her purse and headed back to her classroom. Recess wasn't over yet, but she could use a few minutes alone to think about what she was going to say to Patrick later at her house—and what she'd say to Steven to mitigate the damage without backpedaling on her position if . . . or when . . . their paths crossed again.

Because while she wasn't thrilled about him finding out her stand on the cannon in such a public manner, her views on the matter were strong and built on solid moral ground.

And therein lay the problem.

In light of some of the questions Steven had asked her Sunday about her pro-life views—and their brief if spirited discussion about capital punishment on his boat the day they'd met—they weren't anywhere close to common ground on sanctity of life issues.

Another huge detriment to romance.

Couples could disagree on many subjects, but conflicting positions on moral issues were apt to cause a huge rift.

She tucked her purse into a desk drawer and watched through the window as her first-grade students played in the schoolyard.

So carefree.

So innocent.

So insulated from the kinds of dilemmas adults faced.

Not that childhood was without angst—but at their age, the complexities of adult relationships were years away.

She sat, picked up a pen, and doodled a heart on a scrap of paper.

Perhaps—if she viewed this through the lens of logic—she should be grateful the cannon had washed up on shore and she'd been pulled into a public declaration about it. Marci's request may have been a literal godsend. A message from the Almighty that she should be cautious about letting herself become too enamored with a man whose past was shadowed in mystery.

Kind of the same warning her mother had given her.

And this time she would heed it. She wouldn't apologize for her views, and she wouldn't seek Steven out. If they met again, it would be by happenstance—or initiated by him.

Like that would happen.

She put an X through the heart.

What she ought to do was X the man out of her mind—her top priority going forward.

Trouble was, she couldn't control her dreams—and the intriguing ex-soldier had been infiltrating them on a regular basis.

Just as he'd infiltrated her heart.

And how did you banish a person from your subconscious?

Especially if deep inside, you didn't want to.

That had been awkward.

As Patrick followed Holly next door, he swiped off the sweat beading on his upper lip.

Maybe he shouldn't have broached the subject, but how could he not have mentioned the article about the cannon when everyone in Hope Harbor had either already read it or soon would?

Too bad he couldn't have gotten Steven's take before this appointment with Holly. His brother's parting from her at the door on Sunday—and Cindy's opinion that sparks were flying between the two—suggested a budding romance. If so, he didn't want to jinx it.

Personally, he couldn't care less what Holly thought about the cannon. And hey, if the town didn't want it, he and Cindy could always put it in the backyard.

But the notion of a historic marker that told Jedediah's story was beginning to grow on him. While his great-great-great-grandfather hadn't been a pacifist, he'd lived a virtuous life that ought to be celebrated. If public display of the cannon helped do that, he was all for it.

That didn't mean he and Holly had to squabble, though—as he'd told her within minutes of showing up at her door. Everyone was entitled to their opinion.

His frankness had seemed to surprise her—but while she'd said Marci hadn't told her who owned the cannon when she'd agreed to write the piece, she hadn't suggested that fact altered her opinion.

The question was, how would Steven feel about this unexpected development?

Given his military background, that was tough to answer. If he liked her as much as Cindy was convinced he did, it was possible he'd be able to overlook their different viewpoints—or sway her toward his opinion.

Whatever his response, though, being blindsided wasn't going to help matters.

Patrick pulled out his cell and skimmed his texts. No response to the one he'd sent a couple of hours ago, alerting Steven to get a copy of this week's *Herald* ASAP.

Bad news.

If his brother ran into Holly before he was up to speed, it could be—

"You may have to do a bit of a sell job here." Holly stopped at the step to her neighbor's small front porch and dropped her voice. "Pete can be rather crusty and off-putting, but I think he could use a few friends. I get the feeling he's been keeping to himself since his wife died. And he has no family. As far as I know, I'm the only one in town he's met."

Patrick stowed his phone and shoved his hands in his pockets to hide the trembling that had nothing to do with nervousness about meeting Holly's neighbor. It was another sneak attack of the shakes—and a headache was also beginning to thump in his temples.

Rotten timing.

But he'd have to muscle through and pull out the charm if he wanted this job.

"I'll do my best to wow him."

"Let's hope he's in a receptive mood. I know another lawn job would help you, and he could use more human interaction." Holly gripped the railing with her uninjured hand, maneuvered up the one step, and rang the bell.

Two seconds later, the door opened—as if the owner had been watching them through the window.

The older man was on the scrawny side, with thin silver hair and sharp blue eyes. Despite his air of fragility, however, his handshake after Holly introduced them was firm.

"Here's that taco I promised you, Pete." She handed the man a brown bag. "I'd wager a week's pay this will rouse your appetite. And now I'll leave you two to discuss business." She stepped off the porch. "Whatever time works for you tomorrow is fine, Patrick. I don't have to be here. But be careful with that gorse bush. It has a strong defense system."

"No worries. I'll come armed for attack."

As Holly continued down the walk, he angled back to find Pete Wallace appraising him.

"I understand you lost your job because of alcohol."

O-kay.

Lucky Holly had told him that both she and her neighbor were aware of his problem, or the man's abrupt comment would have caught him more off guard than it did.

Obviously Pete wasn't a pussyfooter—and he was living up to the "crusty" badge Holly had given him.

This could be a short interview.

"Yes sir, I did." No reason not to be honest. Most of the town had gotten wind of the truth at this point. "But I'm seeing a counselor and working hard to get another shot at the mill. I haven't touched alcohol since I was laid off."

"When was that?"

"Eight days ago."

"Not a very long record of abstinence."

In truth, it felt like a lifetime.

"I consider every day a victory." He straightened his shoulders. "And I don't intend to lose this war. I have a wife I love and two children who mean the world to me. I view the layoff as a wake-up call. A gift, almost. It's a second chance, and I don't intend to blow it."

Pete studied him for a few moments, and Patrick met the man's gaze steadily, willing the headache to remain at bay for the duration of this informal job interview.

"Hmph." Pete's nose twitched, and he lifted the brown bag clutched in his hand. Sniffed it. Crimped the top tighter. "I won't have any drinking on the job. I expect you to show up on schedule. I require diligent work, including thorough cleanup."

"Understood."

"You want to walk around the yard and give me a price?"

"I sized it up while I walked back to your neighbor's gorse bush." He quoted the man a dollar amount. "But I'm willing to negotiate."

Pete squinted at him. "You're underpricing your services."

"I need the work."

"I'll make you a counteroffer."

At the figure the man suggested, Patrick's eyebrows rose. "I think the bargaining process is supposed to work the other way."

"I don't believe in underpaying reliable people who do high-quality work. If the work's not up to par, we'll have another discussion."

"It will be. Do you want me to start tomorrow? You're due for a cutting." Past due, given the length of the grass.

"That'll be fine. My equipment's in the shed. You're welcome to use it or bring your own. Knock on the door after you're finished and I'll write you a check."

"Thanks. I appreciate the chance."

"See you tomorrow." Without waiting for a reply, Pete closed the door, leaving behind the aroma of Charley's tacos.

Patrick backed up.

In general, that smell sent his salivary glands into overdrive.

Not today.

The pounding in his temples intensified, and he carefully turned, trying to keep his head steady as he walked back to his car, doing his best to eradicate a sudden craving for alcohol.

Gatorade and a cold shower would help.

ASAP.

Focusing on what mattered was also critical.

Fingers trembling, he pulled out his wallet and flipped to the family photo.

This was his motive for staying sober.

He had the very things Steven envied—a beautiful, caring wife . . . two precious children . . . and a home filled with love.

No way was he letting all that slip through his fingers. While the battle was taxing and the temptation fierce, he was holding his own.

Keeping busy helped—and as of today, he had two new customers. Lawn jobs weren't enough to pay all the bills, but one by one they were adding up—and with Cindy's increased hours, they'd make it through the six weeks as long as he didn't slip up . . . or slide back.

And he wouldn't.

Instead, he'd keep in mind all the tips the counselor had given him—along with Reverend Baker's timely sermon on Sunday. Directing his energies outward as well as inward could help him over the hump. As the minister had said, instead of obsessing over our own tribulations, if we shine a light in the life of someone who's trapped in darkness, our own trials can become lighter and easier to bear.

Patrick paused beside his car and glanced back at Pete's house. Holly had seemed worried about the man's solitary existence—and now that he'd met him, her concerns seemed legit. Not once had the older man's lips flexed a fraction of an inch to hint at a smile.

Mom had had a saying about that. What was it again?

Oh yeah—people who smile the least are often the ones who need smiles the most.

From what he could tell, Pete was in that camp.

So while he was here tomorrow, he'd put his own issues on the back burner and see if he could add a touch of cheer to a stranger's life.

It might not help either of them much—but it sure couldn't hurt.

17

Tucking the latest edition of the *Herald* under his arm, Steven dipped his head against the chilly Wednesday morning wind, boarded his boat, and tightened his grip on his thermos. Too bad the Perfect Blend didn't open until seven—but after all his years in the Middle East, he knew how to brew potent coffee. Thick, strong, and straight—with a hint of cardamom—it always charged his batteries for the day . . . or the mission . . . ahead.

He ducked into the canvas enclosure on deck and poured himself a cup. Sipped.

Bliss.

He set the java down and flipped through the *Herald*. The whole family knew the cannon feature was supposed to be in this week's edition, so why had Patrick texted him a reminder yesterday afternoon—and again last night—that it was out . . . and to pick up a copy ASAP?

Too bad he hadn't checked his phone until it was too late to call or he could have asked him about the urgency.

Whatever the reason for his brother's persistence, however, he now had the edition in hand. Since Sweet Dreams opened early and sold the paper, a quick stop en route to the dock hadn't been a problem.

He paged through, eyebrows arching as he stopped at the center spread.

Wow.

The editor had given the story excellent coverage and primo placement. She'd used two of the photos Patrick had taken on the beach, as well as a few historic shots—including the one of Jedediah standing on deck beside the cannon.

No wonder his brother was excited.

And anything that got his mind off of—

Steven blinked. Stared at the byline on a piece headed simply, "No."

Holly had contributed to the feature?

He scanned the write-up. Switched to the piece on the other side titled, "Yes."

Two different citizens had voiced opinions about whether the cannon should occupy a place of honor in a public location—and Holly was in the negative camp.

His stomach bottomed out.

Given everything she'd shared with him, her opinion wasn't a surprise—but it was one more reason to consider her off limits. Family had to come first. He needed to stand with Patrick on this—and that wouldn't endear him to her.

He took another fortifying swig of the robust coffee and reread her short piece. It was articulate, to the point—and infused with her pro-life stance . . . especially the last paragraph.

> I'm new to Hope Harbor, so I can't speak about the town from a long-term perspective. But one of the things that drew me here was the upbeat vibe. A one-for-all sense of community, a caring spirit that filled me with optimism and made me feel safe and happy and excited about the future. No matter how historic, a cannon doesn't embody those qualities. A weapon of war . . . of carnage and destruction and violence . . . seems more fitting for a battlefield than our lovely wharf pocket park—or any other public

place in a town bearing the name *hope*. This is a community that should celebrate life, not death. I hope citizens take a long, hard look at what a cannon symbolizes before they install this one in such a peaceful spot.

Steven leaned back. This was the Holly he'd come to know—and it was consistent with everything she'd told him on Sunday.

But why hadn't she mentioned her article? It didn't—

He grabbed his phone as it vibrated against his hip. A last-minute cancellation, perhaps?

Given his sudden downshift in mood, that wouldn't be a bad outcome—even if it left him a few hundred dollars poorer.

It wasn't a customer's name that flashed on his screen, however.

He put the cell to his ear, greeted his brother—and got straight to business. "Everything okay?" In general, only a family emergency would compel Patrick to call at this early hour.

"Yeah. Did you get my texts yesterday?"

"Yes. But my battery was low and I put my cell in the charger after I got back to the apartment. It was too late to call when I checked texts and messages."

"Have you seen the *Herald*?"

No emergency—at least not of the family variety.

"I'm reading it as we speak."

"Did you notice Holly's piece?"

Hard not to.

"Uh-huh."

His brother waited, as if hoping he'd offer more than that non-committal answer—but he couldn't talk about this new development until he digested it.

"I saw her late yesterday afternoon, about the lawn work at her house." Another pause.

Fine. He'd ask the question Patrick was obviously expecting. "Did she mention the article?"

"I brought it up, actually. In case you're wondering, she had no clue we owned the cannon when Marci asked her to write that piece."

Somehow, that gave him a modicum of comfort. "She say anything else worth passing on?" He kept his tone neutral.

"No—but I got the feeling she was rattled by our connection to the story once she saw the printed feature. I can think of only one reason that would be the case."

Steven folded up the paper and stuck it in a waterproof compartment.

His brother was fishing—and he didn't intend to take the bait.

"There could be a bunch of reasons. Like . . . some of her fellow teachers may have cornered her to say they disagree with her position."

"You and I both know that's not the reason I'm talking about."

Steven didn't respond.

"Cindy thinks the two of you have potential."

"She's wrong." He took another sip of his brew, but the spicy, citrusy flavor of the cardamom was suddenly too acidic on his tongue.

"You could do worse, from what I hear. Jonah raves about her, and Cindy said she's heard nothing but positive comments. Not to mention she's a looker."

"You don't have to sell me on her charms. But she's not for me." Or, more accurately, he wasn't for her.

"How do you know?"

"Trust me on this. Did her neighbor hire you?"

A beat ticked by.

"In other words, a discussion about Holly is off limits."

"Bingo."

"That's telling, you know."

Steven frowned, suppressing a sudden surge of annoyance. "Practicing armchair psychology now, are we?"

"It doesn't take a degree in psychology to detect clues in human behavior. The fact you don't want to talk about this says you care about her."

"Get real, Patrick. I met her less than a month ago."

"I knew Cindy was the one after our first date."

"Holly and I haven't dated." The impromptu lunch in the park and the chance meeting at Starfish Pier didn't count, right? A date was a planned event—and none of their encounters had been premeditated.

"You could fix that."

"Let it go, Patrick."

"Listen . . . you might not want to write her off too fast. You may be able to work around the obstacles."

Steven gritted his teeth. Patrick could be as tenacious as the pesky seagulls that hung around his boat, hoping to wrangle a few scraps. "So . . . did you get the job with her neighbor?" He enunciated each word.

His brother huffed out a breath. "How come you can help me, but I can't help you?"

"I don't need help."

"Maybe you do, and you're too close to the situation to see the obvious."

Steven opened his mouth to respond. Shut it.

He'd offered Patrick that same assessment not long after he'd come to town, and his brother had blown him off, widening the rift between them.

It would be foolish to make the same mistake.

"I'll take that comment under advisement. Did you get the job?"

After three silent seconds, Patrick let the subject go. "Yeah. I'm going to work on both yards later today, after my counseling session."

"Glad to hear it. You holding up all right?"

"So far."

"You need me, don't hesitate to call. Day or night. Especially if Cindy isn't available."

"I will."

"You certain of that? Because the Roark I-can-do-it-on-my-own mind-set can be a curse as well as a blessing."

"Says the man who once tried to clean out a den of insurgents by himself and ended up pinned between two rival factions until a Night Stalker managed to extract him."

Another story he shouldn't have shared with his brother on that terrible night four years ago.

"I've learned a few lessons since then."

"I promise I'll call if necessary. Are we all still on for dinner in Coos Bay on Saturday night?"

"Yes. I already made a reservation at the restaurant you and Cindy picked."

"Don't worry about it breaking the budget. We can't go anywhere too upscale with two kids in tow."

"We adults will do upscale another time. For my first treat, I wanted to go as a family."

"Fine by me. You aren't going to bail again on church Sunday, are you?"

"Last week was an emergency. Which service are you attending?"

"Late. It's hard to get the kids up, dressed, and fed fast enough for the early one. Why?"

"Just wondering." If fate was kind, Holly would go early this week.

"Holly always goes to the late service, according to Cindy."

He exhaled. Now his brother was a mind reader. "We closed that subject."

"The subject may be closed, but your interest isn't. I saw how you looked at her. You may have decided you aren't in pursuit mode, but that doesn't mean you wouldn't like to be. You want me to see if Cindy's willing to give the early service a shot?"

Yeah.

However . . . it wouldn't be fair to his sister-in-law to ask her to get up at the crack of dawn on the one day a week she could sleep a little later.

"No. Late service is fine. I'll see you on Saturday."

After they said their good-byes, Steven pulled out the article and skimmed it again, his spirits plummeting as the plaintive blare of the foghorn at the end of the jetty offered mournful consolation on this misty morning.

He'd already written off Holly. The article should make no difference.

But if, somewhere deep inside, a tiny spark of hope had still burned, her passionate piece had snuffed it out.

So from this day forward, he would focus all his thoughts and energies on reestablishing ties with his family—and forget about the courageous, optimistic woman who for one, brief shining moment had reignited his belief in the possibility of love.

The man was a hard worker.

Pete watched through the window as Patrick climbed the ladder propped against the spruce tree that had shed the large branch during the storm. Several limbs were on the ground already, and several more were hanging by a thread, poised to drop in the next big wind.

But while Patrick had called his attention to the condition of the tree on Wednesday after cutting the lawn, edging the grass, and sweeping the patio, he hadn't asked for the job. His comment had been positioned more as an FYI.

So why had he jumped all over it? Asked Patrick to tackle the job as soon as possible? Especially when he could have passed the information on to his landlord, let him deal with the problem.

Pete scowled.

It didn't take a genius to figure out the answer to that question.

Like Holly, the man was pleasant to be around. Despite the addiction he was battling, he had an upbeat attitude that was contagious. Also like Holly.

Patrick and his neighbor must drink the same joy juice.

Whatever.

All he knew was that the stories Patrick had shared about the antics of his children had entertained him, and the history he'd related about his great-great-great-grandfather and the cannon Holly had mentioned had been fascinating.

Long after he'd finished the yard work, Patrick had hung around chatting. It had been such an enjoyable interlude he'd hated to see the man go.

That, in turn, had prompted him to suggest a return visit to tackle the spruce tree—and perhaps share a few more stories.

True to his promise, Patrick had arrived promptly at one o'clock on this sunny Friday.

Pete wandered over to the cabinet and pulled out two glasses. Filled them with ice cubes and lemonade. Opened the back door.

On the threshold, he halted. Mashed his lips together.

Engaging this young man in further conversation would break his cardinal make-no-friends-here rule.

Yet loneliness took a toll. Until Sal died, he'd enjoyed being around people. Enjoyed socializing and sharing a few laughs with like-minded spirits.

Patrick fell into that camp. Despite the significant age difference between them, the sense of kinship on his end was strong. It was almost as if they'd been destined to meet.

At the notion of destiny, he snorted.

What a bunch of rubbish.

And getting all fanciful didn't change his reality. His course was set.

But until he followed through on it, what was the harm in being kind to a young man who was facing trials of his own? Perhaps part of his legacy could be a few words of encouragement that might boost Patrick's spirits and fortitude. Nothing wrong with going out on the heels of a good deed—even if that deed had the side benefit of brightening his own life too.

Cane hooked over his arm, he pushed the door open with one shoulder and crossed to the patio. "Why don't you take a break for a few minutes?" He called out the invitation to the younger man as he set the glasses on the table. "I have lemonade, if you're interested."

A large branch dropped to the ground, and from his perch high up on the ladder, Patrick waved. "That would be great. Thanks."

Pete sat while Patrick descended and wiped his hands on a rag. "Pardon my sticky fingers. This sap is like glue—only worse."

"There may be a can of paint thinner in the shed, if that would help. I haven't poked around much in there."

"I've got it covered." Patrick dropped into a chair at the table. "I brought cooking oil for cleanup. It's in the car—and it works like a charm." He picked up the glass of lemonade, took a long swallow, and surveyed the sea. "You've got a world-class view here."

Pete perused the scene.

Funny.

All the days he'd sat out here, he'd never paid much attention to the scale and scope of the beauty. Oh, sure, he'd noticed the waves crashing against the rocks in the distance, and the silver-white harbor seal that liked to sun itself on a flat boulder offshore, and the occasional ship passing by on the horizon.

But taken in aggregate, it *was* a spectacular setting.

"I suppose I do."

"I wouldn't mind waking up to this view every day. Although I can't complain about the view I see every morning." He grinned. "That would be my wife, Cindy."

A pang echoed in Pete's heart. "I felt like that about Sal."

Sympathy softened the other man's features. "Holly told me you lost her a few years ago. I'm sorry. I can't imagine life without Cindy."

"It's hard."

"I expect that's a vast understatement. I don't know how people survive a loss like that. I admire you for carrying on, settling into a new town. You couldn't have picked a finer place than Hope Harbor."

"Doesn't much matter where I live. I won't be here long."

Patrick's glass froze halfway to his mouth, his brow knotting. "But . . . I thought you just moved in."

Stupid comment, Pete. Now you'll have to dig yourself out.

"I did." He waved a fly away from his glass. "But I'm, uh, older. The road ahead could be short."

"Or long. Unless . . . I don't mean to butt in, but do you have health issues?"

At the genuine concern on the younger man's face, Pete's throat tightened. Holly had had the same look the day she'd seen the paperwork in his kitchen.

Yet with her, he hadn't been in the least tempted to discuss his condition.

So why the sudden urge to tell Patrick about it?

Could be his dad's fault. *Never worry the womenfolk, son*, his father had always said—and he'd lived by that rule. All his life he'd kept his aches and pains to himself rather than cause Sal any anxiety. A chauvinistic attitude these days, he supposed . . . but somehow it had stuck.

Given all the troubles this man had, though, maybe he *should* tell him the truth. Not to solicit sympathy, but to help him realize that while the battle he was fighting was difficult, there were far worse traumas he could face.

Steeling himself, he nodded. "As a matter of fact, I do. I have lung cancer. At best, I've got six months left."

Shock flattened Patrick's features. "I would never . . . that's not . . . I didn't expect that. I'm sorry."

Pete gave a stiff shrug. "It is what it is."

"How long have you had it?"

"Three years. I was diagnosed two months before my wife died."

"Isn't there anything that can be done?"

"I had surgery, chemo, and radiation—the treatment plan my oncologist laid out. I started it before Sal died and followed through. The cancer came back. Showed up in my last scan a few weeks ago. I'm done fighting the inevitable."

"Have your doctors given up hope?"

He gave a dismissive wave. "Doctors are always happy to do more cutting or order another test or write half a dozen prescriptions. But I'm tired of being sick. I'd rather be with Sal. That's why I moved here."

Confusion clouded Patrick's eyes. "I don't understand."

He fisted his hands in his lap. "I'm here because assisted suicide is legal in Oregon."

Patrick's complexion lost a few shades of color, as Holly's had. "Isn't that . . . extreme? I mean, I realize you're sick, but you seem to be functioning fine."

"It won't last. And I don't want to deal with what's coming—especially since I don't have what you have—a wife, a family, a future." He leaned forward. "Count your blessings, Patrick. You may be facing a tremendous challenge right now, but you can look forward to a tomorrow surrounded by people who care about you. That's a priceless gift."

"I know—and I *am* grateful. That's why I'm determined to overcome my addiction." He swirled the ice in his glass. "When are you . . . how long are you planning to be here?"

"Not long. I have several more steps to take, but I should finish them soon."

The crevices on Patrick's forehead deepened. "Are you certain you've exhausted all of the options? What about, like, a clinical trial?"

A spot in his heart that had long lain cold warmed at the man's concern—as it had at Holly's. It was touching that virtual strangers were worried about him.

"There's nothing left for me here, Patrick. I'd rather be with Sal."

"Would she want you to do this?"

His lungs balked, and he picked up his glass to buy himself a moment to gather his thoughts.

No, of course she wouldn't. With her zest for life and upbeat outlook even during the most trying times, Sal would have told him to wring every ounce of joy out of his remaining days—and never, ever to willfully cut them short.

And if she were here, he'd have done that. Explored every option and endured any treatment that would buy him one more day in her company.

But without her, what was the point? One more day just meant another twenty-four hours of loneliness. Why continue in a life that was purposeless and empty of love?

"I think I know the answer." Patrick continued to watch him intently.

He stiffened. "I have to do what's best for me."

Patrick turned toward the sea . . . squinted at the horizon . . . finished his lemonade in three long gulps . . . and stood. "If you don't mind, I'd like to come back tomorrow afternoon and finish that job." He motioned toward the tree. "It's going to take longer than I expected, and I have to pick up Jonah from school."

"No problem." He stood too, trying to get a read on Patrick's mood. Was he angry? Upset? Disappointed? Impossible to tell from his guarded expression. "I'd appreciate it if you didn't mention what I shared with you to anyone. Holly knows, because she saw the paperwork on my counter, but I haven't told anyone else."

"Do you mind if I tell my wife?"

"Can she keep a secret?"

"Yes."

"Fine." Most spouses in a solid relationship shared everything, so the man's request wasn't out of line.

"I'll put the ladder and saw away. Thanks for the lemonade." Patrick set the glass on the table and jogged toward the spruce tree.

Pete picked up the glass, hooked his cane over his arm, and returned to the kitchen, keeping an eye on Patrick through the window as the younger man collapsed the ladder, gathered the branches he'd cut into a neat pile, and hauled his equipment toward the shed, out of sight around the corner of the house.

A few minutes later an engine came to life, signaling his departure.

Pete hung the dish towel over the edge of the sink, shoulders drooping. Had telling Patrick about his plan been a mistake? Had his candor given the young man more perspective on his own situation, or simply depressed him?

No way to know. He'd have to wait and see how this played out.

At least the doctor he'd visited yesterday hadn't been shocked by his choice, as everyone else appeared to be. The man had been sympathetic and supportive, if a bit clinical. Their conversation had been very businesslike, like they were discussing plans for an upcoming trip.

And, in fact, they had been. A trip into the unknown, yes—but whatever lay on the other side of death had to be better than his life here on earth.

He wandered back to the window and gave the panoramic view another sweep. It really was stunning. If he was healthier and Sal was here, Hope Harbor would be a pleasant place to live. The setting was gorgeous, and the people he'd crossed paths with here at the house and on his brief forays into town had all been friendly.

Too bad he and Sal hadn't found this community on one of their coast vacations. It would have been a perfect spot to spend their retirement.

But a massive stroke had snatched away her golden years, and the gilt on *his* so-called golden years had tarnished.

He sighed and rested his hands on the windowsill, letting the majestic beauty before him seep into his soul.

Of all the random spots on the map his finger could have landed when he was choosing an address in Oregon, he couldn't have ended up in a nicer place to spend his remaining days. Perhaps he should try to appreciate what it offered instead of insulating himself in darkness. The view of the endless blue sea. The friendliness of the people he ran into. And maybe another one of those amazing tacos his neighbor had brought him that had, for a few brief minutes, jump-started his appetite, as she'd predicted.

Sal would approve of that approach—if not his ultimate goal.

Out on the offshore rocks, the harbor seal flopped into a more comfortable position to sun itself, the picture of contentment.

Wouldn't it be wonderful to bask in the warmth like that without a care in the world?

Not happening in *his* world.

Not anymore.

But he did have a cushioned lounge chair in the tool shed, retrieved at the last minute from the donation pile at the old house for reasons he hadn't fathomed at the time.

Maybe it was meant to be here. On this patio.

And while his days would never again be as carefree as that seal's, perhaps in the weeks he had left he could try to soak up some of the comforting ambiance, contentment, and hope that had long been absent from his life but which seemed to pervade the very air in this charming little town he now called home.

18

What was Steven doing at a Helping Hands project on a Saturday afternoon?

Holly stared at the jeans-clad ex-soldier as he strode up the walk toward the house the organization was repairing and repainting for an elderly resident—then ducked behind a rose trellis.

If there was an escape route, she'd take it—but from the corner she'd wedged herself into, she'd have to climb over the side railing and drop five feet to freedom.

Not the best idea with a sprained wrist—or anytime for someone with SB.

She was stuck.

Besides, she couldn't leave. She'd signed up to help with this project two weeks ago, and injured wrist or not, she wasn't reneging on her commitment.

But Steven's name hadn't been on the volunteer list.

She peeked around the rosebush that screened this side of the porch from the street.

Close on Steven's heels was his sister-in-law.

Hmm.

Had Cindy strong-armed him into helping today?

Or maybe strong-arming hadn't been necessary. Based on what Eleanor Cooper had said after the pro-life dinner auction committee meeting two weeks ago, Steven had a charitable streak a mile wide. Gratis grass-cutting for an older resident, hiring a refugee who needed a job even if he hadn't needed a helper . . . perhaps giving up his military career to come to Hope Harbor and assist his younger brother.

According to one of the teachers at school, he'd also volunteered for a search party last year after two little girls in the current kindergarten class ran away from home.

All of which made his initial reluctance to donate a fishing trip to the pro-life benefit so puzzling.

She edged back into the shadows as he and Cindy chatted with the volunteer coordinator on the front lawn.

Of more immediate concern, however—what was she supposed to say to him about the cannon issue that had fast become a hot-button, divisive topic among residents?

According to Marci, the city manager had been inundated with calls after the article came out. Posters were appearing in many of the shop windows representing both sides of the argument, a petition was circulating, and a town meeting was in the works to discuss the anonymous offer and decide whether a vote was necessary to settle the issue.

She should have kept her opinion to herself that day at the taco stand.

The conversation on the lawn ended, and Steven ascended the steps, paint can and brush in hand, while Cindy circled around to the back of the house.

He'd been assigned porch duty.

It figured.

The instant he spotted her, he came to an abrupt stop.

"Hi." She offered him a tentative smile.

Twin furrows creased his brow.

Not a promising start.

"Why are you painting with a sprained wrist?"

"I'm right-handed. It's no big deal. I didn't want to leave them shorthanded. Pardon the pun."

His lips didn't budge.

"So . . ." She called up her perkiest smile. "I didn't see your name on the sign-up list."

"I was a last-minute addition. Cindy said they could use more hands." He narrowed his eyes in the direction his sister-in-law had disappeared. "And after we got here, she volunteered me for the porch." The latter comment was tinged with suspicion. As if he thought she'd had an ulterior motive.

That was possible. Both his sister-in-law and Patrick had witnessed the almost-kiss on her porch last Sunday.

Holly reined in a groan. They did *not* need the interference of a matchmaker, no matter how well intentioned.

"As the old saying goes, many hands make light work." Somehow she held on to her smile.

"Yeah. This place needs a ton of TLC." He set down his can of paint, his focus on her, not the weathered wall in front of him. "Thanks for hiring Patrick—and lining him up with your neighbor. The two of them appear to have clicked."

One piece of positive news on this Saturday, anyway.

"I'm glad to hear that. Pete could use another friend."

"He may have a couple more after today. While Cindy volunteers here, Patrick's going back to his house to finish a job, with both kids in tow."

"Perfect. Nobody could resist Jonah—and while Beatrice and I aren't well acquainted, she seems like a sweetheart."

"She is." He ran a thumb over the bristles of the pristine brush. "Listen . . . Patrick told me you weren't aware of our connection to the cannon when you wrote that piece for the *Herald*. I may not agree with your position, but from what I know about you, I wouldn't have expected anything less."

Was that a criticism . . . a simple statement of fact . . . or a compliment?

Impossible to tell—but unlikely the latter, given their divergent opinions.

She dipped into the can of paint and transferred her attention to the thirsty wood as she stroked on color. "I was afraid a former military man might take offense." Not a question, so he could ignore her comment if he chose.

"No." His response was immediate. "But it does highlight the difference in our moral compasses." She turned her head, and his gaze caught—and held—hers. "I believe fighting oppression and evil is a noble activity. If that fight sometimes requires the sacrifice of life, I consider it justified."

"I assumed that would be your position—and a lot of the fighting in a war is self-defense. Kill or be killed." She swallowed. "It's an ugly business. I abhor violence, but I can appreciate what you're saying in theory."

"As I recall, even Jesus got violent with the moneychangers and merchants who defiled the temple, driving them out and overturning their tables."

"No one died in that incident."

A muscle ticced in his cheek. "Do you think God wants us to stand by and watch while extremist groups slaughter innocent people? Or murder Christians? Or turn children into suicide bombers? And don't suggest negotiation or dialogue. Those techniques don't work with fanatics."

At the intensity in his eyes and the chill in his voice, her heart stumbled.

This was a new side of Steven. The soldier side.

This was a man who'd faced the enemy he'd described, who'd put his own life on the line in the service of justice and freedom.

This was a man who'd seen horrors that were the stuff of nightmares. Who'd witnessed man's inhumanity to man up close and personal—and had perhaps experienced it himself. Who knew what atrocities he'd been exposed to overseas?

It wasn't fair for her to preach to him from the safety and peace of Hope Harbor about the brutality and barbarism he'd experienced in the Middle East.

"I see your point. And I don't know the answer to your questions. It's a . . . murky subject."

His nostrils flared—and he slowly let out a breath. "I suppose that's progress."

She tipped her head. "What does that mean?"

After a brief hesitation, he swiveled away to examine the wall. "It doesn't matter." His tone was flat.

"What doesn't matter?" She moved closer and touched his arm.

He stiffened—and she drew back.

"Whether or not you change your mind about the justification of using violence to fight violence." A muscle clenched in his jaw. "It doesn't matter."

"I think it does." Especially if his sorrow over the loss of his wife subsided and he opened the door to romance. Hadn't he said if he was in the market for a relationship, she'd be top on his list?

"If you're thinking about *us*, don't get your hopes up." Some of the starch went out of his shoulders. "We're too different. I've done things you would never approve of."

"I think many people regret some of their choices in wartime. It's a high-pressure environment that requires split-second decisions."

"That's the problem. I don't regret my choices. I never will. On the battlefield, anyway."

What did *that* mean?

"Excuse me . . . could I steal one of your cans of paint?" Michael Hunter hustled up the porch steps and joined them. "We're running short out back."

Could the timing for this interruption have been worse?

"Sure." Steven bent, hefted his can, and passed it to the Helping Hands director. "Even the top guy is pitching in today, huh?" He offered the facsimile of a smile, but the strain underneath was apparent. To her, if not to Michael.

"It's the lull before the storm at the cranberry farm. Tracy's handling a broken pipe in the irrigation system today, but in another month it will be all hands on deck. Even after adding two new beds, we're having difficulty growing enough berries to keep up with the demand for our cranberry nut cake—or finding any downtime." He pulled out his cell and frowned. "And calls to Helping Hands—like this one—are also increasing. Suffice it to say, there are days I feel like a juggler. Let us know if you run out of paint." He put the phone to his ear and retreated.

Holly caught her lip between her teeth. How could she route them back to their previous discussion?

Given that Steven was examining a peeling window frame, it didn't appear he was inclined to continue their conversation.

But she wanted to know more.

Needed to know more.

"Steven."

After a moment—and with obvious reluctance—he turned back to her.

"Can we pick up where we left off?"

"There's nothing more to say."

There was *loads* more to say . . . but she'd have to ease back into it.

"Can I at least ask a question?" She didn't wait for him to respond. "If you felt what you were doing overseas was important, why did you leave the military?"

His nostrils flared, and a muscle in his jaw clenched. "I didn't like the person I was becoming. My job was intense and entailed duties that required a certain . . . detachment. That distancing began to carry over into my personal life. I knew I had to decompress, get back on a more normal track—and Patrick's issue gave me an excuse to leave. But I can't erase my history . . . and I don't want to create false expectations."

She'd only been on the receiving end of one break-up speech in her life, but this sure seemed like a kiss-off.

Somehow she managed to coax up the corners of her mouth. "My ego is taking a hit here. I thought you had to be a couple before someone could throw you over."

"Trust me, Holly." His tone was grim. "You'll thank me for this in the long run."

He could be right. Those few hints at dark secrets, while lacking in details, *were* unsettling.

Still—Steven was going to church now. He was a Christian. How far apart could their moral standards be? Wasn't that worth exploring?

But pushing too hard would get her nowhere.

"I realize you have concerns, and I—"

"Steven, we could use your muscle power in the back. Can you lend us a hand?" Reverend Baker stuck his head around a porch post.

"On my way." He set his brush beside the can of paint. "Sorry to desert you."

While his comment was straightforward, the look he gave her wasn't. It was filled with equal parts regret, melancholy, and longing.

He wasn't just talking about the painting job—or physical distance.

He was also removing himself from her emotionally.

As he clattered down the steps and disappeared around the house, Holly leaned against the post near the arbor, staying a safe distance from the prickly canes of the climber.

Steven was prickly too—and he bore more than a faint resemblance to the anemones at Starfish Pier that closed up tight if anyone got too close.

What secrets was he hiding that were so dire he thought they'd be a deal breaker between them?

And given the banked fire in his eyes when he looked at her, was he using grief as an excuse to keep her at arm's length because of those secrets?

Holly retrieved her paintbrush. Dipped it in the can of Evening Glow Yellow the homeowner had chosen for her house. The color was bright. Cheerful. Optimistic.

None of which described her future with Steven, given their exchange during the past few minutes.

But while their opinions about the justification for war and violence did reflect different perspectives, there was another impediment at play here. His comment about having no regrets over his *military* career suggested there were parts of his past he *did* regret.

Those were the ones he was afraid they couldn't overcome.

While that might be true, it was impossible to know for certain unless he shared them with her.

Sad to say, that didn't seem to be in the cards.

And unless she could come up with a plan to convince him to give her a chance to determine for herself whether his secrets were an insurmountable obstacle, Steven Roark was going to disappear from her life as fast as a mole crab disappeared under the sand at the first sign of danger.

"These cookies are good."

Pete refilled Jonah's glass of milk, checked on the baby sleeping in the portable crib Patrick had deposited in his kitchen, and sent a disgruntled glance toward the man who was back up in the tree, finishing the job he'd begun yesterday.

Babysitting hadn't been part of their agreement—but after Patrick had explained about his wife's charitable commitment this afternoon, what could he say?

Besides, the kids were cute. And Jonah was smart and inquisitive, if the questions he'd been throwing out since they'd arrived fifteen minutes ago were any indication. Everything from what kind of seal was on the big rock offshore to picking his brain about the types of sailing ships that had once plied the waters off the Oregon coast.

"I'm glad you like them."

"My mom bakes awesome cookies. She's busy at the Myrtle, though, until my dad goes back to the mill. Did you ever work at a mill, Mr. Wallace?"

"No." He took a store-bought oatmeal cookie for himself and sat at the table across from his diminutive guest.

"Where do you work now?"

"I don't work. I'm retired."

Jonah scrunched up his face. "What does that mean?"

"It means I got too old to work."

The boy cocked his head. "So what do you do every day?"

Wait to die.

Not an appropriate answer for a six-year-old.

"I like to read."

"I'm learning how to do that. It's hard." As he chomped on the cookie, crumbs rained on the floor. "What did you do before you 'tired?"

"I owned a landscaping company."

"What's that?"

"It's a business that helps people plan what kinds of trees and flowers they want to plant in their yards, or at their offices."

"So you got to work outside?"

"A fair amount."

"I like being outside, but I have to stay in sometimes on account of my asthma." He wrinkled his nose. "Do you have asthma?"

"No." But he'd trade it for what he did have in a heartbeat.

"Sometimes it's scary. I have a thing that helps me breathe, though." He dug into his pocket and pulled out an inhaler. "See?" He extended his hand.

Pete leaned forward and examined it. "That's a handy piece of equipment to have."

"Yeah." He shoved it back in his pocket. "Do you have any kids, Mr. Wallace?"

A pang echoed in his heart. "No."

"How come?"

Leave it to a child to ask straight out the question adults always danced around.

"God didn't give us any."

Jonah's brow knitted. "Did you ask him to?"

"Yes." With heartfelt prayers . . . year after year after year.

Another request that had gone unheeded.

"How come he didn't?"

The same question he'd asked himself for decades.

"I don't know—but he did give me a wonderful wife. We had fun together."

"My dad said she went to heaven."

"Yes, she did."

"Do you miss her a bunch?"

"Yes."

"I'd miss my mom and dad too if they—" He sniffed in Beatrice's direction and faked a gag. "She pooped. You'll have to change her."

Change a baby?

A wave of panic rippled through him. "Uh . . . I'll get your dad. I don't have any practice changing babies."

Like none.

He rose and hastened to the window. Peered at the tree.

Patrick was high up, sawing on a branch.

In other words, he was in no position to run in and attend to his daughter.

"It's not hard." Jonah trotted over to the diaper bag Patrick had deposited inside the back door and picked it up. "Everything's in here."

"I think I'll wait for your dad to come down."

As if she'd understood the gist of their conversation, Beatrice screwed up her angelic face and let loose with an ear-splitting wail of protest.

"She doesn't like to be messy." Jonah plopped the bag on one of the chairs at the table.

To borrow one of Holly's phrases—well, crud.

But really, how hard could this be? And if he did it wrong, Patrick could fix it later.

"Let's change her on the bed in my room." He approached the portable crib and gingerly picked up the yowling baby.

Jonah followed him down the hall, the oversized diaper bag slung over his shoulder.

In the bedroom, he leaned over to lay the baby on the bedspread, but the boy stopped him. "Wait. You should put this down first. She can make a mess." He dug out a disposable pad and spread it on the comforter.

After Pete laid the baby down, his helper went to work, handing him a bottle of hand sanitizer and a clean diaper.

"Thank you."

Jonah shrugged. "I've watched Mom and Dad do this a bunch. You're gonna need a lot of these." He pulled out a package of baby wipes.

"Why don't you give me a few more tips while I do this?"

"Sure." Jonah edged back as Pete unsnapped Beatrice's tiny garment and prepared to unfasten the diaper. "Get ready for a stink bomb."

The baby began to squirm and whimper, as if to say, *Get this disgusting thing off me!*, and he picked up the pace.

Stink bomb didn't begin to do justice to the stench that wafted up as he removed the diaper.

"I see what you mean." He folded the foul-smelling diaper in half, took the baby wipe Jonah handed him, and launched into the cleanup chore.

Beatrice calmed down and began sucking on her finger, watching him with big, trusting blue eyes.

His throat tightened.

This is what he and Sal had missed. Caring for a tiny babe . . . creating a safe and nurturing environment that instilled compassion and confidence . . . watching a child grow and develop under their love and guidance.

How different life could have been if he had a devoted daughter or son who cared whether he lived or died.

"You pull those tapes—there." Jonah indicated the tab fasteners.

Pete throttled his melancholy musings, finished the job, and stepped back to assess his work.

Not bad for an amateur.

And Beatrice's contented gurgle suggested his customer was satisfied.

"Let's put this little lady back in her crib."

He used the hand sanitizer again and picked her up.

Jonah followed him into the kitchen.

"Watch her while I clean up, okay?"

"Sure." The boy wandered over to the crib and began to tickle the baby.

Five minutes later, when Pete returned to the kitchen, Jonah was eating another cookie. The trail of crumbs between table and crib suggested he'd followed instructions and monitored the baby.

"We're doing a project at school about backyard plants." The boy climbed back into his chair. "Since you know all about that stuff, could you help me figure out what's growing at my house?"

Pete deposited the soiled diaper, changing pad, and wipes in a plastic bag, sealed it, and tucked it in the trash. As he applied more hand sanitizer, he joined Jonah at the table. "I'm sure your mom or dad would be happy to do that."

"They're busy—and they don't know half the plants in our yard. I bet you do."

It was hard to say no to the boy, but visiting a virtual stranger's house wasn't part of his plan.

"When is this assignment due?"

"Tuesday. I was gonna work on it this weekend."

"I'll tell you what. I'll give your dad my email address, and if he'll take four or five pictures with his phone, I can try to identify what you find."

"I 'spose that would work." But Jonah didn't sound convinced.

"It would be easier if you came over, though." His brow wrinkled and he pushed the cookie crumbs on the table into a tiny pile. "I could maybe pretend you were my grandpa for a while. All my friends have grandpas."

Pete's throat clogged at the indirect compliment, but he cleared it at once and mashed his lips together. Sentiment had no place in his life anymore.

"People do all kinds of things by email these days." He squinted out the window at Patrick. Near as he could estimate, the man wouldn't finish for another hour.

How did you entertain a first-grader for sixty minutes?

Patrick had said the boy could watch one of the DVDs he'd brought—but kids spent too many of their waking hours in front of a screen as it was.

"You know any card games?" Pete refilled his coffee cup.

"Crazy Eights. Mom and Dad and me play sometimes."

"Want to teach it to me?" He felt around in one of the drawers for the deck of cards he'd brought with him from Utah but had never used.

"Sure. It's easy." Jonah launched into an explanation about the finer points of the game.

They were still at it an hour later as Patrick wrapped up the job outside and joined them after a brief knock on the door.

"Hey, Dad. I taught Mr. Wallace to play Crazy Eights."

"Who's been winning?" Patrick grinned and walked over to Beatrice.

"Me."

"Sorry, Pete. I raised a card shark." He bent to stroke a finger down his daughter's cheek. "Everything okay in here?"

"Beatrice pooped." Jonah gathered up the cards as they finished their hand.

Patrick headed for the diaper bag. "I'll take care of her and we'll—"

"Mr. Wallace already changed her." Jonah tapped the cards into a neat stack. "I watched. He did real good."

Pete stood, the corners of his mouth twitching. "I'm a fast learner."

Dismay flattened Patrick's features. "I didn't expect you to do diaper duty. You should have called me."

"You were busy. I coped. And I was rewarded for my efforts with an expert lesson on Crazy Eights."

"He learned it real fast, Dad. Did you know he used to work with plants?"

Patrick angled toward him, and Pete took the cards from Jonah. "I was a landscaper."

"Our garden club here could use your expertise."

There was no way to remind Patrick he wouldn't be here long without raising Jonah's antennas, so he let it pass.

"I asked him if he could help me with my school project." Jonah jumped back into the conversation. "You know, the one about backyard plants? He said maybe you could take pictures and email them to him." Jonah's eyes brightened. "But I have a better idea!" He swiveled around. "Why don't you come and eat with us tomorrow and I can show you our yard?"

The invitation seemed to surprise Patrick as much as it did him . . . but the other man wasted no time seconding it.

"I think that would be great. I know how to cut grass and trim trees, but I can't tell one flower—or weed—from another. Neither can my wife. This project will require serious research on our part. If you could help Jonah out, you'd earn our undying gratitude—and a delicious meal. Cindy may not be a gardener, but she's a wonderful cook."

"Yeah! Mom makes the best desserts ever!"

As the two Roarks waited for his answer, the automatic refusal that formed on his lips died.

A home-cooked meal would be a treat after all the frozen dinners he'd ingested over the past three years.

Strange, but since he'd eaten that taco Holly had brought him, long-absent hunger pangs were beginning to return.

Why not accept? It was only one evening. A couple of hours, max. After that, he could retreat into his cave.

Or not.

Throwing away what little life he had left could be a mistake. Being around people like Holly and Patrick and Jonah—even baby Beatrice—could brighten his final days.

"I was partial to tasty desserts in my day."

"Does that mean you're coming?" Jonah's expression was hopeful.

"Yes."

"Awesome!"

"My sentiments exactly." Patrick grinned and began gathering up all his paraphernalia.

Pete helped him, then walked the trio to the door.

Five minutes later, with the children secured in the car and Jonah calling another enthusiastic good-bye out the window, he waved and watched the car roll down Sea Rose Lane.

Only after it disappeared did he amble back inside.

As he passed the urn on the coffee table, he rested a hand on top. "It seems I have a dinner engagement, Sal."

She didn't respond in words, of course—but a warmth enveloped him. A sense of her presence . . . and approval.

It was a buoyant feeling.

But it wouldn't last.

Because his ultimate plan hadn't changed . . . even if it was somehow beginning to feel wrong.

19

She was *not* going to run after any man—even if Steven had gotten under her skin.

Holly closed her hymnal and watched the Roark clan out of the corner of her eye as they exited a pew on the other side of Grace Christian and filed down the side aisle.

Steven didn't look her direction.

Not once.

If she'd harbored any hopes that his failure to return to the porch yesterday at the Helping Hands project hadn't been personal, his stoic, head-forward departure quashed them.

He wanted nothing more to do with her.

Spirits diving, she gathered up her purse and sweater and stood as Cindy peeled off from the rest of her family, who continued toward the back, and cut through a pew to join her.

"Morning, Holly."

"Hi." She tried to call up a smile—and ignore Steven's broad back disappearing toward the rear of church.

"I know you've taken your neighbor under your wing, and I wanted to let you know he and Patrick hit it off."

"Steven implied that yesterday. I'm glad."

"I can see why you're concerned about him." Cindy lowered her volume and leaned closer. "Pete shared his plan with Patrick yesterday, and gave him permission to tell me. He said you already knew."

A surprising development, considering Pete had sworn her to secrecy.

"I thought he wanted to keep that under wraps."

"I don't think he intends to announce it in the *Herald*, but I suppose he doesn't mind a few people knowing. Anyway, Patrick's convinced that if he had a support system here, he might rethink his decision."

"I came to the same conclusion. That's one of the reasons I introduced the two of them. The more people he gets to know, the more involved he becomes in the community, the more likely he'll realize he has other options. I told him he'd be welcome here at Grace Christian too, but he didn't bite."

"Church attendance could come. In the meantime, Patrick invited him to dinner tonight, and he accepted."

Another bit of news to brighten her day. "That's wonderful!"

"I agree. Since he knows you, I wondered if you'd like to join us too. It can't hurt to have a few familiar faces around the table. He may feel more comfortable—and be open to a repeat invitation."

God bless Cindy for her kindness. But . . .

"Are you certain you don't mind another mouth to feed?" With money tight, every dollar could matter for the Roarks.

"We're not having a fancy meal, and I always make a huge pot of stew. We'll have leftovers whether you come or not."

"If you'll let me contribute to the dinner, I'll be happy to join you. Could I bring dessert?"

Cindy grinned. "Jonah already promised Pete I'd provide that—but how about bread or rolls or biscuits to go with the stew? Would that be too much trouble?"

"Not at all. My mom's biscuit recipe is super. I'll whip up a batch and we can pop them in the oven at the last minute at your house. Give me a time and an address."

After they worked out the details, Cindy continued toward the rear of the church.

Holly waited a few extra minutes in case the family had lingered in the vestibule, and when she left at last, none of the Roarks were in sight.

Good. After yesterday's encounter, it was too soon to cross paths with Steven again.

Especially after he'd ignored her for the past hour.

"Holly! Happy to see you. How's the wrist coming along?" Reverend Baker extended a hand as she approached the exit.

"Improving." She returned his firm shake.

"Thank you for honoring your commitment to Helping Hands yesterday despite your injury."

"I was happy to pitch in. The organization does excellent work."

"I couldn't agree more. I also wanted to commend you on that piece you wrote for the *Herald* about the cannon. It was very thought-provoking."

"I don't know." She sighed. "It seems to have created a ton of controversy. People on both sides of the issue are up in arms—pardon the pun. A town meeting is going to be scheduled in the next couple of weeks."

"Controversy isn't always bad. It can force us to think about moral issues we too often gloss over. You may have done a public service by taking a stand."

"What's your opinion on the cannon?"

The minister linked his fingers behind his back and pursed his lips. "It's still in formation. Hope Harbor is such a haven of peace. I'd hate to see that disrupted. I know we can't ignore the violence and evil in the world, but I'm not certain we have to have a reminder of it staring us in the face every day."

More congregants joined them, cutting the conversation short, and after a quick good-bye, Holly continued toward her car.

Outside, the sun had broken through the earlier mist, and the warmth lifted her spirits.

The situation with Steven might be a bust, but at least her minister wasn't offended by her write-up on the cannon—and even saw some merit in it. Plus, Pete had agreed to have dinner with Patrick and Cindy and their children—suggesting he was rethinking his reclusive ways. If they continued to interact with him, convince him he had a support system, it was possible he'd also reconsider his decision and leave God in control of his destiny.

But that would take time—and the clock was ticking.

She could only pray he'd see the light before his health worsened and he took the final, fatal step that had prompted his move to a town filled with strangers who wanted to be his friends—and who were already his brothers and sisters in the Lord.

"Why are there six place settings?" As the number of plates registered, Steven stopped filling the water glasses and angled toward Cindy.

In the background, Patrick's expression grew sheepish, and he slipped into the kitchen.

Bad vibes began to ripple through him. The kind that had always sensitized his nerve endings in the presence of danger.

"We're having other company today besides you." Cindy set salt and pepper shakers on the table, her manner breezy. As if the other guests were of no consequence.

But they were. He could sense it.

"Since when?"

"Since yesterday for one, this morning for the other. Don't worry. There's plenty of food." She smoothed a wrinkle in the tablecloth and turned to go.

"Wait." Executing a fast maneuver, he stepped in front of her. "Who's coming?"

She arched an eyebrow at him. "You have an issue with us extending hospitality to two people who would otherwise eat dinner alone?"

“Not in principle. Who’s coming?”

“Pete Wallace accepted our invitation yesterday. Do you know him?”

Pete Wallace . . . Pete Wallace . . . Oh, right. Holly’s neighbor. The one she was worried about.

“No—but I know who he is. Who else—”

The bell chimed, and Cindy skirted around him. “I have to answer the door.” She hurried toward the front of the house.

Planting his fists on his hips, he scowled after her.

Fine.

He’d corner Patrick.

He found his brother hiding in the kitchen, pretending to monitor the stew.

“What gives?”

Patrick held up his hands, palms forward in surrender. “I want you to know I had nothing to do with this. I invited Pete, but asking Holly to join us was all Cindy’s idea.”

A jolt rolled through him.

Holly was coming?

The woman he’d run from yesterday like a scared rabbit?

The woman who’d kept him awake half the night as images of her strobed through his mind?

The woman who’d dominated his dreams after he’d finally fallen into a restless sleep?

He bit back a word he tried not to use anymore.

“Why didn’t you tell me?”

“Cindy didn’t mention it until ten minutes before you got here—and I was afraid you’d bail if I called to alert you.”

“I still might.”

“Cindy would be upset—and she means well. Cut her some slack. You don’t have to stay long.”

Conversation filtered in from the living room. A male voice he didn’t recognize, and Holly’s sweet, musical tones—which were growing closer by the second.

He stiffened as Cindy appeared around the kitchen door and tossed him a guilty look, followed by Holly, who was toting a covered pan in her good hand.

Her jaw dropped and her step faltered as their gazes collided.

"Patrick, why don't you introduce Steven to Pete while Holly and I get her biscuits going? I left him in the living room with Jonah." Cindy flashed him a nervous smile. "I don't think introductions are necessary in here."

Steven glared at her.

"Sure." Patrick headed out of the room, leaving him to follow.

Holly edged away from the doorway. "Hello, Steven."

"Hi."

"I, uh, didn't expect to see you here today."

"Likewise." It was important to make it clear he'd been blindsided too, lest she wonder if he'd been a party to this awkward setup. Cindy bore all the blame for that—and she was going to get an earful about it later.

He maneuvered past Holly, catching a faint whiff of the pleasant floral scent that always perfumed the air around her—and never failed to undermine his resolve to keep his distance.

Gritting his teeth, he continued toward the living room.

He'd made his decision yesterday at the Helping Hands project, after he'd found her on the porch sporting that tiny streak of yellow paint on her cheek and had had to summon up every ounce of his willpower not to finish what he'd started at her house last Sunday as they were parting.

Being around her was dangerous. The spark between them was potent. It wouldn't take much for it to ignite—and that would only lead to heartache for both of them.

It was safer to keep his distance.

A plan he'd intended to follow until Cindy had decided to become a matchmaker.

He tried to focus on the older man in the living room as Patrick introduced them. Attempted to join in the small talk.

But knowing Holly was steps away in the kitchen was a major distraction.

Fortunately, Patrick and Jonah kept the conversation moving.

Fifteen minutes later, Cindy announced dinner. Steven took a deep breath and stood, psyching himself up for the next encounter.

If Cindy had put him next to Holly for the meal, he'd have to eat—and leave—fast. A manufactured emergency on the boat would suffice as an excuse.

At the table, however, he found himself seated next to Jonah, with Holly across from him, beside Pete.

That ought to be more manageable.

Or not.

Because once they all sat, she was front and center in his line of sight. Had she been beside him, he could have ignored her. Or tried to.

Patrick offered a brief blessing, and as Cindy ladled out the stew, his brother picked up the conversational ball.

"Tell us about your career as a landscaper, Pete. How did you get into that business?"

The older man buttered a biscuit he'd taken from the basket being passed around the table. "It was chance, really. I always assumed I'd follow my father into law. But during high school, the only summer job I could find was at a nursery. As it turned out, I enjoyed the work—and after the owner saw I had a knack for design, he took me under his wing. I ended up getting a degree in landscape architecture, went to work for the nursery full-time, and bought him out when he retired."

"How did you meet your wife?" Cindy bit into her own biscuit.

Pete's features softened. "She was the daughter of one of my first customers after I graduated. I went to her parents' house to discuss a landscape job, and she and her mom wanted to plant azaleas. I tried to discourage them. The soil in Utah is too dense and alkaline. But Sal looked me in the eye and said, 'There has to be a way to make azaleas and Utah dirt compatible.'" He gave a soft chuckle and dabbed the corner of his mouth with his napkin.

"Was there?" Cindy leaned forward.

"Yes, but it took a lot of work—and it was an ongoing effort."

"How did the azaleas do?" Cindy continued to give Pete her full attention.

"Fine, as long as we kept a careful watch over them, made certain they got the nutrients they needed, and took steps to accommodate changes in the weather."

"Sounds like a recipe for a happy marriage." Cindy leaned back.

"No argument there." Pete took another bite of stew. "Sal and I often thought about that first meeting whenever an issue arose between us. She'd always say, 'Remember the azaleas. We can work this out.' And she was right. If two people are committed to each other, they can find a way to smooth over differences."

Steven felt Patrick glance his direction.

He ignored him.

"Kind of like plucking the weeds on the garden path." Holly took a sip of water and regarded him across the table.

Steven had no clue what that meant.

But Pete obviously did. "You remembered my story."

"It was worth remembering. Too many people today bail as soon as a relationship hits a rocky patch." She continued to focus on him.

He took an oversized bite of his biscuit. Chewed. "These are great, Cindy. The stew is too."

"The stew I can take credit for. Holly brought the biscuits. Honey, why don't you share your latest news?" Cindy motioned to Patrick.

All heads swiveled his direction.

A faint flush bloomed on his brother's cheeks. "I don't know that I'd call it news."

"My modest husband." Cindy sent him an affectionate smile. "Can I tell?"

He shrugged. "If you want."

"Brent Davis called yesterday and asked Patrick to make a presentation about his great-great-great-grandfather and the cannon at the town meeting."

Across the table, Holly fidgeted in her seat. Even though he and Patrick had both assured her there were no hard feelings because of her stance on the issue, the topic clearly made her uncomfortable.

As he prepared to step in and change the subject, Pete spoke.

"That would be fascinating. I'll try to attend. I wish I'd seen the cannon before it left town for restoration."

Holly stared at him. "I thought you didn't like weapons of war."

"The stories Patrick told me about his great-great-great-grandfather gave me a different perspective." He turned to his host. "How do you feel about doing a presentation in front of half the town—or more?"

"Nervous."

Cindy waved his concern aside. "You light up when you talk about history. You'll have everyone mesmerized."

"I hope so. I don't have long to prepare. He wants to have the meeting next week."

"You could do it tomorrow if you had to." Cindy rose. "Anyone want more water?"

As she refilled glasses, Steven risked another peek at Holly.

She was concentrating on her dinner, chin dipped, brow pleated. No doubt plotting a fast escape from a subject that was awkward and a man who'd given her a Dear Jane speech yesterday.

He'd save her the trouble. As soon as the meal was over, he was out of here.

And he was going to tell both Patrick and Cindy to put a lid on any future matchmaking that involved him and their son's lovely teacher.

When it came to fast exits, Steven had broken the world record.

Holly carried another small stack of dishes into the kitchen as Cindy, Jonah, and Pete disappeared out the back door to collect plant specimens for his homework assignment.

"You don't have to help clean up, Holly—especially with a bum wrist. KP is my job. It's the least I can do after Cindy cooks dinner." Patrick stopped loading the dishwasher to motion toward the back door. "Go on outside with the rest of the crew if you want to."

"I don't mind lending a hand in here—and helping one of my students with a homework project could be viewed as preferential treatment."

"I see your point." Patrick went back to stacking. "Listen . . . I'm sorry if having Steven here was uncomfortable for you. I had no idea Cindy was going to invite you after church today."

"It was a delicious meal. I enjoyed every bite. And you've both been clear that you aren't offended by the piece I wrote for the *Herald*, so everything's good." She began scraping plates into the trash, favoring her sore-but-improving wrist.

"I meant the matchmaking angle. Steven told me there were—impediments—to a relationship between the two of you, despite the obvious attraction."

Her cheeks warmed, and she shifted sideways to hide the flush. "He thinks so, anyway." Why deny the obvious? Both Cindy and Patrick had witnessed the almost-kiss at her front door. And as long as Patrick had brought up the subject, why not see what else he'd offer? "We talked a bit about it yesterday. He's convinced some of the assignments he had during his years in the military are problematic, but it's hard to fault a man for doing what he believes is right."

"I can see where he's coming from, though, given what you wrote in the *Herald*." Twin creases scored his forehead. "I mean, even people who support the mission of wiping out insurgents and extremists could have difficulty wrapping their mind around what Delta Force snipers do."

Holly froze as Patrick's words echoed in her mind.

Steven had been a special forces *sniper*?

A trained killer who'd put distant, unsuspecting targets in his sights and pulled the trigger?

She groped for the edge of the counter as his comment yesterday about his job requiring a certain detachment suddenly took on new meaning. From what little she'd read about snipers, killing for them was mechanical. Emotionless.

No wonder Steven considered finding common ground with a woman who abhorred violence, who believed in the sanctity of life, an insurmountable obstacle.

And maybe it was.

"Holly?"

Somewhere in the distance she heard her name—but only after Patrick touched her arm and repeated it did she pull herself out of her daze and focus on his face.

"Sorry. I-I zoned out for a minute."

The furrows on his brow deepened. "You didn't know, did you?"

"I . . . not about his specific job."

Patrick muttered a self-deprecating remark. "Now *I'm* sorry. From what you said about your conversation yesterday, I assumed he'd told you." He forked his fingers through his hair. "Man, is he going to be furious with me."

Sorry as she felt for her host's predicament, she couldn't find the words to reassure him. Not while she was busy trying to mesh the kind, generous, caring charter fisherman she'd come to know with the sniper behind the trigger in the Middle East.

It wasn't computing.

"Listen—I'll tell him what happened, okay? That way, when the two of you meet up again, he'll already know. This is my fault, and I'll take the fallout."

With her mind reeling, it was difficult to think about next steps. "I suppose that . . . that would be helpful."

The likelihood of them bumping into each other after Patrick told his brother what had happened, however, was slim. Steven would make a concerted effort to avoid her rather than risk facing the condemnation he would expect.

But condemning a man for following government-sanctioned orders to fight militant jihadists for reasons he himself believed were just and honorable felt wrong—even if the deed, in abstract, turned her stomach.

How did you reconcile two conflicting moral objectives—respect life and fight evil?

The tangle in her brain was giving her a headache.

As if sensing her mental anguish, Patrick changed the subject.

Yet an hour later, after she drove herself and an unusually upbeat Pete home, that nagging question returned.

Along with one other troubling uncertainty.

If Steven didn't regret the sniper work she was still having difficulty coming to grips with, what had he been referring to that could be *worse* when he'd indicated he harbored other regrets?

Tonight had been the most pleasant evening he'd spent in years.

Pete yawned, padded barefoot into the spare bedroom that housed his computer, and eased into the chair at the small desk. Most of his email was junk these days, but on occasion his financial advisor sent him investment information to review, and he hadn't checked for a while.

As he waited for the laptop to boot up, he searched through the drawers. Somewhere in here he'd stashed a few thank-you cards, and he ought to send the Roark family one for tonight's dinner.

While he was at it, he ought to send one to Holly too. She'd been more than kind. Baking him cookies, sharing her tacos, introducing him to Patrick. His neighbor had brightened his life with her thoughtfulness these past few weeks.

He found a package with three thank-you notes. Those ought to cover him for his remaining days.

After removing two, he logged into email.

He had one message—from Patrick. Sent less than fifteen minutes ago.

Huh.

The man had asked for his email in case Jonah had any questions as he completed his assignment—but the "FYI" header didn't appear to refer to a homework project.

He clicked on the email and leaned forward to scan the text.

We enjoyed having you over for dinner tonight, Pete. Let's do it again soon—without any homework!

I've been doing research on clinical trials for lung cancer. I don't know the details of your diagnosis, but the links below provide excellent guidance on locating trials. I'm sure your doctor would be happy to help too.

I hope you don't think I'm overstepping, but I want you to know my family is willing to provide support in any way we can should you decide to continue treatment . . . or to let the disease run its natural course. I know Holly feels the same. And we have a wonderful organization in town called Helping Hands that would also be happy to assist. So you don't have to face whatever is ahead alone. Please think about all this as you reflect on your options.

I'll be back next week to cut your grass—and arrange another dinner!

Pete leaned back in his chair, pressure building in his throat.

How strange—and touching—to find so many caring people in this small town where he'd come to die in anonymity.

But none of them could replace Sal . . . or fill the empty place her passing had left in his heart.

And it wasn't as if he was contributing anything anymore—other than helping a child with his homework.

"Maybe you could *contribute if you looked for opportunities. There may be a reason you're supposed to linger."*

Sal's gentle prod wasn't new. He'd heard her sweet voice often during the past few months as he'd struggled with his decision, urging him to reconsider. He'd just chosen to ignore her message.

It had been harder to do that here in Hope Harbor, though.

First Holly, then Patrick, now Patrick's family—despite his

resolve to keep to himself, he was making connections, building relationships.

Changing his mind at this juncture, however, would require a radical shift in mind-set. He'd made his peace with his decision, laid all the groundwork, was down to the final steps.

Still—once he had the medication in hand, the exact timing was up to him. He didn't have to lock a date in stone. He could think through this a little more first.

Not that he was having second thoughts.

Not quite.

Yet for the first time since moving to this charming seaside town, he began to listen to the question that had begun to niggle at his subconscious with increasing regularity.

Should he follow a different path?

20

The cat was out of the bag.

One of the cats, anyway.

Steven hit the end button, slid his cell back into his pocket, and sat on the gunwale of his boat as two gulls wheeled overhead.

Unhappy as he was with Patrick for assuming Holly was aware of his Delta Force assignment, getting mad at his brother would accomplish nothing.

And truth be told, maybe it was good she knew. That piece of news ought to convince her they were incompatible without having to reveal the other dark secrets that would probably be even less acceptable to her.

The ones that continued to eat at his soul, day after day.

As the boat gently rocked beneath him, he expelled a breath and pulled out yesterday's folded-up church bulletin. Reread the notice that had caught his eye—and his interest.

> For the past several years, we've been fortunate to have Michael Hunter at the helm of Helping Hands. But with a growing family and a thriving business to manage, he has elected to step aside. We will begin a formal job search for his replacement soon, but in

the meantime if you know of any qualified individuals who might be interested in the director position, please ask them to contact Michael, Reverend Baker, or Father Murphy at one of the numbers listed below.

Steven lowered the bulletin and gazed out over the placid harbor, toward the horizon. Running a charter business for the past twelve months had given him the respite he'd needed after his high-intensity tenure in The Unit, but it was time to chart a new, more permanent course.

Could this be it?

While he didn't have a degree in nonprofit management, a Wharton MBA ought to count for something. He knew how to run a business, and the management skills he'd honed in The Unit would transfer well to the nonprofit world.

The opportunity to do work that helped those in need was also more appealing than starting a for-profit business or working for a large company up in Coos Bay—about as far as he was willing to commute for a job. Hope Harbor was home now, and leaving behind the only family he had to pursue a career in a far-off place wasn't an option.

But how would the two clerics who'd founded Helping Hands feel about hiring someone with his baggage?

No way to know without asking—his next step, if he wanted to pursue this.

Scratch that.

There were no ifs about it.

From the instant he'd spotted the notice in the bulletin, his interest had been piqued. He *did* want to pursue this.

Whether it panned out remained to be seen—but what did he have to lose by talking to Reverend Baker and Father Murphy? Worst case, they'd tell him to forget it.

As for keeping his past a secret—if you couldn't trust a cleric to honor confidences, who *could* you trust?

Without laboring over his decision, he pulled out his cell again, tapped in the minister's number—and crossed his fingers.

"Afternoon, Pete!" As her neighbor exited his house, Holly called out the greeting from behind the stack of papers she was grading on her patio and gave him a cheery wave.

He lifted a hand in acknowledgment, his lips curving up. "Beautiful day."

"Yes, it is. Enjoy this unseasonably warm weather while it lasts."

"That's my plan. I'm going to catch up on my reading." He continued to the cushioned chaise lounge that had appeared on his patio over the weekend, lowered himself into it, and opened his book.

His smile was promising—and his tone had been more upbeat than usual.

Perhaps the kindness campaign she'd launched—reinforced by Patrick and his family—was beginning to pay dividends.

If she could just convince him to join her at Grace Christian, he—

Her cell began to vibrate, and she pulled it out of her pocket. Skimmed the screen. Put it to her ear. "Hi, Mom."

"Hi, honey. How's the wrist?"

"Healing. Anything new on your end?" Not likely, since they'd talked yesterday afternoon . . . and the afternoon before.

At least her parents weren't calling quite as often anymore, now that they were satisfied she'd settled into Hope Harbor and was coping on her own.

"No—but your dad and I have a hankering for Charley's tacos. We were thinking about coming down this weekend. Would that work for you?"

"Sure. I'm at loose ends."

"No hot date?" Her mother's inflection was half teasing, half serious.

"Not this weekend." Sad to say.

"I thought you and that fisherman might be getting better acquainted since he came to your rescue at church."

Her mother's tone remained conversational, but Holly heard the worry underneath. Understandable, given Mom's comments after meeting Steven. Her keen intuition hadn't faded with age, as evidenced by how fast she'd picked up on the shadowed past Steven had alluded to.

"No. I run into him here and there, but it doesn't appear romance is in the cards."

"Not for lack of interest on his part."

More proof of her mother's sharp instincts.

"He thinks we're too different." Why not be honest? With him in full retreat, it didn't much matter if she shared a few more details with her mom.

"What do *you* think?"

"I agree we're different—but some differences can be overcome."

"And some can't."

"You sound like you're in *his* camp."

"No. Firmly in yours. Always. But you can open yourself to a world of heartache by falling for the wrong man and hoping you can work out issues later."

"Part of a relationship is accommodation, though, right?"

"Accommodation, yes. Capitulation, no. For example—I've learned to accommodate the differences your father and I have on occasion in the political arena. But on fundamental issues, we've always been in sync. That's a basic building block of harmony in a relationship."

Holly rested her elbow on the table and propped her chin in her palm, watching Pete shoo away a persistent fly. "I suppose that's true." It was essentially the same message Steven had delivered—and the conclusion she herself had come to less than a week ago after acknowledging the two of them appeared to be worlds apart on a major moral issue.

"No supposing about it. However—I have to admit I'm impressed if this man is backing off for selfless reasons. A guy without ethics would forge full speed ahead rather than discourage a woman who attracted him. His willingness to protect your heart at the expense of a fling that would go nowhere is admirable."

True.

Which just made her *more* interested in him—despite their differences.

She sighed. "He's a nice man, Mom—with many fine qualities."

"Offset by ones that aren't so fine?"

"I don't know. He doesn't let people get close. I think there are things in his past he's not proud of . . . but people can change."

"Yes, they can—but only time can tell if the change is permanent. How long have you known this man?"

"Several weeks." A stretch at best.

"Why don't you slow down, watch and wait, and pray about it? If God intends you two to have any kind of future together, he'll let you know. Listen for his voice—and be patient."

"Easier said than done."

Her mother chuckled. "Don't I know it. Even as a child, you never wanted to wait for anything. I remember the one Christmas you . . . whoops! Your dad is giving me the high sign. We've got a dinner reservation at six. I have to run."

After they said their good-byes, Holly set the cell on the table, mulling over the conundrum her mom had referenced.

Accommodation or capitulation—which would be required with Steven?

On the surface, the sniper issue appeared to require capitulation. For a woman who believed in the sanctity of all life, it was hard to justify killing for any reason.

Yet the evil perpetrated by extremists took life too. Often innocent life. Killing in the name of preventing that kind of evil seemed defensible. Maybe she could never do what Steven had done—but he'd risked his life to eradicate evil, doing a job he himself suggested had taken a personal toll. And he'd gotten out when he recognized the negative effect it was having on him emotionally and psychologically.

After she wrapped her mind around the bombshell Patrick had dropped yesterday, did more thinking and praying and research on the topic, Steven's military history might not be the stumbling block he thought it was.

But there was another piece of his background he continued to regret.

One that could be more daunting.

One he seemed to consider a deal breaker.

So what should she do?

Leaning back in her chair, she perused the far horizon, where a ship sailing for unknown ports was steadily chugging forward despite the chop in the waves.

Perhaps the best approach would be to lie low for the next few days. Give them both space to sort out their feelings.

Then, if she could make peace with his past as a military sniper, she could let him know that—and encourage him to share any other roadblocks he felt stood in their path.

After all, if she could manage to reconcile dating a former sniper with her pro-life position, wasn't there a chance she could also accommodate his other secrets without having to compromise her values?

This was it.

Steven stopped outside Reverend Baker's office and smoothed a hand down his dress shirt. He could have added a tie—but this wasn't a job interview. It was an exploratory discussion that could go nowhere.

If they ever progressed to a real interview, he'd dig out the tie.

Tightening his grip on the slim folder in his hand, he knocked.

"Steven. Come in." Reverend Baker smiled as he pulled the door open and ushered him into the compact office.

A man in a Roman collar stood and held out his hand. "Kevin Murphy. A pleasure to meet you."

He returned the affable priest's handshake and followed the minister to a small round conference table in the corner, declining the man's offer of a beverage.

"I was just telling Kevin how you volunteered at our holiday food drive and signed on for the Helping Hands house project last weekend. Not to mention your generous donation to our dinner auction." Reverend Baker indicated a chair and sat in the one next to it.

"Very commendable." The priest retook his seat. "Our pro-life initiative is especially near and dear to my heart."

Steven's stomach twisted.

This might go south fast.

"I appreciate you both working me into your schedules."

"Helping Hands is always a high priority with us. Besides, I could use a break from writing my homily. This one's giving me fits." The padre leaned back and linked his fingers over his stomach.

"If you need any Bible citations to support your theme, let me know." The minister's lips twitched.

Father Murphy sniffed. "I can manage to find my own, thank you very much." The priest angled away from the reverend and focused on him. "So what would you like to discuss about Helping Hands?"

Steven opened the folder he'd set in front of him. "I saw the notice in yesterday's bulletin that you were looking for a new director. I'm interested in the job." He withdrew the two résumés he'd printed out. "I don't have specific nonprofit experience, but my professional and academic background should qualify me to run an organization like that." He handed each of them a résumé.

"I must say, this is an unexpected development." Reverend Baker scanned the first page. "I was afraid we'd have to employ a search firm to find someone to replace Michael."

"That may still be necessary. I'm not a perfect fit."

"You have an impressive background." Father Murphy flipped to the second page.

"Thank you—but there are a few pieces of information not on there that could be stumbling blocks from a moral standpoint." The two clerics looked up in unison. "I asked for this meeting to both express my interest in the job and explain the possible impediments. Could this discussion be kept confidential?"

"Confidentiality goes with our job." The priest laid the résumé on the table. "Right, Paul?"

"Yes. What's said here will stay here."

"Thank you." Steven took a steadying breath. "Let me start with the easiest part—not that any of the things I'm going to share are easy. During my final years in the service, I was a member of Delta Force, the army's special forces unit. My job was sniper—and I make no apologies for what I did. The enemy we fought was monstrous."

He braced, waiting for censure.

It didn't come.

"That must have been a very difficult assignment." Reverend Baker's demeanor reflected compassion, not condemnation.

Empathy radiated from the priest. "Killing is hard for any soldier, but being a sniper requires a dispassion that can eat at the soul."

Steven took a few seconds to digest their reaction. "I have to admit, I didn't—that wasn't the response I expected from men of the cloth."

"Of course neither of us condones killing—but protecting freedom and preserving the life of innocents can sometimes require extreme measures. I believe Kevin would agree." Reverend Baker ceded the floor to his counterpart.

"Yes." Father Murphy gave a vigorous nod. "I'm also certain

that type of work exacts a price on people of honor and principle. That it leaves scars no one can see."

"Yes, it does—and that's one of the reasons I left." Steven blanked out the disturbing images strobing through his mind—a luxury he didn't have with the dreams that often disrupted his sleep. "My involvement in Delta Force and my role as a sniper are not a subject I'll ever discuss in public. But it's relevant to a job in a humanitarian organization like Helping Hands. What I did in the Middle East is at the other end of the spectrum from that sort of work."

"Maybe not." Father Murphy tipped his head and fingered a corner of the résumé. "We're helping people in need. You were fighting people bent on destroying everything we believe in. Different day-to-day objectives, but the same ultimate goal of making the world a better place."

"It's a moral dilemma of the first magnitude, because at its core Christianity is a faith of peace." Reverend Baker's tone was sober. "But philosophy and practicality can sometimes collide. I believe every possible measure should be employed to solve differences before implementing the use of force, but based on everything I've heard and read, militants and terrorists can't be stopped by anything else."

"That's true—and I can speak from firsthand experience." Steven folded his hands on the empty folder. "What I'm hearing you say is that my military background may not be a disqualifier."

"I believe that's a fair assessment." The priest glanced at Reverend Baker, who dipped his chin in assent.

"In that case . . . let me move on to the other potential stumbling block. This one relates to my personal life."

Digging deep for courage, he stared at the black folder in front of him and shared his story with these two men of God.

When he finished, there was silence in the room.

As the seconds ticked by, he forced himself to look up.

Neither man appeared shocked—but both wore serious expressions.

Reverend Baker spoke first. "I can understand your angst over the decisions you made—and I'm picking up a sense of deep regret and repentance."

"Not a day has gone by in the past four years that I haven't wished for a second chance to make things right." His voice rasped, and he cleared his throat.

"Have you spoken with the Lord about this? Sought forgiveness?"

"No. It seems too much to ask. To be honest, I don't feel worthy of forgiveness."

"None of us are. God doesn't forgive because we're worthy, but because he loves us. And no sin is too great to be absolved—if contrition is sincere. It all begins with an earnest 'I'm sorry.' Wouldn't you agree, Kevin?"

"Yes." While the priest's response was immediate, the furrows remained on his brow. "But I do see your concern about a possible conflict with Helping Hands, given the nature of some of the organization's work. Do you feel you could fully support all of our efforts?"

"I do. I have a slight issue with the opposition to capital punishment, which I believe is legitimate under certain circumstances, but I agree there are alternate methods to deal with dangerous offenders and I would be happy to promote those through the organization. Everything else I'm behind 100 percent."

"I agree with Reverend Baker that it would be wise to take your offenses and regret to God and ask forgiveness. Once you do that, the burden of guilt and remorse you've been carrying will lessen and you can go forward with a clean slate."

Steven shifted in his seat. One more hurdle to lay on the table. "Since Helping Hands is a faith-based initiative, you should also know that God and I haven't communicated much for a while—but I *have* returned to church." Not for the most noble reason, but being back in the Lord's house each Sunday was giving him an unexpected sense of homecoming and comfort.

"An excellent way to reconnect," Reverend Baker said. "And Kevin and I are both available if you ever want to discuss spiritual matters. In the meantime, why don't you give us a few days to review your résumé, think about your proposal, and discuss next steps?"

"That's fair." More than fair, in truth. They could have thrown him out on his ear.

The two clerics rose, and he shook their hands.

"We'll get back to you on this soon." Father Murphy indicated the résumé on the table in front of him.

"If you have any other questions, let me know. I realize there will have to be a formal interview process if you decide to proceed, but I didn't want to initiate that without giving you both my background."

"We appreciate that." Reverend Baker walked him to the door, closing it behind him as he exited.

Back on the street, Steven let out a long, shaky breath.

The meeting had gone smoother than he'd expected—and the two clerics had been more than cordial—but who knew what they were now discussing behind the closed door of the minister's office?

After careful consideration, they could both decide that a former sniper whose personal history was far from spotless wasn't worthy for inclusion on the short list of candidates for the Helping Hands job.

He wouldn't blame them.

So in the meantime, he needed to give serious consideration to other options for the rest of his life—and think about getting right with God.

Because until he did that, it wasn't likely he would ever find the peace of mind—and heart—that would allow him to leave the past behind and forge a new future.

Surfacing from the depths of a deep sleep, Cindy forced open her heavy eyelids. The drugged-like stupor she'd fallen into the instant her head had hit the pillow last night after her double shift at the café was hard to shake off.

So what had awakened her at—she squinted at the bedside clock—one thirty on this Tuesday morning?

She rolled toward Patrick's side of the bed.

Empty.

Her pulse lost its rhythm.

Lord, please let this not be a repeat of the evening Steven came to dinner, after Patrick swore off alcohol for the weekend! Please!

Swinging her legs to the floor, she tried to contain the panic threatening to shut down her lungs.

Fingers clenched at her sides, she padded down the hall toward the kitchen. Stopped in the doorway.

Patrick was standing at the dark window, his back to her—and there was a bottle on the table.

But it contained water, not scotch.

Thank you, God!

"Honey?" She spoke softly.

He swung around. "I'm sorry. Did I wake you?"

"No." She moved toward him, assessing his condition. Most of the withdrawal symptoms had subsided, but insomnia and headaches continued to plague him. "Bad night." It wasn't a question.

"Yeah."

She touched his arm. "Why didn't you wake me?"

"You were exhausted."

"Patrick." She cupped his face with her hands. "We're in this together, remember? If you want me to hold you at night, tell me. Don't try to get through the bad stuff alone."

"You need your sleep."

"I need you—healthy and alcohol-free—more."

"I've been too much of a burden as it is."

"Don't say that." She gave him her fiercest look. "Helping someone you love is never a burden—and I have as much to gain from this as you do."

He leaned a shoulder against the window frame, fine lines of fatigue radiating from the corners of his eyes. "I ought to be able to handle this on my own."

"You *are* handling it—but there's nothing wrong with leaning on people who care about you. It can make all the difference. How come you can see the importance of that for Pete, but not for yourself?"

"Our situations are night and day. He doesn't think he has anything to live for, or anyone in his corner. I know I've got the best support system around, plus a future to look forward to. That's what gets me through the days. I just don't want to cause you any more worry than I already have."

"Oh, honey." She slid her arms around his waist and laid her cheek against his chest. "Worry goes with the territory if you love someone. I worry more when you *don't* tell me what's going on." She leaned back to look up at him. "Finding you gone from our bed—and with a bottle in the kitchen—took ten years off my life."

"It's water."

"I realized that fast. But I wish you'd told me you were having a bad night. You don't have to face temptation alone. It's easier to resist if someone's got your back."

He pulled her close again and rested his chin on top of her head. "I'm not going to give in to the cravings, Cindy. I have too much to lose. I will *not* be my dad. I want to grow old with you and watch our kids marry and give us grandchildren." He tightened his grip. "I know it took a crisis for me to admit I have a problem with alcohol, but now that I have, booze isn't going to win. I'll beat this. I promise."

Her vision misted at the conviction in his voice. "I know you will. You've got the strength and fortitude to see this through—but even if you don't need me for pep talks or prodding, I can always hold your hand."

"At the very least." He gave her a weary wink and wove his fingers through hers. "Let's go to bed. You have to get some sleep."

"You'll stay this time?"

"Yeah."

She let him lead her back to their room, then cuddled up behind him in bed, holding tight to the man who'd won her heart long ago.

Life hadn't turned out to be quite the fairy tale she'd hoped—yet Patrick was a good man who loved her and tried his best. Yes, he had flaws. And yes, there would be struggles ahead.

But they'd tackle them together, plucking the weeds along the path of life like in the story Holly had related from Pete—and in the end they'd find their happy ending.

She wasn't settling for anything less.

Neither was Patrick, given what he'd said tonight.

And with prayer and love and commitment to sustain them, how could they fail?

21

He had to have another one of those tacos.

As Pete pulled into a parking space on the wharf, locked his car, and set off for the white truck near the park where the town was thinking about putting Patrick's cannon, the enticing aroma wafting toward him activated his salivary glands.

The Latino man behind the counter lifted a hand in greeting as he approached. "Morning, Pete."

His step faltered.

How did this guy know his name?

As if he could read minds, the man grinned and motioned him over. "Small towns have active grapevines that bear much fruit."

Oh.

That could explain it.

He continued toward the serving counter. "I'd like an order of tacos." He scanned the interior in search of a menu, but the sole printed sign bore just two words: cash only.

"Coming right up. I'm Charley, by the way." He pointed up, where his name was spelled out in colorful letters on the side of the truck, above the serving counter, and extended a hand.

"Nice to meet you." Pete spouted the standard line and returned his hearty grip.

"Likewise." The man opened a cooler, pulled out fish fillets, and set them on a grill.

"Um . . . is there a menu?"

Charley displayed his white teeth. "Yes. A new one every day. Cook's choice. Today I'm serving halibut with cilantro and my special seasoning and sauce. If you don't like the result, I offer a money-back guarantee. So how are you enjoying our little piece of paradise?"

"It seems to be a pleasant town."

"The people are special too." Charley pulled out several tortillas. "Your neighbor is new here, like you, but she falls into that category."

Pete squinted at him.

There was a rational explanation for how the man could have learned his first name—but why was the taco maker privy to his address?

Charley continued cooking and answered his unspoken question without missing a beat. "Holly mentioned you had tree problems. Ongoing issue here, with the wind. I'm glad Patrick's been lending a hand."

Good grief.

This man knew more than the local newspaper!

"Yes, he has."

"The Roarks are a wonderful family." Charley flipped the fish and sprinkled it with seasoning. "Salt of the earth."

"I agree."

"Have you met many other residents yet?"

"A few." If the clerks at the local market counted.

Charley angled toward Dockside Drive. "I see our clerics have a hankering for tacos today too."

Pete pivoted. Two clergymen involved in an animated discussion were approaching the stand.

He stifled a groan. Conversation hadn't been on his lunch menu.

"Have you met our local men of the cloth?"

At Charley's question, he shifted back toward the stand. "No."

"Fine gentlemen. I expect they're either haggling over Bible verses, discussing the finer points of golf—or debating the merits of a cannon in our park, like everyone else in town is." Charley chuckled. "You'll like them. Everyone does." He began to assemble the tacos.

Pete gauged Charley's progress.

Unfortunately, the order wasn't going to be ready fast enough to let him escape before the clergymen arrived.

He kept his back to the duo, though—until Charley greeted them and began making introductions.

Pasting on a smile, Pete faced them and went through the usual pleasantries as the clerics welcomed him to town.

"You two were in deep discussion as you approached." Charley added a dollop of sauce to each taco.

"I was questioning a strategy my friend here used to get out of a sand trap during our golf game last Thursday." The priest nodded toward his companion.

"It worked, didn't it?"

"Barely. I've seen better form in an eighty-year-old wielding a weed whip."

"Very funny." The minister straightened his collar. "Do you play golf, Pete?"

"Used to."

"We have superb courses in the area."

"Pete's new in town. It's not easy to meet golfing partners, and I don't imagine playing alone is much fun." Charley began wrapping the tacos in white paper.

"You should come with us tomorrow, play a round. We'll introduce you to the regulars. Right, Paul?" The priest tossed the conversational ball to the minister.

Whoa.

This was getting out of hand.

Before he could decline, the reverend jumped in. "Absolutely! You'll love the course."

"An inspired idea." Charley slid the tacos into a brown bag and set it on the counter.

Pete dug out his wallet. "Um . . . I wouldn't want to impose—and I don't walk long distances anymore."

"No imposition at all—and we ride, don't we, Kevin?"

"Yes. Thursday is homily-polishing day for me. Riding picks up the pace of the game and gets me back to my office faster."

"And he needs all the time he can get to whip those homilies into shape." The minister winked.

A chuckle bubbled up in Pete's throat—but he suppressed it. Getting to know Holly—and Patrick's family—was one thing. Getting chummy with the town clerics was another matter entirely.

"I appreciate the offer, but I'd slow you down on the course."

"No worse than Paul's putting." The priest gave the minister a good-natured elbow jab.

"I'd go if I were you, Pete." Charley leaned on the counter. "For the entertainment value, if nothing else." He grinned, but the compelling intensity in his dark eyes was persuasive.

Three against one wasn't fair.

Plus, the notion of getting out again on the links was suddenly all too tempting.

Change the subject, Pete.

"Um . . . how much do I owe you?" Near as he could tell, there weren't any prices posted on the taco stand either.

"First order for newcomers is on the house." Charley gave him a megawatt smile.

"Seriously?"

"A long-standing practice—and very commendable. Makes people feel welcome." Father Murphy gave Charley a thumbs-up. "So how about that golf game? We'll be happy to swing by and pick you up."

The three of them gave him an expectant look.

He crimped the top of the bag in his fingers.

If he said yes, he'd be creating more links in the community. Initiating new friendships.

If he said no, he could spend tomorrow alone—and lonely—on his patio . . . as he'd spent most of his days in Hope Harbor.

All at once, the latter prospect held zero appeal.

Maybe he wasn't long for this world—whether by choice, if he followed his original plan, or by letting nature take its course if he didn't—but why deprive himself of human contact for his remaining days?

"Thank you. I'd enjoy a game of golf."

"Wonderful!" The priest clapped him on the back.

Once they agreed on a pickup time, Charley went back to cooking. "What do you gents think about the prospect of that cannon in our waterside park?"

"I'm leaning against it," the minister said.

The priest stared at him. "You never told me that."

"I've been thinking about it. In Ezekiel, God instructed us to put away violence and destruction. And the Beatitudes are straightforward on the subject—blessed are the peacemakers."

"How is that inconsistent with a cannon in our park?"

The minister's eyebrows rose. "Isn't it obvious? Cannons wreak violence and destruction."

"They can also be used to *stop* violence and destruction—and to usher in peace. Think about Paul's letter to the Romans. He's clear that God empowers governments to bring wrath on those who do evil."

"But do we want a reminder of violence in our peaceful town park?"

The padre turned toward him. "What do you think, Pete?"

If he got into the middle of a theological argument, he was sure to lose.

"I think there's a certain amount of merit in reminders from the past. As Winston Churchill said, if we don't learn from history, we're doomed to repeat it—though I believe he borrowed that thought from someone else. Also, many battles have been fought for honorable reasons. A cannon can symbolize war and destruction—or the noble sacrifices made by those who fight for peace and freedom. Viewer's choice."

"Well said." Charley saluted with his spatula.

The perfect exit cue.

"I'll see you two tomorrow. Thanks again, Charley." He gave the bag a small shake.

"My pleasure. Enjoy."

The debate behind him faded away as he ambled toward his car, surveying the planters spaced along the sidewalk that followed the curving wharf. Beside them, flowers in nursery containers were waiting to be placed in their new home. Two gray-haired women in jeans had already filled the first planter and moved on to the second. Garden club volunteers, perhaps?

He studied the flowers. They were using impatiens . . . lobelia . . . pansies. There could be nasturtiums in the mix too.

Hmm.

Those planters would benefit from height variation in the flowers. A few spikes here and there would add visual interest, and it wouldn't hurt to—

Pete huffed and picked up his pace.

Conversing with his neighbor, going to dinner at Patrick's house, and playing one game of golf was more than sufficient social interaction. There was no reason to add gardening with the local club to his activity list—even if his fingers suddenly itched to sketch the ideal composition for those waterfront planters.

What he should do was go home and enjoy the tacos that were emitting a mouth-watering aroma.

And he would *not* think about gardening.

Even if he did allow himself one last peek at the planters over his shoulder as he slid behind the wheel of his car.

The high school gym, where the town had decided to hold the cannon meeting, was packed.

From her position inside the back door, Holly paused and took a fortifying breath. Hard to believe she'd launched all this furor with a simple comment at Charley's taco stand.

Thank heaven she'd refused Pete's offer of a ride. She might want to hightail it out of here fast if the mood became nasty.

"Hi, Holly!"

At the cheery greeting, she swung around. Marci waved and bounded over, a camera slung around her neck, notebook in hand. "Amazing turnout, isn't it?"

"Yes."

"I've never seen the town this riled up—except when the lighthouse was in danger. But at least we were all on the same side with that one. I can't believe an antique cannon generated such passion." She motioned toward the front. "We've got news coverage from Coos Bay *and* Portland. This could go into a national feed."

Holly inspected the dais that had been set up for the event. TV crews were stationed on each side.

How in the world had this gotten so out of hand?

"It must be a slow news day."

"Nah. Small-town stories have human interest appeal—especially if citizens are on opposing sides of an issue. I wish we could have gotten this kind of coverage during the lighthouse crusade." She leaned sideways and peered through the crowd. "I want to talk to Patrick before the news crews descend. And be prepared—they have your name from the *Herald* story. I'm betting they'll try to get you on camera."

With that, Marci plunged into the crowd.

Holly eyed the door, fighting back a wave of panic. She did *not* want to go on camera about the cannon—or any other subject.

Low profile was her middle name. She'd drawn enough attention during her younger years to last a lifetime, thanks to her SB—a sizable amount of it unpleasant. Curious stares, pitying glances, the cruel sort of teasing common among children. No wonder she'd become an introvert.

She may have learned to tame her shyness and put up a self-confident front as she'd matured, but she was much more comfortable with her first-graders than she'd ever be in a crowd of adults like this.

And the very thought of being thrust into the spotlight of a TV camera knotted her stomach.

For an instant, she toyed with the idea of bolting.

But that would be spineless. She'd started this. She should be here for the finish.

That did not, however, mean she had to call attention to herself. She could sit—okay, hide—in one of the last rows and leave as soon as the meeting was over.

She claimed a seat in a far corner, slouched down, and buried her face in her cell until Brent called the meeting to order at seven o'clock on the dot.

Once all the attention was focused on him and the chatter in the crowd subsided, she straightened up.

The city manager didn't waste time. He gave a brief background on the discovery of the cannon, the anonymous offer for restoration—and the stipulations it entailed—and introduced Patrick.

Although Steven's brother seemed tense at first, his passion for the subject soon dispelled his nerves. As Cindy had predicted, he had the audience mesmerized in a matter of minutes by both his captivating delivery and the compelling images in his PowerPoint presentation.

For the next twenty minutes, every eye was riveted on him—as they should be. His command of the subject was impressive, and without ever directly appealing to the audience to support his position, he built a convincing case for displaying the cannon in the town park.

And he pulled it all together in his conclusion.

"I want to thank all of you for coming out tonight to hear about my great-great-great-grandfather. Whatever your position on the cannon, I hope you can appreciate the service he gave to his country on the USS *Shark* and as the keeper of our beloved lighthouse. While his early days as a sailor involved conflict, at heart he was a peace-loving man. The merchant ship he purchased did have two cannons—but they were never fired under his watch. Yet he understood that battle was necessary on occasion."

The image on the screen changed from the shot of Jedediah on board his ship to a photo of old, faded writing, penned in the elaborate script of a bygone era.

"This is a page from his journal, written near the end of his life. I know it's difficult to read, so let me translate it for you. 'As I look back, I am most proud of my service in the navy aboard the USS *Shark*. She was built for a noble purpose—to suppress slave traders and pirates. While force was sometimes necessary to fulfill that mission, I believe it was justified. I will never forget the slave ships we encountered, where men were crammed into airless compartments and treated worse than animals. I am honored to have played a small role in disrupting such a dreadful business and stopping those atrocities. I have always believed the fight we waged on behalf of human dignity vindicated the loss of life it entailed—but as my days on this earth wind down, I leave that final judgment to God.'"

The screen went dark, and Patrick regarded the audience. "I hope the town will put the cannon in a place of honor as a symbol of Jedediah's contribution to our country's history—but if that doesn't happen, it will have a place of honor on our property, and anyone who would like to see it is always welcome to stop by. Thank you all for your interest and attention."

As Patrick stepped back and Brent returned to the platform, the audience erupted in applause.

Holly joined in.

It was difficult to judge how many hearts Patrick had touched tonight with the tale of his long-ago relative—but he'd touched hers.

And changed her mind.

After listening to the story of a navy sailor who'd disliked violence but had nevertheless fought in fierce battles to stop the slave trade . . . who'd owned a merchant ship equipped with cannons he'd never used . . . who'd lived out his days tending a lighthouse in a bucolic, serene setting . . . how could she not see the cannon in a different light?

Not as a symbol of oppression and death, but of freedom and life.

It was a two-edged sword, yes. Weapons could be used for good—or for evil.

But sometimes, they were the only way to *fight* evil—as Steven had said when he'd talked about the battle against extremists in the Middle East. Force was the one language they understood.

The applause continued, and she looked toward the front row, where Steven sat with Cindy and Jonah. Nothing but the back of his head was visible, but he had to be proud of the well-deserved ovation Patrick was receiving for his stellar presentation.

As the clapping at last subsided, Brent took center stage. "The meeting is now open to comments and questions. We have a mic set up in the center aisle, so please come forward, state your name, and let us hear from you."

Several people rose as the TV cameras swiveled around to capture their comments.

All of those who came forward commended Patrick on his presentation, but a few still expressed misgivings about having a cannon in the park—even after Brent reminded everyone it would be put in context with an accompanying plaque honoring Jedediah.

When one of the naysayers referenced her anti-cannon piece in the *Herald* and praised her rationale, Holly cringed and sank lower in her seat.

Her reasoning may have been sound in the abstract—but she hadn't been privy to the extenuating circumstances in this particular situation.

She slid lower after a second person referenced her write-up.

Well, crud.

Who'd have thought the paltry few paragraphs she'd penned would be that influential?

She peeked at the cameras, all trained on the current speaker, recording every syllable.

If anyone else got up to state their disapproval, momentum could build and the negative tide could swell.

Unless she, the instigator, stood up behind that mic and did some damage control.

A wave of nausea rolled through her.

Impossible.

No way could she put herself in the spotlight in front of a crowd of people *and* news cameras.

But if you've changed your mind about the cannon, you should let everyone know, Holly. That's the ethical course of action.

At the nudge from her conscience, she squirmed.

Yeah, it was.

Except it would thrust her galaxies beyond her comfort level.

"We'll take two more comments or questions and call it a night."

As Brent made that announcement, another resident approached the mic. Someone else could do the same at any moment—and who knew what side they'd be on?

It was now or never.

Cobbling together every scrap of her courage, Holly forced herself to stand and walk to the center aisle.

All attention was directed toward the mic, and from the front, Steven's gaze caught hers.

Surprise . . . admiration . . . perhaps even a touch of tenderness? . . . flashed across his face before the bright lights from the TV cameras blinded her.

She tuned out the current speaker as she tried to compose an articulate statement—but all too fast he moved aside and it was her turn.

There was nothing to do but wing it . . . and pray God gave her eloquence.

She introduced herself, doing her best to ignore the murmur that ran through the crowd.

"Several people tonight have referenced the negative piece I wrote for the *Herald* about displaying the cannon in our park—or anywhere in Hope Harbor." Her words quivered, and she swallowed. Took a deep breath. *Hold it together, Holly. You can do this.* "I want to state publicly that after hearing Patrick Roark's presentation tonight, I've changed my mind." More whispering in the assembly. "While I will never be in favor of glorifying war or violence, I do support honoring those who fight oppression and terror and evil. Jedediah Roark did that—and as long as the plaque gives him credit for that, I think the cannon is worthy of public display."

Flashbulbs went off, and she blinked. Backed away from the mic.

A shout of "Hear, Hear!" from a voice that sounded a lot like Eleanor Cooper's rang through the gym as she returned to her seat, praying her shaky legs wouldn't collapse.

Brent took over again as she dropped into her chair. "I'd like to get a show of hands on this issue to help me determine whether we should draft a referendum for a vote. All those in favor of accepting the donation we've been offered for restoration and putting the cannon on public display, please raise your hand."

Holly lifted her hand and gave the room a sweep. Near as she could tell, the response was overwhelmingly in favor of proceeding.

Her impression was confirmed when Brent called for nays. At best, a dozen hands out of the crowd of two or three hundred people went up.

"I'd say that's definitive." Brent smiled at the group. "Thank you all for coming. This meeting is adjourned."

As Holly stood, one of the reporters in front pointed to her, motioned to the camera crew, and began weaving through the crowd in her direction.

Uh-oh.

Unless she wanted to have those blinding lights aimed her direction again, she had to get out of here.

Pronto.

However . . . plowing through the throng in the back that was in no apparent hurry to depart felt like swimming through molasses.

As the dogged reporter bore down on her, making faster progress through the crowd than her quarry, Holly braced. Given the woman's determined expression, she wasn't going to be satisfied with a no-comment answer.

So barring a split in the horde in front of her that mimicked the Red Sea parting for the Israelites, she was going to be back in the media spotlight again before this night ended.

22

The news crew was descending on Holly—and despite her frantic attempt to escape through the crowd, she was getting nowhere.

"I have to go." Steven tossed the comment to Cindy as he struck out toward the back of the gym. "Tell Patrick I'll call him later."

His sister-in-law grabbed his arm. "Hey! We all came together, remember? Aren't you riding home with us?"

Gritting his teeth, he bit back a term she wouldn't appreciate.

He should have followed his first inclination and driven his own car—except Patrick had needed all the moral support he could get, right up to the moment of his introduction.

After that, he'd been fine.

More than fine.

The kid really knew his stuff—and even for someone who found most history dull and boring, Patrick had brought the story of Jedediah alive.

His brother ought to have a road show.

And he sure didn't need him now, while he held court with the media and the Hope Harbor residents who were swarming him. He was handling all the attention like a pro.

That wasn't how it would play out with Holly if the TV crew

got to her before she could escape. Not after her admission that she struggled with shyness and avoided being in the limelight.

Which made her willingness to stand up in front of the town tonight and acknowledge she'd been wrong about the cannon that much more incredible.

But she didn't have to subject herself to further scrutiny.

His mission was clear: intercept and deflect.

"Earth to Steven." Cindy gave his arm a slight shake. "Aren't you riding home with us?"

"I don't know. If I'm not here when you're ready to leave, I'll find other transportation." He tracked the progress of the news crew. They were gaining on Holly. "I have to go."

Cindy followed his line of sight—and loosened her grip. "Ah. I get it now. But . . . Patrick told me you weren't interested in pursuing her."

He spared Cindy an annoyed glance. "I'm not. This isn't a date."

"Uh-huh." Her smug expression said she wasn't buying his denial.

Whatever.

He tugged his arm free and took off at a jog. "Don't wait around for me."

"We won't. *Our* business for the evening is finished."

He ignored the implication.

All that mattered was getting Holly out of hostile territory.

Despite his excellent maneuvering skills, trying to fight upstream against the crowd surging toward Patrick was a challenge. Plus, he was working from a disadvantage. The reporter and her crew had a significant lead.

By the time he reached Holly, the newswoman had thrust a microphone in front of her and was rattling off questions about stirring up a hornet's nest with her piece in the *Herald*.

Holly's gaze connected with his.

It didn't take a Delta Force operator trained to analyze body language and facial nuances to recognize her plea for help.

If, however, he happened to be reading her wrong and she got mad at him for stepping in, he'd deal with it later. It wasn't as if they had a relationship to damage.

Unfortunately.

"I don't believe the lady has any comment." He wedged himself between the reporter and Holly, shielding her from the glare of the spotlight on the minicam.

The woman did a double take at the intrusion . . . then narrowed her eyes as she scrutinized him. "You're the brother. One of the owners of the cannon."

"Patrick's the historian in the family."

"You were in the army. A military man." She shoved the mic in his face. "How do you feel about all the opposition to the cannon being put on public display?"

She'd done her homework if she knew his background—and her ability to switch directions after encountering a roadblock was a useful skill in her line of work.

But she wasn't going to get anywhere with him either.

"The opposition appears to have melted away." He pushed the mic aside and took Holly's arm. "If you'll excuse us, we have another commitment."

He shouldered past the crew, keeping Holly close. The reporter followed for a few steps, tossing out more questions—all of which he ignored.

Not until they exited the building did he pause. "Where did you park?"

"There—near the end." She motioned toward the far side of the packed lot, now beginning to thin.

"I'll walk you over."

Holly scanned the milling crowd behind her. "I don't think you have to bother. She seems to have given up."

Not necessarily.

But with the imminent threat contained, it might be best to ease back on the heavy-handed tactics.

"Reporters can be persistent." He switched to a conversational tone. "Unless you want to risk another encounter, you may want to let me go with you."

She caught her lower lip between her teeth. "I suppose it couldn't hurt. The lot isn't very well lit, and I'd hate for her to launch a sneak attack in the dark." She looked up at him. "Thank you for coming to my rescue, by the way. Talk about answered prayers. I was pleading for a miracle—and there you were."

He gave a mirthless laugh. "I'm no one's answer to a prayer—and no miracle."

"You were for me tonight."

"And here I was worried about offending you." He shoved his hands in his pockets and coaxed up the corners of his mouth. "Some women wouldn't appreciate that kind of take-charge approach."

"This was an emergency. A TV camera brings back all the bad feelings I had as a kid who drew unwanted attention wherever she went."

"Which makes your public statement tonight all the more remarkable."

She shrugged. "It was the right thing to do. I formed an opinion without complete information, and that was a mistake. You can't make sound choices if you're in the dark." She resettled the strap of her purse on her shoulder. Moistened her lips. "Speaking of that . . . I'm glad we have this chance to talk tonight, despite the circumstances. I've been thinking about what Patrick told me in terms of your job in the military. You knew he'd shared that, didn't you?"

"Spilled is more like it—but yes. He admitted the slip."

"Well . . . I wanted to tell you that I understand why the military believes your job has to be done—and I appreciate the mental and emotional toughness required to deal with that kind of traumatic assignment."

There was no condemnation—nor a hint of censure—in her tone.

Not what he'd expected.

A departing group jostled him, and he took her arm again. "Let's get out of the traffic."

He led her toward her car in silence, trying to absorb this new development.

Despite her pro-life stance, Holly not only accepted what he'd done as a sniper, but recognized the justification for it . . . and the toll those missions took.

That was more or less the same response he'd gotten from the clerics.

And it raised a vital question.

If Holly could reconcile that part of his past with her pro-life beliefs, was it possible she'd also be able to live with the other mistakes that continued to haunt him?

The ones he would never try to defend, as he would always defend his sniper duties?

The ones that had tarnished his soul so badly he was still unsure he could ask God for forgiveness, despite the encouragement of the minister and priest?

If she could . . . if she was somehow able to look past that black mark on his soul . . . might they have a chance at a relationship?

Hope surged within him despite his fierce attempt to contain it.

"I'm over there." Holly pointed toward her Civic and hit the autolock button on her keychain.

He walked with her to the door—but it was too soon to let her go. She'd suggested miracles were in the air this night, and he wanted his chance at a share of them.

"I'd invite you for coffee to continue this conversation, but the Perfect Blend is closed." He called up a smile, hoping the dim light hid the strain beneath it. "Besides, I don't have wheels. I rode here with Patrick." If she was willing to extend the evening, he'd come up with another location . . . and see where their conversation led. But he'd let her make that call rather than push.

Holly responded without one iota of hesitation. "I can take you home."

He was just as quick on the uptake. "That works." He opened her door for her. After she was behind the wheel, he circled the car and slid into the passenger's seat.

Now what?

They could drive up toward Bandon and stop for a pizza at Frank's if she was hungry—a distinct possibility. With tonight's meeting looming, she may have been too nervous to eat much dinner.

But that could be a bad idea.

If he decided to tell her his other secrets—and her reaction was as negative as he feared—the drive home could be very, very awkward.

"Do you want to go directly to your apartment?" She twisted the key in the ignition and put the car in gear.

No. Why rush back to those empty, lonely rooms?

Yet it was smarter to have the discussion closer to his place. That would save them an uncomfortable drive if what she heard turned her stomach . . . and turned her against him . . . and she wanted to escape fast.

"Yeah. I have a full charter tomorrow, and we're already getting past my bedtime. I never minded the early hours or long, sleepless stretches overseas, but these days they bother me."

"I can relate to wanting a full night's sleep." Yet there was no missing the disappointment in her inflection.

A positive sign.

"If you're game, though, I could show you the nighttime view of Starfish Pier from the dunes at the end of the road. On a clear night like this, with a full moon, it's beautiful. And we could continue our conversation away from this crowd." He tacked on the last as he swept a hand over the parking lot and gym, lest she think he was angling for something more hands-on than a chat.

A romantic rendezvous was *not* on his agenda for this evening, despite Cindy's insinuation.

Much as he wished it was.

"I'd like that."

Somehow he managed to engage in small talk during the short drive, asking questions about her students, her parents, and her neighbor.

And a few minutes later, after they passed his apartment complex and reached the end of the road, Holly appeared to be far less stressed than she had been at the gym.

That made one of them.

For as she set the brake and he slid out of the car to get her door, a high-stakes decision loomed.

Tell her his story and hope she reacted as the clerics had—or close up like the anemones they'd seen on their last visit here and protect his heart from the very real possibility of rejection?

This could be it.

While she waited for Steven to open her door, Holly filled her lungs.

Her anxiety over the close encounter with the TV world was waning, but her nerves were kicking in about what could transpire in the next few minutes.

In view of the fact that Steven had seemed surprised . . . and relieved . . . after she'd told him her feelings about his sniper job—then invited her to continue that conversation—had her reaction given him the comfort level he needed to risk sharing his other secrets?

And what could she do to give that comfort level a boost?

No.

Back up.

The real question was *should* she try to give his comfort level a boost?

What if he opened up, led her down what would likely be a scary road—and it ended up being a dead end? Whatever skeletons he had in his closet could turn out to be unacceptable.

But unless they took that leap, there was no chance of a relationship anyway.

Her door opened, and Steven extended a hand.

Go for it, Holly. You have nothing to lose.

Shoring up her courage, she placed her fingers in his. His grip tightened as he helped her out of the car, his touch sure, strong—and gentle.

Kind of like the man himself, once you got past the tough exterior.

"I have a blanket in the trunk, if you want to bring that along. Otherwise, we'll take part of the beach home with us." She tried for nonchalance—no easy feat with a hammering pulse.

"I like a woman who's prepared. Let me grab it."

She pushed the trunk release, and he retrieved the blanket.

As he rejoined her, he took her arm again. "How's the wrist?"

"Almost back to normal."

"Are you certain you're up to scaling a dune?"

"As long as I have a strong arm to hang on to."

One side of his mouth hitched up. "Then let's do this."

With a serious assist from him, she scaled the small mound of sand—and once on top, she let out a soft *oh*.

From her patio at the house, the partial view of the sea and sky at night was beautiful—but here, on a height, the expanse of star-sprinkled heavens and shimmering water was vast and unobstructed. The full moon illuminated the beach and bathed the curling waves in silver, while the exposed rocks in the tide pools glistened in the lunar glow.

It was magical.

Best of all, they had the place to themselves.

If this location wasn't conducive to the sharing of confidences, nowhere on earth would be.

"You weren't kidding. This is spectacular."

He spread the blanket on top of the dune, helped her down, and sat beside her, keeping a respectable distance between them as he drew up his legs and linked his fingers around his knees. "I come down here once in a while at night if I don't have a charter the next morning. The immensity of the scene helps restore my perspective. Reminds me that despite any gnarly problems I happen to be wrestling with, in the giant cosmos of creation they're paltry—and we're all nothing but microscopic specks."

"Yet God calls each of us by name and loves us as sons and daughters."

"That's a hard concept to grasp."

"I know. Trying to understand the mystery of God is like digging a hole on the beach and attempting to transfer the sea into it, bucket by bucket. It's never going to happen. That's why trust is integral to faith. And really—would a God that the finite human mind was capable of fully understanding be worthy of worship? That would put him at our level, and he's so much bigger than that."

"I never thought of it that way."

"I heard a sermon on the topic once, and the rationale stuck with me. I pull it out often when I'm struggling to understand how particular events make sense from a divine perspective. They always do—but we may not be privy to God's reasoning. We just have to trust . . . and accept . . . they happen for a purpose." She hesitated. Braced. Might as well put the topic he'd broached in the parking lot back on the table. "Like, for example, a pro-life woman meeting a man who appeals to her, only to discover he was a sniper."

He angled toward her. "I appreciate what you said back there, about how you've come to view my job in The Unit. I didn't know if you'd be able to accept what I did."

"I didn't either." If ever there was a time for honesty, this was it. "Had someone told me a few weeks ago I'd make peace with that, I doubt I would have believed them. But having a face and a personality to go with a situation can give it a whole different slant. I always assumed a sniper would be an emotionless, cold, detached machine—but that's not you."

"It's part of me. And that description pretty much nails me during a mission. You have to have those qualities to do that job."

"It's not *all* of you, though. There's much more below the surface. You care about your brother and his family. You contribute to charitable causes—both money and sweat. I've watched you interact with your niece and nephew, seen your kindness and gentleness. It's a dichotomy—like you're two different people—but I'm learning everyone has many layers . . . and one or two don't define us." A chilly breeze swept past, and she buttoned her jacket, suppressing a shiver.

"Cold?"

"No." That was a lie—but cutting short this rare chance to talk to Steven one-on-one would be crazy.

Without missing a beat, he slipped out of his own jacket and draped it around her shoulders.

"I can't take this." She tried to shrug it off. "You'll freeze."

He held it firmly in place. "Believe me, I'm not in the least cold—and I've been in conditions far more frigid than this with less to keep me warm. I don't want the weather to interrupt this conversation."

They were tracking the same direction.

Maybe it was time to broach the subject of his other secrets.

Snuggling deeper into the jacket infused with his body heat, she tried to psyche herself up to take the plunge. After all, a shy woman who hated the limelight yet found the courage to stand up in front of a crowd—and TV cameras—ought to be able to talk to one person.

But this was harder in many respects than what she'd done earlier, given that the outcome of this conversation had a bearing on her entire future.

As her mom had always told her whenever a new surgery was imminent, though, the only way to secure a better future was to tackle the hard stuff in the present.

That was as true on an interpersonal level as it had been for her physical challenges through the years.

A stray, passing cloud covered the moon, casting a black shroud over the scene—and under the cover of darkness, she broached the subject he'd been avoiding for weeks.

"Steven—can I ask you a question?"

Beside her, she could feel him tense. "I guess."

"You said once that if you were in the market for a relationship, I'd be at the top of your list. I thought you were pushing me away because you were grieving over your wife—but I have a feeling it's more than that."

Only the muted thunder of waves crashing against the jagged offshore rocks broke the silence as she held her breath.

Finally he responded. "That's not a question."

And that wasn't an answer.

"You know what I'm asking."

"Yeah. I do." He exhaled and scooped up a handful of sand. Let it sift through his fingers. "Your intuition is correct. It's more than that." Lifting his head, he surveyed the horizon, giving her a view of his strong, shadowed profile etched against the dark water. "I haven't told anyone else this yet, but I met with Reverend Baker and Father Murphy a few days ago to let them know I'm interested in the director position at Helping Hands. At their request, I also talked with Michael Hunter."

At the non sequitur, she frowned. "I don't . . . how is that relevant to our discussion?"

"I was worried my history could be a deterrent for that job—like it could be a deterrent for us."

"How did they react?"

"They were more open-minded than I expected. They're considering my application."

"And you don't think I'd be willing to do the same—for a different, more personal position?"

"Given who you are, and your own history—I'm not certain."

His response was slow and deliberate, as if he'd already given her question a great deal of thought.

"Then why don't you tell me and let me decide?"

He turned to her, and despite the dim light she could feel the intensity of his gaze. "You want the truth?"

"Yes."

"Because I'm afraid you'll bolt—and the possibility that you could disappear from my life scares me."

The air whooshed out of her lungs.

The man was laying it all out there. Exposing his deepest feelings. Putting his heart on the line.

Before she could formulate a response, he continued.

"From the instant I laid eyes on you, my world shifted. For years I was a loner, doing my job, wrestling with my private demons, living a solitary, isolated life. Meeting you made me want more. Chemistry may have ignited the spark, but as I've gotten to know you, that spark has flamed into a blaze I can't quench. When I'm not with you, I think about you. When I *am* with you, I want . . ." His voice hoarsened, and he raked his fingers through his hair.

As the silence lengthened, she touched his hand. "What do you want?" A husky whisper was all she could manage.

He dipped his chin. Stroked an unsteady finger across her knuckles, the caress whisper soft. "Too much."

Holly stopped breathing.

Waited.

But he didn't make the obvious next move.

If romance was in the cards for this evening, apparently she was going to have to initiate it.

Her pulse picked up.

Could she be so bold?

Should she be?

Maybe he was the wise one, thinking this through instead of taking a step that would lead them into new territory and forever change the landscape of their relationship. Maybe she should exercise restraint too. Maybe she'd live to regret it if she followed her heart and took the initiative.

Yet she wanted this as much as he did. Wanted a memory to hold forever if this ended up being a farewell kiss rather than the beginning of a grand romance.

As it very well could be, depending on what he was so afraid to share with her.

But if it was, at least she'd have this moment to remember—and savor.

Pushing aside her doubts, Holly slowly leaned toward him.

He didn't back away.

Instead, with a slight groan—and a sigh of surrender—he met her halfway and lowered his mouth to hers, his lips tender yet demanding. Gentle yet hungry. Giving as much as taking, both leading and following, seeming to know exactly what she wanted and how to please her.

Mercy.

This man knew how to kiss.

Major league.

As the embrace went on and on . . . as passion surged . . . she lost track of time.

Or maybe it stopped.

Hard to tell, when the world around you ceased to exist. When you were alone in a universe of your own, spinning through the firmament, propelled by a powerful surge of emotion as impossible to stop as the tide.

Until all at once Steven wrenched free and spoke ragged words that brought her crashing back to earth in a hard landing.

"I'm sorry, Holly. That was a mistake."

23

Talk about a colossal tactical error.

As shock, dismay, and embarrassment chased away the tender warmth that had softened Holly's features, Steven's gut clenched.

Great way to win a lady's heart, Roark. Why don't you throw in a few other insults while you're at it—or kick her in the teeth?

Holly's breath hitched, and she started to pull back.

He gripped her shoulders. "Wait. Let me rephrase that." He chose his words more carefully this go-round. "The kiss wasn't a mistake—but it was premature. I told myself I wouldn't do that until . . . or unless . . . you gave me a green light after you were fully briefed on my background. Somehow my emotions overpowered my self-discipline—a rare occurrence that speaks volumes about the strength of your appeal. As for the kiss . . . if you want a repeat performance later, I'm all in."

Beneath his fingers, the tension in her shoulders diminished. "Thanks for clarifying. I was afraid my kissing wasn't up to your standards. I haven't had all that much practice."

The knot in his stomach loosened. She wasn't going to hold his stupid comment against him.

He could only hope she'd be as generous as the next few minutes unfolded.

"Then you have incredible natural ability." He released her and repositioned himself to get an optimal view of her reactions. Body language was often more telling than verbal cues. The darkness hid subtle details, but there was sufficient luminous light to reveal clues that would help him gauge her reaction to his story.

A reaction that could very well be negative.

It was possible the glow in her eyes, generated by far more than reflected moonlight, would vanish—and he had to be prepared for that.

But what was he going to do if she walked away forever?

His stomach bottomed out.

Reconnecting with Patrick and his family had eased his loneliness, but that didn't take the place of a family of his own. Or of Holly—and the bright future he could envision with her.

A surge of panic swept over him, as powerful and relentless as a riptide.

What if—

"Steven." She rested a hand on his knee. "Just tell me."

He reined in his turbulent emotions.

Yeah.

That's what he needed to do.

Playing out what-if scenarios had been helpful in The Unit, but his life wasn't in danger here. Only his heart.

And unlike combat situations, where decisions had to be immediate, he'd have time to develop a survival plan after the fact if his worst fears came to fruition.

"My story isn't pretty."

"I didn't think it would be."

"It may not be one you can live with." No sense dancing around the danger.

"I'm aware of that. But I learned long ago during my surgical cycles that delaying the inevitable is useless—and can sometimes make matters worse. If there's hard stuff to deal with, it's better to get it over with . . . and hope the outcome is positive. If it's not—you pick yourself up and move on."

"An admirable philosophy."

"Developed in the school of hard knocks." She offered him the flicker of a smile.

"I know." While Holly's life had been far more sheltered than his, she'd endured her share of trials—and they'd forged a strong spirit. She was a survivor, like he was. She'd be able to handle what he had to tell her.

Perhaps with more grit and grace than he would handle her reaction, if this went south.

"The floor . . . or the dune . . . is yours." She gave him her full attention.

Steven gripped the edge of the blanket and filled his lungs with the briny air. "I've only told this story to three people—and even they don't know all the details. I'd ask that you keep this confidential."

"That goes without saying. And thank you in advance for trusting me with such personal information." Warmth infused her voice.

He acknowledged her comment with a dip of his head. "I told you my wife died four years ago—but I never told you the circumstances. The story actually begins eleven months before her death . . . with a pregnancy neither of us expected."

Twin furrows appeared on Holly's brow—but she remained silent.

"It happened while I was home on a brief leave, after being deployed a few weeks into our marriage. When the leave ended, I went back to the Middle East—and two months later, I got the news in an email."

Somewhere in the distance, the mournful whistle of a train echoed in the night, and the coil of tension in Steven's stomach tightened. "This isn't . . . it's harder than I expected to spit this out." An apt description for how he felt about exorcising the vile truth.

"It doesn't have to be, if you let God walk with you and follow where he leads."

"Following isn't my style. I'm used to being in charge."

"Or thinking you are."

Her correction was gentle—but she had a point.

He took a mental step back. Recalibrated.

Okay, God, I'm acknowledging you're in control here. That you run the show. Please guide me through this confession.

"I'll keep that in mind." He plunged back in, forcing out the words. "I have to admit, I'd never given much thought to being a father. Not that I was opposed to it, but I always envisioned parenthood somewhere in the far distant future. My focus in those days was on my career. I'm ashamed to admit even Laura took second place to The Unit—and she realized that not long after we were married."

Confession number one was out.

He swallowed . . . and for a brief instant he had an inkling of how potent Patrick's cravings for alcohol could be. For the first time in four years, he longed for a stiff drink to soften the edges of his ragged emotions.

"You're doing fine." Holly touched his knee again, the warmth of her fingers seeping through his slacks, her encouragement propping up his faltering fortitude.

Keep going, Roark. You've defeated enemy insurgents in life-and-death battles. You can crush your fears and get through this.

He fisted his hands and continued.

"When I got Laura's email, I was shocked. We'd both agreed the timing wasn't ideal to start a family, and we'd taken precautions. As the doctor told her, however, no form of birth control is infallible except abstinence."

"How did she feel about the pregnancy?"

"She was stunned too, but after she got over the initial surprise, she was happy about it. Me—not so much. I figured I had seven months to get used to the idea, though, and that I'd come up with a plan to juggle a wife and family with my work in The Unit. Then, four weeks later, I got another email." He paused.

Holly waited a few seconds. "Something happened to the baby?"

"No. Not in the sense you mean. But a screening test during Laura's first trimester showed a marker for Down syndrome. A follow-up test confirmed that diagnosis. She was shattered and distraught. I was upset . . . and angry . . . and frustrated."

"I expect all of those were normal reactions." Holly's expression didn't change, but a slight note of caution had crept into her tone.

"Maybe. And being thousands of miles apart didn't help. We were each dealing with the crisis in isolation. I did tons of research on the condition, and most of what I read was discouraging—and scary." He braced for confession number two. "In the end, I concluded that given the demands of my job and my inability to provide much moral support in the immediate future, we should . . . terminate the pregnancy."

That was the phrase he'd used with Laura too. It sounded less callous than *kill the baby*.

But that's what abortion did—as the woman sitting inches away well knew. She could have become a statistic herself, given the abortion rate for children with spina bifida.

"Did your wife agree?" Holly's question was subdued, and her complexion had paled—unless the moonlight was playing tricks on him.

"Not at first—but I built a compelling case. Listed all the potential medical problems for children with Down syndrome. Told her this was the decision made by the vast majority of couples in our situation. Painted a dismal picture of how difficult it would be for her to cope with all the physical challenges our child would have. In the end, she caved under my pressure."

"Did you come home?"

"I offered to try and get a leave, but she said she'd handle it. And she did. The whole experience took a toll on her, though—and on us."

Holly didn't say anything.

She didn't have to.

Any decent man would have moved heaven and earth to be with his wife during such a traumatic experience.

Keep going, Roark. Get it all out there. Every last, ugly piece.

"I take full blame for the decision. I pushed Laura into it. I wish I could say my motives were noble, that I wanted to spare the child all the difficulties that condition can entail—but the truth is, I wanted to spare myself. It was a selfish decision, one born of fear and an unwillingness to be inconvenienced." He swallowed past the lump in his throat. "I know this doesn't change the past or undo the mistake, but if I was faced with the decision again, I'd make a different choice."

Only the waves crashing against the rocks filled the silence that stretched between them as he waited for her reaction.

At last Holly exhaled. "I didn't expect . . . this wasn't on my radar screen. I mean . . . I knew whatever you were keeping from me would be a challenge to deal with, but I didn't . . . I guess I never expected it to hit this close to home. It's a lot to process."

And he wasn't through yet.

If he was going to bare his soul, he had to put every transgression on the table so there were no dark secrets between them that could lead to conflict down the road.

He had to confess sin number three.

"There's more."

Her head jerked up, like a dazed boxer trying to prepare for the second of a one-two punch. "More?"

"Yeah. I told you, it's not a pretty story." He crossed his legs and gripped his knees. "After the abortion, I was relieved . . . but Laura was plagued by guilt. She began taking meds for depression. When I came home on leave, I began to worry she was becoming dependent on drugs to get her through the day—and guilt began to eat at *me* over what I'd more or less forced her to do."

"She could have refused."

Steven was tempted to agree to lessen his culpability—but that would be disingenuous.

"I'm not certain that's true, given all the pressure I put on her and the scare tactics I employed about what we—mostly she—would be facing with a Down syndrome baby."

"Did you think about leaving the service?"

"No. Another failure on my part—and another indication of my selfishness. All my life I'd wanted to be part of Delta Force, and I wasn't willing to give up that dream for the woman I loved or the child we created. I won't offer any excuses for my behavior. What I did was wrong, plain and simple."

"How long were you home on leave?"

"Three weeks. Not long enough. I did set up a meeting with a counselor for Laura, and I went with her to the first session. She promised she'd continue seeing the woman after I went back overseas."

"Did she?"

"No. I thought she was, but I found out later she stopped after four sessions." He swallowed. "One day I got called in to see my commanding officer. The chaplain was with him. I knew it was bad news—but it was far worse than I imagined. Laura had been found dead from a drug overdose."

Holly drew in a sharp breath—but didn't speak.

"Her death was ruled accidental, but I've never been convinced that was true, given her depression. The depression I caused." He blinked to clear away the moisture misting his vision. "So not only did I destroy our baby's life, I may also be responsible for my wife's death. I should have been there for her. Until the day I die, I'll regret those mistakes." His voice broke.

Steven tried to convince his lungs to continue inflating and deflating as he waited for Holly's verdict.

For almost thirty eternal seconds she looked out over the glimmering moonlit water at Starfish Pier. Her brain had to be in overdrive, trying to digest all he'd shared.

She confirmed his assumption when she finally spoke. "That's a ton of heavy stuff to absorb."

"I know."

He waited for her to offer some reassurance. An indication she might be able to accept this piece of his past as she'd accepted his role as a sniper.

It didn't come.

"I appreciate your willingness to share your story with me, especially since you know *my* story—and the principles I believe in."

"It wouldn't be fair to start a relationship without being up-front about possible impediments. Honesty is the only way to create a strong foundation." Even if the truth ended up being quicksand instead of bedrock.

"I appreciate that too. I . . . I need to think about everything you told me."

"I understand." He rose and held out his hand to help her up, suppressing the powerful urge to pull her back into his arms and beg her to give him a chance to prove he was worthy of her, to believe he'd learned from his mistakes and wasn't the same man he'd been four years ago.

She put her fingers in his and he drew her to her feet, tightening his grip as the sand shifted beneath her.

"Sorry. I'm a little unsteady."

Yeah, she would be—as much from his shocking story as from standing on unstable ground.

"I'll walk you down the dune."

He picked up the blanket, shook it out, and kept a firm grip on her arm as they negotiated the sloping surface.

Once they were on solid terrain, he released her, stowed the blanket—and kept his distance.

"Don't you want me to drop you at your apartment?" She held on to the edge of the car door. Tight. As if she was trying to steady herself.

"No. I'm going to stay here for a while."

"It will be a dark walk back to Sea Haven."

"In Delta Force, night was our friend. Besides, the moon's bright. I'll be fine."

She hesitated. "I'll call you, okay?"

"Please."

She touched her fingers to her lips, as if remembering the incredible kiss they'd shared less than half an hour ago. "I do care for you, Steven. I just . . . we're very different. Our histories are nothing alike. The life you've led is . . . it's worlds away from everything I know. It's a struggle to reconcile a lot of what you've done with everything I believe."

"I realize that."

She slipped off his jacket and held it out. "You'll need this on the dunes."

No, he wouldn't—though he took it from her anyway. A piece of cloth, no matter how insulated, wasn't going to be able to warm the cold place in his heart.

Holly slid behind the wheel, started the engine, executed a U-turn, and drove away.

Steven remained where he was until her taillights disappeared into the night, then turned and considered the dune as tendrils of fog began to drift past.

What was the point of staying here alone, with only the moon and the waves for company while fog rolled in? He could brood just as easily in the warmth of his apartment.

Shoving his arms into the sleeves of his jacket, he struck out through the thickening mist.

Soon the moon and stars would be obscured. In minutes it would be difficult to see the pavement. To find his way home.

The toe of his shoe hit a rock, and it skittered across the asphalt, disappearing into the shadows.

If he wasn't careful, he could wander off the road, become disoriented, get lost in the darkness.

Not a bad metaphor for his life, actually. He'd come close to doing that after Laura died. Again near the end of his tenure in The Unit.

Yet he'd managed to find his footing, continue on.

Surely he could do the same if Holly rejected him.

Couldn't he?

For a decisive, confident man who'd been bested by very few challenges, he suddenly wasn't at all certain he'd overcome this one.

But win or lose, he'd taken the high road tonight—even if the prospect of traveling it alone from here on out left him feeling as cold and desolate as the harsh, barren peaks of the Hindu Kush mountains he'd known all too well during his missions with The Unit in Afghanistan.

24

Give it up, Holly. It's going to be light in twenty minutes, and you have to get up in half an hour anyway. If you lie here, you'll just keep thinking about Steven.

Sighing, she threw back the covers, exchanged her pjs for a T-shirt and sweatpants, and padded toward the kitchen.

Too bad it wasn't Saturday. She could wander into town, pick up a latte at the Perfect Blend and a cinnamon roll at Sweet Dreams, and drown her sorrows in sugar and caffeine.

But the weekend was two days away, and her students were expecting their usual perky teacher in two hours.

Perky.

Ha.

That came nowhere near to describing her mood since her sojourn to the dunes with Steven Tuesday night after the town meeting.

Yawning, she plugged in her one-cup coffeemaker and went through the motions of brewing her caffeine infusion for the day. Tangling the sheets for two nights in a row while her body thrashed and images of the ex-soldier who'd bared his soul strobed through her mind had *not* been restful.

She owed Steven a follow-up call—and a decision about whether to move forward—but when had she had time to process everything he'd told her? Her students demanded every bit of her energy and attention during the day. Last night she'd attended a pro-life dinner auction committee meeting. In between, she'd had homework to grade and lessons to plan.

That's why carving out twenty minutes to sit on her patio this morning and give the situation her full, undivided attention while night turned to day was a priority.

She slipped on the pair of flats she kept by the door for forays into the yard, retrieved her fleece jacket from a hook on the wall . . . and drew in a long, slow breath.

After doing intensive research on military snipers, making peace with Steven's role in Delta Force hadn't been as problematic as she'd expected. The biggest difference between him and soldiers who killed in battle was that he'd had names to go with his targets—specific terrorist leaders whose elimination would help deescalate violence, stop atrocities, and save lives.

It was hard to condemn a man who took on a tough, soul-numbing job for the noble purpose of trying to make the world a safer, more peaceful place.

His latest revelation, however, had struck closer to home.

Maybe too close.

If her parents had felt as he had, she would never have been born.

She bunched the soft fabric in her fists. Leaned a shoulder against the wall.

Even factoring in his regrets, could a woman with her past and a man who'd lobbied to end the life of his own baby ever find a happily ever after?

Impossible to know with absolute certainty.

Meaning a relationship with him would require a leap of faith—and a boatload of trust.

Perhaps more than she could dredge up.

The light went off on the coffeemaker, and she removed her mug, added cream, and lifted the java to her nose. Inhaled.

The soothing scent didn't work its usual magic. Her emotions remained as turbulent as the waters off Hope Harbor on a stormy day.

Surviving one failed relationship had been traumatic—but given the strength of her feelings for Steven, if they got involved and the romance crashed and burned, the impact would be far more devastating.

As a headache began to form in her temples, she picked up a dish towel, slipped through the back door, and crossed the concrete pad to her small patio table. After wiping the mist off a chair, she sat facing the sea, mug in hand.

And discovered she wasn't the only early riser.

Pete was ensconced in his lounge chair, also angled toward the water—and lying still as death.

Her heart stuttered, and she shot back to her feet.

It was too dark to see his face or tell if his chest was rising and falling, but was it possible he'd—

"I haven't checked out yet, if that's what you're wondering."

At his wry comment, Holly grabbed the back of her chair to steady herself. "G-good morning."

"Morning. I like to come out here and watch the sky light up. Want to join me?"

No.

She wanted to think about her dilemma with Steven.

But there was no graceful way to decline.

Besides, in case Pete was having any negative thoughts in this predawn hour, companionship might help settle him.

"I could sit for a few minutes before I have to get ready for school."

She carefully traversed the damp grass and joined him, swiped the terry-cloth square over the chair next to the lounger, and sat. "I see you beat me to the coffee." She motioned with her cup toward the empty mug on the ground beside him.

"First thing every morning. A leisurely cup of coffee is one of life's small indulgences. A simple pleasure even lung cancer can't ruin."

The dark liquid in her cup sloshed at his unexpected candor, and she steadied the mug with both hands. "I . . . I didn't realize that was your diagnosis."

"I haven't shared it with many people. Patrick. You. The two clerics in town."

"You've been to church?" Her spirits perked up. Had the seed she'd planted taken root?

"No. I played golf with them last week."

Huh.

Probably not as helpful as church attendance . . . but God worked in all kinds of environments.

At least her prayers for Pete to connect with others in town seemed to be producing results.

As for his medical issues . . .

"I don't mean to pry, but may I ask if your condition is incurable—or did you just opt not to have further treatments?"

"You and Patrick think alike."

"You've discussed your prognosis with him?"

"Not in any detail—but he's encouraged me to continue the fight . . . and offered the support of his family no matter what I decide. The town clerics did too—although all I told them was that I was pondering my options. I didn't mention the paperwork you saw in my kitchen."

"You know you can call on me too, if I can help with anything. I'm no stranger to medical problems myself." Since he'd shared part of his story with her, she gave him the condensed version of hers.

"I suspected you had some condition like that. But your health issues aren't imminently life-threatening, and you have a strong support system. Including, I suspect, Patrick's brother."

Her jaw dropped.

How had he managed to maneuver around to *that* subject?

And how did he know she and Steven had become close?

A faint hint of pink unfurled on the far horizon, and she focused on that. "Um . . . why do you think that?"

He gave a soft chuckle. "I saw the two of you in the parking lot at the gym after the town meeting. Even from a distance, body language can be revealing. In case you haven't realized it yet, the man likes you. And vice versa."

She appraised him. Pete might be a new acquaintance—and his initial behavior had been off-putting—but now that she was getting to know him, he appeared to be a kind, insightful man.

Maybe the input of an impartial third party would be helpful in this situation—if she could solicit advice without breaching any confidences.

"We do like each other, but we have very different backgrounds . . . and histories."

"That can be problematic—or not."

She squinted at him. "What do you mean?"

"I'm thinking of a story Patrick told me about Jedediah—of cannon fame—and his wife."

"He didn't talk much about her in his presentation Tuesday, other than to mention they were married for more than forty years."

"I don't suppose romance was relevant to the topic under debate. Nor was the subject matter suitable for a family audience. But she and Jedediah had a rocky start."

"How so?"

"Before he met her, she was a . . . what's the genteel term? . . . a lady of the evening."

Holly stared at him. "Seriously?"

"Yes. Patrick found a number of the notes they sent each other while they were courting—or I should say, while Jedediah was trying to convince her to *let* him court her—and they're pretty definitive. She'd left that life behind but felt it had tainted her forever and made her unsuitable to be the wife of a successful shipping merchant who was also a man of impeccable integrity."

"She obviously changed her mind. Any idea why?"

"Patrick showed me the letter he's convinced persuaded her. Jedediah said her past was of no consequence. That if God could forgive her, he could too. All that mattered to him was the woman she was today—and the tomorrows he hoped they could share. It brought a tear to my eye, let me tell you."

"That's a beautiful sentiment." And food for thought.

"I agree. After all, if God is willing to give people a second chance, why should we do any less?"

A loud belch echoed in the stillness, and Holly looked toward the offshore rocks.

The silver-white harbor seal who often sunned himself there gazed at them with doleful eyes.

"Ah." Pete chuckled. "Casper's arrived. He comes most mornings."

Holly's lips twitched. "You've taken to naming the resident marine life?"

"Nope. I mentioned the seal to Charley on my last taco run, and he told me his name."

That sounded like the town's artist. Given his acquaintance with Floyd and Gladys, the man didn't limit his friendships to the human species.

She glanced at her watch, finished off the last of her coffee, and stood. "I have to get to school."

"Tell Jonah I said hi."

"I'll do that. See you later."

Pete lifted a hand in farewell and went back to watching Casper's antics.

As she crossed the damp grass, she scanned the heavens. It appeared they were in for fine weather today. The sky was turning blue, and soon the sun would rise above the hills and dispel the last of the mist, allowing for a clear view far into the distance.

That's what she needed too—a clear view of what lay ahead so she'd know how to proceed.

Sadly, that wasn't as simple as the sun sweeping away the fog. No one could predict the future.

But Pete's story about Jedediah and the woman he'd loved was worth mulling over as she pondered next steps.

Steven paused outside Reverend Baker's office, resettled his sport jacket on his shoulders, and adjusted his tie.

Not his usual wardrobe on a Thursday afternoon—or any day—but a job interview wasn't part of his normal routine either.

And why else would the minister have called yesterday and asked him to meet with Father Murphy, Michael Hunter, and himself? The three of them wouldn't waste their collective time if he wasn't under serious consideration for the director job. Any one of them could have phoned or texted him with a thanks but no thanks.

If a future with Holly wasn't to be—and given her silence since their impromptu visit to Starfish Pier Tuesday night, that seemed the logical conclusion—at least the Helping Hands job still appeared to be a possibility.

He lifted his hand and knocked on the door.

A few seconds later, Reverend Baker pulled it open. "Come in, Steven—and please excuse the casual attire. Our golf game ran long today, and Kevin and I didn't have a spare minute to change."

The golf-shirt-clad priest rose as he entered. "It ran long because I spent half the game waiting for my friend here to dig himself out of sand traps. How are you, Steven?" He extended his hand.

"Fine, thank you. Michael." He shook the third man's hand too.

After declining the minister's offer of a beverage, he claimed the seat at the table Michael indicated.

"We shouldn't be too long—and I apologize for not telling you dressing up wasn't necessary." Reverend Baker sat. "This isn't a job interview."

Steven's stomach dropped, but he did his best to maintain an impassive expression.

So much for his hopes that—

"What my colleague here is trying to say is that the job is yours if you want it." Father Murphy gave the minister an exasperated look. "You could have started with that, you know."

The two men indulged in good-natured banter for a moment, but Steven tuned it out as he digested the news.

They were offering him the job.

But also much, much more.

They were giving him a new beginning, in a career that would allow him to do worthwhile work that fed his soul.

While he might never be able to fully atone for all his mistakes, this was an opportunity to begin making amends.

"I think we've surprised him." Michael smiled his direction.

He refocused on the conversation. "Yes. I was concerned my background would work against me. The best I hoped for today was a chance to ace an interview and plead my case."

"The three of us met the day after you and I talked." Michael linked his fingers on the table in front of him. "After seeing you around town during the past year, hearing stories about the low-key behind-the-scenes assistance you've provided to residents in need, and reviewing your credentials, it didn't take me long to conclude you'd be an excellent fit for the organization."

"We felt the same," Father Murphy said. "We didn't see any reason to prolong the process or broaden the search. Of course we realize you may want to explore other options. Nonprofit jobs like this won't make you rich—in worldly goods. We've prepared salary and benefit information for you to review, and we'd be happy to reconvene in a few days after you've had an opportunity to think about it."

Reverend Baker slid a slim folder across the table toward him.

"Give me a minute." He flipped it open.

The salary was front and center on the first sheet. No, it wasn't a fortune—but it would provide a comfortable living.

He skimmed the rest of the material. The benefits were more than adequate.

Plus—barring an emergency—he'd never have to get up in the wee hours of the morning again to take out a fishing boat in rainy, cold weather. A huge positive at this stage of his life.

The only hitch was the charter trip he'd donated to the pro-life dinner auction—but he'd make that a sales contingency on his business . . . or pilot the trip himself if the boat and business hadn't sold by then.

He closed the folder. "There's no reason to reconvene from my end. I'm happy to accept the terms and the job."

"Wonderful!" Father Murphy beamed at him. "I'm glad we were able to find someone here in town to take over from Michael. I wasn't relishing the involvement of a recruiting firm."

"You and I can work out a start date that's reasonable, and I'll stay on board for the first couple of weeks to brief you on the routine and the inner workings," Michael said. "But in light of your military experience, I expect you're a fast learner. Given the dicey situations you dealt with, I doubt any of the crises we encounter will throw you. And I'll be a phone call away indefinitely if you have questions."

"Thank you. And thank you all for trusting me with the helm of such a worthy organization."

"We're the lucky ones." Reverend Baker checked his watch and stood. "I hate to break this up, but I have a sick call to make."

"And I have a homily to polish." The priest stood too.

Steven followed their lead.

"Let the news sink in, and call me in a few days to talk about timing. I expect with a charter business there are reservations to consider—and we're flexible if you have to juggle both jobs for a while to fulfill your obligations. We don't want any disappointed fishermen." Michael smiled.

"I do have quite a few bookings over the next two weeks, but the majority of my customers are last-minute. I should be able to get rolling without much delay."

He shook hands all around again, and three minutes later he

was walking toward his car in the parking lot adjacent to Grace Christian with a new job in hand.

Literally.

Tightening his grip on the slim folder that held his future, he lifted his face to the warmth of the afternoon sun.

So many pieces had fallen into place over the past few weeks.

Patrick was on the road to sobriety.

The perfect job had dropped into his lap.

He was more at peace with his past than he'd ever been.

There was only one shadow on the future he looked forward to in this little seaside community that had become home.

He'd fallen for the wrong woman.

No, that wasn't true.

He'd fallen for the right woman—but she'd decided he was the wrong guy for her.

What other explanation could there be for her silence?

She'd said she'd call—and he had no doubt she would . . . once she figured out how to phrase her rejection in the least hurtful way. That had to be why she hadn't made contact. If she'd decided to take a chance on him, there'd be no reason to wait.

He opened the door to his jeep and slid behind the wheel, setting the folder on the seat beside him as he perused the steeple on the small church.

There *was* one other piece of unfinished business on his plate.

Perhaps it was time to do what the clerics had suggested and ask God's forgiveness. Begin his new life with a clean slate.

And what better place to commune with the Almighty—and seek forgiveness—than out on Pelican Point, beside the soaring lighthouse once tended by his great-great-great-grandfather that had guided countless lost souls home?

He twisted the key, backed out of the parking spot, and aimed the jeep toward the headland north of town.

Prayer had been too long absent from his life, as his return to church had reminded him—and according to Scripture, it wielded immense power.

It could even salvage lost causes.

So while he was out at the lighthouse, why not throw in one extra prayer about Holly?

She might not be in God's plan for him—but it couldn't hurt to ask for guidance.

For both of them.

25

Why had he let Father Murphy talk him into this?

Pete set the brake on the car in the parking lot at St. Francis church, heaved a sigh, and read the sign beside the rose-covered arbor that marked the entrance to the meditation garden.

All are welcome.

Nice sentiment—except he didn't want to be here.

He should never have let his guard down during the golf game last week with the two clerics and told them about Sal. And the cancer. And his career as a landscape architect.

But they'd been easy to talk to. Had seemed interested in his story, and truly distressed to learn he was ill.

As kind as they'd been, how could he refuse Father Murphy's invitation to stop by and see the meditation garden Reverend Baker had said his Catholic colleague lavished with TLC?

He was under no obligation to stay long, though. Ten minutes ought to do it, tops.

Leaving the car behind, he approached the arbor where the priest had suggested they meet.

Father Murphy was nowhere in sight.

Not a problem.

This would give him a chance to look over the garden first and formulate some polite, complimentary remarks about the man's efforts.

Shifting into landscape architect mode, he stepped through the archway and set off along the stone, circular path that meandered through the tucked-away bower.

A variety of annuals and perennials, along with bushes of different heights, gave the space visual interest. The hydrangeas would provide vivid bursts of color later in the season, and the buds on the large rhododendrons were beginning to show a hint of pink. A fountain stood in the center, the soft splash of water enhancing the aura of peace and tranquility that pervaded the space. Two inviting wooden benches spaced along the path provided a view of the bird feeder dangling from the branch of a tall Sitka spruce, where a yellow-rumped warbler was enjoying a midafternoon snack.

Pete settled onto the bench beside a small statue of Francis of Assisi and breathed in the evergreen-scented air, his tension melting away.

No need to conjure up compliments. The priest had done an excellent job converting the space into a sheltered, private haven conducive to contemplation and reflection. Any praise he offered for this labor of love would be sincere.

"There you are!" The jolly cleric barreled through the arbor, dressed in work clothes, a bucket and trowel in one hand, a nursery container holding a sword fern in the other, a wide-brimmed hat shading his face. "Sorry I'm a few minutes late. As I was on my way out the rectory door, the phone rang. One of our more garrulous parishioners wanted to discuss the potluck supper we're planning in a couple of weeks. I got off the phone as fast as I could after debating the merits of mustard-based potato salad versus mayo-based." He rolled his eyes.

"Don't worry about it." Pete stood. "I enjoyed spending a few minutes here. You've created a lovely spot. Did you do all the work yourself?"

The priest joined him and set the bucket, trowel, and nursery container on the path. "Most of it. When I was assigned here, this was nothing but a patch of spotty grass, except for the spruce and a few bushes. I could see it had potential, though."

"Which you've realized."

"High praise, coming from a man with your background. Or are you just being kind?" The priest grinned.

"I'm being honest. You've done a fine job selecting plants, and the layout is very restful."

"Thank you. I like to think of this as a little piece of heaven on earth. But it remains a work in progress—as we all are."

"Is that a new addition?" Pete motioned toward the fern at the man's feet.

The priest's eyes lit up. "Yes. I've been meaning to add a sword fern over there for months." He indicated a shady spot in the back of the garden. "While I was out and about earlier, I passed by the native-plant nursery down near Sixes and decided this was the day. I'm going to plant this baby, then pull weeds for a while—a never-ending job."

"I hear you." Pete surveyed the garden again. There was no reason to delay his departure . . . yet it was such a serene spot. "I don't want to detain you, but to tell the truth, I hate to leave."

"Music to a gardener's ears—and don't feel like you have to rush off. The garden is available to everyone anytime, as the sign says." He indicated the welcome placard at the entrance. "Pick a bench and relax."

"I can't sit and watch you work."

"Wouldn't bother me in the least. I get great pleasure out of seeing people enjoy the garden."

"Maybe I could pull a few weeds." That hadn't been in his plans . . . but why not? He had nothing else to do at home on this Friday afternoon, and the padre was companionable.

"You don't have to do that."

"I'd enjoy it."

"In that case—I accept. I never refuse a sincere offer of help. And it usually benefits the helper as much as it does me and the garden. Working with plants has remarkable restorative and calming properties." The priest picked up the fern. "The area next to where I'm going to plant this could use weeding, if you want to tackle that section. I'll join you as soon as I get the fern in the ground. You sure you're up to this?" The priest laid a hand on his shoulder, a shadow of concern momentarily dimming his joviality.

"Yes. Today's a good day—and I enjoy being in a well-kept garden."

"Then have at it."

The priest continued toward the spot designated for the fern while Pete toted the bucket to the section requiring attention, eased onto his knees, and began to pluck weeds.

True to his word, ten minutes later the priest joined him and they worked in comfortable silence broken only by an occasional comment or the trill of a bird.

An hour passed before Pete thought to check his watch—the most relaxing sixty minutes he'd spent in years.

"What time is it?" Father Murphy swiped the sleeve of his sweatshirt across his forehead.

"Four-thirty."

The priest made a face. "I'm going to have to call it a day out here and dive back into reality. I've got a wedding rehearsal in an hour." He plunked the last weed in the bucket, stood, and extended a hand.

Pete took it. Getting down had been a breeze. Getting up would be more of a challenge.

But with an assist from the priest, he was on his feet with less trouble than he'd expected. "Thanks. These old knees aren't what they used to be."

"I'm beginning to notice that myself. As my father says, if you live long enough, all the parts start to wear out. He has a titanium knee, a cobalt-chromium hip, a pig valve in his heart, and a pacemaker—but he keeps plugging along."

"How old is he?"

"Eighty-five in July."

"That's amazing."

"I agree. After my mom died five years ago, we were afraid he'd give up—and for a while he did. He lost weight, cut out his daily walks, stopped taking his medicine . . . not that he took much. Vitamins and a baby aspirin. He said the Lord was finished with him, and he was ready to check out. Nothing my brother, sister, or I said convinced him otherwise."

"What changed his mind?"

"A note he received from a young woman who worked at the library he frequented. He'd spotted her one day at a nearby coffee shop, sitting in a corner, crying. Dad could never turn a blind eye to anyone who was suffering, so he went over to ask if there was anything he could do. She told him her husband had just left her. Dad spent more than an hour listening to her story, offering a few sage words here and there, I expect. He got the note from her months after Mom died."

"What did it say?"

"That the day he'd stopped to talk to her, she'd been on the verge of a breakdown . . . or worse. His simple act of kindness and caring had boosted her spirits, encouraged her to pick herself up and go on with her life." The priest shook his head. "It goes to show how one small gesture of compassion can have a life-changing impact."

Kind of like Holly's kindnesses had impacted *him*. Her umbrella and soup offer that first day . . . homemade cookies . . . taco-sharing . . . introducing him to Patrick. Nothing earth-shattering—yet they'd all had a positive effect on his life.

Pete shoved his hands in his pockets. "That's quite a story."

"I agree—because the turning point went both directions . . . as it often does. As Dad told me a few months later while I was home on vacation, and I quote, 'After that, I stopped playing God, Kevin. The good Lord gave me this life, and he entrusted me with this body to take care of during the journey. He also gave me a purpose. I may not always know what that is, but *he* does. And until he calls me home, I have to keep on keeping on. That's my job—and my responsibility. The rest I'll leave up to him.'" Father Murphy pushed his hat farther back on his head and grinned. "And *I'm* supposed to be the theologian in the family."

Pete called up an answering smile. "I'm glad it ended well for your father."

"We all were." He extended his hand. "Thank you for stopping by today—and for helping weed."

"My pleasure."

"Come anytime . . . not just to weed, but to enjoy God's creation." The priest gave a jaunty wave and set off at a jog toward the arbor, bucket of weeds in one hand, the empty nursery container with the trowel inside in the other.

Pete followed more slowly. No one was waiting for him. There was nothing major on his to-do list. Nor was there much purpose to his days.

That *he* knew of.

But as Father Murphy's story had reminded him, *God* could have a purpose for him.

Was it wrong to circumvent that by ending the life he'd been given, even if his body was failing?

Could there be a reason he'd been brought to Hope Harbor beyond random chance?

Were there people here whose lives would benefit from his presence?

"You already have *had a positive impact, Pete. On your neighbor Holly. On Patrick and his family. On the minister and priest. Perhaps on the clerk at the grocery store. That kind word you said to her on your last visit, when she seemed down, could have gotten her over a hump. We're all like stones tossed in the water,*

creating a ripple effect with outer limits too far away for us to see. But God sees them."

As Sal's voice echoed in his mind, Pete stopped beneath the rose arbor, where the first buds of summer were beginning to form. In another month, they'd burst into bloom, fulfilling their promise.

Unless someone plucked them off before they had a chance to blossom. To realize their potential.

Was that what he'd be doing if he followed the plan he'd come here determined to implement?

Letting nature take its course might be okay—but was it wrong to intervene in God's plan for him? Wrest control from the creator who'd given him life?

"You know the answer to that, Pete."

Sal again, in her gentle voice.

He sighed.

Yeah.

He knew.

He'd always known.

But until he'd come here and his life had begun intertwining with the lives of people who appeared to genuinely care about him, it had been easy to keep the doubts about his decision at bay.

He fingered a bud, frowning.

Maybe he ought to stick it out. Suck every drop of goodness from whatever time he had left. Seek to make a positive impact on the people he'd met and the community he'd adopted.

The garden club could use his help—and Father Murphy would welcome another pair of hands to keep the weeds under control in the meditation garden. It wouldn't hurt Patrick to have a father figure in his life. Jonah and Beatrice could benefit from a stand-in grandpa, as Jonah had already implied. Holly might appreciate a set of impartial ears to listen to her concerns about that fella she liked.

And who knew if there were others in town who could use a friend—or if there was a task where he could lend a helping hand . . . perhaps through the organization with that very name?

Pete turned back to the garden for one last look.

Father Murphy had called it a little piece of heaven, and that was an apt description. It offered a glimpse of the peace and tranquility the Lord had promised. There was a sense of timelessness about it. Of eternity.

Maybe, instead of trading in the earthly realm before God was ready for him, he could come here, to this tiny slice of paradise, if he needed refreshment and encouragement . . . and let the Almighty decide when it was time for him to transition to eternal paradise.

It was worth thinking about.

And it might not be a bad idea to take Holly up on her suggestion about attending church either.

After all, what more fitting place could there be than a house of God to find the guidance he was seeking?

26

What in the world?

As she traversed the main aisle of Grace Christian a few minutes before the early Sunday service was scheduled to begin, Holly jolted to a stop.

Pete was sitting in one of the last pews on the far side, head down, reading the bulletin.

Had he had a change of heart? Was he rethinking his plans? Had God planted fruitful seeds during his golf outing with the clerics? Had the support she and Patrick's family offered had an impact?

Whatever the reason for his church attendance today, it had to be a positive sign.

That was one piece of happy news this morning, anyway.

She continued down the aisle and slid into a pew, smothering a yawn. Getting up early on Sunday after rising at the crack of dawn all week for school was the pits—but coming to the first service virtually guaranteed she wouldn't run into Steven.

And that was critical.

The high-voltage current that zipped between them whenever they were together was dangerous. It could short-circuit her brain, tempt her to compromise her beliefs to make a relationship work.

That was *not* the recipe for long-term happiness or harmony.

She had to come to a decision before she saw him again. One based on clear, logical thinking.

Slumping in her pew, she focused on a ray of sun streaming into the sanctuary, the usually invisible dancing dust motes exposed to the world in the bright beam of light.

She may have come to terms with Steven's sniper background, but how was she supposed to deal with the devastating revelation about his wife and baby—and the fear that a selfish, uncaring stranger hibernated deep within the man she'd thought she was beginning to know?

And what about their differing opinions on capital punishment? He may have moderated his views on the other issues, but as far as she could see, he hadn't budged on this one. Could she live with that?

Until the past few weeks, she'd have said no.

Now . . . she was less certain.

It was all so confusing.

The organ struck up the opening chords of the first hymn, and Holly stood to add her voice to those around her, singing by rote as her brain continued to grapple with the thorny issues that had plagued her day and night since Tuesday.

Hard as she tried to concentrate on the service, her mind kept drifting . . . until the concluding words of Reverend Baker's sermon suddenly penetrated her mental fog.

"But love isn't always easy, is it?" The minister gave the congregation a slow sweep. "That's because we're all different. We don't fit together as cleanly as the pieces of a jigsaw puzzle. Sometimes there are gaps. Rough edges. Holes. The finished product when we come together isn't always perfect. But as we're reminded in Corinthians, a love that keeps no record of wrongs . . . that perseveres . . . never fails."

He folded his notes and rested his hands on the edges of the pulpit. "As we wrap up our formal worship for this week, let me leave you with one suggestion. If there's someone in your life who hasn't lived up to your ideal—take a second look. As my mother told my sister after she complained about being unable to find the perfect man to marry, 'Honey, if you ever do find him, he'll want the perfect woman—and it won't be you.'"

A titter rippled through the congregation, and the minister smiled.

"I can't say it any more eloquently than she did. Don't let imperfections or petty differences hinder love. We don't all have to agree on everything in order to create harmony within our own circles. We simply have to respect divergent opinions and recognize the good in the imperfect people we love—which more often than not will outweigh the bad." He lifted his hands, palms up. "Now let us rise for the final hymn."

The organist began the introduction, and Holly fumbled for the hymnal in the rack in front of her, mind racing.

Reverend Baker hadn't been talking about romantic love per se in his sermon—except for the story about his mother's advice.

But everything he'd said applied to her situation.

Neither she nor Steven were perfect. Far from it.

Yet they were both good people whose views had been formed after much soul-searching and deliberation. Who were doing their best to live lives of integrity and honor. Who believed honesty and trust were vital to a relationship.

Their opinions on some issues might differ, but that didn't have to be a deal breaker if they respected each other's positions and agreed to disagree.

As for the mistakes Steven had made in his first marriage—Pete's story about Jedediah gave her a road map to follow.

Forget the past. Forgive as God forgave. Forge a new future.

It was the man Steven was today that mattered.

And that man was worth trusting—and loving.

Doubts vanishing as fast as a Hope Harbor mist under the warmth of a summer sun, Holly peeked at her watch. Now that her thoughts had clarified, she had to talk with Steven.

ASAP.

The instant the song ended, she stowed her hymnal and exited the pew. Despite the temptation to stop and chat with Pete, she had an important—and urgent—mission to complete.

Besides, Eleanor Cooper was already engaging him in conversation and welcoming him to Grace Christian, God bless her.

Next thing he knew, the older woman would be dropping off pieces of fudge cake for him.

And that kind of attention and consideration was just what he needed.

In fact, if he was beginning to venture out, she could invite him to accompany her to Charley's next week. Maybe introduce him to Rose in the garden club.

But for today, her focus was Steven—and taking a step that would irrevocably impact the rest of her life.

It was starting to rain.

As a drop hit him on the nose, Steven stopped swabbing the deck and lifted his head.

The dark clouds that had been roiling on the horizon all morning had finally made good on their threat and moved in.

Fine by him. The shift from blue sky to gray fit his mood.

After rinsing and stowing the mop, he ducked into the foldaway canvas enclosure he'd put up for his charter clients on this Sunday morning in case the rain arrived early.

Not that they'd used it. The four high school buddies from long ago were experienced fishermen who didn't mind bad weather or require much instruction. They'd even been happy to clean their own fish and had left in high spirits.

The best kind of customers.

Though truth be told, today he wouldn't have minded dealing with tangled lines or a case of seasickness.

Anything to keep his mind off Holly.

He dropped into a deck chair and watched the raindrops slide down the isinglass windows like silent tears. No reason to hurry home. He wasn't due at Patrick's house for dinner for four hours, and he'd missed the late service at church—unfortunately. But today's fishermen had booked their trip long ago, and canceling wouldn't have been fair.

The sole item on his afternoon schedule was lunch—and that could wait until the rain slacked off.

Unless he had a protein bar tucked somewhere on board.

He leaned forward, flipped the latch, and rummaged through the storage compartment.

His fingers closed over an envelope . . . and he withdrew the birthday card Cindy had sent him last month.

So much had changed in the few short weeks since he'd last read this.

Like . . . everything.

Strange how it had all turned out.

Patrick may have resisted every attempt by his take-charge big brother to muscle into his life, yet in the end they'd connected on mutually agreeable terms . . . mended their fences . . . and Patrick had gone on to tackle his addiction on his own.

Steven leaned back in his chair, weighing the card in his hand. That wasn't at all how he'd imagined the mission that had brought him to Hope Harbor would play out.

Nor had he expected to find his own new beginning. One that had transformed his life as he strengthened family ties, secured a new job, and made peace with his past.

The only piece missing was—

"Hello? Is anyone on board?"

At the familiar voice, Steven jerked upright.

Holly was here?

His pulse vaulted into double time, and he sprang up. No deliberations today about whether to hide from her or not, unlike on her first visit.

He wanted to see her.

Whatever the outcome.

He pushed through the canvas, into the rain. "Hi."

"Hi back." She offered him a nervous smile, her cheery blue slicker and matching umbrella brightening up the gloomy day. "I've been waiting in my car, watching for you to leave . . . but my patience ran out."

"How long have you been out there?"

"Since the last service ended. I waited for you outside church too—after trying your apartment first. When I saw Patrick and his family leave without you, I flagged them down. They told me you had a job this morning. So I came here."

"You went to a lot of effort to track me down."

"This is important."

That could mean only one thing.

She'd come to a decision.

He drew in a lungful of air. "You want to come on board?"

"My sea legs aren't the best." She flashed him another quick smile as she repeated the comment she'd made on her first visit.

"There isn't much motion in the marina." He followed the script too—but deviated once he took her arm and helped her aboard. Instead of directing her to the stern, he guided her into the portable enclosure. "It'll be warmer and drier in here."

He kept a firm grip on her as she inched across the gently undulating deck, but released her once she was seated, then took the chair beside her.

"So . . ." She exhaled. "I've been thinking and praying a lot about our conversation Tuesday night. Like, constantly."

"Me too." He braced for bad news.

"I also had an enlightening chat with Pete about your great-great-great-grandfather and listened to a thought-provoking sermon today."

He curled his fingers. It was impossible to tell where this was leading—and the suspense was excruciating. Good or bad, it was far easier to deal with certainties than with the unknown.

"Just give me the bottom line, okay? The last few days have been—" He bit back the word that leapt to the tip of his tongue. "They've been tough."

She lifted her hand and rested her palm against his cheek, the warmth of her touch zipping straight to his heart. "Sorry. I didn't mean to drag this out. The bottom line is that I think we have potential, and I'd like to explore it."

Steven sucked in a breath as the coil of tension in his gut began to loosen. "Are you—" His voice rasped, and he swallowed. Tried again. "Are you sure about this? Because I'm not a halfway kind of guy. Once I have a mission, it's full speed ahead—and I don't let obstacles get in my way."

She scooted her chair next to his and put her arms around his neck. "I like the sound of that." She tugged, urging him closer. "In case there's any doubt in your mind, I'm officially giving you a green light for a repeat of that mind-blowing kiss on the dune."

Despite a powerful temptation to cave, he managed to corral a wisp of his evaporating restraint. This romance ought to be launched in a fine restaurant with candlelight and music and flowers—not on a wet boat, with only the raucous caw of two circling gulls providing musical accompaniment. Holly deserved no less than a first-class beginning to this courtship. "This isn't the most romantic setting. I smell like fish."

Her fingers inched up to burrow into the hair at the base of his neck, mischief sparkling in her hazel eyes. "What happened to full speed ahead?"

"I can throttle back until I go home, shower, and change." Maybe. Unless she ratcheted up her flirting campaign. "Why don't we regroup for a fancy dinner in a few hours?" He'd have to bail on Patrick and Cindy—but they'd understand.

"Count me in—but I'm going to take a page from your book and not let any obstacles get in my way either. After waiting for hours to see you, I at least want a preview of what's to come. We've been in a holding pattern for too long." She urged him closer again—with a little more force—until their lips were inches apart.

"You're killing me here. My self-control is slipping."

"Let it slip."

He rested his hands on her shoulders, itching to pull her close. "You realize you're going to smell like fish too."

"Small price to pay. Besides, if I'm going to date a fisherman, I suppose I'll have to get used to it."

"My fishing days are numbered."

Her face lit up. "You got the Helping Hands job!"

"Yes."

"I knew you would." She inched her chair closer. "Let me congratulate you."

Without waiting for him to take the initiative, she leaned over and pressed her lips to his.

The last sliver of his resistance crumbled.

Surrendering, he wrapped his arms around her and gave her exactly what she wanted—a kiss to remember.

And as the rain intensified, cocooning them in their own private world . . . as the boat rocked gently in its slip . . . as the gulls continued to circle overhead . . . and as the sweet perfume that was all Holly invaded his senses and overpowered the smell of fish, Steven had one last rational thought.

Despite this most unromantic setting, the incredible kiss they were sharing was definitely the start of something big.

Epilogue

"Helping Hands couldn't have picked a more perfect night for the pro-life fundraiser."

As the warmth of Steven's breath tickled her earlobe, Holly swiveled away from the banquet facility window that offered a panoramic view of the Pelican Point lighthouse on this clear, moonbeam-bathed night.

"The weather definitely cooperated." She gave the man beside her an appreciative head-to-toe. "Have I mentioned how fantastic you look in a tux?"

He grinned. "Twice. But this"—he flicked his bow tie—"is a royal pain."

"It's also crooked." She reached up and adjusted it, letting her fingers linger.

His eyes darkened, and his voice dropped to a low growl. "Keep that up, I won't be responsible for my behavior. And your parents may not approve of us smooching in public."

She peeked over his shoulder and scanned the thirty round, linen-covered tables for ten that filled the space. "No worries. They're on the dance floor." She planted a quick kiss on his jaw.

As she backed off, he grabbed her arms. "Uh-uh. If we're going to flout propriety, let's do a better job of it than that." He leaned down and gave her a real kiss.

"Shall I take a shot of that for the *Herald*? I can see the caption now—'Helping Hands director and local teacher swoon over success of fundraiser.'"

At Marci's amused comment, Holly eased out of the kiss and turned to the editor. "Not unless you're planning to convert the *Herald* into one of those Hollywood-type gossip rags."

"Perish the thought. But I would like to get a photo of the two of you, if you don't mind."

"Happy to oblige." Steven put his arm around her waist and tucked her close as they posed for the camera.

"Thanks." Marci snapped several photos. "And now I'll leave you in peace to carry on with more pleasurable pursuits. Just come up for air in time for the cannon and plaque dedication in the park tomorrow."

Before they could respond, she zipped off as fast as her six-months-pregnant girth allowed.

"I guess the cat's out of the bag on our romance." Holly waved at Pete, who responded with a grin and a thumbs-up from his seat between Cindy and Eleanor Cooper.

"It's been out for a while. Remember, this is a small town—and we've been seen together in public for months."

"Never kissing."

"You started it."

"Guilty as charged—and I'm not sorry."

"Neither am I." He motioned toward Pete, who was having an animated conversation with his tablemates. "I'm glad he's still around. You have a nice neighbor."

"I agree. The experimental drug he decided to try has done wonders. I wish there was a cure, but he's feeling well and is content with remission. It's giving him a chance to spend more time with the wide circle of friends he's made—and Jonah adores him."

"True. Pete's kind of displaced a certain uncle in my nephew's affections."

"Is that a complaint?"

"Nope. I'm glad Jonah has a grandfather figure in his life. And a significant portion of *my* affections are elsewhere these days too." He fingered a wisp of hair that had escaped her fancy updo. "What do you say we escape outside for a few minutes? All the formalities for the evening are over, the auction was a huge success, and we deserve to celebrate."

Holly smiled. "Define celebrate."

"I'll leave that to your imagination—but picture a romantic lighthouse, a full moon, stars strewn across the heavens, the faint strains of a love song in the background . . . and go from there."

A delicious shiver ran through her. "My imagination is running wild."

"As someone once said, I like the sound of that. Let's—"

"Sorry to interrupt." Reverend Baker directed the apology to both of them, then focused on Steven. "But I'd like to introduce you to two of our biggest donors. They have a son in the service and are interested in your military background. I realize you can't say much, but if you could chat with them for a few minutes I think they'd appreciate it."

"Happy to oblige." He touched her arm, and his ardent gaze locked with hers. "Hold that last thought. I'll meet you outside in a few minutes."

"I'll be waiting."

He followed the minister back through the crowd, pausing to exchange a few words with her parents as they left the dance floor. The three of them had hit it off, as she'd known they would once they'd gotten to know each other.

They were all fine people.

She'd always known that about her parents—and over the past five months, as she and Steven had deepened their relationship, he'd proven to be every bit as wonderful.

And she'd fallen for him.

Hard.

After he disappeared into the crowd, she slipped outside into the unseasonably warm air. No wrap necessary tonight, even though her boat-neck satin cocktail dress left her arms bare. The wind on the headland was also behaving itself.

It was a perfect night for a stroll down the short path to the lighthouse.

A few other couples had also come outside, but they were staying on the terrace beside the banquet facility. Most, though, had succumbed to the dreamy ambiance and were hand-in-hand.

As one twosome indulged in a discreet kiss, the corners of her mouth bowed.

That could be her and Steven in a few minutes.

Another tingle raced through her.

Hard to believe that eight months ago she'd been living in Eugene, stuck in a rut, bemoaning the loss of a less-than-worthy boyfriend, wondering if her personal life would always be dull and boring and predictable.

Her impetuous application for the job in Hope Harbor had been like buying a lottery ticket. You hoped for a big win, but given the odds, expected nothing.

Yet she'd hit the jackpot.

She'd found a job that fulfilled her, a town she loved, friends in unexpected places—and an unlikely suitor who'd stolen her heart and made her believe in romance again.

It felt almost like a fairy tale.

In fact, it had all the earmarks of a storybook . . . save one.

But barring some unforeseen glitch, the requisite happy ending was waiting in the wings to make its grand entrance in the not-too-distant future.

This was the night.

Steven fingered the small box in the pocket of his tux as he wove through the crowd at the dinner auction, heading for the door to the path that led to the lighthouse—and Holly.

It was possible he was rushing this, that waiting until Christmas would be more prudent.

But why postpone the future if you knew you'd found the woman you wanted to share it with? Waiting another week or month or year wasn't going to make him any more certain Holly and he were meant for each other.

The only question was whether she was ready to say yes.

If she wasn't . . . he'd retreat and give her the time she needed to be as confident as he was.

From all indications, though, she was as anxious as he was to—

"Steven! Wait up!"

Throttling a groan, he slowed his pace and pivoted toward his brother, who was zigzagging toward him through the crowd.

First Rev. Baker had waylaid him, now Patrick.

He was never going to get outside.

But he tamped down his frustration. He ought to be glad his brother had not only turned his life around and was bright eyed and sober, but that he'd returned to his job at the mill and become a sought-after speaker for groups throughout the state, thanks to the coverage his talk at the high school gym had generated. Not just about Jedediah, either, but Oregon history in general. The kid was a font of information on all sorts of obscure historical topics. Who knew?

And he was fielding history-related photography assignments too. Those shots he'd taken of the cannon, and the ones he used in his presentations, had received attention from publications all over the state—and beyond.

He was doing fine—but that didn't mean a support system wasn't still important.

So he'd give him two minutes.

Max.

"Sorry." Patrick stopped beside him. "You seemed like you were about to make a fast escape, and I wanted to share a piece of good news in case you weren't coming back."

"I'm coming back. Later."

Patrick leaned sideways and peered through the wall of windows. "Is that Holly out there?"

"Yeah."

"Ah. In that case, I won't detain you long. I wouldn't want to stand in the way of young love." Patrick smirked at him.

"Very funny."

"No—very serious. Holly's a keeper."

"Tell me something I don't know. What did you want?"

"Would you rather I catch up with you later?"

"Depends on how long this will take."

"I'll give you the condensed version. I had a call today from a prestigious national speaker's bureau. They think there could be interest all over the country in the stuff I talk about in my presentations—and they want to represent me. Is that amazing or what?"

Steven smiled and clapped a hand on his shoulder. "It's fantastic—but I'm not surprised. You know your subject, and you have a compelling presentation style. I'm proud of you, kid."

A soft flush suffused Patrick's face. "Thanks. I wanted you to be the first to know—after Cindy. I'm gonna tell Pete now. You can share the news with Holly if you want to . . . after you get past higher priority items." He winked and gave him a little shove. "Don't keep the lady waiting."

Not in his plans.

As Patrick made a beeline for Pete, Steven strode toward the door. There would be no more delays.

Holly was angled toward the lighthouse as he exited, the soft folds of her form-fitting deep blue dress molding every delicious curve. Her upswept hair left her neck bare . . . and alluringly accessible.

It was a temptation he didn't intend to resist for long.

Picking up his pace, he moved behind her and wrapped his arms around her waist. "Sorry for the delay. I got intercepted twice as I tried to escape."

She leaned back against him, her hair tickling his jaw. "No problem. I was enjoying the view."

"So was I. From over there, by the door." He nuzzled her neck.

She gave a throaty purr. "Watch yourself, soldier. You're edging into dangerous territory."

"Don't I know it." He allowed himself one more nibble, then stepped to the side and took her hand. If all went as he hoped, they could pick this up again in a few minutes, away from any curious bystanders. "Want to walk out to the lighthouse?"

"Sure. Unlike most of the women here tonight, I'm wearing sensible shoes instead of flirty high heels—by necessity."

He glanced down at her beaded flats. "Those look flirty to me."

"Thanks." She squeezed his fingers. "Shall we?"

They strolled down the gravel path, illuminated with ground-level accent lighting, until they came to the bench closest to the lighthouse. No one else had ventured this far out.

"Shall we sit?" He stopped beside it.

"Works for me." She settled onto the seat.

Pulse picking up, he joined her—and tried to calm his sudden case of nerves.

There was no reason to be anxious. Holly cared for him. Maybe the L-word had never been spoken, but the signs were there. At worst, she might defer her answer. But she wouldn't say no outright.

Would she?

"Steven?" She touched his hand, and he shifted toward her. "Is everything all right?"

"I, uh, had a moment of panic." Why not be honest? As he'd discovered, while he'd mastered the art of masking his emotions during his years in the military, Holly had demonstrated an uncanny ability to see behind any façade he erected.

"Panic?" She frowned. "About what?"

Just do it, Steven. Skip the preliminaries and cut to the chase.

Slowly he withdrew the small square jeweler's box from his pocket and flipped it open. "About this."

Her breath hitched as she gaped at the marquis-cut diamond the clerk had assured him would impress any woman.

But she didn't say a word.

His heart stuttered.

"I've, uh, been carrying this around for the past month, waiting for the perfect occasion to offer it. Settings don't get much more memorable than here at the lighthouse, with us all dressed up in our benefit finery. So the time seems right. But if I'm rushing you, I can save my speech for later."

"No." Her response came out in a squeak, and she cleared her throat. Dragged her attention away from the ring and lifted her chin. "You're not rushing me. I'd like to hear your speech."

She hadn't cut him off.

That was encouraging.

He filled his lungs and launched into the spiel he'd memorized weeks ago. "Patrick is the speech giver in this family, as we're all discovering, but I'll do my best. You know my story—in more detail than anyone else. I realize it could have been a deal breaker for us, given your background. I'm beyond grateful it wasn't. Because meeting you, falling in love with you, has been the best thing that's ever happened to me, and I don't know how I'd survive if you walked out of my life." His voice hoarsened.

"I'm not going anywhere, Steven." She laid her hand on his, her eyes radiant in the moonlight, her soft voice filled with tenderness. "Ever. I love you. You're all my romantic fantasies rolled into one package, and I can't imagine life without you either."

The very words he'd hoped to hear.

"In that case . . ." He slid off the bench, onto one knee. "I love you, Holly Miller, and I would be honored if you'd agree to become my wife."

In answer, she lifted her left hand and held it out.

He slid the ring onto her finger, leaned down and kissed it, then stood and pulled her to her feet, into the circle of his arms. "What would you think about a Christmas wedding?"

She arched an eyebrow. "That's kind of fast."

"Every day will seem like a year to me. I'd marry you tomorrow if you'd let me."

"Do you want to elope?"

"Could we?"

"If that will put you out of your misery."

Tempted as he was, he shook his head. Holly deserved a first-class wedding, with her family and friends around her as they exchanged vows. He could wait four and a half months.

Even if he didn't want to.

"Let's have a real wedding. Can we pull one off by Christmas?"

"If I have to move heaven and earth. My best Christmas gift this season will be spending the holiday with you."

"Then we'll plan the wedding for a few days before. In the meantime . . ." He pulled her close again and let his lips trail down her temple, in the direction of her mouth. "Let's practice for the first kiss at the wedding. We want it to be perfect."

"I may need a lot of rehearsal."

"That can be arranged."

He followed the curve of her cheek all the way down and claimed her sweet, welcoming lips.

And there in the moonlight, in the arms of the woman he loved, he sent a silent thank-you heavenward.

The outcome of his journey home may not have been what he'd expected—but it was better.

Much, much better.

Holly tightened her embrace as she melted into his kiss . . . and he responded in kind beneath the towering lighthouse, once tended with meticulous care by his great-great-great-grandfather, that had guided lost souls home.

How fitting was that?

For here in Hope Harbor, with a woman he suspected Jedediah would heartily approve of, he'd found safe harbor.

For always.

Author's Note

Welcome to Hope Harbor—where hearts heal . . . and love blooms.

If you're a first-time visitor, I'm glad you're here. If you're a regular, welcome back.

When I began this series, my publisher and I hoped my charming Oregon seaside town would become, in the words of *Publishers Weekly*, "a place of emotional restoration that readers will yearn to visit." Happily, that's exactly what's happened. Six books in, readers have embraced the town and all of the characters, from my seagull couple, Floyd and Gladys, to the bantering clerics, to taco-making artist and town philosopher, Charley Lopez.

Best news of all? There are more books in the queue!

During my long writing career, I've been blessed to have amazing support on both the personal and professional fronts, and I owe all of these special people a deep debt of gratitude.

On the personal side, love and hugs to my husband and real-life hero, Tom, who sees up-close-and-personal all the joys and challenges that a writing career entails, and who delights in my success as much as I do. A special thanks as well to my parents, James and Dorothy Hannon—my original cheering section. My dad is still rooting for me every day, and I know my mom continues to hold me close to her heart and watch over me from heaven.

For more than ten years, my publishing partners at Revell have provided incredible support on the professional side—and become friends along the way. Special thanks to Dwight Baker, Kristin Kornoelje, Jennifer Leep, Michele Misiak, Karen Steele, Gayle Raymer, and all the other Revell employees who work so hard to create the best possible book for readers.

So what's ahead? In October, I'll debut a brand-new suspense series. It features three sisters involved in truth-seeking professions who find themselves plunged into dicey situations that lead to danger . . . and romance. And next April, we'll return to Hope Harbor for another heartwarming story on the Oregon coast.

In the meantime, I hope you enjoy *Starfish Pier*!

Read a *Sneak Peek* of a

BRAND-NEW SERIES

Coming Soon from

IRENE HANNON

The package was ticking.

Eve Reilly froze . . . sucked in a breath . . . and gaped at the FedEx box propped beside her front door.

Tick.

Tick.

Tick.

Tick.

The sound was faint—but distinctive.

And was that . . . was that a *wire* sticking out through the tape?

She squinted.

Yeah.

It was.

Heart stuttering, she eased the door closed, snatched up the cell she'd dropped on the hall table, and jabbed in 911 as she bolted toward the back of the house.

The box definitely didn't contain anything as prosaic as the new water filters she'd ordered for her fridge.

"911. What is the nature of your emergency?"

"There's a package on my front porch that's t-ticking—and a wire is hanging out of it." Eve dug through the drawer next to the kitchen sink until her shaky fingers closed over the back-door key for her neighbor's house.

"I'm dispatching as we speak." The woman's voice was calm. Like she dealt with bombs every day. "I want you to vacate the premises and find cover a safe distance away until officers arrive."

"Got it." She pulled open the back door and clattered down the steps while she answered the woman's questions, trying to wrap her mind around this surreal turn of events.

Hate mail was one thing. An occupational hazard you learned to live with in her type of job.

But a bomb?

Way out of bounds.

She skipped the last step and leapt to the ground.

Maybe her sisters were right.

Maybe hosting a controversial talk radio show *was* a dangerous job.

And maybe, in the future, she wouldn't cavalierly dismiss the venom that was sometimes spewed at her by listeners who didn't agree with her opinions.

For now, though, she had to focus on keeping her neighbors safe. Willing as she was to put *herself* in the line of fire as part of her job, it wasn't fair to endanger the innocent residents of this bucolic St. Louis suburb she called home.

The 911 operator finished her questions as Eve sprinted next door.

"I'll stay on the line until officers arrive. Are you moving to a safe location?"

"Uh-huh." Or she would be soon. After detouring to Olivia Macie's. The eighty-one-year-old widow would either be watching TV with the volume sky-high or napping without her hearing aid. She wouldn't hear her phone—and she might not even notice the noise from the emergency vehicles that would soon descend on the quiet cul de sac.

After bounding up the steps to the woman's back porch, she skidded to a stop, set the phone beside the pot of geraniums on the patio table, and pounded on the door.

"Come on, Olivia. Open up. Please!" As she squeezed her other neighbor's key, the first faint wail of a siren keened through the muggy St. Louis August air.

She continued to pummel the door until the spry, white-haired woman at last pulled it open.

"Gracious, Eve." Olivia adjusted her glasses and blinked. "I thought I was being raided."

"Sorry. You need to go down into the basement ASAP." She gave the woman a choppy three-sentence explanation. "Until the police get here and tell us what to do, that's the most secure place."

She hoped.

After all, if subterranean walls of concrete offered protection from tornados, they ought to shield a person from a bomb that was a hundred feet away . . . right?

And it had to be safer than fleeing in the open air. What if the package exploded while Olivia was outside?

Her skin grew clammy as a stream of stomach-turning images strobed across her mind.

"There's a bomb on your front porch?" Her neighbor stared at her as if she'd just said aliens had landed in the yard.

"I don't know for sure—but it's ticking, and I'm not taking any chances. Can you get downstairs by yourself while I stash Ernie in the basement?" Her neighbors to the north would be devastated if anything happened to the coddled bichon frise they'd left in her charge while they attended a wedding in Chicago.

"Of course—but you should take cover too."

"I will." She tossed the promise over her shoulder as she hurtled down the steps and dashed across her backyard to her other neighbor's house, the wail of the sirens louder now.

Please don't let that package blow up while I'm out here, Lord!

With that desperate plea looping through her mind, she zoomed to her neighbor's back porch, breaking every personal speed record.

Once she slipped through the door, Ernie pranced around her feet with a happy yip, then charged toward his food dish and gave her a hopeful look.

"Sorry, buddy." She snagged his leash off a hook and swept him up. "You can chow down later. In the meantime, you and I are going to the basement."

The white fluff ball began to squirm in her arms as if he'd been attacked by a band of marauding fleas.

Clearly the word *basement* did not conjure up positive vibes.

She tightened her grip. "Sorry again, but that's the best place for us until this is over."

Negotiating the stairs with a wriggling fur ball in her arms was a challenge—but self-preservation was a powerful stabilizer.

At the bottom of the steps, she snapped on his leash, secured it to the rail, and set him on the floor.

"Chill, Ernie. We won't be down here for—"

Bam! Bam! Bam!

She jerked, hand flying to her chest as the pounding on the back door reverberated through the quiet house.

Ernie whined, and she gave him a quick pat before starting back up to the main level. "Stay."

Instead of following her order, the pup clambered up on her heels as far as the leash allowed, almost knocking her off balance in his frenzy to avoid banishment.

Tuning out his plaintive howls, she hightailed it to the back door. A police officer in tactical vest and helmet with the visor down was visible through the window, fist raised as if he was preparing to bang again.

He spoke the instant she pulled the door open. "Ma'am, you need to leave the house. We have a possible bomb next door, and we're evacuating the adjacent homes."

"I know about the bomb. I called it in. I live there." As she flapped a hand toward her modest Cape Cod house, his eyebrows rose. "I came over to take care of my neighbor's dog, okay? They're gone for the weekend. I have their key." She held it up. "The basement's safe, isn't it? Because that's where I told my neighbor on the other side to go."

The man pulled his radio off his belt. "I'll give the officer who's working those houses her location." He took her arm and urged her out the door. "We'll get a statement once we're out of range."

"Should I bring Ernie?"

He frowned. "Who?"

"My neighbor's dog." She motioned toward the basement door. "I wouldn't want—"

"He'll be fine. Let's go."

Without giving her a chance to respond, he hustled her across the yard, keeping the houses lining the street between them and the package on her porch.

While the 911 dispatcher had treated her call as routine, the officer from this quiet, local suburb seemed a bit rattled.

At the end of the cul de sac, he handed her off to a County officer inside the yellow police tape that cordoned off the neighborhood.

The uniformed woman introduced herself, but the name didn't penetrate the fog that had begun to swirl through Eve's brain.

"Ma'am?" The officer peered at her. "Are you all right?"

The question registered at a peripheral level, and she forced herself to concentrate. "Um . . . sure. I think so." She tightened her grasp on the key in her hand as police officers swarmed the area, sweat glistening on their brows.

But the hot sun couldn't dispel the cold chill that rippled through her.

"Let me get you a bottle of water." The officer kept tabs on her as she strode toward the emergency vehicles that were multiplying like mosquitoes in a stagnant pond.

Eve suppressed another shiver and tried to tune out the controlled frenzy around her.

Weird how she could pontificate for six hours a week to a quarter of a million listeners around the country about the violence, vulgarity, and vice besetting society, yet when serious nastiness hit close to home, her stomach morphed into a blender.

It wasn't a good feeling.

But she was *not* going to succumb to pressure. Or threats. Or intimidation.

No way.

She'd honor the promise she'd made to herself the day she'd

launched this venture—to seek and stand up for the truth, whatever the cost.

Still . . . a bomb?

Seriously?

Yet if someone was determined to undermine her resolve, an explosive device did have a lot more punch than a nasty letter.

Except the scare tactic wasn't going to work.

She mashed her lips together and lifted her chin.

Whatever the motivation for today's incident, she was sticking with her principles. Tomorrow would be business as usual.

In the meantime, though, she needed to rein in her galloping pulse, get her shakes under control—and try not to lose her lunch.

So much for any hopes of a quiet end to his first week in the Crimes Against Persons Bureau.

Expelling a breath, St. Louis County detective Brent Lange shoved his cell back into its holster, executed a U-turn, and pointed his Taurus east.

A possible bomb hadn't been in his Friday afternoon plans, but if you were the detective closest to the action, you got the call.

And even if it ended up being a false alarm—as most such calls were—he'd be on the job long after the bomb and arson crew called it quits. Someone had to dig in and get all the details, make certain there wasn't more to the story than a silly prank or a simple mistake.

Despite his rookie detective status, after ten years as a street cop he knew how the system worked.

Flipping on his lights and siren, he pressed harder on the unmarked vehicle's gas pedal. It would be much easier to get questions answered before the news crews descended and added to the chaos.

Ten minutes later, as he approached his destination in a neighborhood of older but well-kept middle-class homes, he gave the area a sweep.

In the distance, yellow tape blocked the entrance to the cul de sac where the possible bomb was located. A second perimeter had been staked out beyond that to create a working zone for law enforcement and emergency crews.

Standard protocol for a situation like this.

He flashed his creds at the local officer who was monitoring the flow of traffic into the restricted area, and the man waved him past.

Brent wedged his vehicle behind a County patrol car, slid out of the driver's seat, and surveyed the scene in the outer perimeter.

It took mere moments to locate the 911 caller. Eve Reilly, according to Sarge. As the only civilian inside the yellow tape, she wasn't difficult to spot.

Pausing near the front of his vehicle, he studied her. The slender thirtysomething woman was clutching a water bottle, every toned muscle of her five-foot-sixish frame taut, her free hand clenched. Gray leggings extended a few inches below her knees, delineating a pair of notable legs, and a moss-green tank top outlined generous curves. Her copper-colored hair was pulled back into a stretchy band, but the elastic loop was losing its grip, leaving her short ponytail askew. While the strong tilt of her chin hinted at fortitude, her pallor suggested her stamina had taken a major hit.

As if sensing his scrutiny, she angled toward him.

His cue to approach.

Resuming his trek, he took in a few more details as he drew close.

Gold-flecked irises the same hue as her tank top were fringed by lush lashes. A faint sprinkling of freckles arched over her nose. Her full lips bore no trace of artificial color.

Even makeup free, Eve Reilly was a beauty. The typical girl-next-door, with a hint of exotic glamor.

An intriguing combination.

But nothing in her appearance offered a clue about why she would be the victim of a bomb scare.

Determining that was his next order of business.

Irene Hannon is the bestselling, award-winning author of more than fifty contemporary romance and romantic suspense novels. She is also a three-time winner of the RITA award—the "Oscar" of romance fiction—from Romance Writers of America and is a member of that organization's elite Hall of Fame.

Her many other awards include National Readers' Choice, Daphne du Maurier, Retailers' Choice, Booksellers' Best, Carol, and Reviewers' Choice from *RT Book Reviews* magazine, which also honored her with a Career Achievement award for her entire body of work. In addition, she is a two-time Christy award finalist.

Millions of her books have been sold worldwide, and her novels have been translated into multiple languages.

Irene, who holds a BA in psychology and an MA in journalism, juggled two careers for many years until she gave up her executive corporate communications position with a Fortune 500 company to write full-time. She is happy to say she has no regrets.

A trained vocalist, Irene has sung the leading role in numerous community musical theater productions and is also a soloist at her church. She and her husband enjoy traveling, long hikes, Saturday mornings at their favorite coffee shop, and spending time with family. They make their home in Missouri.

To learn more about Irene and her books, visit www.irenehannon.com. She posts on Twitter and Instagram, but is most active on Facebook, where she loves to chat with readers.

Meet

at www.IreneHannon.com

Learn news, sign up for her mailing list,

and more!

Find her on   

Welcome to

Hope Harbor . . .

Revell
a division of Baker Publishing Group
www.RevellBooks.com

Available wherever books and ebooks are sold.

. . . where hearts *heal*
and *love blooms*

THREE-TIME RITA AWARD WINNER
IRENE HANNON
Pelican Point
A Hope Harbor Novel

THREE-TIME RITA AWARD WINNER
IRENE HANNON
Driftwood Bay
A Hope Harbor Novel

THREE-TIME RITA AWARD WINNER
IRENE HANNON
Sandpiper Cove
A Hope Harbor Novel

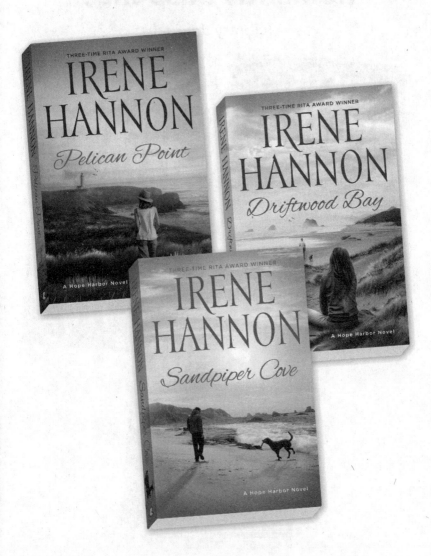

Revell
a division of Baker Publishing Group
www.RevellBooks.com

Available wherever books and ebooks are sold. 

MORE FROM THE

"Queen of Inspirational Romantic Suspense"

(Library Journal)

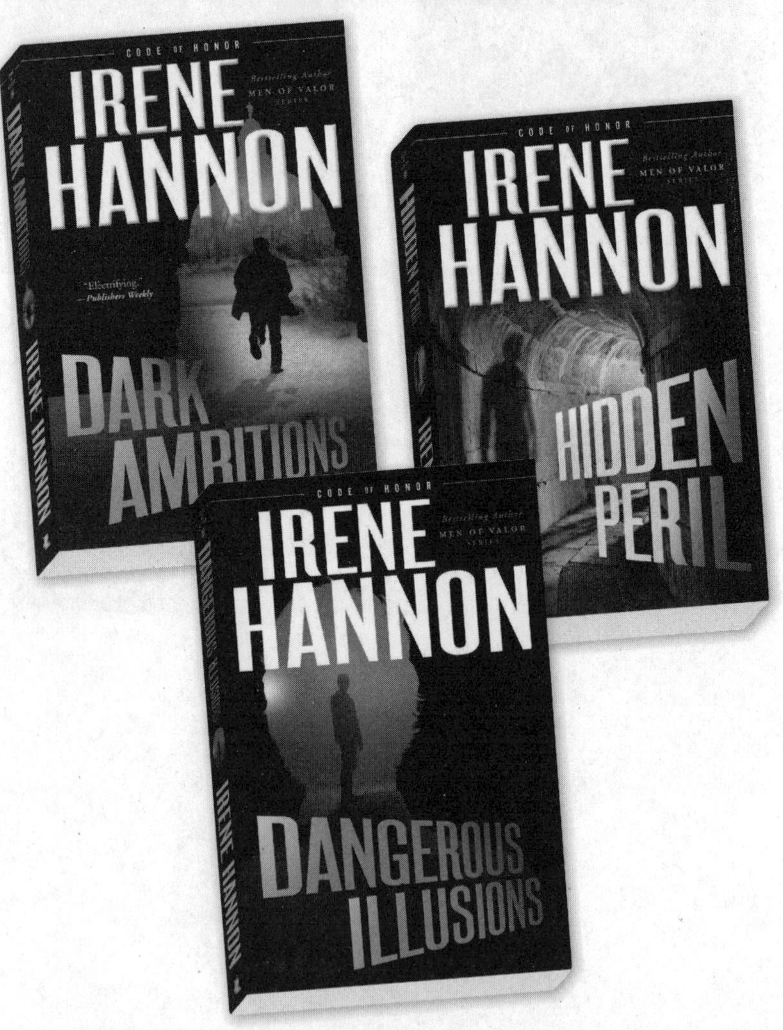

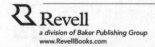

Revell
a division of Baker Publishing Group
www.RevellBooks.com

Available wherever books and ebooks are sold.

DANGER LURKS AROUND EVERY CORNER

Revell
a division of Baker Publishing Group
www.RevellBooks.com

Available wherever books and ebooks are sold.

Be the First to Hear about New Books from Revell!

Sign up for announcements about new and upcoming titles at

RevellBooks.com/SignUp

@RevellBooks

Don't miss out on our great reads!